SOUL SURVIVOR

Also by Katana Collins

SOUL STRIPPER

SOUL SURVIVOR

KATANA COLLINS

APHRODISIA

KENSINGTON PUBLISHING CORP.

www.kensingtonbooks.com

APHRODISIA BOOKS are published by

Kensington Publishing Corp.
119 West 40th Street
New York, NY 10018

All Kensington titles, imprints, and distributed lines are available at special quantity discounts for bulk purchases for sales promotion, premiums, fund-raising, and educational or institutional use.

Special book excerpts or customized printings can also be created to fit specific needs. For details, write or phone the office of the Kensington Special Sales Manager: Kensington Publishing Corp., 119 West 40th Street, New York, NY 10018. Attn. Special Sales Department. Phone: 1-800-221-2647.

ISBN-13: 978-0-7582-9013-7
ISBN-10: 0-7582-9013-6
First Kensington Trade Paperback Printing: October 2013

eISBN-13: 978-0-7582-9014-4
eISBN-10: 0-7582-9014-4
First Kensington Electronic Edition: October 2013

10 9 8 7 6 5 4 3 2 1
Printed in the United States of America

For Bridget and Mom—my biggest cheerleaders

Acknowledgments

As usual, I had a ton of help on this book. I want to take a moment to offer my utmost gratitude to the village that aided in *Soul Survivor*'s creation and growth.

To my critique group—Derek, Krista, and Shauna—not only did you prevent me from crumpling into a pile of angst, but you also tirelessly read and scoured the early drafts for plot-holes, continuity issues, and grammatical errors. Thank you for cheering me on as I rounded the finish line.

My local coffee shops—Red Horse and Roots . . . I'm not quite sure what I would do without you as a sanctuary. Thank you for keeping me caffeinated.

Special thanks to editor extraordinaire, Martin Biro, and the entire Kensington team for their tireless work. I'm in awe of how hard you all work and it does not go without recognition.

Bridget, Bo, Adam, and the kids, for all those Christmases, birthdays, and holidays where I had my nose in a laptop because of a looming deadline. . . . thank you for being so patient!

To my parents—who, despite the naughty nature of this book never once blinked an eye at showing their love and support. I'm so thankful that I have such badass parents that they can come out to the bar, have a drink, and toast to their daughter's latest erotic romance!

And as always, I want to thank my husband, Sean. You are at the heart of every hero I write.

1

The neon-colored lights were blinding as they swooped around the club like laser beams. First purple. Then green. Now blue. It felt like I was in the middle of a lava lamp, watching them spin around me. With the little straw stirrer, I sipped my Long Island iced tea and kept dancing. Sweaty men bumped into me from all angles, each attempting to brush my ass or breasts, in the hopes I might look up and give them even the slightest bit of attention. If only they knew just how deadly my attention could be.

Kayce, my best friend, grabbed my elbow and swung me around, our noses almost bumping in the process. Even with immortal hearing, I could barely make out what she was saying over the thumping of the bass. Grabbing the back of my head, she pulled me in closer, her lips on my ear. "I think I found two!" she yelled.

For normal girls on the town, this could mean anything—two seats, two bucks, two drinks. For two succubi on the town? It meant victims. We prey on the local men and women here in Las Vegas to satiate the raging itch between our legs and sustain our immortal souls on Earth.

With her hand still wrapped around the back of my neck, she turned me toward two college-aged guys who were staring at us, transfixed, while their clammy hands clenched plastic cups spilling over with cheap beer.

My head snapped back to Kayce. "They're so *young*," I said, noting their auras, silver and sparkling. These two were Heaven-bound for sure.

"I thought you didn't care anymore?" Her gaze narrowed.

My stomach twisted, guilt trying to gnaw its way out as if some little animal had burrowed into there. I pushed the feeling aside. "I don't," I shouted over the music with a nonchalant shrug. I was bluffing. If Kayce knew I was lying, then she chose to ignore it.

"What do you say we give them a little something to look forward to?" she said as a devious grin crept its way across her face. She nestled her body into mine, pulsing to the beat of the music. Running her hands through my shoulder-length blond curls, she sent a wicked glance to the two guys watching, their mouths hanging agape. "C'mon, girl," she whispered. "It's show time."

I moved to the music with her, running my fingers down her open, bare back. We turned in rhythm so that I was looking directly at the leaner college kid; he had surfer blond hair that flopped to one side and full lips. An itch surged through my core, shooting between my legs and my mouth went dry. A droplet of sweat tickled its way down the side of my face along my hairline and I quickly shapeshifted it away, making sure to settle my makeup, yet again. Drinking was making me sloppy with my appearance—and I had it much easier than most humans. With one hand, I swept Kayce's curtain of jet-black hair to the side and ran my lips ever so gently up her neck to her ear.

My eyes stayed on the college kid as I darted out a tongue that barely grazed her earlobe.

Her fingers splayed against my scalp, weaving into my hair and she tugged my neck back. "Which one do you want?" she whispered. With my eyes closed, nose aimed at the ceiling, I could feel her kisses as they trailed down my throat. When I finally opened my eyes again, I turned around, still on the beat, dropped myself down the ground, and swiveled my hips back to a standing position.

"Surfer boy. We've been staring at each other," I answered as though I were ordering mustard on a sandwich.

"Okay, then," she answered. "That leaves me with the mocha candy."

The crowd on the dance floor had parted, and there was now a group of people circled around us, watching. Men gazed hungrily and women scowled, eyes red and angry. Their jealousy surged a bolt of energy into me. Even though I used to be an angel, that bad-girl side wins out every time. An angel turned succubus—I was a creature no one in the demon or angel realm could explain. The succubus with a soul.

The song ended and Kayce took my hand, leading me to the two guys. "This is Monica," she said, running a fingernail down the length of the other guy's bicep, which bulged beneath his Hollister polo shirt.

Surfer boy took my hand in his. "I'm Paul," he said. His palm was sweaty and after the handshake ended, I wiped my hand on my slinky, sequined dress, not caring if it stained. That's the beauty of shapeshifting. It took a lot of my focus not to slink away, hoping that none of his other body parts were *that* sweaty.

Kayce already had a leg wrapped around the other guy, pressing herself against him to the beat. I grabbed Paul's hand and pulled him off the dance floor. I wasn't quite the exhibitionist Kayce was. The bathroom was an extremely modern design with clear glass walls that fogged over as soon as you locked the door, so that no one could see in. I tugged Paul inside, locking the door behind me. The glass fogged, encasing us, and making it look as if the entire club on the other side of the glass had filled with mist instantaneously. He grabbed me from behind and turned my hips back to him, his hands squeezing my waist in a way that suggested a carnal need. Our lips rushed to find each other's and his hands cupped my jaw. Bright blond hair flopped forward into his face and I brushed it back, my fingernails running through the silk-like strands. My tongue found his and they twisted around each other.

With my eyes closed, it was easy to pretend for a moment the hair belonged to Drew—my human manager at the cafe where I worked during the day. I pretended that those lips were fuller with a tiny scar slicing across the top. Pretended that this college boy's hands were more calloused and weathered from years of hard work as they circled and caressed my body.

An apelike grunt pulled me back to reality. Cool air tickled my puckering nipples and it wasn't until that moment that I realized he had pulled my dress down over my breasts. A raging erection poked through his jeans against my belly and the contact sent a jolt of electricity through my blood. I needed his life to survive—this wasn't about passion or even sex; it was survival. Never mind that I had had sex the night before as well. Never mind that I had chosen Paul because he had a slight resemblance to the man I loved but couldn't have. Never mind I probably could have gone two weeks without another conquest with all the Heaven-bound men I'd been seducing lately. Right now—all that mattered was the life force in front of me. A morality so strong that its power pushed on my gut causing the air to gush out of my lungs, leaving me breathless.

I shoved Paul against the opposite wall, wrapping my legs

around his waist. As I propped myself on his hips, the dress slid up above my ass and I shapeshifted my panties away. One of the glorious things about having more sex than I need—I have plenty of power for superfluous shifting.

A finger slid inside me and I tensed my sex around him. Again, I captured those pretty-boy lips in mine and drank him in. His soul was glistening, shimmering. He was going to be an amazing fix—the high would be electrifying. Much more so than the assholes and Hell-bound men I used to sleep with. And what's a week off their life in order for me to not be condemned to Hell? A week off their life so that I could maintain a human body and not be a drifting soul in the bowels of Hell. And in exchange, they get a night with me—sex extraordinaire. It's an even trade.

Okay, maybe not even, but it's the closest I can get to justifying my actions. Besides, my broken heart is still on the mend. Anonymous sex speeds up the healing process. Not only had I discovered Drew was working things out with Adrienne, but now she was the apprentice to my Julian. My old mentor back when *I* was an angel. I'd lost both the loves of my life to the same woman.

I shook the memory away, concentrating again on the fix that stood before me. I wasn't against falling in love—but I was against getting involved with humans or angels *ever* again. Demon dates only from now on. And the biggest downside to dating demons—they're a bunch of fucking assholes. But Paul was here in front of me. He was hot. And he wanted me. My job is to corrupt souls for Hell and steal their life force. I used to fight my duties . . . but these days, I was becoming friggin' employee of the year.

His arms, which had been holding me up by the ass, released me back to the ground. We both scrambled to get his pants off. I tore the pale blue polo shirt over his head and threw it on the floor. His hands wound through my golden, soft curls and just as I thought he was going to pull me in for another kiss, he grunted and pushed me to my knees.

Under normal circumstances, this sort of overt lack of regard for my sexual needs wouldn't fly. If I was training him to be a consistent lover at my beckoned need, then I would have taken the time to fight it. But for now, fuck it. I flicked a tongue out and ran it along the tip, then up and down the length of his shaft. His fingers still twisted in my hair, tightening their hold on me. He pulled my face closer to his cock. Done with the appetizer, he wanted the entree.

I grabbed his balls, squeezing perhaps a little too tightly, to where pain turned into pleasure. A gust of air whooshed from his lips, the sudden change from gentle to rough proving too much for him. Amateur. I took his entire length into my mouth, wrapping my lips tightly around his girth. My teeth just barely grazed against him as he fucked my mouth. With the skill of an expert, I used my other hand to grip the base of his dick, rotating my head with a swirl as I reached the tip. His head slammed against my throat.

"Fuck me with those stunning sucking lips, gorgeous." He was growing in size; getting bigger against my tongue. There was no way I was letting him get away with not doing any work. I lowered his hands from my hair and placed them on my breasts. His thumbs rolled over my pebbled nipples sending shock waves through my whole body. The ache between my legs grew and I pulled my mouth away before he could finish.

He groaned and tried to pull my head back towards his cock. Slapping his hands away, I stood, bending over the sink. I flipped my dress up past my hips. "Don't you want this instead?"

His eyes grew wide and licked his dry lips before approaching. Two large hands wrapped around my hips and the sides of my ass. The tip of his finger teased my opening, wet and slick and ready for him. The same hand traced around the curve of my ass and spanked me. It wasn't a hard slap, but I gasped in an exaggerated way. Finally, he pushed himself into me. Reaching around front, he flicked at my clit. My knees buckled with the small, but effective motions. The tension was building and I gripped the sink, body trembling, as an orgasm rolled over my body. The itch between my legs was fierce, reminding me that though it was pleasurable, this fuck was a necessity. I could come a hundred times for him, but until he spilled his seed on me, his soul—his energy—was safe.

Thanks to my succubus senses and inhuman reflexes, I saw him unlock the bathroom door before the fogged walls cleared. Within those milliseconds, I shifted my face to look like someone else. Just because Paul was an exhibitionist, didn't mean I had to be. Modesty might seem silly—being that I corrupt souls by fucking countless men each week—but I didn't like my Hellish duties to cross over into my day job. And even though most of these people here in the club were visiting from out of town, I didn't want to be known and recognized as the girl who was publicly getting it from behind. I did the same thing with my night job as a stripper—shift my looks slightly so that most people wouldn't necessarily recognize me during the day.

The walls around us cleared. See-through. "Oh yeah," Paul grunted and slapped my ass, squeezing it hard enough to leave a mark.

Grabbing a fistful of my hair and yanking my head back, he pushed into me with one final thrust. Sliding out just in time, he came all over my ass. It dripped down into my folds and the rush of his life force was like walking into an air-conditioned room after sweating outside on a hot summer's day. It momentarily took my breath away. His life reeled before my eyes, like I was watching an abridged version being projected before me. He'd graduate cum laude; move to Chicago; work in a boutique marketing firm before marrying and settling down in the suburbs. And lastly, he'd die of a heart attack.

Finally, I released the breath I'd been holding, thankful that I hadn't stripped too much of his life. I pulled my dress back down over my ass and looked into the mirror above me. I was glowing, radiant with the new life force. Paul's life force.

I turned to face him, not bothering to shift back into my original features. He was so drunk on cheap beer, he wouldn't even notice I looked slightly different from before. I glanced quickly out at the line of people formed to watch our little performance, then touched his cheek, running a finger down his jawline. "Thanks, Paul."

His pupils were dilated, eyes wide, ready to party some more. Just a side effect of my poison. He was high on me. "Who says it has to be over?" He grabbed me around the waist, pulling me in for another kiss. The crowd of people watching outside whooped and hollered. I let him kiss me a moment longer before pulling away and handing him his pants.

"I say so," I said quietly, reaching for the door. "Oh, and Paul?" When I looked back over my shoulder, he still had the energy, but a dejected look was etched on his pretty, boyish face.

He straightened as I turned around, eyes wide and expectant. "Yeah?" he said, hopeful, zipping up his pants. Like a puppy, I imagined two floppy ears perking up.

"Never shove a woman's head to your dick without reciprocating the act yourself." His face dropped, all color draining quickly away. On an exhale, my shoulders slumped slightly. I spoke again, a tad more quietly this time. "And lay off the red meat, okay? I mean . . . it's just—it can be bad for your heart."

2

I slipped out of the club, giving a little wave to Kayce, whose body was still entwined with her conquest. She was my ride home, but I really didn't want to wait for her to finish. And who knew if she even *would* finish. She might be intending to take him back to her place—in which case, I'd have to see Paul again. No, thank you. I clutched my purse to my chest and prepared for the walk home. It wasn't a long walk—and the streets in Vegas were always bustling. Checking my phone, I noted that it was only a little past midnight. Not late at all by most standards. Early for Vegas.

There was a chill in the air. A dry, cool October breeze caught my hair, whipping it about my face. Kitschy Halloween decorations adorned all the local businesses—smiling jack-o'-lanterns and witches with green skin hung in the windows. It was a fun holiday—one of my favorites since moving to the states. Being alive for close to three centuries meant you saw a lot of customs and various holidays around plenty of countries.

Seeing the green witch made me immediately think of Adrienne—Drew's ex-girlfriend, a detective who studied witchcraft, who had given her life for me a few months prior. Contrary to popular belief, witches are not immortal beings—*or green*; they are simply humans with a gift. The whole time she and Drew dated, I was certain she was this horrible person . . . a cheating slut. I couldn't have been more wrong; she was Vice and couldn't blow her cover—not even for the man she loved. Drew. *My* Drew. And now she was an angel—that's how good a person she was. Not only Heaven-bound . . . but a motherfucking angel. All of her spell-casting managed to hide that part of her aura . . . especially since she worked to catch so many immortal bad guys; she had to be able to conceal her true goodness as an undercover detective. When she'd died to save me, I'd absorbed some of those powers. As I walked down the street, I practiced snapping my fingers—a small flame igniting at my fingertips.

I lived a few blocks over from the main Vegas Strip, right down the street from Drew's coffee shop. As I approached, there was the tiniest sliver of light coming from inside. It was awfully late for Drew to still be working, but he did sometimes lose track of time while updating the books.

I walked up to the windows, planning to just take a small peek inside to make sure he was okay. I found Drew perched on a ladder, hanging a string of orange paper lanterns from the ceiling. His muscles rippled through his fitted V-neck T-shirt and his carpenter jeans hugged his legs just enough so that you could see the definition of his butt and thighs. I sighed and leaned against the window. *Tap, tap, tap.* I rapped the window with my knuckle. He startled, gripping the ladder, and put a hand to his chest with an exaggerated exhale. Smiling, he held up a finger, signaling me to hold on a moment, and climbed down slowly, carefully from the ladder.

A warm feeling swirled around the pit of my stomach and

spread through my limbs like honey. He walked over, unlocking the door.

"Hey," he said. *Hey.* It was such a simple greeting, but it sent shivers coursing through my body.

"Hey back," I said.

There was a moment where neither of us said anything. We stood there locked in each other's eyes. He licked his lips and the sight of his tongue made my stomach clench. A few months ago, after years of sexual chemistry and denying ourselves physical contact—we finally slept together. I had lost my powers as a result of a power-hungry succubus and a revenge-happy ex on a killing spree. With no repercussions, I couldn't resist his touch. Back then, I wouldn't have dreamt of sleeping with a man like Paul or Drew—or any moral human who was Heaven-bound. But for that one night with Drew, I got to experience what a normal passionate evening should entail. And now we were back to our awkward sexual tension.

I sighed. "Putting up some decorations, I see?" I said, breaking the moment.

He nodded and held the cafe's door open so that I could enter. As I did, he leaned in to give me the ceremonial hello, a half hug and faux kiss on the cheek. It was stiff, and I was getting to a point where I loathed the greeting. He sniffed as he pulled away and looked me up and down. "Tequila?"

I shrugged. "Sure. Among other things."

He inhaled again as though remembering a long, lost friend. As a recovering alcoholic, it didn't occur to me that the smell of alcohol *on* someone would mean something to him.

I walked inside, looking around—the holiday décor was far nicer than it typically was. He's usually among the crowd that buys some plastic, cartoon Halloween icons and using scotch tape, hangs them in the windows. But these decorations were understated and classy. Ceramic pumpkins and cornucopias on each table. Tea lights and paper lanterns in orange and black hung from the ceiling. "Wow," I whispered.

"Yeah," he said. "I know."

"You should have told me you were doing this tonight. I could have stayed late and helped."

He shrugged and his eyes slipped down to my strapless dress that sparkled with hundreds of rhinestones. It was short—came just below my crotch and sat low across my cleavage. "It seemed like you had more exciting places to be tonight." His smile faltered and he cleared his throat, looking away. "Besides . . ."

"Where do you want to carve the pumpkins . . . ?" Adrienne walked out from the back room holding two medium-sized pumpkins in her arms. ". . . oh." She shifted one pumpkin onto her hip and set the other on the counter. "Hi, Monica." She walked over to hug me, only to pull back as though I could burn her. Her eyes raked over me and I knew she could sense my recent hunt. Could probably still smell the sin of him clinging to my body. She leaned in for the hug anyway, keeping as much space between our bodies as possible. Her nose scrunched as she pulled away from the halfhearted embrace. "We were just about to carve some pumpkins, if you want to join." There was a slight edge to her voice that I couldn't put my finger on. I looked her up and down—head to toe. Her hair was still a bright, platinum blond as it had been back in her prostitute/detective days and her skin still bore a slightly orange tan, reflective of too much time in a carcinogenic coffin. But she was beautiful, despite these traits. A beauty that brought bile up my throat.

"Speaking of"—Drew rushed past us toward the back room—"I should grab some of my tools." It was just Adrienne and I, left in a stare-down.

Her eyes shifted under my glare and she cleared her throat. "We've only got two pumpkins, but you and I could share."

I held her stare and my mouth hardened into a frown. "Don't you think we've shared enough for one lifetime?" I forced a sickeningly sweet smile.

She blinked, her own grin flickering away as her eyes darted to the back room. "I, uh—"

"Does he know that you're an angel? That you died six months ago to save me?"

She swallowed and shook her head. "You know I can't tell him any of that."

I snorted, my lip curling back with the noise. "I guess that's what you did best as a human, too. Keeping secrets."

"And what did you do best as a human, Monica? Oh, that's right, Jules told me . . . you just loved to tease the boys in your village."

Jules told her? About my past? My voice was hard and I looked down my nose at her radioactive skin. "I didn't realize they had spray tans in Heaven, too."

One side of her mouth tilted into a delicate half-smile and she shrugged with a nonchalance that only an angel could master. Her eyes were still hard and stone-like. "What can I say? I love my tanning beds."

Drew entered from the back room with a small metal toolbox in hand.

"I'd love to stay, but I've got to get home," I said, back to my normal voice. I knew myself well enough to know that I shouldn't be around Adrienne with a knife in hand.

Drew stepped over to her, picking up the pumpkin that had been set on the table. "Why don't you lay down some newspaper in the back? It'll be easier to clean up in the stock area. I'll be there in a minute."

"Sure. G'night, Monica. Maybe next time, huh?"

"Perhaps."

She turned around, her long, platinum hair fanning out dramatically behind her.

"So," I said once she was gone, knowing that she could still probably hear us. Fucking angels had even better hearing than demons. "You two are back together?"

One shoulder touched an ear as he shrugged and shifted his weight from foot to foot. "Not . . . officially. She's finally back in town from whatever her case was and we're just . . . spending time together. It's the least I can do since we—since I . . ." His voice broke and he stared at the floor as if it had all the answers to the universe.

"Since we fucked on my kitchen table?" I offered him a syrupy smile.

He exhaled a gush of air, head shaking back and forth. "Don't do that, Mon. Don't make it sound so cheap."

I couldn't help but laugh—the noise catching in my throat. "Gotta call a spade a spade, Drew."

His voice dropped to a whisper. "You don't think I owe this to her? After cheating on her? You don't think I at least need to try to make things work between her and me?" His eyes raised to meet mine, catching my chin between his thumb and forefinger. "Please tell me you understand that."

The lump in my throat grew to golf-ball size and I swallowed it down. "You two were breaking up when we—you weren't cheating."

"It felt like cheating. Look, we're just . . . we're reacquainting ourselves with each other."

"So you haven't had sex yet?" I blurted the question out without stopping to think how it would sound. He dropped my chin, his hand pulling away as though I were poisonous. And who was I kidding? I *was.* All those damn Long Island iced teas lower your ability to censor. Angels can have sex with humans, but the relationship should first be blessed by an ArchAngel. And once the two consummate the relationship, if the human betrays the angel, he or she will have a black mark on their soul for which the only redemption is then in turn saving another angel or angel-bound human. It was a dangerous line to cross.

He closed his eyes, taking a deep breath before answering. Hands on his hips, he looked up at me through long lashes. "No. We haven't, not that it's any of your business."

"Well, good," I said pointedly and loudly, in the hopes that Adrienne could hear me. She'd be risking his soul forever for a selfish reason and she should know it. Sex with me might take time off his life, but sex with her ran the risk of banishment to Hell. Take a guess at which would be worse.

"Yeah," he responded, his voice growing louder, scowl deepening. "It *is* good. We're talking a lot more. Discovering things she couldn't tell me before. We picnic together and find the excitement in the little things like holding each other's hand." He continued his rant, every now and then hushing his own voice so that she wouldn't hear. He said the words, but there was a catch in his voice. And I didn't buy it. It was too sickeningly sweet and it didn't sound the least bit like Drew. "I see things differently with her, Monica. Roses for example—she's shown me just how many colors are in a single petal."

"Really, Drew? Roses are red and I had sex an hour ago." I threw my bag over my shoulder and huffed out of there.

He didn't bother coming after me and I didn't bother to look back. There was a time when Drew would have never let me walk away angry, but those days were long gone.

I was only a block and a half away from my house when I heard a shriek—no, more like scream. Shrill and loud in my head, it stopped me in my tracks and I bent over, clutching my temples in pain. As quickly as it had come on, it disappeared. I stood straight, looking around to see if anyone was around to have noticed my weird behavior. On my right at the stoplight was a couple making out—they hadn't seen me and obviously hadn't heard the scream.

I shook away the uneasy feeling and checked my phone. There was a text from Kayce waiting for me.

Where'd you go? George and I are at The Lounge.

I hadn't seen George, my incubus friend, all week. The night was still young and The Lounge was only a few blocks east. I turned past the couple making out, the shrill scream pushed to the back of my mind.

3

It was well past noon by the time I woke up the next morning. I had to work the two to eight shift at the cafe. Never before had I *not* wanted to go to work and see Drew.

My head throbbed and I popped two aspirin in my mouth, downing them with a glass of water. I could still feel the effects of alcohol and the resulting hangover that came with that—though it took a whole lot more alcohol to affect us demons than most humans. While I normally enjoyed the ritual of a hot shower and brushing my teeth in the mornings, after a long night of partying with my friends, I just wanted to be ready without any fuss.

I shifted into a slim-cut pair of jeans and a scoop-neck T-shirt. My hair was dark blond and a little past my shoulders with soft curls that twisted around each other. Looking in the mirror, I thought better of the outfit. I usually dress conservatively for my job, but I wanted Drew to look at me and drool. I wanted him to remember the body that once knelt over his face. I shifted instead into a halter top that was cut low, revealing impressive cleavage that wasn't too over the top. The halter tied at the nape of my neck as well as across my lower and middle back. All that kept the shirt in place were three easy-to-untie bows.

"I liked the first outfit better," a baritone voice said from my bedside and I screamed, reaching for the gun that I kept in my purse.

"Too late," he said. "You'd already be dead."

"Julian!" Fucking angels. Sneaky little bastards.

"For someone who's got a hit out on her, you're not so good with being aware of your surroundings." He was, of course, speaking of the bounty Lexi had mentioned was on my head back when she tried to kill me a few months ago. Hence my gun and holy water bullets. I had definitely been on edge since then, but certainly didn't want my old mentor to know that.

"If it's an angel who's out to kill me, I'd say I've got bigger problems."

Jules meandered around my room, walking over to the bookshelf where I kept a few tchotchkes from the various countries and centuries I've lived as a succubus. He picked up a scarf my mother had knitted for me in my human days. The wool was so old that it was damn close to being brittle. He turned it over in his hand. With a sigh, I walked over, gently took it from him, and placed it back in its spot on my shelf, running a finger tenderly over my family's crest knitted into the base.

"What is it you want, Jules?"

He rocked back on his heels, tucking his thumbs into his front pockets. "Just checking in on a friend. Can't I do that?"

I narrowed my eyes at him. "Uh-huh."

He responded by arching his eyebrows innocently. "What?"

"It just seems unlikely that you would come here without a specific reason."

He said nothing, just stared at me with those intense crystal-blue eyes. After a few more seconds of no response, I sighed and rolled my own baby blues. "Fine, then I've gotta get going."

"Well, there was something. . . ."

"I knew it."

"I wanted to see if there was any way I could convince you to warm up to Adrienne a little? She's trying so hard with you."

I folded my arms. "Is she, now? Tell me Jules—why is it that you were telling her of my human days? Because for someone who's 'trying so hard' she sure has a funny way of throwing my past in my face."

Julian's chest collapsed, shoulders sagging in the process and he ran a hand over his face, across his blond stubble. His hair was blond, wavy, and tickled his collarbone with a shine that models would envy. "I'm sorry. I thought it would help for her to know."

"Did *she* send you to talk to me?"

He shook his head. "No. Not at all . . ." He paused, choosing his words carefully. "She would never ask for my help in such a personal matter. Is it so much to ask that my oldest friend and my mentee get along?"

"Yeah," I answered brusquely. "Actually, it is."

He paused, looking me over from my bedhead-styled hair to my open-toed kitten heels. "I see you're . . . *embracing* your succubus nature. Quite the change, isn't it?" He tipped his chin up, looking down at me through half-open eyelids.

"Yep. You could say that." I grabbed my purse, pretending to be fascinated by which lipstick to take with me. Something we both knew was bullshit since I could affect any shade I wanted. I slid my arm through the purse strap and stood taller, all my weight shifted onto one foot. "Why fight a losing battle?"

His face remained stoic and he nodded. "I believe in you. You'll come out of this."

"Sure you do. Why don't you go work with your replacement Monica. Better keep her away from any vampires . . . it would probably inhibit your chances of being promoted to ArchAngel if you lost another angel mentee to lust. I'm sure I'll see you around." I fumbled around my purse for my keys and when I looked up again, Jules was already gone.

I arrived at the cafe already in a bad mood. Boo-fucking-hoo, Adrienne. Your Heavenly existence is so hard.

So you can imagine just how excited I was to see Adrienne and Damien sitting together having a cup of coffee. Drew stood next to Adrienne's chair, his hand resting lightly on her back. They all looked up as the bells over the door announced my entrance. Mine and Drew's eyes connected, the muscles in his neck tightening.

So much for just slinking past them. I cleared my throat and found the courage somewhere down deep to approach. "Hey, guys." My voice sounded rough, like I had swallowed a fistful of gravel.

Drew nodded with a single head tilt.

Adrienne's smile was brittle. "Hi, Monica."

Damien simply stared, amusement twitching at the corners of his mouth. His olive skin smelled of aftershave and his dark hair looked as though he had recently trimmed it. The layers fell on each other with a precision that looked both sexy and expensive. Gray eyes regarded me with a warmth I couldn't help but feel skeptical about.

I shifted my weight from one foot to the other. "So—you two working?"

Adrienne nodded. "Yeah, we just got a call about another

out-of-town case. This one's in Utah, and we thought"—her eyes shifted to Drew—"you might have a little insight on it."

"Me?" I raised my eyebrows and then looked over at Damien.

He raised his hands in an "I surrender" sort of position. "Wasn't my idea."

Drew chuckled and rubbed his forefinger across his top lip. "I don't think Monica's the right person to help in an investigation," he said quietly as if remembering a fonder time. "Remember when she cut her leg a while ago? The slightest bit of blood and *smack*." He clicked his tongue with a quick twitch of his head motioning to the floor. "She was out."

I glared at Drew, jaw clenched.

At this, Damien leaned back, arms crossing his chest. "Oh yeah? I wouldn't picture you as being one to pass out after a little blood."

"I'm *not*," I said, the heat rising to my cheeks. "That was . . . an extraordinary . . . circumstance. It had been a rough week."

Damien's twitch of a smile was officially a full smirk now.

"Whatever. I need to get to work." I swung around and headed to the back to put my stuff away.

When I finished, I spun around to find Adrienne there with a file in her hand, long acrylic fingernails clutching it tightly. "Please," she said. "Just take a look at this. Any insight you can offer would be helpful. Our chief is on us to help out this other precinct and so far, D and I can't come up with anything new."

I took the file, halfheartedly flipping through it, not even bothering to read. "And why exactly do you think I'll be able to find anything? I'm not a detective. I'm not an angel. I'm not even a blip on Saetan's radar."

"Well," she said, quieter, "we both know that's not true." After a pause, she sighed. "About last night—I'm sorry about what I sai—"

"I'll have a look at the file when I find a little time. My schedule is *awfully* full these days, though. That reminds me—I was going to dance as a naughty cop tonight. Have any suggestions for me?"

Adrienne's jaw clenched and she wrenched the file from my hands, opening it up to an image. "Look—there are runes surrounding her body. They're Celtic—old Celtic magic. I had once tried a spell similar in my witch days, but before I could master it, I—well, *you* know." She looked to her hand, rustling the papers pointedly in front of me. "Julian mentioned that the two of you spent time in Ireland a few centuries ago and that you may be able to help."

"Why doesn't Julian help you? He *is* your mentor."

"He can't interfere with human practices. You know that. Not without the blessing from the council."

"But *you* can?"

"I received permission after I became an angel to continue my work as a detective as long as I was no longer Vice. They felt it would best utilize my natural gifts."

"Ah." I bit the inside of my cheek to keep from saying anything more.

"Please. Just take a look."

I didn't answer right away. Just stood with my arms crossed. She looked so hopeful there with her perfect posture in her classically cut navy blue suit. Her bright blond hair was pulled tightly into a high ponytail with two tendrils framing her face. Her makeup, though subdued, oozed sex. Damn her. Grabbing the file back, I tossed it into my locker and slammed the door shut. "Sure. I'll have a look."

Her face, which had been all business before, lifted slightly into a smile. "Thank you, Monica. I'll go tell Damien you're on board."

* * *

A couple hours or so into my shift, Damien was still sitting at the same table near the window. Adrienne had long since left. Genevieve was working the register and I was making the orders as they came in. Vanilla skim latte. Iced cappuccino, extra foam. Caramel mocha latte. Okay, so that last one was for me. I brewed a double shot of espresso. Quick and potent—just how he likes it.

"You're still here," I said, setting the espresso down in front of him.

He leaned back in his chair, resting his arm over the back casually. "Hello to you, too, succubus."

I sighed. "Ya know, I'm going to start calling you elemental from now on." That's what Damien was—a human who could speak to and hear the elements: earth, air, fire, metal. Though he was still technically a mortal, elementals lived much longer lives than typical humans. Hundreds of years, even. They didn't age like your average human. Hence the reason a succubus, or incubus for that matter, wouldn't be able to steal any portion of their souls.

He looked down at the double shot I had placed in front of him. "I didn't order anything."

"It's on the house," I said. "Drew hates it when people sit for hours and don't order anything."

"Well, then." His eyebrows hung low over his eyes, "I guess I owe you a tip, then, don't I?" His mouth curved into a smile that didn't reveal any teeth.

I leaned on the empty chair next to him. "Or you could just tell me why the Hell you're still here."

He sighed and leaned forward, resting both elbows on the table. "Adrienne seems to think you're gonna be able to help in our next case. I don't have quite the faith in you that she does."

"So?" I let the sentence drop off.

He held my gaze and licked his lips. It was a game of

chicken—who would look away first? He picked up his espresso and took a sip, maintaining eye contact the entire time. After setting it back on the table, he cleared his throat. "I was wondering if you wanted to get dinner with me sometime." His hands clasped in front of him and he straightened his back, shoulders squared directly at me.

I laughed out loud, laughed right in his face. "You've got to be fucking kidding me."

"Is that a no?"

"Considering you've spent the past six months either ignoring me or sending me hateful glares from across the room—I'd say, *yeah*, that's a no." I narrowed my eyes and turned my head to look at him from the side. "What changed? You wanted nothing to do with me after the battle at my place."

"Adrienne is like a sister to me . . . and when I thought she died saving you, I needed someone to blame. But now she's back and she's fine." After another moment of holding my gaze, he sighed and fell back in his chair. "C'mon. Just go to fucking dinner with me. You obviously want to—you bought me a coffee."

"Technically Drew bought you that coffee. Take him to dinner instead."

He smirked again from behind his cup. "I would, but he doesn't seem the type to put out on the first date."

My heart dropped as I stared into those gray eyes. "And I do?" I ran my tongue across dry lips. "Something tells me I should be insulted, Detective Kane."

A growl reverberated from deep in Damien's chest. "Calling you wildly and unapologetically sexual is far from an insult, succubus." With his small smirk, a dimple formed at the corner of his mouth. "And if you call me Detective Kane again, I won't be held responsible for what happens here"—his eyes flicked down—"on this table."

I opened my mouth, tempted to call his bluff as something struck me. Damien didn't seem the type to date, nor did he seem like the kind of guy who would ask a girl out to dinner in order to wine and dine her. He could easily find a bedmate any night of the week with hardly a wink. I opened my mouth to answer when I heard a door shut behind me. I turned to find Drew coming out of his office, a stack of papers in his hands. His eyes found mine, a sad smile tipping his mouth—until he saw me talking to Damien. The hint of a smile immediately dropped, and he shuffled away, glancing back down at his paperwork. And away from me. I looked back over at Damien, who still stared at me with knowing eyes. They were half lowered and an amused smirk slid across his face.

"No, Damien. My answer is no."

I finished the rest of my shift with no more excitement. Damien left shortly after I turned him down and Drew pretty much avoided me for the rest of the day. A little after eight o'clock, I was grabbing my stuff from my locker. I glanced over my shoulder before shifting into a leather jumpsuit that zipped up from crotch to cleavage.

Head down, I stalked out to the front and collided with Drew. I bounced off his tight pecs and, in my three-inch heels, almost fell backwards. He reached out a hand, grabbing my elbow just before I toppled over. His eyes landed on the tight leather buckling around my breasts, and his mouth stayed open. When he finally brought his eyes back to my face, he swallowed. "Off to work?"

I nodded. "Of course." I gestured to the outfit.

He gave one breathy laugh—which was hardly a laugh at all—before answering. "It's hard to tell these days."

"There's not exactly anyone to hold back for, anymore."

"You have friends." His eyes softened at the corners.

It was my turn to snort a laugh. "Like Kayce? Who do you think encourages me?"

Hands clenched on his hips, he let one rake through his hair and then fall to his thigh. "Why do you have to make everything so hard, Monica? You know I didn't mean Kayce. I meant me. *Me.* Your friend. I am still your friend."

"Are you?" My voice was soft, throat closing with the threat of tears. "Because I don't believe it these days."

"*You* were the one who said you didn't want anything outside of our one night together. That was your choice, not mine." He wiped his palm over reddish blond stubble. "I don't get you. We were friends before. . . . Why can't we be friends now?"

"Because you made your choice, Drew. You chose her. And you can't ride a tricycle without having a third wheel." I went to move past him and one hand darted out to grab my elbow. My skin beneath his hand sizzled at the touch. A heady electricity hung in the air between us, and I felt myself panting as I looked up into his green eyes. His wet lips pressed together and he swallowed, Adam's apple bobbing up, then down. I closed my eyes and memorized what his hand felt like on my body. I never knew if it would be the last.

"I haven't chosen anyone. Not yet. I'm just—"

"Shut *up*," I snapped. "I don't want to hear it anymore. I get it. You feel guilty for fucking me so you're with her out of pity."

His eyes flashed, anger resonating between us. He dropped my elbow, knuckles turning white with clenched fists. "I am not with her out of pity," he spat.

I crossed my arms, narrowing my eyes at him. "Well, then, what would you call it?"

His voice was dangerous. On edge. "If you're going to make life so miserable for both of us here, why don't you just quit?"

I opened my eyes again and his were hard with nostrils flaring as he waited for my response. It was a question he had asked me numerous times over the past six months. A question I always gave the same answer to every time. It was a well-rehearsed dance we did.

"If I make *your* life so miserable, why don't you just fire me?" I said the words quietly, but with no less intensity. I moved to push past his shoulder, but stopped just as our bodies connected. Looking up, our noses were so close that one slight movement from either of us could have resulted in our lips touching. "We don't all get happily ever afters, Drew."

4

The drive to Hell's Lair from the coffee shop is only about twenty minutes, depending on traffic. Lucien, the ArchDemon of Nevada and the closest thing to a brother I've got, is the owner and my boss. He's a pretty intimidating guy to most, but not to me.

The place was already crawling with the lowest of the lows when I slipped in through the tinted glass doors. Both humans and immortals frequented the club, so we had to be careful not to let our guard down too much just because it was a known demon bar in the immortal realm. As soon as I stepped foot in the club, my foot slid into a questionable puddle. It pooled into my strappy high heels, squishing between my toes.

"Ugh!" I screamed and shook my foot. Mystery fluid splattered off of me.

"You're late again, darlin'." I looked up to find T, our bouncer and bartender, looking at me, arms crossed, eyes thoughtful. He wore big gold jewelry that came right from the *Mr. T* catalogue and he was a big guy—huge, actually. Lots of bulk that might be half muscle, half fat. I honestly never took the time to find out. Either way, he looked scary and could probably beat the shit out of most people.

"Yeah, yeah. What else is new?"

"Lenny's been looking for you."

I checked my phone. 9:22. "I'm only five minutes late! Damn, he's picky."

"You know Lenny. Late is late."

I looked at T without turning my head. "Anyone looking right now?"

He shook his head. T's a man of few words.

Thank Hell. I stepped to the side of the mystery puddle and shifted my shoe and foot clean. "You gonna clean that up?"

"Already sent for the mop."

"And do I even want to know what it was?"

His eyes caught mine, his smile a mere apparition. "Nope."

Janelle, our newest dancer, came up to T with a mop and bucket. Setting it down next to him, she let her hand trail from his shoulder down to his lower back. "Here you go, baby," she said, her eyelids half closed and a serene smile splayed on her face.

And then, something so odd happened that it made my breath catch in my throat. T smiled. A full-on, all-teeth-showing smile. As long as I've known the man, I've never seen him grin that widely. Janelle smiled wider, too, and scrunched her nose.

"I'll see you later, right?"

He nodded and she ran off backstage.

"Well, I'll be damned," I said, leaning casually against his shoulder.

"You already are, girl."

Just as I was about to get the details of the recent developments, Lenny's nasally voice rang out from my right. "Monica! You're twelve minutes late!"

I sighed and when I turned to look at him, I noticed he was wearing a new shirt. I could tell because he had left the size sticker on the arm. If I was a nicer person, I would have torn it off. Or at least told him about it. "Actually, I'm five minutes late. I've been here chatting."

"Until you're in costume and ready to go on stage, you're considered late!"

I gestured to my leather jumpsuit. "What exactly do you think I'm wearing, Lenny? You think I go around dressing like this for kicks?"

He opened his mouth to retort, but thought better of it. My job was certainly more secure than his and he knew it. I walked slowly past him, staring down my nose at his little, ratlike features. "See ya later, T," I said over my shoulder after staring down Lenny.

T gave me a quick nod and went back to mopping up the mystery puddle.

With the foul mood I was in, I chose an angry, energetic song to dance to. "Black Betty" pounded through the speakers and I started at the pole in the center of the stage. With the hard pulse of the first few beats, I straddled it, mimicking what I would do if it was a man I was riding. The guitar lick began and I climbed the pole, allowing my body to slide down in a spiral head-first. Using the energy of the music, I swirled my hips and thrust my ass in the air.

As I walked to the front center stage, more and more men were gathering around. I turned my back to them and lowered my body into a straddle, bending over so my ass, still leather-clad, was in their faces. Bills were being tossed onto the stage and I hadn't even taken anything off yet. I spanked myself, the sound of skin hitting leather ringing out over the music. Still in the straddle position, I pulsed my hips from side to side. I looked over my shoulder at the man standing right behind me.

"Spank me," I said. His eyes grew wide, with fear or nerves I wasn't sure. No one was supposed to touch the dancers. "It's okay. . . . I've told you to." I ran my tongue across scarlet red lips. "C'mon." My voice grew more demanding. "Spank it. Hard."

He raised a hand and struck me across the ass, squeezing my cheek at the end. I exaggerated my cry for the performance and hollered out in faux ecstasy. Standing upright again, I turned to face the front right side of the audience and unzipped the front of my jumpsuit in jerky motions that mimicked a hand job. Underneath, I wore a black, lace push-up bra and I peeled away the leather from my body, shifting my skin so that no lines or moisture from the leather showed. I unclasped the bra and my breasts fell out. They were full but not overly large. I found that the more attainable I made my body, my looks, the more tips I got.

I circled the audience, allowing the men to put the money in my G-string. I even let most spank me as I passed. The more the audience realized I'd let them touch me, the more likely they were to buy a lap dance later, I rationalized.

One man particularly caught my eye sitting at the front left side of the stage. He had a beautiful bronzed, olive skin tone—maybe of Cuban lineage—and dark hair that was cropped short. Large, chocolate eyes stared back at me with an intensity that almost made me stop in my tracks. I was wearing nothing but my thong at this point. Doing a back bend, I allowed my head to fall off the edge of the stage, and snaked my body so that I was lying on my back before him. My breasts heaved just below his chin.

He held a fifty-dollar bill pinched between two fingers, and I glanced down at my thong, signaling where he could put it.

His eyes held mine, not bothering to look at my body, but he ran the edge of the bill from the center of my collarbone down between my breasts, circled it around each nipple allowing enough time for them to pebble. Then he ran the money down my tight abs before slipping it into the front of my thong. He let his hand linger, caressing the top of my landing strip until he pulled away. I gasped as he touched me, goose bumps covering my flesh. Even with that tiny bit of contact, I could tell this guy was skilled, an expert in his own right. His eyes remained on mine. There was something in his face that was familiar, though I knew I had never before met the man.

The song was coming to a close. I pulled myself up for a big finish upside down on the top of the pole. When I looked into the audience again, Damien stood at center stage. His hair was messed, as though he had been running his hands through it all day. The dark gray button-down shirt was unbuttoned to the middle of his sternum and he wore his signature leather jacket, even though the club was unseasonably warm inside. His dark, brooding stare directed straight at me. His eyes flicked to my Cuban big tipper, then back again at me.

When I came out of my dressing room, I was back in the leather jumpsuit, so tight that it clung to me like a second skin. Damien was waiting for me, leaning against the stage door like some sort of Johnny. He ran a tongue along his top teeth as I walked out and kicked himself off the wall. "Well, that was quite the performance."

"Are you stalking me now?"

One eyebrow arched and the corner of his mouth tilted up. "I used to frequent this club all the time before you knew who I was."

"So, then, that's a yes? You're a stalker."

"Who said I was here to see you?"

"Well, are you?"

"Of course." He smiled and sipped his beer.

Crossing my arms, I lowered my eyes to a scowl, but I was pretty certain my lips still held the slightest smile regardless of how much I tried to give him my bitchiest frown. "I'm really not interested in dating *anyone* right now."

His silver-ish eyes flashed with—something that I couldn't quite put my finger on. "Good. I'm not really looking to date either." His smile was an erotic proposal.

"Really? Then what the Hell is all this about?" I gestured dramatically at the two of us.

"I may not be so good with the romance," he said with a flippant hand gesture, before stepping in so close that I could feel his pulse; the pounding of his heart strangely similar to another sort of pounding I knew we both desired. "But, Monica—I know a hundred different ways to make you come. And I want to show you each and every one of them."

Damien's face was hard, his expression broad and resolute. Before I could speak, he gently placed a finger on my lips. "Before you object, take a good look at me, Monica. Do I look like the sort of man who's easily dissuaded?"

Our bodies were pressed together and I throbbed for every hot, hard inch of him. And judging by the annoying smirk he bore, he knew I did. My breasts were heavy and all too sensitive and my clit ached for attention, beating along with my thrashing heart. *It's just my succubus senses taking over.* I closed my eyes, trying to convince myself this was true. Finally, I stepped back. I needed air and being this close to Damien was sucking all the oxygen out of me. His hand darted out, grabbing at my bicep.

"Excuse me, ma'am." The lumbering voice came from my left with the slightest hint of an accent—a Creole drawl. Both Damien and I flashed a look to the third person. It was the big-tipper from earlier. Damien's glare lowered and he exhaled long and slow. A warning. The stranger's smile was all charm. "Is this man bothering you?"

"Nope," I said, pulling my arm from his grasp. "Actually, he was just leaving."

"The Hell I was," he growled.

Lenny scurried past us and Damien grabbed his shirt collar from behind. "I'm buying a private dance. With her." He gestured at me.

"Interesting," the stranger said. "I was about to do the same."

Lenny's eyes glistened at the mention of a sale. "Well," he said, "she is on the clock for a few hours. Who was here first?"

"I was," Damien said, flashing a triumphant glance to the stranger.

"I'll pay double to go first," the Creole man answered.

"Triple," Damien said through gritted teeth.

The stranger smiled in a smug way. "I'll match that and I'll personally tip *you* as well as the lady here." He gestured to Lenny, who brightened at the mention of a tip. "And trust me, I am a very generous man." His large chocolate-brown eyes glistened and he glanced at me, licking his lips. It's not every day a fat, sweaty fuck like Lenny gets offered a tip in a female strip joint.

"Well, then," Lenny said, "let me get your name, sir. . . ."

"Luis," he said, sending a sheepish smile in my direction. I couldn't help but return it. That damn Southern charm.

"Wait" Damien shot out a hand, placing it on Lenny's clipboard. A low hum resonated through my body and I recognized it immediately as Damien speaking to an element. "Well, well, well . . ." He slid a sideways glance to me before leaning in and whispering something in Lenny's ear.

Lenny's face dropped, turning a ghostly pallor. He cleared

his throat and looked down at his clipboard, marking something. "I'm sorry, sir," he said, looking at Luis. "I'm afraid this gentleman was first. You can of course have the next dance."

Luis cast another look toward me. "Perhaps another night, *mon cherie*." He took my hand and brushed his lips across a knuckle. "I don't like being anyone's sloppy second." After standing up straight, he pulled out two more bills, handed one to Lenny and the other to me. "For taking up your time." The bill he placed in my hand felt stiff and when I unrolled it, I could see the hint of a business card inside. I tucked it into my cleavage.

"Thank you, Luis."

"My pleasure." He tipped an invisible hat to each of us—even Damien—and turned to leave the club.

Damien mocked the hat tip with a middle finger aimed at Luis, muttering some sort of expletive under his breath.

I put a hand on my hip and sighed. "You better be a good fucking tipper, Damien. You might have just cost me a month's rent." I grabbed his hand and pulled him into one of our back rooms.

Once inside, I shut the door behind me and held out a hand, palm up. "Okay, pay up. Triple the cost. And don't forget the tip."

"You seriously going to make me pay triple the amount?"

"Isn't that the deal you worked out with Lenny?"

He smirked again. "No, I think Lenny and I came to another understanding."

I dropped my hand, tilting my head. "What did you say to him if it wasn't in regard to money? Lenny's only language is the dollar bill."

"I told him that if he didn't give the first dance to me, I'd tell Lucien he was skimming money off the top." He folded his arms dramatically across his chest.

It was hard to be mad at anyone who stuck it to Lenny, the little weasel. "You sneaky little bastard," I said, mirroring Damien's crossed arms.

"Yep. So I could probably get away without paying you *anything*."

I slowly walked toward him and pushed his body into the chair sitting in the middle of the room. "But you *will* tip, right?"

He fell back into a seated position and shifted his body so that his groin was easy to access. "I guess that all depends."

My eyebrows arched. "Oh? On what?"

"Whether or not you'll join me for dinner. And with the dirt I've got on Lenny—I can keep coming back for a dance every night without paying a penny."

"I thought you didn't do romance?"

"I don't. Dinner would consist of you, spread on the table, as my main course."

"You certainly don't beat around the bush."

"I don't imagine you having any sort of bush down there, babe."

"Don't call me babe." I slowly shifted the jumpsuit zipper open to my naval so that the edges of my breasts popped out, just shy of the nipples, from underneath. I had lost the bra after my dance. I traced my silhouette with a finger, up and down from my décolletage to my belly. "And what if I told you I *wanted* a bit of romance? To get me in the mood?"

His breathing was getting more and more shallow, chest rising and falling in a faster pattern. "I'd bring you roses and chocolate and take you to the most damned expensive restaurant I could find."

"Mmm." I knelt over him, and an impressive erection pushed into my crotch. I peeled the leather slowly from my body, catching the tip from Luis just as it fell from my cleavage.

I tossed it behind me, making a mental note to grab it later. Then, standing in the chair, I allowed him to take the rest of the body suit down past my thighs. I stepped out of them; first one foot then the other, and kicked it to the floor, leaving me in nothing but my thong.

I shifted myself to look like Pamela Anderson. "Who do you feel like being with tonight? A blond bombshell?" I shifted to a waif-like model that graced all the *Vogue*s this year. "Skinny runway model?"

He shook his head, a smile lilting at the corners. "I just want Monica. That's who I'm paying for."

With a shrug I turned back into myself. "If you say so, elemental. You're giving up something that every man in the world would love to experiment with."

His smirk grew. "Ask me again in a century."

Kneeling back down again, I was acutely aware that all that kept my skin from his pants was a small triangle of sheer fabric, not much thicker than floss. I pressed my sex against his firmly. He grunted and threw his head back. Lowering his mouth to my nipple, he circled his tongue around the sensitive nub and then nipped, pulling a hand up to squeeze.

I grabbed his hair with the force of someone much stronger than I looked and jerked his head back. In a hoarse voice, I whispered, "You don't touch me unless I say you can."

He swallowed, laughter dancing in his eyes.

"Understand?" I asked, eyebrows arched.

He gave a nod so slight that it was almost imperceptible. "Yes."

"Yes, what?" My voice had a tough-as-nails edge to it and I was pretty sure that Damien was just humoring me. But the bottom line was it didn't matter what dirt he had on Lenny. One scream from me and T would be in here in a flash, kicking his elemental ass to the curb.

"Yes, ma'am," he said with a mocking Southern accent that made me immediately think of Luis.

"That's more like it." I tapped his jaw with my fingertips. It was a half-smack, half-pat gesture. I rolled my hips over his erection, the size of it causing me to gasp involuntarily. He was *huge*. I groaned, imagining what he would feel like inside of me.

He chuckled, knuckles white, gripping the sides of the chair. "Impressed already, succubus?"

My hardened nipples brushed against the starchy fabric of his shirt and I twisted my fingers into his hair, tugging hard enough to elicit a grunt out of him. I smiled. "I'll ask the questions. How are you with a little pain, elemental?"

He blinked once. Twice. Full lips pressed into a line. "Better than you, I'm sure."

"I suppose we'll never find out."

"I wouldn't be so sure about that."

I slithered my body up his chest so that my breasts were back in his face. Exaggerating my breathing, I heaved them up and down, merely a tongue's length away from his mouth. Damien closed his eyes and inhaled deeply, lips parted.

"You're a breast man," I whispered and ran one nipple down the side of his face and along his parted lips. His tongue darted out, licking his lips as if he could taste the remnants of me.

"With you, baby, I'm an everything man."

"And you say you're not romantic," I muttered in his ear and nipped at his neck.

His hands moved to my hips and he hooked his thumbs into my G-string. I pulled away, instead kneeling on the floor and unfastening his leather belt, pulling it swiftly from the loops at his waist. "What did I say about touching, Detective Kane?" I snapped the belt dramatically.

"I'm sorry, *ma'am*. You're hard to resist." The playful smile tugged at his lips, but didn't quite reach his eyes.

With the belt in hand, I sauntered to the back of the chair and ran my hands from his shoulders to fingertips. Holding them tightly in mine, I pulled his hands behind the chair and, fastening some makeshift handcuffs, belted his wrists together behind him.

"There. That should hold you . . . for now." I pulled his pants down to his ankles, taking a step back to admire him, sitting there in boxer briefs, the smallest bit of chest hair peeking out from his shirt collar. His gray eyes glistened as he looked at me through a spiderweb of long lashes.

I slid my panties down past my hips and thighs. They landed in a pool at my ankles. With a sharp breath, he inhaled the slightest gasp. I bent over slowly and purposefully, making sure to give him a view of my backside as I did so, and lifted the thong from the floor.

Holding out my hand in a theatrical way, I whispered an incantation and within seconds, I held a roll of electrical tape. With a catlike grace, I walked slowly, rolling my hips from side to side toward Damien. His eyes were wide, and when he opened his mouth to say something, I shoved my panties inside and taped them in place, wrapping the roll of tape around the back of his head several times before ripping it with my teeth.

In the back dance rooms, Lucien has a chest of drawers with various toys and costumes. Mood-inducing things. I fished around the top drawer until I found a couple of candles, matches, and a blindfold. "So you think you can handle pain better than me?"

Setting the toys on the floor beside him, I unbuttoned his shirt, revealing a set of tight abs and a perfectly sculpted chest. The look on his face was one to memorize—a mixture of fear and lust. I lit one of the candles, letting the wax heat up and pool around the middle. "Who's first? You or me?"

He grunted a response—the words themselves were unimportant at this point.

When there was enough scorching wax, I tilted my head back and let the hot liquid drip down my chest. I gasped as the burning sensation rolled over my skin. As quickly as it came, it was gone. The hardened wax clung to my body. "Now you." I walked in circles around his chair and slid the blindfold over his eyes. "But where you get it will be the surprise." Leaning down, I ran my lips up the length of his neck and he tensed as he felt me, immediately relaxing as he realized it wasn't wax—just me. "I could do it here," I said and ran my tongue along his salty skin.

Walking to the front, I trailed my fingernails down his chest and over his tight nipples. "Or here."

An evil grin crept over my face. It was almost too mean—could I actually be that girl? Oh, yes. Yes, I could.

In one swift movement, I grabbed the waistband of his boxer briefs and pulled them down to his ankles. "I think you deserve it right here." I cupped his balls in my hand and took notice that he had recently groomed himself. Expecting to get lucky, I see. His erection stood so strong in the air that it took all my restraint not to take him into my mouth right that second. The itch raged between my legs and I forced myself to ignore it. It's not like I could gain any life force from an elemental anyway. . . . Then again, it also meant that he in return would not be harmed by my poison.

His protests began, muffled cries from behind my panties that sounded vaguely like "no." He was actively trying to pull his hands from the leather belt and I knew that with his superhuman strength, that belt wouldn't hold him for more than thirty seconds. Not when he really wanted out.

"Here it comes." I set the candle down and picked up his

beer. Turning it over, the ice cold frothy liquid poured all over his erection.

He screamed out, body tensed, then relaxed as he realized he wasn't in any pain.

I shifted the jumpsuit back on and leaned down, my lips to his ear. "Dinner tomorrow. At McFlanagan's. If you think you're man enough to take me on."

And with that, I walked out.

5

Ireland, 1740

The field was colorless, sparkling with ice and frost, despite the harvest season. Stalks that should have been leafy and green lay withered and parched beneath the frozen prairie. Julian stood next to me, rationing the little bit of water left to the various humans we had saved from dying in the streets.

I wore white. A garment that was full and long and not decorative at all. "Why would God do this?" I asked Julian, attempting to tie a dirty apron around my waist. Not that dirt mattered; as angels, we were unaffected by germs.

He walked over, taking the apron strings from my hands, fingers brushing against mine gently. He hovered to the right of my shoulder, his lips mere inches from my neck as he spoke. "This frost was no act of God. It was Carman. She enjoys the devastation; knowing we cannot interfere in a battle, she mocks us all." His voice was dark and rough and when I snuck a glance back at him, his hardened stare sent a shudder through my body.

"And God cannot do anything? There's nothing to stop her?"

"We hope that other sorcerers who use their powers for good

will step up. God has sent us angels to help the humans. But for weather—no, God cannot reverse her spell." He spoke softly; the words were not loud enough to fall on mortal ears. With a sigh, his features softened and he looked back down at my apron strings, taking his time tying the bow. His fingertips traced the outline of my hip as he finished.

A chill crept over my flesh as I turned my attention out the window again. In the middle of the field, gliding across the frost as if she wore blades on her slippers, was a deathly pale woman. Fiery red hair frayed from her face like a coarse, curly halo. It was long and stuck out in a way that suggested she had not seen a comb in ages. "Oh, dear." I pulled back from Julian's touch, throwing the door open and running barefoot into the snow. The ice felt cool on my feet, but could not give me the same chill it did humans. I ran to her, calling out in Gaelic. She did not respond, but continued to glide across the ice slowly, eyes straight ahead.

I called out in Celt to her—a language I'd thought hardly anyone used anymore. "Ma'am, come inside, please! Warm yourself by our fire!" I caught up to her—a mere arm's length away—only she wasn't walking. Her feet, clad simply in little slippers, floated above the ice. Her dress was clean but tattered, hanging in shreds around emaciated shins.

A crack sounded and she swiveled her head to stare directly into my eyes. As suddenly as I'd seen her movement, she was before me, but a breath away. The stench from her mouth was rancid. Death. Tilting her head to the side, she stared at me inquisitively in a way that almost suggested that she remembered me from another time. Her eyes were ice blue—so fair that they almost looked blanched of color. They had a cloudy film covering them from corner to corner. With a gasp, I stepped back. Away from her milky gaze. Away from her rancid breath. Away from her.

Despite the horror that ran through my body—I found her

beautiful. A terrifying beauty that shot goose bumps from the back of my neck to my fingertips. With no warning, her mouth opened and with jaw unhinged, she let out a wail. The high-pitched noise was one from my past. I had never seen that face. But in my human days—I had heard that scream. I had seen that fiery red hair passing by the window at night.

Julian grabbed my shoulders, shaking me from the trance. "Monica! Monica, are you all right? What is it?"

"The-the woman . . ." When I turned back around, she was gone. "The red-headed woman. She was here just a moment ago."

Julian's brow furrowed over two concerned eyes. "Just now?"

I nodded. He knew I wasn't lying. By our very nature, we couldn't. Omission of truth, absolutely—but not an outright lie. A chill slid over my body, colder than the snow beneath my feet.

"You couldn't see her." It was a statement, not a question as I stared at the empty space next to me where she stood seconds before. "She had the strangest eyes—milky white and a pale blue like . . ."

". . . ice." Julian finished my sentence for me. I swallowed and closed my eyes, not wanting to look at him just yet; not wanting him to see the fear she injected into my veins. Angels were not supposed to feel fear. We were supposed to put our faith in God without doubt, yet this was growing harder and harder with each human who died in my arms.

"Did she scream?" Jules's voice pulled me back from the abyss.

I slowly opened my eyes, noticing just how close he was standing. How good his body felt pressed up against mine. I pushed the tingle he created away. "Yes. It could shatter your bones."

His face dropped as he nodded. "You saw a Banshee. The Irish Faery of Death."

"A Banshee?"

"Yes. They are souls that have been imprisoned to be the bearers of bad news. Typically, it's a sort of limbo state for the soul until they commit a selfless act to free their soul. They are destined to walk the Earth, bringing death and sorrow to those around them."

"So she appeared to tell me someone's going to die? That's no news. People all around us are dying."

"Perhaps the death will not be a human one."

"We cannot die . . . can we Jules?"

"We can in spirit." He took my hand leading me back to the cabin. But that face—her face was one I could never forget.

I woke from my dream—the memory was one I had not thought of in ages. The Banshee's scream echoed in my head and I clutched my temples, curling up in the fetal position until it went away. The memory from Ireland was one I had pushed away for so long. The scream from the other night—it had been the Banshee. That's why no one else on the corner had heard her. She was back.

The dream woke me up at 4 AM and I managed to fall back asleep for a few more hours. Finally, at nine, I threw my covers to the side and padded into the kitchen.

I plopped onto my couch with a bowl of cereal and turned on the TV, hoping for an episode of *SpongeBob*. As I turned on the television, a banner ran along the bottom of the screen, flashing *Breaking News.* I changed the channel. I didn't really care about what craziness humans were getting themselves into this week. But as I kept flipping, I noticed it was on every major network. Finally, I stopped to see what the Hell was going on and why in fuck it was keeping me from watching morning cartoons.

A vanilla-looking woman with a blond bob haircut and a gray suit stood in front of some sort of town-square-looking area. "We have breaking news just in—a mutilated body was discovered in Salt Lake City, Utah, at five-fifteen this morning. The coroners have yet to give an estimated time of death. It appears to be some sort of ritualistic killing. Authorities have yet to confirm if this death is in any way linked to the victim found off I-15 two weeks ago. The victim, a sixty-four-year-old local farmer, Moe Kaelica, seems to have been brutalized sometime late last night or early this morning and left naked for dead here in Salt Lake City. According to friends and family, Mr. Kaelica was a God-fearing man who lived a simple, hard-working life. Right now, they are preparing to move his body out of the area." The cameraman turned the focus over her shoulder where a human body was outlined beneath a sheet. Leave it to Salt Lake City's coroner team to not even have a proper body bag. This town probably hasn't dealt with a brutal murder in ages. Two men with uniforms labeled CORONER lifted the stretcher, and as they did an arm slipped out from under the sheet, dangling stiff and lifeless over the edge of the gurney. The bowl of cereal slipped from my hands, spilling multicolored milk all over my hardwood floor. On the inside of his wrist, he had a Gaelic symbol carved into his flesh. My human family's crest.

6

Though I didn't often think of my family crest, I still recognized it immediately. After years of my parents teaching me to knit the crest onto our clothing and branding our sheep with that symbol, it wasn't something I could easily forget.

I immediately thought back to Adrienne's case—didn't she say it was out of town in Utah? Why did I have to be so petty and not bring the file home? Though I hadn't had any intention of helping initially, if this case had anything to do with my family lineage, I had no choice but to look into it. Was it a warning to me? About the bounty on my head? Curiosity kills the damned.

I mopped up the spilled cereal and grabbed my things, making a mad dash for the cafe. Could it be the same serial killer Adrienne and Damien were looking for? I didn't think she had mentioned anything about the killings being quite so public, but then again, I hadn't given her much time to say anything about the case. I was *supposed* to read about it.

As soon as I walked into the cafe, I could hear muffled shouting coming from Drew's office. I recognized Adrienne's voice, calmer, but tension broke with each word. When I looked to my left, Damien was sitting at a table with his chair leaned back on two legs. He looked at me, taking a long, slow sip of his black coffee. "They're having a fight."

"No, shit." I replied. "About what?"

"We have to leave again. On that case she was asking you about yesterday."

"Where are you going?"

"Salt Lake City."

"So the news today—that *was* your case?"

He rolled his eyes. "So I guess you didn't take a look at the file? What the Hell is it with you and reading those files?"

Tension set in my jaw and I gnashed my teeth. "I was a bit too busy last night working to read a case I'm not even getting paid for. You know, that little job I have every night."

"Ah, yes. *Working*." There was a pause as he stared at me and I couldn't help but picture him bound naked to the chair. It was rare that I felt self-conscious, but the scrutiny of his gaze was enough to make me shift my weight back and forth. "I managed to make it home all right, in case you were wondering." His gaze held mine, his eyes flickering like a flame.

I smiled and hitched my bag higher onto my shoulder. "I never doubted you for a second, Detective Kane." Then I added, more quietly, "At least you had that wood chair to keep you company. She can be a real talker, huh, elemental?"

"She wasn't the only wood I had to keep me company." He cleared his throat, gray eyes crinkling at the corners. "By the way, I'm going to have to cancel dinner tonight."

Though his voice sounded regretful, there was the smallest quirk to his mouth as if his erratic schedule was somewhat amusing. I hated that little translucent smile. He was so cocky. "That's all right," I replied, "I already arranged a backup."

His barely-there grin dropped immediately. "What? Who? That Cajun son of a bitch?" he growled. *Territorial bastard, isn't he?* It was of course a bluff; I had no man waiting in the wings, but he and I both knew I could find one faster than a heartbeat.

I leaned in, my breath blowing the hair above his ears as I spoke. "You don't need to know who."

He closed his eyes, inhaling deeply. "Woman, you will be the death of me," he murmured so quietly that I wasn't sure I was even supposed to hear it.

Turning to walk back to my locker, I heard the clack as he placed his chair's legs all on the floor. I grabbed the file from my locker and rifled through the papers. The first victim had been found on the side of the road, hung across a highway sign, naked, and drowned. As though someone had strapped her down and forced water down her throat with her nose closed. A strange death, indeed. She had then been left on a highway sign for all passers-by to see in a very public and similar manner, like the farmer from this morning.

I flipped through the pictures of her body—there were some wide shots, interiors of the car found next to the crime scene, and close-ups of each body part. I stopped when I came to a macro image of the inside of her thigh. Two puncture marks were bloody and gaping. My hand instinctually touched my leg where I still bore two similar marks. Though most people who saw them initially thought they were birthmarks, they were in actuality scars. A constant reminder of the night I became the succubus standing here today. A shiver slithered down my spine, hitting each vertebra like a step on a staircase as the visual of my family's crest carved into the farmer's arm popped back into my mind.

I tucked the folder under my arm and headed back out front. With my supernatural hearing, I could still hear the fight in Drew's office, but it had quieted down significantly. So much that I was pretty sure Damien and I were the only two who could hear them now.

Walking back out to the front, I sat down across from Damien. "Change of plans," I said. His eyebrows arched, but he said nothing in return. There was a flash of something in his eyes—anger, maybe. "We're going to have that date after all."

"Is that so?" There was a coldness to his voice. He lifted his empty coffee mug to his lips and then, as though remembering he had drained the last of it, dropped it back down onto the napkin. "And just how are we going to swing that with you in Sin City and me in Mormon-ville?"

"We're keeping our date because"—I held his gaze, the corners of my mouth twitching into a small smile—"I'm going with you to Utah."

"You two are dating?" Drew's voice made me jump, and when I turned, I came face-to-face with one hundred and seventy-five pounds of stern mouth and muscle.

As if forgetting that his girlfriend was right beside him, he shook his head and pulled his gaze from mine, turning back to Adrienne. "I want to come along, too."

Adrienne's head flopped down, defeated. "Drew, you can't tag along. This is an investigation—"

"And you're a civilian," Damien finished for her, his voice vibrating with authority.

"And just what is Monica?" Drew said, eyebrows hooded low over his eyes.

"She's a . . . consultant. On the case." Damien answered with the same commanding tone.

I sent Drew a shaky smile, which he didn't bother returning. "Were you even going to ask me for time off? Or did you just assume you'd have a job whenever you chose to return?"

I stood back up, my nose coming to the middle of his sternum. "Fine. Drew, may I please have a few days off to do some freelance work?" I said in a mocking tone.

"No." I stumbled back a step—there was something on his breath. Whiskey? Wine, maybe?

I stared at him through narrowed eyes and lowered my voice. "Drew, are you—are you drinking again?"

"What?" His voice roared through the cafe and he instinctively took his own step back.

On a sigh, I let the argument go. This was neither the time nor place to call attention to his alcoholism. "C'mon, Drew. You're being petulant. Just give me the fucking time off. How often do I request vacation days? Besides, *you're* the one always telling me I'm better than *this*." I gestured around the cafe. Then, with a sweeping hand movement across my body, added, "And *this*. Then when I try to take time off for a legitimate job, you say no?"

He crossed his arms, jade eyes hardening into a stare. "You're not even giving me any notice. My answer is no."

His sudden dominance was both infuriating and sexy all at once. Goose bumps rose on my arms as I remembered our night together, how he'd held me down while thrusting into me.

"No?" I arched an eyebrow and almost imperceptibly shifted myself so that my hair was glossier, eyes brighter, skin glowing. "You sure about that?" I released the succubus pheromone that I so often held in. My irresistible glamour wrapped around his body like silk sheets, coaxing like a soft purr and crooked finger.

Adrienne inhaled sharply to my left and I immediately broke the spell, casting an apologetic glance her way before I could even stop myself. Yeah, I hated her, but so blatantly sexualizing Drew in front of her was a low even for me. As if nothing had happened, Drew's angry gaze returned. "Yes, I'm sure. You really want to go . . . ? You can quit."

It was our bit again. The same conversation we had had over and over the past six months. He stood in front of me, tapping a foot waiting for my rebuttal.

"Fine," I said quietly. His mouth tipped up into a triumphant smile.

"Good." His voice brimmed with arrogance.

I raised my chin, staring into those sparkling eyes. "Fine, I *quit.*"

His arms, which had been crossed in front of his chest fell to his sides. "What?"

"You heard me. I fucking quit."

His face flushed red and Adrienne rested a hand on his forearm, her touch so soft, fingers merely fluttered over his skin. An instant calm rolled over Drew and he took a deep breath, exhaling it through softly parted lips. Damn that angel magic—the ability to calm people with a simple look or touch. It was one I missed.

"Monica. You don't have to do that. You'll give her the time off, right Drew?"

Though he was visibly calmer, anger still brewed beneath the surface.

"No need," I said. "I've been meaning to move on from this place anyway."

Drew's face flushed red at that. Adrienne swallowed and turned her attention back to him. "Okay, Drew," she said in a willowy voice. "You can come along with us to Utah."

"What?!" I shouted.

"You've got to be fucking kidding me." Damien's shoulders thumped against the back of his chair. "He is a civilian, Adrienne." *Thank Hell for Damien*, I thought and stood back, letting him handle this one.

Her cheeks plumped with a slight, gentle smile, one that suggested she had dealt with Damien's tantrums before. "Drew's right—Monica's a civilian, too."

He stood abruptly, his shoulders squared to her. "That is *different* and you know it."

Her smile deepened and the tiniest creases formed around her eyes and mouth. They might have made another woman look weathered, but on Adrienne, they were charming. "Perhaps. But"—her voice dropped to a whisper even though I was pretty sure Drew could still hear her—"I think he should come along." Something passed between the two—an unspoken language. "Besides, you'll stay out of the way, won't ya?" She nudged Drew playfully with an elbow.

"The answer is *no*." Damien's voice sliced through the air with an edge that made the back of my neck itch.

Adrienne just held his stare, not glaring, but not smiling either. The two continued like statues until finally, Damien spoke. "Fine. I suppose it would be nice to have someone to make us our lattes in the morning. I take my espressos as a double shot, Drew." His muscles relaxed and he fell back into a slouched position in the chair. "Tell me, barista, do you even know how to button a shirt?" He looked up and down Drew's simple Hanes T-shirt, an arrogant grin tickling the edges of his lips.

"What are you doing?" I hissed at Damien through a clenched jaw. He glanced in my direction, then right back at Drew again, ignoring my question.

Drew's eyes narrowed. "Gee, I don't know. I guess I can always have Adrienne button it for me in the morning." He snaked an arm around her waist, glaring at Damien as he pulled her in for a tight embrace.

"What the Hell are you going to do in Salt Lake City, Drew? We're all going to be working and you'll be . . . what? Sightseeing? It's not exactly a city known for its party scene."

"Well, lucky for me, I'm not a man known for my partying." The loving look he'd sported with Adrienne disappeared, replaced with a hardness that was rarely ever directed at me. "Besides, Salt Lake City is a recovering alcoholic's dream."

"Are you so sure that's what you are these days?" The smell of alcohol was faint, but it was definitely there. And if I could smell it, I was damn sure Adrienne could, too.

Adrienne shot me a look that could make flowers wilt and

squeezed him closer, nuzzling into his chest. "Let's go get you packed, huh?" The two walked hand in hand back to his office, but not before she sent me another glare over her shoulder.

"A week with them, and I'll stake *myself* to the center of town square." I muttered, rubbing my temples with two stiff fingers.

"Me fucking too," Damien agreed.

7

Another amazing perk of being a succubus . . . you don't have to pack anything when going on a road trip. Not even a toothbrush. I stood in my closet, looking around at my various things. Yes, all of it could have been shapeshifted, but there's still something special about actually owning your clothing. Like owning a piece of history. It's a fine line to tread though—being alive for almost three hundred years, you could become the most interesting hoarder ever, ending up with dozens of storage units all over the world.

If it had just been Damien, Adrienne, and me going on this trip, I could have gotten away with packing nothing. But with Drew tagging along, I'd at least need some sort of bag with me. Something that alluded to me being like every other woman. I grabbed a duffel bag from the top shelf and threw in a couple pairs of jeans, a dress, some T-shirts, and my favorite pink, fuzzy robe. I can't leave home without it.

A sizzle echoed quietly through my bedroom, sounding like bacon on a frying pan. And just as I registered what the noise was, Lucien's power slammed into me, physically knocking my back against the wall.

"Were you planning on telling *me* that you were leaving?"

I coughed, sputtering out an answer. "Yes, of course." I had actually completely forgotten about asking Lucien for a leave of absence, but that was the absolute last thing he needed to hear at the moment.

"When? From the road? From the plane? Maybe you were going to send me a postcard from Utah with a picture of a bunch of fucking Mormons smiling and waving at me?"

Damn, I'd forgotten how pissy Lucien could get. He almost never exudes such potent power around me—then again, I've been particularly bitchy lately. But considering the stellar work I'd been doing for him and his sector, you'd think he could fucking ease up a little. "Could you scale the power play down?" I said through a raspy breath. "I can barely breathe."

The power whooshed out of the room as quickly as it had come and Lucien stood before me, arms crossed. Bushy eyebrows were so low over his eyes, wrinkles were forming between them. He was muscular and his raven hair was pulled into a ponytail at the base of his neck. Lucien had never revealed all of his backstory to me, but I did know that he came from Romania originally. And he was old. Like, really, really old.

I took a deep breath, allowing it to fill my lungs and exhaling before answering him. "Look, I was going to ask you . . . after I packed."

His face softened into a crotchety smile. "Packing?" He peeked into my bag using his pointer finger to poke around inside. "Oh, yes. That's right. . . . Your human is going, too."

"He's not *my* human," I said, crossing my arms.

"I don't give a fuck about him. Or this trip. Or the 'murder case' you want to investigate. I'm not losing my best dancer." I noted how he said *murder case* as if it was an alleged thing.

"Fucking Hell, Lucien!" I threw my hands up. "I'm not leaving forever. A weekend . . . five days at the most."

He snorted and pushed my duffel bag to the side. "No." He growled and looked at me, his eyes darkening to almost black.

I grabbed the duffel bag and zipped it up. As if that would prevent him from looking inside again if he wanted to. A thought popped into my head and I looked up at my boss; from the skeptical look that slid over his face, I must not have hid my epiphany very well.

"What is it?" he said, turning his head to the side.

"I'm going to be in Salt Lake City."

"Yes, I know." He rolled his eyes and tucked his hands into his front pockets as if he was already bored of me.

"Yes—what if I, er, acquired some souls up there for you? Some Mormon Tabernacle Choir boys would certainly get you noticed by the bigwigs in Hell."

His eyes flashed with something—greed? Power? And he ran one hand across his stubble. "Some good ol' Christian boys, huh?"

It was appealing to him. I'd known the idea would be. I held his gaze, refusing to look away first.

"But it's not my sector." He scowled.

"When has that ever mattered to anyone in Hell? A soul's a soul."

"Demons are very territorial. It might start a war."

He was right about that. Fucking demons were babies about their lands. "So, let's work out a deal with the ArchDemon there. Let her bring a couple of her girls down here for the weekend. That way you're not left shorthanded, too. Kayce and I will go up to Utah—"

"No," Lucien boomed. "Not Kayce." I arched my eyebrows, suppressing the smile that threatened to spread across my face. "It seems you're territorial over more than just land, I see." Kayce and Lucien just needed to fucking get together already. They both so clearly wanted it.

"Bring George. It'll look even better if he gets some guys to come out of the closet."

"And you'll take care of the ArchDemon up there?"

"Oh, yes. Claudette and I go way back," he said with a smirk. "By the way, you forgot to pack underwear." He gestured to my luggage.

Folding my arms below my chest so that it pushed my cleavage even higher, I replied "As it is, it doesn't look like I'll be needing any, anyway."

By that afternoon, I was "packed" and ready to go. I waited in line at a chain coffee shop at LAS airport for the group to reconvene. I ordered my usual—a caramel mocha latte—and the baristas stared at me as though I had ordered pizza at a coffee shop. "It's easy," I explained. "Make a latte and add a shot of caramel flavoring and a shot of mocha syrup. Drizzle some warm caramel on top." Once it had been made, I found a table close to our gate and dragged my stupid duffel bag behind me. Damn, clothes could get heavy! Under my breath, I whispered in the foreign language of Adrienne's witchcraft, which I had been practicing. A handkerchief materialized in my pocket and when I pulled it out, couldn't help frowning at the sight of the ugly ninety-nine-cent Wal-Mart square of fabric. I had definitely been going for something silky and pretty. I had to remind myself that I was still new at this; even shapeshifting can take a while for a fledgling succubus to learn. And witchcraft was not a skill I was adept at yet. But that's the beauty of being immortal. You have eons to perfect a new talent. There wasn't much I wasn't good at anymore. And that's not a statement on how awesome I am—more of how old I am.

"Excuse me," a man's voice said from my left and when I looked up, I was staring into blue eyes and sandy brown hair that was cut military short. "Awfully large table for such a small woman." His eyes flashed. Honestly, I didn't know what gave men such blatant sexual courage. Yes, he was attractive and sure, I was interested. But man, come on a little strong, why don't ya? "Mind if I share the table with you?" he asked, then gestured around to the rest of the seating area. "There's nothing else open."

I took a moment to look up at him and into those blue eyes, so dark that they almost looked brown from some angles. He was attractive—wearing a uniform with little wings pinned to his lapel. It meant he was either a flight attendant or a pilot. On one hand, a male flight attendant wasn't all that appealing of a career choice. On the other hand, I wasn't sure he looked old enough to be a pilot, and heaven help us all if our lives were in this boy's hands.

I narrowed my eyes at him. "I'm actually waiting for some people."

His full lips twisted into a half-smile and took a sip of his coffee, the other hand resting on his small rolly-luggage suitcase. "Of course you are," he said as though he were in on some sort of secret. "But I could keep you company while you wait."

"Are you a flight attendant?" I asked rather brazenly, even for me.

The question seemed to catch him off guard and he rolled back on his heels instinctually. "No," he said, pointing to the wings on his lapel, "a pilot. First officer."

I shrugged and pulled my duffel bag off of the seat next to me. "Have a seat. But I really am waiting for people."

A smile arched across his face as he sat down. "Sure you are."

I dropped my jaw in exaggerated shock. "I am. Would I lie to *you*? A pilot?"

"I guess I wouldn't know, now, would I?"

"I suppose not." I smiled behind my coffee cup and took a

sip. His aura was okay—not perfect, but good enough. There was a hint of something magical about him—but it was barely even a trace. I wondered if even he knew he had abilities.

"Where you off to?" he asked, craning his neck to read my ticket.

"Salt Lake City," I replied.

He raised an eyebrow. "The 6:24 flight?"

I nodded and he slapped a hand to his thigh, all smiles. "No kidding. That's my flight."

An icy chill ran through my body and I froze, spine stiff. Coincidences didn't used to startle me, but now I didn't trust them. "No kidding," I said, monotone, mocking his response.

"Small world, huh?" He smiled and held out a hand, palm up. "Let me see your ticket."

I pulled the strip of paper closer to my body. "Why?" My voice was no longer fun and flirty, but a dangerous purr.

"Just trust me." He nudged his hand closer to me. When I didn't respond, he rolled his eyes. "C'mon, seriously. What could I possibly do with your ticket? If I lose it, you just go see that nice lady there and she prints you another." He pointed to a desk with a woman in a navy suit typing at a computer.

"Okay, fine." I slapped the ticket into the palm of his hand and he examined it, reading.

"Oh, no. This won't do. A pretty thing like you can't be seated right in front of the bathrooms." He stood and held up a finger, signaling for a moment. After talking to the woman behind the desk for a few minutes he came bouncing back over, a proud smile on his face.

"Here you go." He presented the new boarding pass as though it were made of gold. "First class. Have whatever you like—food, drinks. It's all on me." Those full lips turned up into a smile and he placed his hands on hips, emphasizing two well-defined biceps. The sight sent a tremor down to my torso, my nipples tightening. I crossed my legs and held in my pheromone. I could not take time off our pilot's life. What if I did and the result was he died while flying the plane? No. Too many lives were at risk.

"Thank you." My anxiety melted away as I clutched my new boarding pass.

"Anytime." He took his seat across from me again and leaned on both elbows. "So, you know what I do. What about yourself?"

I shrugged. "I have a few jobs."

"A Jane of all trades, huh?" He chuckled and continued to lean in as though he was captivated by this dull conversation. "What's bringing you to Utah?"

"A . . . gig," I wasn't really sure how to define my role on this case. "I guess you could say I'm a freelance detective."

Damien's deep voice resonated behind me, so low that it reverberated through my body. "You're a detective now, huh?"

I jumped and when I turned around, Damien stood close behind me—too close. I could have leaned my head back on his stomach.

"Shit! Don't creep up on a girl." My shock quickly turned into annoyance. "This is Damien. . . . Damien, this is . . ." I paused, realizing I didn't know the stranger's name.

He stood, holding out a hand. "Aaron."

"Uh-huh," Damien grunted. And instead of taking his hand, he grabbed the coffee cup Aaron had been drinking from and placed that in his palm instead.

"Right." Aaron looked down at his to-go cup, then back at me. "Well, I need to go prep the plane for our flight. Enjoy your first-class ride. I'll be in Salt Lake City all day tomorrow—if you're free. . . ."

"She won't be," Damien growled.

I glared at him, then brought my eyes back to Aaron. "Yes. Maybe. I'm not sure how busy work will be."

"Very," Damien interjected again.

I darted my head back to him. "You don't *know* that."

"Yes, I do. I'm your boss."

Clicking my tongue, I rolled my eyes. "I will let you know if you give me your numbe—"

"I wrote it on the back of your boarding pass," he said with a presumptuous smile. "At the very least, I'll see you on the flight, Monica." He nodded at Damien and headed off to the gate.

Damien plopped down across from me. "Well, that was rude," I said crossing my arms.

"Babe, you haven't even seen rude yet," he said through clenched teeth.

"Don't. Call. Me. Babe," I said slowly, hitting each word dramatically.

The tension in his jaw dissipated and he leaned back in the seat. He was wearing a Ramones T-shirt that crinkled as he folded his arms. "Man, you are awfully moody lately, succubus. If I didn't know better, I'd ask if you were on your period."

I rolled my eyes, giving him one of those looks. You know, the look that implies one more word might result in my foot up his ass. "I'm just really not looking forward to this trip."

"No?" An eyebrow arched above a steel-gray eye, and he smirked in that sexy way of his. "I have to admit that I am. Since Adrienne and Drew are sharing a room—that means you and I are left to share. I call the left side of the bed."

"Sounds cozy. You on the left, me on the right . . . and George in the middle."

"What?" His smile wilted like a flower that hadn't been watered.

"Oh yeah." I thumped a palm to my forehead, exaggerating. "George is coming along. And the only way I could convince Lucien to give me time off was if I promised to fuck multiple Heaven-bound boys. George, too. So keep a lookout for a sock on the door."

His eyes darkened. "Maybe I'll get my own room."

"Maybe that's best," I said.

I managed to avoid Drew and Adrienne for most of the preboarding stuff. And even now, as we were in line to get our seats on the plane, I stayed at the front of the group and they hung in the back.

I hiked my bag over my shoulder, wishing not for the first time that I had thought to pack a bag that rolled. I had more strength than most humans—so it wasn't that the bag was heavy. Just an annoyance.

"I still can't believe you managed to get a first-class upgrade. Bitch," George said beside me, nudging my shoulder with a smirk. "Five minutes with me and that straight boy would have been playing for another team."

Damien snorted. "It is going to be a long, *long* weekend."

I shifted the bag to my other shoulder, changing weight on my hips.

"Need a little help with that?" Damien's breath on my neck quivered deep within my belly. Sex was a drug for me. One that got deep under my skin making me ache for it. The more I had it on a frequent basis, the more I craved it. The stirrings of my itch began between my legs and I swallowed, suppressing the urge. It wouldn't be satiated with Damien anyway, so what was the point? *For pleasure, you idiot*, said a little voice in the back of my head. I pushed it away. Sex was a means of survival; that was it.

"I'm fine." But even as I said it, I could feel my neck muscles tense.

He wrapped a finger into my hair, twirling it around, and let his fingernail graze my jaw. "Well, well, well, I didn't realize I had such an effect on you." His finger slid against my moist skin, slick with a sheen of sweat. I shifted it quickly away.

"We would now like to welcome our first-class passengers,"

a woman's voice echoed over the intercom. I took off, leaving the group behind me and made a beeline for my seat on the plane. I just needed to get comfortable in my leather chair with a glass of crisp, white wine. After stuffing my bag in the compartment above, I collapsed into the seat, shut my eyes, and crossed my legs in a weak attempt to satiate the itch raging between them. The leather was cool beneath me and no one else came to sit in the seat beside me. I couldn't help but wonder if Aaron had arranged for that as well.

"Hey again." Aaron slid into the seat next to mine. He was so tall that his knees were at a forty-five-degree angle while he sat.

I couldn't help but smile when I saw him. "Hi, back. You're nothing if not persistent, huh?"

He returned my smile and brushed away a piece of hair that I had purposefully let fall into my eyes. Guys were always a sucker for that. "I was going to ask you before the angry guy interrupted us—did you want to come hang out in the cockpit? My captain said he wouldn't mind if you wanted to chat in there while he took care of pre-flight preparations."

My smile spread even wider at the absurdity of the question. I was, of course, already a member of the mile-high club . . . but never from within the navigation area.

"Are you saying you want to show me your *cock*pit?" *Oh, this could be fun. . . .*

His smile fell into a needy look that make all my hairs stand on end. "That's exactly what I'm saying." He leaned closer, eyes flashing with something deprived and determined.

"Is there any way to see inside while we're in the air . . . ?"

The question registered on his face with shock, and his mouth dropped before he answered. As he blinked, the lust faded from his eyes and they brimmed with a new hesitation. "Uh—well, we have pretty strict rules. I-I don't know. . . ."

"That's okay," I cut him off. Maybe he was more innocent

than I had originally thought. Besides, as I'd thought before—it truly was a bad idea to take time off the life of the man who was flying my plane. I wouldn't die, but a plane crash would hurt like a bitch.

"No, wait." He looked panicked and held a hand up, palm out. "We each take breaks once we get to our desired altitude. We take fifteen minutes to get water, stretch, use the restroom, etc. I could get you in while he's on that break—but"—he swallowed, eyes darting around the plane and lowered his voice—"we'd have to be quick about it."

My mouth twitched and I suppressed a smirk. "Quick about what, Aaron?" I asked, eyes wide, head tilted. Again, he opened his mouth to answer, but seemed at a loss for words. I put a hand to his face and brushed my thumb across his bottom lip. The itch flashed from deep in my core and I closed my eyes ignoring her pleas. "It's probably a little risky, huh? Maybe we should wait and meet up properly. After we land, I could probably grab a drink somewhere, if you're interested?" It was an absurd question; of course he was interested.

There was a droop to his eyelids. A sadness, perhaps at the thought I wouldn't be joining him for some in-air playtime. "Promise? A drink when we land?"

He was a little stalker-like, sure. But I'd need to stock up on energy reserves somewhere.

"Sure. After we're on the ground."

8

Ireland, 1740

"I found a warlock," Julian rushed in from outside, shutting the heavy wood door from the frost, chilly air gushing in with him.

I ran to him, taking some of the wool he'd brushed from the few sheep we had managed to keep alive.

"Someone who can reverse Carman's spell?"

"We can only hope. He certainly has status and monetary means to accomplish it. As of yet, he is our closest chance."

"You must go to him. Immediately. I can tend to the ill."

Julian's face tensed, eyes shining. "I'm not going to him. You are."

I took a step away from my mentor. Surely he had misspoken. "You cannot put the fate of these people in my hands," I whispered, gesturing behind me to where the sick lay in pain. "I have no idea what I'm doing."

"We have little choice in this matter, Monica. We can't teleport into the grounds—only right outside it. I already attempted to discuss matters with him." Jules's face darkened, a grimness

settling over his features and he suddenly looked weary. "But his footmen demanded that you be sent in my place."

"Me? How did they know me?"

He shrugged and a tension set in his jaw and in his beautifully manicured eyebrows. "I wish I knew. They asked for you by name."

The door blew open with a frigid gust of wind and I hugged my body, shivering as Julian ran, using all his body weight and supernatural muscle to force it shut against the pressure of Carman's angry winds.

He glided forward and his large arms encompassed me in an embrace. He rested his chin on my head and moved his hands up and down my body from shoulder to wrist. "You must go. We have no choice. Believe me, I don't want to leave you in the hands of this sorcerer, but I have faith you are ready to take on this mission. If something goes wrong, all you have to do is call for me and I can be there before this warlock blinks."

"We both know that it takes less than a blink for a warlock to cast a spell—especially one powerful enough to take on Carman."

"You mustn't think that way. He's powerful, but he's no match for an angel."

I turned my nose to the center of his chest and inhaled his spicy scent. Like peppermint. "You could barely shut the door just now."

"A little faith, seraphim." One hand stopped moving against my arm and clasped my palm, weaving his fingers through mine, pulling my body even closer to his. "Carman is a force to be reckoned with. I could take her—but restrictions prevent me from doing so. We cannot interfere directly with the day-to-day dealings of humans. All we can do is be here to help aid in their sickness. This warlock will have his work cut out for him." The

other hand traced my clavicle up the curve of my neck before landing on my jaw. "Hold on tightly, seraphim."

A crack echoed through the air and when I opened my eyes, we stood on Dame Street in Dublin. Julian's hand still held mine, the other rested on my jaw. "You are here to see Lord Buckley," he whispered, leaning his head to mine. Jules nuzzled my temple as he took a deep breath, his chest expanding into my nose. "Be careful," he whispered, his lips dangerously close. His nose brushed the length of mine and my mouth went dry. A sharp inhale escaped him as I ran a tongue over my lips, his body stiffening beneath my hand.

"I must go." His voice was harder. "The sick need one of us there."

He unlocked his fingers from mine, taking two steps back. His eyes were sad as the crack sounded through the air. He'd disappeared so quickly one would have thought I had been standing alone in the street the whole time.

Turning, I faced the castle. Two men flanked the entrance, standing guard with eyes straight ahead. An outdoor roof was built over the gate and shaded the sun from directly hitting them. The one on the right—with eyes so dark, they almost looked black—glanced at me, his gaze tracing down my face and landing on my neck. My heart beat so loudly, I was certain he could hear it hammering against my ribs. There was something unsettling about the men. Something dangerous and supernatural. A warning shimmied across my skin as I looked upon them. Vampires.

A gust of wind sliced across my face and whistled in my ear. The whistling transformed into a scream. A shrill cry that brought the memory of fiery hair and hollow, milky eyes to the forefront of my memory once again.

9

I awoke with a start, popping up and out of my seat, the scream still echoing throughout the cabin. I covered my ears with two palms and the sound quickly dulled. My clammy skin stuck to the leather and it felt as though I were covered with a thin film. Shifting the sweat away, I stole a glance over my shoulder around the first-class cabin to see if there were any witnesses to my sudden wake-up call. Once again, no one else had heard the scream. Of course they hadn't.

From what I could see, everyone was either reading or watching the little televisions plastered to the seats in front of them. In an instant, the anxiety melted away and I let my head fall back against the seat. The last thing I wanted to do was fall asleep again. Though it didn't seem to matter whether I was awake or asleep; the Banshee reared her ugly head whenever she damned well pleased.

The seat belt clicked as I threw it to the side. As much as I enjoyed first class, right now all I wanted was company. As I stood, a flight attendant came rushing to my side.

"May I help you with something, miss?"

She looked to be in her forties with chemically processed red hair. Attractive, but only one cigarette away from looking haggard.

I smiled sweetly back at her. I had done the flight attendant thing back in the golden days—a Pan Am girl. It was a tough job, made even more difficult by annoying and disgruntled passengers. Granted, in my day it was made more difficult by handsy businessmen who existed before sexual harassment was a thing.

"No, thank you. I was just going to head to the back to chat with a friend of mine I'm traveling with."

"Well, there's plenty of room up here if he decides he wants a row to himself. Any friend of Aaron's . . ." Her words trailed off, eyes dropping to the floor.

I thanked her again and dipped myself beneath the curtain that separated the two areas. As I walked down the aisle, I felt a little bad for how cramped the others must have felt. All the passengers looked like adults being stuffed into children's furniture. Their legs up by their chests. Arms forced in their laps. Maybe I should invite George up front with me. Then Damien could have his own row and I'd have someone to keep me company.

A lump caught in my throat as I approached, seeing Drew and Adrienne. They were sleeping, Adrienne clinging to his arm, head against his shoulder. And Drew's body was angled away from hers, sleeping against the window. The small light above shined down on Adrienne, creating an angelic glow with bits of dust that shimmered and sparkled within the beam of light. Their hands were clasped together in a tangled web of affection; the intimacy was enough to bring bile up my throat. It felt so voyeuristic, watching them asleep together. Like I was a fly on the wall in one of their bedrooms late at night.

"Hey, you," George whispered.

"Hey." My voice sounded dead. Void of emotion and even his voice didn't manage to break the trance I felt while staring at the two.

"What are you doing back here? Shouldn't you be sipping champagne and eating food so rare it can only be hunted in international waters?"

I swallowed, still not able to tear my gaze from Drew. Tears pooled at the base of my eyes threatening to spill down my cheeks.

"Hey," George said again, not a greeting this time, but a consolation. He took hold of my hand, giving it a reassuring squeeze.

With a sniff, I swiped the back of my hand across my nose and brushed across my cheeks. "I'm fine," I said, louder, and finally tore my eyes away from the scene. "Just wanted to say hi." I scanned for Damien and didn't see him.

George nodded in the direction of the back bathroom. "He's back there."

"If you wanna come up to first class, there's plenty of room." My eyes darted to the *happy couple* again. "But just you," I added. "No one else."

My heart felt like a black hole these days. A black hole that continually sucked away any and all happiness. And for the first time in months, I thought it might actually be smart to quit the cafe. Though the threat had been conceived out of stubbornness, perhaps it was the best thing. For both Drew *and* me.

"Sure," George said. And his eyes flickered with sadness—no, sympathy. For me. The thought of someone feeling sorry for me burned through my veins, bringing my blood to a low simmer. There were a lot of people in this world to pity—I was definitely not one of them.

"I might not be there, though. I've got . . . matters to attend to." My voice had a hardness to it that hadn't been there moments ago.

George's eyes narrowed, a tilted smile curving to his eyes. "Matters? Might these matters be currently flying our plane?"

I swallowed and in lieu of an answer, pivoted, making my way to the cockpit.

"That's my girl," George said, releasing his hold on my fingers.

Back in first class, I went to my seat, waiting for the right moment. The flight attendants packed the snack cart and went into the economy class to start serving drinks.

Just as I'd suspected, within a few minutes, the captain came out, stepping into the restroom. Ducking down in my seat slightly, I shifted to look like the flight attendant and surreptitiously stood, walking over to the galley. The bathroom door banged shut behind him as he exited and came over next to me. He had lots of gray hair and a little belly poking out from under his uniform.

"Hi, Captain," I said with a little salute.

"Hey, Meg," he answered with a sigh, grabbing a water bottle.

"Rough night?"

He ran a hand across his face, skin sagging beneath his heavy touch. "Just exhausted. It's my third flight today."

"I talked to Aaron earlier. He seems very refreshed—and there's an empty row right up there." I gestured to the first row in first class. "You could probably sit for twenty minutes or so." I lowered my voice to a whisper. "I won't tell anyone."

"Really?" His eyes widened. "That would be great. . . ." His words faded off as he looked at me through narrowed eyes. "You're usually such a stickler for the rules. What's going on?"

Shit. I shrugged and sent him what I hoped was a nonchalant smile. "I'd just rather have my captain rested during a flight." He didn't say anything else, but nodded in agreement. "Get yourself a blanket and pillow. I'll go tell Aaron where you'll be for your break."

"Thanks," he said, heading to the first row.

Still in Meg's flight attendant uniform, I turned to the cockpit, shifting my face back to myself and slowly turning my hair back to blond. I rapped a knuckle on the door and entered. Once the door shut, I shifted my hair completely back to its normal shade.

"Quick break," Aaron said, not taking his eyes off a book in his lap.

I kept Meg's uniform on, making sure my hair was rumpled and sexy with big, soft curls that flowed just below my shoulders. "We've only got fifteen minutes. You better make it count, First Officer."

His eyes widened to the size of quarters, the book falling out of his lap. "How did you—how did you get that outfit?"

I, of course, had shifted the skirt tighter and shorter and wore a blazer that dipped dangerously low into my cleavage with no shirt underneath. "You like it? May I get you a beverage? Some peanuts?" Taking my time, I strolled over to him. It was a short walk and I was soon swinging a leg over his lap to sit facing him. "I could offer you warm tea—as long as you save the tea bags for me."

His shocked face melted quickly into one of lust, and grabbing the back of my neck, he pulled my face toward his. His kiss was urgent and almost as hard as he was.

Aaron groaned, two large and capable hands massaging my breasts through the blazer. They eventually landed on my hips, squeezing my ass. "They said you were good—but I didn't think you'd be this good."

I froze, an icy chill creeping up my spine. As quickly as the theories formed in my head, Aaron had my wrists clutched in his hands and pinned them to my sides.

"I wasn't initially planning on fucking you before killing you—but now that we've started, I think this might be worth losing a few days of my life."

My body trembled and I flailed my arms wildly about in an attempt to break his hold on me. With my superhuman strength, I should have been able to break his grasp as easily as one peels a banana. A chant that I immediately recognized as witchcraft came from his beautiful lips, barely moving. The foreign language slid easily over his tongue and teeth much in the same way one plays a tune from memory on the piano. My strength was nothing compared to the spell he had just cast.

When he finished the incantation, he tutted in a condescending way.

I closed my eyes, using the power stored from past sexual conquests to shift into a three-hundred pound man. When I opened them again, he was pinned beneath my massive body, face stricken with panic. "Still wanna fuck me before you kill me?" My voice had dropped several octaves.

"You bitch!" he shouted, letting go of my wrists immediately, and I pulled myself off of him, shifting back into my typical human body.

He was now standing at the other end of the cockpit, panting heavily. Relief? Fear? Who the Hell cared. I raised my chin. "The bounty. You've been sent to kill me?"

"Of course," he barely blinked.

I almost laughed. "They sent a human? To kill a demon? You poor fool . . ." I muttered the last part under my breath.

"You're being naïve if you think I'm merely human."

"Even as a warlock, you're still a mortal man. You have no idea what you're up against."

"Ulikai Magen Etu Euto Ulikai Magen . . ." He eyes shut during the chant and a debilitating pain seared through my insides as though a fire were spreading across my organs. Clutching my stomach I fell to my knees, crying out.

His words faded away and so did my pain. I was afraid to look up into those eyes again. Afraid at what I'd see. He knelt down, taking my chin between a thumb and forefinger. "So beautiful," he whispered.

"Can I ask who sent you? At the very least, I deserve to know who's behind my death."

"All I know is they came to me knowing my flights are based out of Vegas. Someone else local turned the gig down."

Someone local.

"And how much are you getting paid?" *Keep him talking. . . .*

"I'll be fairly compensated, upon . . . completion of the job." I gulped, in an attempt to swallow my fear. "But I'll also receive whatever assets you have tied up, as well. And from what I've heard, you've been around for some time and have been quite the little saver."

"So . . . what? You're going to explode my insides with some crazy witchcraft?"

"I have a spell I've been perfecting for quite some time now. Something that will help eradicate the world of your kind."

"Looking to go down in the history books, are you?"

His eyebrow arched in place of an answer and a smile spread to reach his eyes as they flicked to the clock on the dashboard. "I'd love to keep chatting, darling, but we're almost out of time."

He began a different chant this time, one that hung low in his throat, and wind started rushing around us as if someone had opened a window. My hair whipped my cheeks and neck as if someone were lashing my skin. A thin line of fire circled around where I stood, and I froze as I realized what was next to come. Salt. And once I was encased within the salt and fire, I'd be trapped; he'd be able to send me anywhere he wanted in a blink.

My own incantation escaped my lips before my brain could stop it and the wind that was swirling around the room funneled directly to the fire, blowing it out.

Aaron's eyes darted around the room and he stood staring at me, ready to pounce if needed. "How did you do that?" he shouted.

I smirked in an equally evil grin that mirrored his. "Guess we've both got our trade secrets, huh?"

His eyes were wide; terror. "No, it's not possible. A succubus's abilities end with shapeshifting."

"Do they?" I smiled. Oh, this was turning out to be fun. Granted, he was far more advanced in witchcraft than me. But I was now certain that I could at least stave him off until the captain returned.

He advanced toward me—not quite a run, but faster than your average walk. The space in the room was shortened, and his legs were so long, it would only take him mere steps to reach me.

"Shantu Kii Meremeii," I spoke while envisioning a knife. Instead, a broadsword materialized in my hand.

With the momentum he was moving toward me, Aaron was unable to stop and the sword sliced through his body with an ease I hadn't realized was possible. It was easy to forget that human lives were so fragile. His mouth hung open and he gurgled something that I didn't understand as he fell to his knees.

"Oh, shit," I whispered falling with him. "Oh shit, oh shit. I didn't mean to kill you—I just wanted to fight you off."

He still couldn't speak and fell farther to the ground on his side, legs curled in a fetal position. The sword stuck out from his body like a skewered piece of meat. With one last gurgle, his eyes glazed over and the muscles in his face relaxed. "Oh shit," I whispered again while running a hand over his eyelids to shut them. I'd killed him. I hadn't meant to—but in the end, that didn't really matter, did it?

My hair whipped at my neck as I frantically looked around the cockpit for something to get me out of this mess. The captain would come back any minute now to find a dead man on the ground and a sexed-up stewardess busting out of her uniform. I felt around in Aaron 's pocket where his phone was and pulled it out. Sure, they say not to use your phones on a flight, but this was clearly an emergency. I dialed Lucien's number. It rang once before he picked up.

"This is Lucien."

"Get here. Now. I'm in the cockpit."

"Monica? What the—"

I didn't give him the chance to say no. I hung up the phone and tossed it onto the seat. I knew he had placed a constant tracker on me ever since we'd dealt with a murderer in his sector; he could find me in an instant. Part of me wanted to continue holding Aaron's lifeless body. The other part—the self-preservation side—made me lower him out of my arms back to the floor. If I hadn't killed him, he would have murdered me. I'd had no choice. A crack sounded and Lucien appeared in front of me.

"Do you know how hard it is to teleport onto a flying plane, Mon? This better be . . ." His words faded away as he stared wide-eyed at Aaron, sprawled across the floor, sword sticking out of his chest like he had lost some Arthurian battle.

"You've got to be fucking kidding me." His head snapped around to look at me, arm flailing wildly to Aaron's corpse. "How'd this happen?"

I shrugged and tears threatened to spill from the corners of my eyes. "He's an assassin—was scheduled to kill me tonight. I-I don't know; I didn't mean to kill him, but he lunged at me and I tried to conjure a knife, but instead got a sword in hand. At that point it was too late. He ran right into it." I sniffled to keep the tears from exploding.

"Conjured? What the fuck are you talking about . . . ?"

I held up a hand, cutting him off. "Look, we don't have much time. The captain will be back any minute. Can you get his body out of here?"

Lucien snorted and looked me up and down. "Of course I can." He lifted the body with ease and threw him over a shoulder. "Nice outfit, by the way."

"Shut up," I muttered before shifting to look like Aaron. Medium height. Sandy brown hair. Muscular with dark blue eyes. "Close enough?"

Lucien nodded. "A fucking mirror image. You really going to land this plane?" an eyebrow lifted with the question.

I shrugged. "I'm hoping the captain will do the brunt of the work."

"You owe me for this."

"What else is new?" I said under my breath.

Crack. Lucien was gone just as the door to the cockpit slid open.

10

The captain stood in the opening of the doorway staring at me, fake Aaron, with forehead crinkled. "What are you doing standing there?"

"I . . . was just going to page for you."

"From a standing position? Several feet away?" His narrowed eyes darted to our seats at the front of the tiny room.

It took all my power not to glance down at my feet, the bloody carpet below squishing beneath my shoes. Thank Hell for dark carpeting. "No," I said, taking a moment's hesitation. I shifted a cut that looked deep on the palm of my hand. "I cut myself." I held up my palm to show an open, gaping wound. "And I needed to run to the bathroom to clean it quickly." Not only would it explain the blood below me (if anyone took the time to notice), but maybe I could get out of landing the plane.

"Christ, Aaron. Go, but hurry. We're scheduled to land soon."

Classic. He takes an extra long break, then blames the younger kid for needing the bathroom. As I exited the cockpit,

I almost ran directly into Damien's shoulder, speaking with Meg, the flight attendant.

"What do you mean you haven't seen her? She must be here *somewhere*. We're fucking thousands of feet in the air."

Oh shit.

"Excuse me." I touched his arm and his neck whipped around aggressively in my—well, Aaron's face. He cracked his knuckles.

"What do *you* want?"

I cleared my throat and stepped so that Meg wouldn't be able to see my face.

"You're looking for your friend in first class, right?"

"Yes," Damien snarled. "What did you do with her?" He stepped as if he were going to lunge at me.

I shifted my eyes back to blue like Monica's briefly so that he would notice. Shock, then recognition softened his angry eyebrows. "I believe she went to sit in the back with her friends. If she's not there at the moment, she's probably in the restroom."

He nodded slowly, grasping that something was up he needed to just go along with. "Uh-huh."

"We have video monitors up in the cockpit—I was of course keeping an eye on her and saw her back there just a minute ago."

Damien swallowed, jaw clenched. It was most likely pretty jarring to see someone you were attracted to as a six-foot-something man. "Well"—he clapped his hands together in forced jovial tone—"I guess we're good here, huh?" He clapped Meg on the shoulder and she scowled at him. Then he looked again at me. "Thanks for letting me know." He shook my hand in a gentle way that could only be interpreted as sweet. Then, turning, he went back to the economy cabin.

Meg looked at me, creases all over her forehead. "Some people, huh? I wouldn't mess with that girl, Aaron. She's got way too many men protecting her as it is. She smells of trouble."

Oh, Meg. If you only knew.

When I returned to the cockpit, the captain sat waiting for me. "All right, rookie. Ready?"

Ready? Rookie? "Uh—sure." I took the seat next to him, my fingers twitching in my lap.

"Well, let's land this plane." The captain grabbed a fishing magazine from next to his seat and flipped through a few pages.

After staring at him for a few moments, I grabbed Aaron's iPad. "Um, okay." They had autopilot for when they were at the correct altitude. . . . Maybe they had an auto-landing program now, too. It had been some time since I'd been privy to the inner workings at an airline.

"What are you *doing*?" the captain shouted just as I pushed the button to turn on the iPad.

His loud voice boomed through the tiny enclosed space and I jumped, almost dropping the expensive electronic device. "I'm—er . . . landing?"

"Gonna be a smart ass, I see . . . ," he grumbled before grabbing a headset and speaking a bunch of coded nonsense into it.

"I just really don't think I'll be of much use with this hand. It's really in bad shape." I shifted the gash to look even worse, making sure some ligaments and bone could be seen.

"Jesus Christ, kid. Was it that bad a few minutes ago?"

I shrugged. "Must've been, right?"

He shook his head. "Shit. Guess I'll be landing this thing on my own tonight."

I smirked on the inside. Lazy bastard had had a break *and* a nap—he sure as Hell should be landing it, even if Aaron were still here to help. I watched as he maneuvered the controls and the tower with an ease that could only be described as fascinating. Like watching a skilled gymnast perform a flawless routine. As the wheels touched down, I had to stop myself from clapping.

We exited the cockpit and watched all the passengers leave the flight. Damien walked by and caught my gaze. As subtly as I could, I shifted my gaze to the luggage compartment above my would-have-been seat. With an eye roll, he nodded and reached in to grab my duffel bag.

After everyone had left, the captain clasped my shoulder. "You're lucky that was the last flight of the evening for this plane, kid. Otherwise, you would have been stuck here for an hour with post-flight tasks. Go get that hand stitched up."

I nodded and turned to leave. "Hey," he said . . . the tone in his voice giving me pause. "How'd you get that cut, anyway? Pretty nasty one considering how safe these flights are."

I swallowed and turned to meet his eyes. They were narrowed and he had both hands in his pockets, leaning against the door frame. I shrugged. "It's pretty embarrassing. I—I was learning how to knit. And the needle sliced through my hand."

You would have thought I'd told the man I'd taken up puppy hunting by the look on his face. "*You* knit?"

I held up the gashed palm. "Not anymore, I don't. Guess that's why us guys are supposed to leave that task to the women, huh?" I elbowed his belly in a friendly gesture and turned to make my escape once more, rolling Aaron's luggage behind me with his iPad tucked under one arm.

11

I found the group waiting for me right outside the airplane, each with their own suspicious glare. Damien was seething to a point that if you poured cold water on him, steam would have erupted off his body. George had his "what the fuck" face on, Adrienne was wringing her hands, and Drew just looked confused.

"Well? Where is she?" Drew asked the group, eyes tilting down at the corners. My stomach wrenched as I walked past them still in Aaron's body. "If she's not out in another minute, I'm going back in there."

"No!" everyone yelled so loud it made *me* jump.

"Drew, you'll get arrested if you try to go back on the plane," Adrienne said calmly, placing a hand on his forearm. "Let's just give her a few minutes."

The men's room was just a few feet ahead, my sanctuary. Just a few more steps and I could shift back into me. Damien's gaze burned into my back.

"Excuse me!" Drew's voice bellowed from behind me and I sped up the pace. I heard him call out again, but he sounded farther away. I didn't bother looking back, and instead slipped into the men's bathroom. A few men stood at the urinal and as though it was habit, forced themselves not to look up as I entered. One man's eyes twitched in my direction and we made eye contact before he quickly diverted his attention back to the matters at hand.

I slipped into a stall, pulling Aaron's bag with me. After locking the door, I shifted. It was like an immediate comfort; not too dissimilar from taking off a tight dress after a long night of dancing. My breathing was heavy and I sighed, leaning against the side of the stall. Even with having a lot of sex lately, that shift had sucked up a lot of my energy reserves. When I looked down at my fingernails, they were glossy and long—even without my making them so. A telltale sign that my body was compensating for depleted reserves. The more energy we need, the more beautiful we naturally are; a beautiful bait strung up on Saetan's fishing line.

Once I caught my breath, I opened the stall with the intention of just slipping out quietly. It was as though every man at their urinals forgot the unspoken rule of not making eye contact while taking a piss and in unison they looked up and directly at me.

On an exhale, I raised an eyebrow and smirked before strutting to the exit. My confidence shattered as Drew walked in, almost bumping into me.

"Oh, excuse me," he said before it registered whom he was talking to . . . and *where* we were talking. "Monica! What—what are you doing in here!" He dropped his voice, eyes shifting at the other men who were all now staring at us, mouths agape. "This is the men's room, Mon," he whispered as if I didn't already know that.

A nervous laugh strangled in my throat. "Right, I know. I mean—I didn't know at first. And then I came in and, uh, oops?" Clearing my throat, I beelined it away from there. Drew was at my heels.

"We were all pretty worried about you. Where've you been?" The concern in his voice caused a pang in my heart.

"I was the first off the plane," I said over my shoulder. Keep the lies simple. Don't get caught in a web of intricacy. "First-class luxuries, you know."

He grabbed my elbow, spinning me to face him. Drew's green eyes were tilted and his face registered a mixture of emotions ranging from anger to sadness. "Monica," he whispered, a frown marring the space between his eyes. "That pilot—I-I don't know. . . . There's something about him I don't like. Just . . . be careful."

The words were a bee sting on my heart. "Oh," I said with a bitter laugh. "There's a shocker—you don't like someone I'm sleeping with. Takes a genius to dissect that."

His jaw dropped, brows pinching as he registered what I had just said. The muscles in his throat tightened and for all of a minute, my heart broke for him. "You slept with him? Already?" His eyes darted to the bathroom door and his features hardened as though one by one they turned to stone. "So that's what you were doing in there. An airport bathroom. That's classy." His eyebrows twitched with the sarcasm and he tucked both hands into his pockets, backing away from me. "Even for *you*."

My face flamed. He had no right commenting on my choices. Not anymore. "I am a shattered vase, thanks to you. I am thousands of glass shards and you don't get to tell me how to piece them back together when you're the one who broke me in the first place. Besides—" I arched an eyebrow and folded my arms across my cleavage, making sure to push them just a touch higher. He swallowed, his eyes not leaving mine. We were in a standoff, each with loaded guns, ready to draw.

"Why would I need to resort to bathroom fucking? Aaron and I already took care of that in the cockpit."

Drew's face turned bright red, pain flashing across his chiseled features. His lips pressed together in a thin, white line.

"There you are!" George interrupted and stepped between us. He looked at me with apologetic eyes and gently ushered me away from Drew. Wrapping me in a hug, he kissed my temple. "What do you say we get to the hotel?"

George's arms took the place of Drew's as I rested my cheek on his shoulder.

Drew and I managed to ignore each other for the rest of the evening. Within a couple of hours, I had filled Damien, Adrienne, and George in on what had happened in the cockpit and we were checked into the hotel. I collapsed into bed, not even caring that it was only ten o'clock. Not caring that I desperately needed to hunt. And not caring that Drew was in the next room sharing a bed with Adrienne.

The feeling of someone watching you is always startling. I woke with a start, gasping and sitting straight up. The hotel comforter was coarse and scratched against my skin. A breath, short and ragged, caught in my throat and I glanced at the clock. A little before three in the morning. I was about to throw back the covers to splash some water on my face, when I noticed someone at the foot of my bed. She was facing the other way and I could just barely make out the back of her head—red fiery coils of hair. A scream strangled in my throat as she turned slowly to face me, spinning with the grace of a practiced ballerina. She hovered at the foot of my bed, head bobbing up and down, milky eyes regarding me with a stony glare. As if trapped in a block of ice, I froze. A whimpering sound crackled through the air. I was surprised to discover it was my own soft cry.

She cocked her head like a puppy who didn't understand my

fear. I slid a glance to George's empty bed—he was out hunting, no doubt. Panic gripped my throat like two meaty hands and I hesitated before bringing my attention back to the Banshee. Her hair spread out, framing her face like a bunch of red serpents. She parted her lips and I cringed, anticipating the scream.

Instead, she puckered her lips and blew, a stream of black fog escaping her mouth and surrounding my body.

The fog split and instantaneously, her face was in front of mine, close enough to kiss. I clamped a hand over my mouth to stop the scream. Putting a finger to her lips, she shook her head back and forth. Blood stained her fingers as she lowered her hand.

Veins pulsed in my neck, my heart jackhammered against my chest. My throat felt dry despite the full glass of water I had drunk before bed. Her bloody finger moved to my face. I shook my head, desperation in my eyes. *Please don't touch me, please don't touch me. . . .*

She paused, eyebrows twitching together. What could she not understand about this? How did she not realize I didn't want an omen of death touching me?!

With a deep breath, I looked closely at her. How long had it been since she was human? Her features, though terrifying, retained the traits of what once could have been a beautiful woman. A dainty nose and scarlet lips that matched her hair. High cheekbones. Even those milky eyes could have been at one point a bright, luminous blue. She was like a wild animal that had been trained to do a task. A feral cat put in a home for the first time, not knowing how to receive or give affection.

She glanced down at her bloody fingers, then back into my eyes. Did she have any concept that I wasn't human either?

I shifted myself to look like the mirror image of the Banshee, the rush of it making me breathless. I would definitely need to find a conquest soon. Her wild red hair was now mine. Pale skin. Milky eyes. She blinked, her neck twitching at the sight and she raised her hands to her face, feeling her nose, her chin, her cheekbones. Red smears covered her powdery skin. Her mouth tilted into a frown and I couldn't help but wonder if she'd never before seen her appearance. One hand moved to my face, the other still on her own jaw.

I shifted back to myself before she could touch me and her hand jerked back, surprised at the sudden change.

"See?" I whispered. "I'm not human. Why are you coming to me?"

She opened her mouth to speak, a grunt escaping in lieu of words. She sounded like a hound that had had its vocal chords snipped. Teeth clicked together as she snapped her mouth shut and her jaw clenched, lines forming on her flawless porcelain skin. She clapped her hand to her chest and tapped it a few times with her palm, using the other hand to point at me.

With a deep breath, I shifted to look like her again. This time those big milky eyes regarded me in fascination. She tapped her chest again, lighter this time with only her fingertips, and turned her head to the side as if asking, *Me?*

Nodding, I pointed to her. "Yes. This is you." I whispered.

Those milky eyes brimmed with fluid. They weren't your typical tears—they were a translucent gray. Like murky bath water falling from her eyes. Like a rising tide, they spilled over onto her cheeks and the blood on her face mixed with the odd tears, creating an even bigger mess. Her hand stretched out toward my face again and before I could stop it, her still bloody fingers brushed across my lips. Those red coils of hair were the last thing I remembered seeing before I fell into darkness.

12

The rest of the night was just blackness. I slept without dreams; slept without nightmares; slept without worry until the blaring sound of the hotel phone ringing startled me out of the darkness. I shot up out of my deep sleep, gasping for breath.

"Calm down. It's just the wake-up call." George stretched and said through a yawn.

After taking a moment to look around the room, I threw the covers aside, in search of the little coffee maker that comes in these hotel rooms. I looked on the desk, next to the TV, on the vanity mirror . . . there wasn't a single self-service coffee pod anywhere.

George approached as I was looking through the closets where they kept the ironing board and extra hangers. "What in the Hell are you looking for? The magical door to Narnia?"

With a sigh, I sat back on my heels. "I can't find the coffee-pot. I'll just have to pinch my nose and drink Starbucks, I guess."

"Baby girl, hardly anyone in this damn city drinks coffee—that's considered devil-juice."

"What?" I shot to my feet, grabbing George by his T-shirt. "George, if I don't get coffee this morning, I will not be a tolerable person!"

"And how is that different than any other day?" he asked, flicking my hands from his shirt as though they were a mere piece of lint. He shifted into his outfit for the day. A button-down shirt and pinstriped pants. And of course, his newsboy hat. The vibrant blue shirt paired with his mocha skin and perfectly coarse ringlet hair was absolutely delectable. "You finish getting ready. I'll meet you in the lobby in ten minutes—and I promise to have a cup of coffee for you."

I perked at the mention of caffeine. "A latte?"

"Don't push your luck." The door slammed behind him.

I actually changed clothes myself—physical clothes that I had packed with me—as well as did my own makeup. I managed to get just enough energy to shift my hair into something manageable, but even that left me a little breathless.

There was a quiet knock on the door and when I stood to answer, darkness closed in on the edges of my vision. After a deep breath and another knock from outside, I finally managed to open it.

Damien leaned against the door frame. The scent of arabica beans flooded my nostrils and I closed my eyes, breathing it in. "Now that is a sight for sore eyes," I said.

"Why thank you." Damien's smile was cocky and lopsided as he handed one of the cups to me.

"I meant the coffee, jackass," I answered but couldn't suppress my own smile.

"Sure ya did," he winked. He took his time looking me over and my skin tingled under his gaze. "Everything okay today?"

"After a sip of this"—I held the coffee cup up—"it will be."

His smile slipped, revealing more concern than he usually let on. "You look . . . tired. Beautiful, but tired."

With a shrug, I grabbed my purse from the bed. "I'm going to need to power up again tonight. I didn't get anything from Aaron before I—well, you know." Swallowing, I didn't want to talk any more about how I'd murdered a man. Not even to save my own life.

Damien nodded, another smirk spreading along his face. "Well, if you need help in that department . . ."

"And just how would a night with you do me any good? It's not like I can recharge off of you."

His grin widened. "Oh, it would do you good. Trust me."

Giving his arm a playful nudge, I swung my purse over my shoulder and guided him out of my room. "C'mon, Casanova. Don't pretend you could handle me."

He grunted. "Oh, baby. I could handle ten of you and still have enough stamina to take you dancing after."

Damien and Adrienne had arranged all the proper clearances prior to our arrival. They handed me a temporary badge along with industrial-strength pepper spray and a walkie-talkie.

"Really?" I looked at them through an eye roll. "A walkie-talkie?"

"We have a low budget," Adrienne said before walking into the morgue.

When we arrived at the coroner's office, Damien held my elbow, pulling me back from the group. "Oh, there's one more government-issued item." He pulled fuzzy hot pink handcuffs from his file fax and clipped them to my belt loops. "Got them just for you, puddin'."

Should I have been insulted? Maybe. But mostly, I just found it endearing. Even if he'd done it to get a rise out of me.

"In case you need to restrain someone . . . this time you won't have to use their own *belt*."

"Cute," I said. "But I already have leopard-print ones at home." I turned and followed Adrienne into the coroner's office. She and George were already inside shaking the hand of a tall, white-haired man who was round at the midsection but otherwise in decent shape for his age. If we were anywhere other than Salt Lake City, I would have thought the belly was a result of too much beer.

"Has there been an autopsy on the first victim yet?" Adrienne's voice interrupted my observations.

The coroner—Jed—as I came to learn, handed her a file. "Just the other day. Mr. Kaelica has not yet had an autopsy. It's on the schedule for today."

Damien nodded. "Well, let's have a look at him first."

My stomach flip-flopped and I caught Damien's arm just as my knees started quaking. "We're looking at a corpse?" I hissed.

He looked at me as though he were talking to a five-year-old. "What else would we be doing at a coroner's office?"

Damn, if we were going to do this dating thing for real, he'd have to learn to be a bit more empathetic. My mind went immediately to Drew—the way he used to just hold me when I was having a bad day. I quickly pushed him from my thoughts. He hadn't held me like that since the whole Adrienne drama six months ago.

With a shudder, I forced down the sick that was threatening to surface and stiffened my legs, hoping to calm the quaking coming from down there.

"You can always wait out here," Damien said with just the slightest trace of annoyance, "but then I'm not quite sure why my department is paying you for this little visit."

Every muscle in my face clenched and I spoke through gritted teeth. "I am *fine*. Let's go."

"Are you sure, Monica? You don't look so . . . ," Adrienne started.

"I said *let's go.*" If I'd been sure I could walk ahead of them without vomiting everywhere, I would have stomped forward.

A hand on my elbow made me gasp and I released a breath when I saw it was just George. "Hey there," he said softly, taking the empty paper coffee cup from my hand. "Glad to see you're caffeinated." He winked and his full lips curved to his eyes. My George. My rock.

His shoulder was firm against my cheek—not the most comfortable, but I rested on him anyway. "Let's go," he said. "If we lag behind too long they'll think you backed out."

The room was frigid—a giant ice box. But the perishables weren't food. At least not to anyone other than a vampire. And even vamps had standards—they liked their blood pumping. No one liked a frozen dinner.

There were several surgical tables with people covered in sheets. "I was just about to prep him for the autopsy this afternoon," Jed said while peeling away the white cotton sheet.

I bit back a cry at the sight of the dead older man on the table. Damien and Adrienne circled the corpse like a couple of vultures, their gloved hands lifting, poking, and stretching various body parts. His body was covered in slash marks . . . like he'd been hit repeatedly with a switch. His deeply lined face was slackened, but despite being dead, he still looked tense. Runes surrounded his body like faint swirls all up and down his skin. They looked Celtic or of some sort of ancient Irish magic. Taking a step forward, George followed. "He looks . . . familiar," I said to no one in particular. "There's something about him."

Jed held out a box of surgical gloves. "Please," he said, "before getting any closer."

I nodded, and George and I each took a pair, popping them over our hands.

Damien and Adrienne exchanged a look, and he gave her the tiniest little nod. She moved to Jed, her smile turned on like a five-hundred-watt lightbulb. "Dr. Spencer, would you mind if we had a few minutes with the body? We work so much better when we can just brainstorm aloud and our superior would hate for someone not on our team to hear our blathering ideas."

"Well, Detective, I'm really not supposed to . . ."

"Oh, I know," she cooed, slipping the latex glove off and placing a hand on his arm. "And I wouldn't dream of asking you to do anything you weren't comfortable with."

"Son of a bitch," I whispered as his eyes glazed over. A mixed look of adoration and worship overcame his gentle features.

"Of course, Detective. If that's what you need to get the job done."

"So you'll wait for us to call you back in, yes?"

"Yes." Like a zombie he exited the room, the door clamping shut behind him.

Damien snickered once he'd left and Adrienne popped the glove back on. Back to her normal voice. "Well, let's get started for real."

"Having a partner who's an angel really comes in handy." Damien winked at her. "Then again, in your prostitute days, you could accomplish almost as much."

She shrugged. "Might as well use the powers we've got at hand."

Damien pulled the overhead light down to Moe Kaelica's inner thigh. "Look what we've got here. Just like victim number one, he has a vampire bite."

All feelings of queasiness disappeared. I was suddenly alert. "Let me see," I said, pushing my way forward. I moved between Adrienne and Damien. Sure enough, there were two open wounds in the same area. My scars tingled, though I was certain that was entirely in my head. I knew that wound better than I knew how to make a latte, and something about the one in front of me was not right.

"I think we have a vampire murderer on our hands," Adrienne stated, flipping open an iPad. She pushed it into George's hands. "Make yourself useful. Take notes."

"Man, you're a lot bossier when you're on duty," he muttered, sitting in a chair at the corner of the room.

"Not so fast," I cut her off, holding a hand up. "Do you have a ruler?"

The two detectives exchanged looks. Fist to his mouth, Damien cleared his throat. "It's an autopsy room. I'm sure they do."

"Here." Adrienne pulled out a small measuring tape from her purse. I couldn't help the way my face twisted. I mean, who carries measuring tape? As if reading my mind, she answered with an eye roll of her own. "It's for my knitting."

"Of course it is, Pollyanna," I muttered while measuring the distance between the teeth marks. "There. Almost three inches. Who the Hell would have a mouth that big between canines?"

Damien looked at Adrienne, who shrugged. "There are lots of people who have large jaws."

"Really?" My eyes narrowed. It was as though he was opposing me just to be difficult. "Smile wide for me. Let's measure your chompers."

"Could you wash off the tape first?"

After soaping it up and rinsing it off, I held the tape up to his teeth. "There. See? You're an average-sized man . . ."

He scoffed with a crinkle of his brow. "Sweetheart, I'm anything but average."

I chose to ignore the interruption. ". . . and your measurement was just at about two inches. So, we're either talking about a giant . . . or someone is trying to make it *look* like a vampire murder."

Adrienne smiled, and from behind her George gave me a wink. "That's great, Monica. Really . . . good work."

Damien held up a hand. "Whoa, whoa. We can't rule vampires out entirely. We could just have an exceptionally large vamp on our hands."

"We could," Adrienne agreed. "But I'm not about to hedge my bets on that. We'll keep an open mind for now."

"And just who made you the one running this investigation?" His knuckles were bleached of color, clenched onto his hips.

"I could ask you the same question."

After a moment's silence, Damien cleared his throat. "All right then." He chewed his top lip in a very uncharacteristic way. "Anything else on his body that's noteworthy?"

I studied Moe and lifted his left hand. It was stone cold and even harder than I'd imagined it would feel. I turned the hand over—and there it was, my family's crest.

"We saw pictures of this symbol in the file last night. It looks like some sort of old Celtic—"

"It's a family crest," I said, swallowing. Squeezing my eyes shut, I pushed the memories to the back of my mind. It was so long ago, I had to dust away the fog just to remember snippets. I couldn't even really recall what Mama looked like. But her smell—she'd always carried the scent of flour and cedar. My sisters and I would play in the field and as a little girl, I would pretend the sheep were a sea of dragons holding me prisoner. "Or more accurately, it's *my* family crest," I added, quieter. "I wanted to be sure before I said anything." I lowered Moe's hand and raised my eyes to meet Damien's.

His mouth hung open and he clamped it shut at the realization that he was gaping. Quickly diverting his eyes back to his notepad, he scribbled something.

A sudden touch startled me. It wasn't until acrylic nails circled my back that I realized it was Adrienne's hand offering comfort. "Are you sure?" she asked. "It must be years since you've seen it. . . ."

"I'm sure," I snapped. "I have it knitted onto a scarf my

mama made when I was a child. It's back at my apartment if you need to see it. This is sloppy, but it's my crest. Without a doubt."

Damien and Adrienne's eyes locked as if they could communicate without words.

"You mentioned that the first victim had Celtic runes too, right?"

Adrienne nodded. "Yes. We haven't seen her in person obviously, but that's what we were told. We'll finish here and then go see her, as well."

After clearing his throat, Damien pointed out some of the other slashes along Moe's body. "These lashes look like they were made with a switch or something that would have hit hard and fast. It's not the work of a knife or a blade of any kind."

"They're erratic and wild," Adrienne continued for him, looking closer at one slice particularly. She looked again at her file in hand. "We'll have more information post-autopsy, but for now the cause of death is being cited as suffocation."

"In a public square?" The doubt must have been evident on my face because George started rubbing my back in circles, taking over where Adrienne left off.

"We're just going off of what's in the file, Monica," she said quietly.

"May I see it?" I held out a hand, palm up.

"What? You're actually going to *read* one of the files?" Damien said.

I rolled my eyes and snatched it from his hand. "Don't be sarcastic, Damien. You don't wear it well." He smirked and bent to look closer at the body. We both knew I was lying. He did sarcasm in the hottest way possible.

I sat in the chair by the door and started flipping through the pictures. Because of the death's public display, there were crowds of people surrounding Moe's body. He had been staked to a bulletin board in the middle of the town in a Christ-like fashion—hands outstretched, feet bound together. It was the sort of community board where people could hang flyers and business cards. "He was just a farmer," I murmured. "How the Hell does he tie into another murder of a young woman?"

"Could just be random profiling. No rhyme or reason to why he chooses his victims," Adrienne said while looking under his fingernails. "It looks like he put up a fight. We'll find out if there's any DNA under here soon enough."

I remembered what Damien had said back in April—many times, the surrounding scenery holds the clue, not just the body itself. Something as simple as the dirt from the murderer's shoe can be enough to convict. Scanning the picture, I looked at the pavement. The statue. The crowd. Swimming in a sea of faces was one I recognized. In the front row to the right of the body—those hard black eyes. Chiseled, angular features. Skin so deathly pale, it was almost translucent. The mystery man who had helped save me six months ago. The vampire who had turned me from angel to demon. Dejan.

13

Ireland, 1740

The door slammed shut behind me, the heavy wood echoing in the stone entranceway of the castle. With chin raised high in the air, I took two steps inside.

"Hello?" The greeting strangled in my throat and after a cough, I tried again. "Hello? Lord Buckley? You sent for me."

A flame popped from one of the many candles lining the hallway. My stomach clenched as I took yet another step inside. The pads of my fingers were slick against clammy palms. At the end of the hallway, there was a dim light casting a golden glow. I followed it, careful of how I stepped. A sorcerer's power was not one to test.

A beautiful melody, soft and alluring, played somewhere near the light. The talent was so striking that for a moment I simply wanted to lean against the marble and listen with closed eyes. And forget that I had a terrifying job to do. But I pressed on, moving closer and closer to the lyrical noise. At the entranceway, I stopped, peeking my head around the corner.

He was seated at an ebony piano, his back to me. Brown hair reflected the candlelight, creating a subtle glint of auburn. The ends fell to the middle of his neck, curls twisting around each other. His white shirt was loose and billowed as his arms moved along the ivory piano keys, fingers fluttering like butterflies over a rosebush. I'd expected him to be in tails and a waistcoat. Something fitting of a lord serving his own castle.

The song finished on a chord that angels themselves couldn't have sung more perfectly. "That was lovely." My voice, though barely above a whisper, echoed through the room.

It was a slow routine, one I could tell he did daily. He closed the piano, stretched his neck to each side, and stood to a startling height of at least six feet. When he did finally turn to greet me, the smallest half-smile ticked at the corners of his mouth. "Thank you." His English was flawless but there was a twinge of a French accent.

"My name is Mo—"

His bright green eyes flashed and the half-smile tilted even more. "Yes, Monica. I know your name."

Silence settled like a thick fog between us and I cleared my throat, looking around the room, pretending to be suddenly fascinated by the stone flooring.

Worn shoes padded loudly against the stone flooring as he strode toward me. "It's lovely to finally meet you." His hand grasped mine firmly and he bowed, lowering his lips to my knuckles. Hair flopped forward into his flawless face when he bent, and as he stood again, the shirt fell open revealing a smooth and muscled chest. A heart-melting grin spread across his face, and he gestured to himself with a sweeping movement. "I apologize for the attire. I was tending to the sheep all day. When the music calls, I have little choice but to do its bidding. Time got away from me."

I turned my head, my hand still cradled in his. "You tend to your own sheep? Don't you have servants for such labor?"

His boyish grin faded, twitching with—what was that? Em-

barrassment? "I do. I grew up on a farm—the eldest son of a shepherd." He shrugged with one shoulder, tilting his head with the movement. "I still enjoy the task. The sheep were always my friends as a boy."

My eyes narrowed. "I was the daughter of a shepherd. I know what you mean—I loved our sheep almost as much as I loved my sisters."

His grin deepened, a dimple darkening one side of his cheek. That smile—heavens. It warmed my belly and sent shivers down my spine. "Then you understand my plight. Sure, my laborers could do the work—and I'll confess they do some—but when I'm out in the field, I think of my father."

"And your sheep are faring well in this frost?"

"I lost a few, but yes, overall they are quite well. Then again, I have the means to shelter them more than most farmers here in Ireland. You lost a few sheep the other day, did you not, Monica?"

I froze. Just how much did he know? Fine hairs all over my body stood to attention. "How do you know of me?"

There was a storm swirling behind his eyes even though on the exterior, he seemed so put together. I wondered about his childhood. Just how long ago it had been—as a sorcerer, he could have been the same age for many years. Existing for as long as some of us did, we'd seen so much through the years. Enough to haunt us daily.

Settling in at the doorway, he leaned against the other side of it and crossed one foot over the other. "I saw you in a vision," he said it as though it were as normal as saying he saw me once at market.

"I have a favor from the high council to ask of you." My voice trembled. He seemed so lovely. Genuine and happy. It was easy to forget the terrible times that were just outside these castle walls. I was here for a job. One I could not fail.

Full, rosy lips curved into a full smile and he licked my body with his eyes, taking in everything from my clothing to my hair. "Come." He pushed off the door frame holding out a hand, palm up, for the taking. "We both must dress for dinner. I have extra clothes in the guest room."

"Thank you, Lord Buckley, but I do not need to change."

The playful smile stayed but his eyes swirled with—something. "That was not a request." His unwavering smile glistened. "Tonight is a celebration." His hand, still held out before me, twitched. "Follow me."

"A . . . celebration?" Did he have any idea of how our people are suffering?

"We will talk business, I promise you. But neither of us is properly attired to do so at the moment." He stepped in closer, breath deep and labored as he stared down at my white dress and apron. "This . . . fabric is rather sheer," he said, pinching it and circling the cloth between two fingers. "It will be quite distracting, wouldn't you agree?"

When I opened my mouth to speak, his own flesh, peeking out at the open V of his shirt, caught my eye. He was correct—it was incredibly distracting. Tiny beads of perspiration gathered at his sternum and my breath strangled at the back of my throat.

He chuckled in a deep, throaty way. "I see I'm not the only one distracted."

I quickly averted my eyes down to the floor again, shame burning my cheeks. "My apologies, Lord Buckley."

"None necessary, Monica. I'm rather pleased that you like what you see." I could feel the hum of his voice. Feel the rise and fall of his chest with each shallow breath. The stirrings in his britches thrummed through my body as he brushed against me. An accident? Perhaps. Also quite possibly a purposeful movement.

I stepped back from his person. Hesitantly, I lowered my fin-

gers into his palm. His smile widened as he led us both out of the room. "Wise choice," he whispered.

I didn't bother mentioning that I could create any dress of the finest silk faster than he could chant a spell. This knowledge was best kept secret until I knew more of Lord Buckley. He didn't seem terrifying at all. He seemed—young. Playful and boyish. Full of vibrance and life that I craved daily.

He led me to a boudoir with heavy velvet drapes, and with a gesture of his hand, all the candles lit. His arrogant smile was one that made it clear he was trying to impress. And I hated to admit that he did. Very much so.

"Thank you," I said. "Do you prefer a specific dress?"

Pulling a gown out from the back, he held it up to examine it. "I do believe this would be most striking on you." He fingered the gold embroidery on the bodice, face softening as his touch roamed over the gown. "It was my mother's," he added quietly.

It was gold brocade, layers upon layers with the most lovely cream accents. There was a slight trace of the arcane twisting around the dress like translucent vines embracing it. The sentimental gaze snapped away and he looked back to me, smiling once more. "The gold will complement your eyes most beautifully."

"Will it fit?"

He nodded as he draped the dress across my arms. Amusement flashed across his chiseled features. "I can guarantee it."

Insecurity and confusion trailed down my spine. I wasn't quite sure what he meant by that. "Very well. I will be ready shortly."

With a bow, he took one of my hands in his and looked up at me with those sparkling green eyes. "I will wait in the dining hall." He pressed another lingering kiss to my knuckles, licking his lips as he pulled away, as though he could still taste me upon them.

A few minutes later, I stepped into the gown and pulled it up and over my bodice. A magic surrounded me like two large arms in an embrace and the dress began lacing itself up. My hair, which hung just below my shoulders, bounced into ringlets and swept at the top of my head in a fine twist.

I stepped back and looked at myself in a full-length mirror that rested in the boudoir. The final strings tugged on the corset, taking my breath. A soft knock at the door startled me. "Yes?" I called, slightly annoyed at his impatience.

"M'lady," a gruff voice called from the other side. It did not sound at all like Lord Buckley's and held a Balkan accent. "When you are dressed, I will escort you to dinner."

I opened the door to find a man with powdery skin. It was sallow, and the bags under his eyes, blue and bruised. My angel senses tingled and unease crept over me. He was one of the guards who had stood outside when I arrived. With a shiver, I rubbed my arms. The man before me was a vampire. "In the name of God, I implore you to stay back!" My voice quivered and I held out a hand. I wasn't the most prestigious angel yet, but I knew I could take a vampire.

"M'lady," the vampire said while casting his eyes to the floor. "I assure you I am no threat." His dark eyes met mine again and I could see red circling dilated pupils. He had not fed for a while. His features, though sickly, were beautiful and a part of me couldn't help but explore his person with my eyes. A strong nose and jaw, high cheekbones, and a dimpled chin—they were royal features. "I am one of Lord Buckley's servants. I will take you down to dinner when you are ready."

I looked upon him through narrowed eyes. Vampires were not to be trusted and I was suddenly very aware of the blood rushing through my body, the pulse of every vein. He was dangerous and the thought of that brought a rush between my legs that I desperately tried to push away. I clenched my eyes shut.

"M'lady," the gruff voice whispered, "I beg of you to breathe.

Your . . . anxiety is making your pulse quicken." When I opened my eyes again, his were transfixed on my neck. "I have not fed in quite some time."

After a deep breath, I swallowed, my brain pleading with my body to calm itself. "I can see that," I returned. While Lord Buckley was handsome in a refined, aristocratic way, this vampire was dark and brooding. Exotic. "I apologize. Does Lord Buckley not allow you to . . . feed?"

"Not very frequently," he said, pressing two dry lips together. "None of us."

"There are more of you?"

He nodded. "Yes."

"But why?"

"You will have to ask my lord over supper." He extended an arm, which I took with caution. He was so cold that beneath his suit jacket, I could feel his icy skin permeating the wool. He leaned in close to my ear and dropped his voice. "And when you discover the answer, please let me know as well." His nose dipped a fraction closer to my hair and he inhaled deeply with a longing that made me both excited and nervous.

"What is your name?" I didn't exactly like the vampire—and I certainly didn't trust him—but I had never before encountered such a civilized demon. It was an opportunity to learn more about our opposing sides. One that I was certain my Julian would have taken advantage of as well.

He looked down at me, neck muscles clenched so tightly that blue veins were visible beneath the blanched white skin. "Dejan." His head dipped.

"Dejan," I repeated, rolling the foreign name around in my mouth. "I'm Monica."

"M'lady." He walked me into a formal dining area with a long, heavy table adorned with the most beautiful flowers. "Bon appétit." Though his words were simple enough, his eyes

were pleading, and I couldn't help but tilt my head, eyebrows knitted together. Why was he so concerned for me?

"That will be all, Dejan," Lord Buckley snapped, glaring at the vampire.

After a quick bow, Dejan backed out of the room. A tremble shivered through my body. I was in a castle filled with vampires being controlled by a sorcerer. What had I gotten myself into?

14

We found Jed and with the help of Adrienne's charm, he brought us to Lena's body. The room was filled with what looked like giant filing cabinets and he threw the door open as simply and easily as though he were showing us the coatroom. "Here she is," he said, gesturing palm up. "Need me to move her to an exam table for ya?"

Adrienne ushered him out of the room once again with one arm around his shoulder. "No, no, that won't be necessary. We'll call you when we're done." She locked the door behind him, then, with a flick of her hand, Lena's body lifted and she was levitating over to one of the exam tables.

"Show-off," I muttered under my breath. She and George both darted a glance in my direction—damn supernatural hearing. I mean, sure . . . no one really knew about my witchcraft yet. But it still annoyed me that her power had developed so quickly as such a fledgling angel. Years of practice as a witch must have aided her advancement.

Adrienne cleared her throat, purposefully ignoring my

petulant banter. Which made me hate her even more. "After we finish with her, her body will be released to the family to have a proper burial."

Once Lena was on the table, everyone immediately noticed that she, too, wore the marks of a vampire on her inner thigh. Damien measured the distance between the marks this time. . . . It was a little over three-inches. "Shit," he muttered and ran a hand through his dark hair.

Crossing my arms, I couldn't help the haughty smile that curved across my face. "I've never heard of teeth spaces getting *smaller*, have you, D?" George snickered from the corner and Adrienne acted as though she didn't hear me. Something we all knew to be bullshit since she could have heard a pin drop onto carpet in the Toyota parked across the street. When Damien didn't answer, I simply continued. "Because I certainly have never heard of such things. So, we may have two vampires working together on these murders?"

"That would be unlikely," he said through gritted teeth. "Vampires can barely stand to live with their own covens . . . much less share a kill."

"Lena Vlasik," Adrienne said aloud in a noble effort to change the direction of the conversation. "She was drowned in a rain storm, then was left hanging on a road sign."

Damien played with the latex glove, snapping it against his wrist. "Her lungs were filled with water and her jaw was locked in an open position when they found her on the road." He tilted her jaw back to inspect her nose.

George pushed off the wall in the back of the room, walking forward without getting too close. A sharp intake of breath came from over my shoulder as he peeked at the body.

"Her car was wet on the inside—as though the rain had flooded it. Then it was abandoned on the side of the road," Adrienne continued.

"Shouldn't you already know all of this?" I asked.

She looked up at me from behind the folder. "I do. I'm repeating it for *you*."

Celtic runes surrounded her body; the arcane was subtler than with Moe's, but then again, she had been dead for longer. The inside of her wrist had a different family crest—one I didn't recognize. Damien held the hand up by the forearm. "Yours again?"

I shook my head no.

"Is it Irish?"

I looked closer and didn't recognize anything from my heritage or culture about it. "Not that I can see. But it's so raw, it's hard to tell."

"Damn," he said, dropping her hand to the table.

"Vlasik isn't an Irish name—why would Celtic runes be surrounding her body?" Adrienne asked while tucking an errant hair away from her face. Her eyes turned down at the corners as she gently cradled the girl's face, her dark hair spilling over the end of the table. She was beautiful, twenty-nine, and had had a lifetime ahead of her. The tragedy of it caught in my throat and I had to look away.

"If we found her car in the impound lot, could you talk to it?" I asked Damien.

"It's always worth a try."

The room turned suddenly cold and I shivered while rubbing the gooseflesh that rose on my arms. When I looked up, the Banshee stood directly behind Damien and Adrienne. She opened her mouth, unhinged her jaw to let out the deafening scream I'd been coming to know so well.

"No!" I shouted, holding out a hand. The entire room jumped, all faces turned to me. Even the Banshee's, and she cocked her head slowly in that same curious way.

"Monica," Damien said. "What the fuck?"

I didn't bother looking at him, but kept my eyes fastened onto the Banshee's. "Shut up, D," I said, quieter. He darted a look over his shoulder to where the Banshee floated, but his eyes registered nothing. "No more deaths." I shook my head hoping to whatever God would have me that she could understand me. "I know. I know it's your job, but just let us figure this out first." As I closed my eyes, my breath was short and my lungs constricted with a tightness that I wished would go the fuck away. When I opened my eyes again, she was in front of me—so close to my face that I could smell the stink of death on her breath.

"Monica." George's gentle voice was behind me and I felt a hand on the small of my back.

"Give me a minute, George." I didn't dare break my eyes away from hers again.

Her head tilted to the other side and she looked from me to Damien, her head spinning slowly and evenly, then back at me. And as if seeing the body on the table for the first time, she froze.

"Monica—what's going on?" Damien's voice boomed through the cold room.

Holding up a hand, I shushed him with a look that I hoped showed that I meant business. "What magic is this?" I asked the Banshee and gestured to Lena. Murky tears fell down her cheeks once more and I was getting used to the gruesome visuals she provided.

Once more, she blew a breath from puckered lips and a black smog encased us. Her crazy eyes and porcelain skin were still crystal clear despite the fog. My friends' voices became distant murmurs and I was suddenly standing amidst a crowd in the center of town. Cops ushered people away and yellow tape sectioned the people away from what they were chattering about. To my right stood the Banshee, her feet never touching the ground—merely floating an inch or so above, her feet limp at the ankles. To my left stood Dejan. His face was stony and revealed no emotion whatsoever.

"Go on, go home. There's nothing more to see here," one cop said as he walked along the line. Dejan pushed people aside with a massively large shoulder as he made his way to the front of the crowd. The Banshee and I followed.

"You, too, buddy. Go home."

Dejan grabbed the cop by the shirt uniform and growled. "Show me the scene." His voice was low and menacing. The same dangerous purr that I remembered from centuries before.

The cop's eyes became dilated, an inky black. "Please, sir, right this way." The officer escorted Dejan to the bulletin board, which he looked over rapidly for clues. His head was a blur with the fast search. His gaze stopped suddenly. Just below a smear of blood was a newspaper clipping—more specifically, a personal ad. He snatched it in his rough, dirty hand, lip curling back as he read. I leaned over his shoulder to see for myself what had caught his attention.

Wealthy royalty seeking strong-minded, sexually free woman. Should have blonde, wavy hair and blue eyes. Must possess the ability to strip my soul with a mere kiss. Immortality preferred.

The vampire growled and crumpled the paper into his balled fist before shoving it deep in the pocket of his duster. Could that have been for me? Some sort of clue about my connection to the victim?

Without moving my feet, I was being pulled back from the scene, the Banshee's hand on my shoulder. Faster and faster we moved until I was back in the coroner's room, lying flat on my back on cool linoleum flooring.

A gasp caught in my throat and I looked up into three sets of very concerned eyes.

Damien was the first to exhale, hand to his chest. The sudden relief was soon replaced with an angry scowl. "Your penchant to black out on me during investigations is rather unsettling, succubus."

George held my hand, pulling me to a sitting position. "You okay?"

"Oh, you know me. I'm just an attention whore," I said, swiping a hand over my face.

"You got the whore part right," he said, pinching my cheeks playfully.

"What happened, Monica?" Adrienne's melodic voice sang through the room. She looked genuinely concerned.

"The Banshee. Again. She was here and she showed me—well, it's kind of hard to explain."

"Try us," Damien grumbled and Adrienne put a calming hand on his arm. He shrugged away her touch. "Stop that! Maybe I don't want to calm down. Ever think of that?"

Adrienne's face twisted and her eyes pinched. She quickly blinked, looking away, and I couldn't help but feel bad for her. In an effort to change the subject and perhaps take the heat off the angel, I went into the story. The personal ad. Dejan in the picture. The Banshee bringing me to the past.

When I finished, Damien looked just as angry as he had before, if not maybe more so. He stalked to his file fax and pulled out Moe's file, flipping through it until he pulled out a close-up image of the bulletin board. Then, pulling the magnifying glass that hovered over Lena's body, he looked closely at all items on the board. "Well, I'll be damned," he whispered before looking back up at me. "Do you think this is meant for you?"

I felt my shoulders touch my ears in an involuntary shrug. "It's too much of a coincidence along with my family crest carved into Moe's wrist, don't you think?"

Damien's phone rang just as the Banshee's shrill scream reverberated in my head.

Everyone gave me another strange look as Damien answered. After hanging up, he looked around at all of us. "We've got another murder. Let's go."

15

We said good-bye to Jed and he gave us a sad wave, as though his life were so void of the living he could hardly bear to see us leave. He stared particularly hard at Adrienne as she sent him a flirty wave over her shoulder.

Damien filled us in on the little he knew as we drove to the crime scene. "The recent victim was found by some hikers in a section of a trail called Gobbler's Knob." He slid a glance at me in the rearview mirror, and with a slight tilt to his head, his lips curved into a smile. "Yes, that's the real name. And it just might be my new nickname for you, succubus."

A guttural sound rolled in the back of Adrienne's throat. "You're disgusting sometimes," she huffed.

"I'm not the one who pretended to be a prostitute for months, hun."

She rolled her eyes and punched him lightly on the shoulder. The sight of those two together, acting so familial, twisted my stomach. She had her little meat hooks in every man I liked. Granted, Damien and Adrienne were more like siblings than anything romantic, but still. It was unsettling. I wasn't used to having to compete for anyone's attention. And I didn't much care for it.

Grasping George's sleeve, I pulled him close to me. "You cannot become friends with her. Ever. Got it?"

"Damn." He brushed my fingers off his lapel with mocked annoyance. "Calm down, girlfriend. You're the only blonde I've got eyes for." After holding my smile for a moment, his gaze quickly shifted out the window. "Except for that blond hottie. Hel-*lo*!" I followed his eyes to a well-built blond man standing in the parking lot of the park. "Please tell me this is the trail we need to take!"

Damien pulled into a spot and read an old, rickety sign. "Alexander Basin," he said aloud. "Yep, this is it."

George was out of the car before any of us had even unbuckled.

"So how do we get to this place?" I asked. "Do they chopper us in or something?"

Damien shook his head, face twisting in amusement. Honestly, you'd think I'd just asked if the police chief would give us his Swiss bank account number or something. "We hike it," he said. From his tone, I imagined him throwing a *duh* after it.

I quirked an eyebrow and crossed my arms under my breasts. "You're kidding, right?"

Damien looked down at my heels and another haughty smile splayed on those delicious lips of his. "Don't you worry, succubus. I can piggyback you there if you want."

I considered this for a moment. My body pressed against his back, legs wrapped around his body. On an exhale I grabbed the hiking map from his hands and examined it closely. "Gobbler's Knob, you said?" Adrienne looked over my shoulder, and as if both scheming at the same time, we caught each other's eyes.

"We'll see you there in"—I looked back down at the map—"about two and a half miles." Tossing the map at his chest, Adrienne followed me as I stepped over a few logs and twigs to a secluded area just inside the woods.

"Aw, c'mon, you guys!" Damien called after us. "You're really just gonna leave me here?"

With a *crack,* we did just that.

We both shifted to invisible, just in case we appeared in front of a ton of uniformed officers. Luckily, we were just far enough outside of the action that we could go back to being visible and walk the quarter mile to where yellow tape blocked off a large section of the beautiful trail. White screens were up around what I assumed was the body.

Adrienne walked toward the officers with a determination I'd never seen in her before. Then again, I'd never seen her on the job. She held up her badge as we ducked under the yellow tape. "Who can fill me in here?"

I followed at her heels, feeling completely out of place. A nervousness settled in my stomach and as we walked closer to the body, a stench of charred flesh and innards flooded my nose. I wasn't sure if I'd be able to keep my coffee down.

A younger officer came rushing over to Adrienne's side, his eyes sliding to her badge. Or maybe her rack. I couldn't quite tell. "Are you Detective Kane?"

"I'm Detective Lauriette. Kane is my partner." She glanced back at me and hitched a thumb in my direction. "This is Monica Lamb. She's a special consultant we've hired to assist."

The officer gave me a strange look, eyes settled on my belt. When I looked down, the fuzzy, pink handcuffs dangled there. "Oh, shit," I mumbled, unclipping them and shoving them in my bag.

"Really, Monica?" Adrienne's face was a hardened scowl.

"Blame your partner," I said through gritted teeth.

Thank Hell the officer interrupted us, giving Adrienne something else to focus in on. "Is Kane on his way?"

"He should be here within an hour. I can fill him in when he arrives."

"The victim, Sonja Thomsen. Age twenty. A student at BYU. Family lives in Tennessee. She left to go on a hike yesterday morning, early around six a.m. according to her roommates. Was found this morning around eight a.m. by the Morgansons over there, who were taking their dog off the trail. Her lower body is charred, yet the face and sternum are very well intact. Damned strangest thing I've ever seen."

Around our feet were the ashes of crispy, fallen leaves. "Forest fire?" I asked, clearly new at these questions based on the dumb looks I received from both Adrienne and the officer.

"No way," he said. "There's no way a forest fire would be so contained. It's as though someone lit her on fire and only burned her bottom half until she died."

"What was the time of death?" Adrienne asked, sending me daggers from her eyes. Clearly she wanted to do the questioning. I bet if Damien were here, *he'd* let me ask some questions.

"We won't know for sure until the medical examiner is finished, but we think somewhere around five this morning."

"So someone kidnapped her for twenty-four hours? That seems weird, doesn't it?"

"Monica!" Adrienne snapped. "I will ask the questions." After a pause, Adrienne cleared her throat. "Do we have any leads yet?"

"There's a boyfriend she hasn't been getting along with lately. And her mother's ex-husband who was apparently always a little too affectionate with her. A restraining order was involved. But, again, he's from Tennessee." The officer shook his head. "We think this is definitely the work of the Crest Killer. Another symbol is on the body."

I cringed. *Please don't be my family crest. . . .*

"And there's no connection yet between the victims?" Adrienne swiped her finger along the iPad.

"None that we've found."

She nodded. "Thanks. I think we got it from here."

He scurried away from the area as quickly as he could. Clearly he'd seen enough of the victim for one day.

At the edge of the second string of yellow tape was a box of gloves. Adrienne tossed me a couple, which I snapped on along with her. "You ready for this?"

I nodded yes, but my head screamed no.

With narrowed eyes, she scrutinized me from head to toe. "This will be gruesome. I can already tell. You can wait over there if you want."

I should have said yes. I should have kissed her on the lips for giving me an out. But instead, I clenched my jaw and shook my head. "Nope. I'm here to help." After another deep breath, I opened my eyes to find Adrienne's were still glued to my face. "Let's go."

We slipped under the tape and around the white screens. And thank Hell for those. This sight was not one for random passers-by. I thought of the poor, unsuspecting couple who had found this girl. She was tied to a tree limb by bound wrists, a dangling torso. A pile of leaves and ashes lay at where her feet should be, a few embers still orange and glowing. Her body was burned to nothing from her rib cage down, leaving a dripping carcass from head to breasts. Someone had washed the dirt and ash from her face and neck prior to leaving her hanging there. Her head lay limply, chin to chest, cheeks slackened, eyes wide and horrified. She had beautiful blond hair that was styled in a clean ponytail and crystal blue eyes. A pinched nose that lots of women pay good money to a plastic surgeon to achieve—in short, she was a stunning, young woman.

The smell of crispy flesh flooded my nose and a wave of nausea climbed my throat. I clamped my eyes shut, pushing away the horrifying image and breathing deep through my mouth so not to focus on the putrid scent. After spending a moment composing myself, I opened my eyes again to the horrific sight.

Sure enough, another family crest was on the body. This one wasn't nearly as crude as the other two. It was branded onto her skin in angry blisters just between her breasts.

Adrienne knelt and pinched the ash between two fingers, bringing it to her nose and inhaling deeply. "No kerosene. No lighter fluid. I can't even trace the scent of a matchbook," she whispered.

I could see tendrils of dark magic twisting around her body and up from the ash like thorny vines surrounding her. From a distance, we heard a faint *crack* and I assumed it was George. A light brush on my arm startled me, making me jump nearly out of my skin.

"It's me," said a voice so quiet, only immortal ears could hear it.

"Julian?" I whispered back.

"Hey, Jules," Adrienne said, and judging by her wide eyes, she was as surprised as me to see him here. "What are you doing?"

"Just having a look," he answered, cryptic as ever.

Adrienne took a few pictures on her phone, made some notes, and bagged a few of her own samples. "Let's go talk to the couple who found her."

We exited the area and Adrienne held up the yellow tape just a touch longer to allow Julian time to exit.

"What are you doing here?" I muttered through the corner of my mouth.

"Later," he whispered back.

A listless breeze coiled through the trees, rustling leaves and bringing a deep, savory scent of ash and pine. A couple sat on a fallen tree, the female holding a large yellow lab in her arms. His snout was covered with soot and dirt caked all the way up its legs almost to the belly. She nuzzled her face in his neck, not caring at all about the dirt, dried tears staining her cheeks. Her husband sat beside her, hands wringing around each other and staring vacantly at the ground.

"Mr. and Mrs. Morganson?" Adrienne stalked toward the couple.

The man cleared his throat and stood. "Yes. That's us."

"I understand you two found the body this morning?"

Mrs. Morganson nodded and scratched the dog's ear while standing as well. "That's right," she said. "We had Baxter off leash and he headed off the trail."

"Which isn't all that unusual," her husband interjected. "We go off the trail all the time around here."

She nodded with him. "We followed Baxter and found him with the girl."

"Then what did you do?" Adrienne asked, her eyes trailing down their ash-covered clothing.

"I-I tried to grab her so that if she was still alive, she wasn't hanging by her arms. But—" Mr. Morganson's voice cracked and his wife ran her hand in small circles over his back. After a moment, he composed himself. "But as soon as I touched her, it was clear she was already dead."

"It wasn't already clear considering she only had half a body?" Adrienne raised an eyebrow. I nearly gasped as I shot a look in her direction. Her biting sarcasm was cruel and unnecessary to these poor people.

Mr. Morganson shook his head. "I . . . well, no. I-I mean, I guess it should have been obvious, but I j-just wasn't thinking."

Adrienne made a note. "There was no fire blazing under her?"

Mrs. Morganson answered this time. "No, it was mostly out when we arrived. Not much smoke either. I called for 911 as Rick ran to her."

"You didn't notice anyone around? No one on the trail that stood out to you?" Adrienne's voice was stern. I was amazed to see her lack of empathy with the people who had discovered the victim.

Both shook their heads no. "We only passed one other person. We've seen him on this trail a couple of times over the past month. He didn't look suspicious or anything if that's what you're asking," Mrs. Morganson answered. Adrienne's gaze narrowed. "But . . . but the trails aren't very busy this early," Mrs. Morganson added, eyes cast at Adrienne's iPad.

"And what did he look like? This other person on the trail?"

"White male, taller than me by maybe an inch or so," Mr. Morganson answered. "Dark hair . . ."

"Well, that describes just about forty percent of the population," I muttered.

"He was a large guy . . . easily had an extra sixty pounds on me. Muscle."

Adrienne slid a look to me, lips pressed into a small line. "Any distinguishing marks? Scars? Birthmarks?"

Both shook their heads. "He had eyes so dark they almost looked black," Mrs. Morganson offered. "And he was pale. Like, really, really pale." I slid a look to Adrienne. Dejan. It had to have been Dejan.

"Okay." Adrienne snapped her iPad case closed. "Thank you very much. The police should have your information and if we need anything further, we'll be in touch."

Adrienne turned away and then quickly spun back to the couple. "Oh, just one more thing. Where were you yesterday morning? Around six a.m.?"

All jaws dropped—including mine and I swear I heard Julian's, too.

"Adrienne," I whispered.

The look she sent me was frigid. A cold, hardened stare that was enough to shut me up instantly. Fair enough—she was more of a veteran at this than me for sure. It just seemed so . . . accusatory. Not just the question, but *how* she asked it.

"We . . . I—well . . . ," Mrs. Morganson stuttered.

"Were you hiking yesterday morning?" Adrienne asked, stone-faced.

"I was." Mr. Morganson said. "I took Baxter alone yesterday because Heather wasn't feeling well."

"Uh-huh. And what time was that?" Adrienne had her iPad back out and was taking notes again.

"I left the house at . . . I don't know, what time was it, honey?"

"A little before six, I think," she answered for him.

My gaze slid to Adrienne, whose face still revealed nothing. "And what time did you get home?"

"I stopped to pick up some tea and oatmeal for Heather and some coffee for me on the way. I think I was home by seven-thirty or eight."

A pause. "Which was it, Mr. Morganson? Seven-thirty or eight?"

He swallowed. "Closer to eight, I'd say."

"And you didn't see anyone else on the trail? Did you see the victim yesterday morning? Or the tall, pale man from today?"

"There were a couple of people jogging." His eyes traveled in the direction where Sonja's body hung. Even though she was covered with protective screens, his eyes glazed over. A trembling hand covered his mouth and swiped under his nose. "I honestly don't know. I come up here to escape people and tend to keep my head down."

"And this morning? Where were you at four a.m.?"

The couple both looked as though they might crack any second. Mrs. Morganson's tears had long been spilling down her cheeks and Mr. Morganson was close behind her. "*This* morning? We left the house together around seven. . . ."

"Did I ask you about seven a.m.?" Adrienne clipped. "Where were you at four a.m.?"

"We were asleep. In bed." Mr. Morganson answered.

"Thank you." Adrienne's smile slithered up her face in a snakelike way that made me shiver. "We'll be in touch."

She turned and stalked away back to where the police were still gathered. I followed her, needing to jog to keep up. "That was a little harsh," I whispered.

"Monica, it's my *job* to be harsh." She stuffed the iPad back into her bag. "And maybe you didn't notice, but there was dirt embedded under his nails. Grabbing our victim wouldn't have embedded the soot that much."

"Yeah, but they were hiking. That could be from anything—"

"And the scratch marks on his neck? Did you see those? They were peeking out from under his shirt."

Damn, I am really not good at this detective thing. I need to start really looking at everything. "Also, could be a lot of things. It could be from his dog or tree branches, or he might enjoy rough play or—"

"Or it *could* be from Sonja trying to fight him for her life. It's my job to look at all possibilities. And if you're going to be a consultant, I suggest you start doing the same."

After a long pause, Adrienne finally spoke again. "So, what are you doing here, Jules?"

The voice came from between us. "The family crest—it's mine. From my human days."

"Oh, Julian," Adrienne whimpered, eyes closing and hands clenched to her narrow hips.

"What does that mean, exactly? Is Sonja part of your family or something?"

I could feel his nod beside me. "Something like that, yes."

Adrienne looked back at me. "We need to find out whose family crest was on Lena. Find what the link is here."

"Yeah, no shit," I said back.

There was a rustling behind us and Damien and George walked up from the trail, panting. I looked George over from head to toe. "*You* hiked?"

He shrugged. "The hot blonde was headed the same way. . . . Besides, I didn't want to leave your mister here walking alone."

Damien's jacket was slung over his arm, sleeves rolled to the elbow. "Thanks for that," he muttered. "Had to listen to him hit on some hiker for about thirty minutes."

My breath stalled in my throat as I took in Damien's whole look. Sweat beaded over his face and down his neck. Not the gross sweat—but the sexy sweat. The kind that reminds me of a hard workout and two bodies rolling around together in fine Egyptian cotton sheets. I inhaled his musky scent, a slow, warm thrill uncoiling in the center of my belly; that scent, it was all Damien.

"What are you staring at, succubus?" he grumbled while wiping his face with the palms of his hands.

"Well, we're actually pretty much done here," Adrienne said, and I wanted to kiss her for snapping me out of my aroused fog. "If you want to look around a bit, we'll see you back down at the bottom."

"Oh, no you don't," he snapped and grabbed on to Adrienne's elbow. "You're not leaving me here to hike this shit back. I know there's a way to teleport me, as well, right?"

"Sorry, dude," George offered with a shrug. "There's no way I'm hiking a second time. I linked my arm in his, and George, Adrienne, and I walked over to a hidden wooded area.

"Motherfuckers," Damien growled just before we disappeared.

16

The ArchDemon of Salt Lake City had her office stationed in a mall. A *mall.* She owned a little celestial jewelry shop nestled between The Gap and a Foot Locker.

"Is this for real?" George asked with a flippant gesture toward the storefront.

I shrugged and trudged forward. "Only one way to find out, I guess." There was a sensor on the door that pinged with our entrances. A young, pretty girl smiled at us from behind the counter.

"Good afternoon." She sounded as if her vocal chords had been dipped in sugar.

"Er—hi." I noted some unique-looking stones hanging on leather cords. Crystals shimmered under the lights creating a discotheque look. "We're here to see Claudette. Is she in?"

"Oh, yes." The girl's head nodded up and down like a bobblehead. "Claudette is always here." She stared vacantly at us, eyes glazing over.

I darted a look to George, whose lip was curling back as

though the pretty girl repulsed him. "Um, could we *see* her, then?"

"Ah, oh yes, of course."

"Jane, no need, I'm right here."

Jane's eyes widened as the tall, willowy woman glided into the room. Her auburn pixie-cut hair had bangs that flopped into her eyes slightly. "How do you always do that?" Jane asked, then looked to George and me. "It's like she can always sense when someone is looking for her." Claudette smiled in the same way a mother would at an infant discovering its hands for the first time. "You must be Monica." Claudette shifted her smile to me and I took her outstretched hand in mine.

"That's right. And this is George."

"Hi." He flashed his dimples at Claudette and even though I was sure she'd seen it all, she still seemed to brighten under his attention.

"I'm Claudette. Please, follow me." She nodded her head toward the back and we followed.

Her office was plush and bright with entirely white furnishings and accessories. Much more what I would imagine for Julian's office than a demon's. Even Claudette herself coordinated with the neutral/white tones in her taupe pants and white silk button-down shirt. "Please, have a seat."

Like school children, we did as told. Even though she wasn't our ArchDemon, we certainly didn't want to cross anyone more powerful than ourselves.

"So," she continued, lowering herself into a large white leather office chair and crossing her legs at the knees. "Tell me, dear ones. What are you doing in my sector? Did Lucien send you here to spy on me?" Her voice was brittle with a faux sweetness that made my stomach clench.

George and I looked at each other—both at a loss of what to say. George was the first to speak. "No, not at all. We're here working on official police business. Lucien actually had very little say in whether or not we were coming—"

"We only checked with Lucien as a courtesy."

Her lips twitched at the corners, but didn't even resemble a smile. It was hard to tell if this fact pissed her off *more* or simply amused her. "So—any souls you acquire while you're here go to . . . who exactly?"

"I believe that's something you and Lucien should work out for yourselves. He has a couple of your girls, right?"

Her cool smile sent an icy shiver down my arms. "That's correct. I assume you are both working to corrupt the well-known religious population we have here?"

Leaning back on the couch, George swung an arm over the back. "That's right. We're already joining a Bible Bowling League tonight."

"We are?"

He flashed me a look. "Yes. Did I forget to mention that?"

Claudette's laugh was terrifyingly beautiful and heartless all at once. "Good luck with that. Considering none of us can touch anything holy. My girls have been working to infiltrate these groups for decades. It takes time and patience, and it is certainly not as easy as it seems."

"I think we can handle it." George's smile was equally beautiful and chilling, if only for the effectiveness of his charm.

Air expelled through flared nostrils, tension tightening the insides of Claudette's eyebrows. "Of course. Good luck to you both, then. Report back to me if you are still here on Tuesday, please."

She stood, showing us out. We ran into Jane again as Claudette strolled back into her office.

"Thank you for coming!" Jane called with a wave.

As we made our way to the front of the store, a dark but shimmering stone caught my eye. My blood turned cold as I moved to examine it more closely. It was a deep blue, similar to that of a lapis lazuli, but with more shimmer. It was the same type of stone Lexi and Wills had given to me six months ago. A rare type of stone that has the ability to strip a succubus of her powers. I was pretty certain it wasn't the exact one seeing as Lucien and Jules had promised to take care of it. But the type of stone was rare, one that came from Lilith's time in the Garden of Eden. And seeing how none of us had figured out how Wills and Lexi had gotten the stones in the first place—it seemed even stranger that we should find one here in Claudette's store.

17

Ireland, 1740

The dinner table was large enough to seat well over twenty and the cavernous room echoed with each clattering plate and utensil. The silence between us was torturous. I sipped my soup quietly, glancing up occasionally at Lord Buckley through my thick lashes. Each gaze was met with a lopsided smirk. The man should terrify me; his very power and presence should have me trembling at the knees. But he was so boyish and charming, it was hard to imagine him as terribly dangerous.

The castle glowed in the candlelight and a fire across the room cracked and popped. It was far from cold inside, but a shiver ran down my spine regardless. The fate of Ireland was in mine and Lord Buckley's hands alone at the moment. And he seemed more interested in sharing playful glances across the table than discussing business.

Dejan's presence in the house was distracting, perhaps even more so than Lord Buckley's. I didn't have to turn around to know he was approaching. His bloodsucking presence tingled through my angel senses. Frigid skin brushed my arm as he reached across to clear my empty soup bowl.

"Did you enjoy your soup?" Lord Buckley boomed from the other end of the table, his smile arching across his face.

"Yes, very much." I paused. "Lord Buckley—is it—would it be possible to sit closer? It is difficult to discuss the matters at hand when we have a table's length between us."

His face split into a grin, regal features brightening. I was a lamb inviting a wolf to dine with me. "Of course, m'lady. I agree it feels so foolish to sit so dreadfully far apart." With a small but effectual clap, he gestured to his place setting, hard eyes holding Dejan's gaze. Standing, he flipped his coattails behind him and glided to my end of the table. He took the seat beside me, leaning his elbows on the table. Wavy hair flopped over one eye and he brushed it back with one hand.

"My god," he whispered. The candlelight caught a glint in his green eyes and they shimmered like emeralds. "You are stunning."

"My beauty comes from within," I answered. "You are merely seeing God's light within me."

A laugh grunted and his smile twisted. Pain. Discussing God caused this beautiful man pain.

"You don't believe that at all, do you?" I asked the question out of reflex. I clearly knew the answer already.

"Answer me something, my angel. Are these your human features? Or did you change when you became an angel?"

I hesitated. "These are . . . my human features, yes. Though the best version of my human self. I died younger than the body you see before you."

"Is that so?" He asked the question in a way that suggested he'd already known that as well. "Monica is not an Irish name. Did you change it?"

Most angels change their names after their human lives end. Something I was certain Lord Buckley knew already. His questions were testing me; toying with my very emotions. "Just how much do you know about me, Lord Buckley?"

His smile was sharper than a knife's blade and could just as easily slice me open. "As I said before—I saw you in a vision. And that's precisely what you were—a vision." His eyes squeezed shut and he tilted his head as though recalling a meaningful memory. "A sight for my sore eyes." Eyes blinking open again, he brushed the back of his knuckle over my cheekbone, and tucked a curl behind my ear, smile softening. Perhaps I was wrong about him. Maybe he, too, was a sheep, lost and in search of a herd.

"But—you do believe in God, do you not?"

"Can one believe in angels and not a God?"

I studied his face, beginning at his thick hairline, smooth forehead, and eyes that despite years of battle seemed to soften around me. I was determined to discover the reason. "You are adept at answering a question with a question, I see."

One side of his mouth tilted farther up. "It is an art."

Dejan brought the main course—a sort of mincemeat pie filled with hearty beef, mixed vegetables, potatoes, and a flaky, buttery crust on top. The vampire's presence again chilled the room. If Lord Buckley noticed my discomfort, he was quite good at hiding it. He placed his napkin over his lap and picked up his fork. "Thank you, Dejan. This looks delectable."

I followed his movements with my own fork and napkin and took the first bite, the food melting on my tongue. Dejan's footsteps faded and I looked up to ensure he was in fact gone. Even if I lowered my voice, there was no guarantee that the vampire wasn't listening in. I wasn't entirely privy to vampire secrets, but I was pretty sure their hearing was significantly good—perhaps not quite as sensitive as that of we angels, but obviously better than humans'. That was a certainty. "Why vampires, Lord Buckley? Why risk it?"

His fork froze halfway to his mouth, breath fogging the gold utensil. After finishing his bite and chewing slowly, methodi-

cally, he tapped his napkin to either corner of his mouth. "That is an easy question to answer. When I lived in France, vampires were running rampant. Everywhere I looked, I saw lives lost." His gaze shifted somewhere beyond my shoulder, staring into a vacant pit of nothing. After a pause, he continued. "I had a family once. Back in Paris. A wife. Two children. And I came home to find them slaughtered. New vampires, I was told. They are the only ones who feast so rabidly." Instantly, it was as though his trance expired and his eyes snapped back to mine. "So, when I came to Ireland and I saw similar killings, I enslaved the murderers. It keeps the savages contained and I get servants I would otherwise need anyway."

"And you don't let them feed?" I whispered, my voice barely audible. "That seems rather cruel, doesn't it?"

He laughed, voice cracking with the bitter sound. "My dear, you don't have to whisper. They can't hear us. I have enchantments on every room. They can only hear what I want them to hear." His chuckle dissipated and I shifted my eyes around the room warily. "I keep them hungry as a reminder to them that I am in control. They do my bidding if they are close to starvation because they know I am their only hope for a next meal." He paused, taking a sip of whiskey, rolling the amber liquid around in his mouth before swallowing hard. "Besides, they are weaker when they are hungry."

I blinked back my confusion. "But . . . how? How can you physically stop a vampire from feeding?"

"I cannot reveal that. Not even to you, my angel."

"Very well," I said, my voice taking on the authoritative tone I'd heard come from Julian during meetings. "Let's discuss business, then. You are clearly interested in helping mankind as demonstrated by your containment of vampires. We are facing a catastrophe here in Ireland. Carman's frost is devastating our

people. And you, Lord Buckley, you alone have the power within you to end it. Please say you'll help us."

He leaned back in his seat on an exhale, eyes shimmering. The playful, charming boy who had been interested in courting me almost entirely disappeared. "I will help you."

The exhale hissed out of my mouth and I, too, fell back in my chair. A smile broke out across my face, the action feeling old and creaky. How long had it been since I felt true elation? "Oh, Lord Buckley, thank you . . ."

He held up a silencing hand. "On a few conditions." My smile froze; if you had hit it with a mallet, it would have shattered into a thousand tiny pieces. Of course. Nothing ever came without stipulations . . . especially not with a power-hungry sorcerer.

"State your conditions," I said, my tone stiffening with my spine, "and I will see what I can do."

"Well, clearly I am powerful. But even Carman may be too much for me to handle on my own. She comes with her three sons, as well. I need the help of you angels."

"Sons? Lord Buckley, surely you know we cannot assist in this. We are not allowed . . ."

"I'm not talking of you taking any action. But I require your presence. Here at the castle for the duration of the battle. Without your presence, Carman and her boys could attack me specifically at any moment. But with your company, it becomes harder for her and her awful children."

I sat back in my seat. "Three sons," I repeated.

"Well, two that are a threat. The one should not be an issue as he is trying to maintain a low profile and claims to have nothing to do with this frost. He's even offered to help where he can."

"You've been in contact with him?"

Lord Buckley shrugged, but did not answer.

"So . . . you would like an angel to live here. With you."

"No . . ."

"But you just spoke of—"

He hand fell on top of mine, his warm touch silencing me almost immediately with a gasp. "Not just any angel. You. I require you to live here during the duration of my battle with Carman."

"You want me to stay here with you and several vampires? This is very unorthodox. . . ."

"And yet—part of you wants to say yes, doesn't it?" His thumb moved in circles over my skin, a gentle caress.

A breath hitched in my throat. I did want to say yes. I wanted to live with this man and learn his secrets. A burning between my legs pulsed through my core and I closed my eyes, not daring to answer him. I couldn't answer that without lying. And I certainly couldn't admit the truth. "I am not authorized to make this decision." His heady scent flooded my nostrils and I inhaled him deeply.

"Yes, yes," he replied with a flippant hand gesture, returning to his pie. The absence of his touch left me feeling achingly empty inside. I wanted his hands on me—touching me in places I was not supposed to be touched. "Go and ask your council."

I stood from the table, the heavy chair scraping along the stone floors with a horrid noise. His eyes rose to mine, startled. "Where are you going? I did not mean right this moment. For heaven's sake, stay. Finish your dinner."

"No thank you, Lord Buckley. I will have an answer for you in the morning."

With a wariness that wasn't there before, he stood as well, flipping his coattails out behind him. "Very well."

"I would like to change before leaving."

His smile was soft and he took my hand, running a thumb along my knuckles. It sent tingles up my arm and I resisted the shiver that threatened my spine. "Keep it for now. It's far too cold to be running around in tatters."

"Thank you," I said softly. "Whatever their answer is, I will see you tomorrow."

He bowed and as his head dropped, Dejan's cold eyes stared at me from beyond the doorway, hungry and wanting.

18

The panic attack was coming on strong. That stone—that damn stone. It had been the catalyst for so much that went wrong six months ago. Breathing was becoming increasingly difficult and George stared at me, eyes tinted with concern.

"Monica?"

I couldn't come out and say anything about the stone—Claudette was bound to hear anything we spoke within the store. With a deep breath, I forced my raging heart to calm down; the blood rushing through my head was a violent river. I walked over to the stone and being sure not to touch the damn thing, pointed to it. "Isn't this beautiful," I said to George pointedly, doing my best to give him the ol' "something bigger is going on here" eyes.

Initially, he just stared at me in confusion; then, finally, recognition washed over his fine features. "Oh. Oh! Um, yeah, that's really striking."

Jane came rushing over, sensing a sale like a vulture can sense death. "Oh, isn't it just beautiful?" She yanked it off the rack and held it up to my collar. "Would you like to try it on?"

I crumpled away from the piece in the same way a vampire would shrivel away from the sun. "No! I mean, um, yes, it is, but . . . I meant . . . *that* one." I pointed to another stone necklace that had been right next to the blue one.

"Oh!" she exclaimed, still as cheerful as ever. "I'm sorry. I could have sworn I saw you pointing to this one." She put the wretched stone back on its hook. "Claudette gets most of her jewelry from the most unusual places. The stones themselves are all acquired by her own family." Jane grabbed a second necklace, this one red and matte, holding it up to my neck. "Would you like to try this one on?"

"Oh, I really shouldn't." If I had to spend any more time with this girl, the only thing I wanted her slipping around my neck was a fucking noose. "We should really go."

I left the store, dragging George behind me. "Holy shit!" he exclaimed when we left and I clamped a hand over his mouth, putting a finger to my lips. Who knew how far her hearing stretched?

It wasn't until we were safely in our rental car, driving back to the hotel that I allowed him to speak. "Holy shit!" he said again. "Do you think *she* has the hit out on you?"

"How should I know? I've never even *met* her before. Why would she want me dead?"

He shrugged, managing to keep his hands positioned at ten and two on the wheel. "I don't know, baby girl. Aren't we under her protection while we're here, though? Technically, Lucien doesn't control us while we're under her territory."

The thought sent a fearful tremor through my body. "Maybe the stone just came from her store. It doesn't mean she is the person behind this whole Lexi/Wills thing, does it?"

When George didn't respond, I had my answer. Coincidences were rare in our world. That stone being here in the same city where all these murders were taking place meant something. Though what that something was baffled me to no end.

The rest of the drive was quiet and when we pulled into the hotel, I could see Drew and Adrienne at the hotel bar sitting at a high-top table, hands entwined. I groaned, falling against the brick outside.

"What now?"

"Inside. Drew and Adrienne. Being all—you know. Affectionate and shit."

"Oh, affection and shit. That is a bad combo," George said with a smile.

I sent him a tired one in return. "You know what I mean. I just don't want to deal with them right now."

He shrugged. "So don't. Teleport to the room."

"After my battle with Aaron, I barely had enough energy to style my hair this morning. I won't make it to this evening if I use my remaining powers to avoid Drew."

"I arranged for us to go to this bible study, bowling night thing. We'll definitely be able to get you recharged there. I could really use your help. Rob is wary of me—if we can get him to hook up with you first, I can ease my way in."

My head dropped in my hands. "I'm not really sure what that means, my head is so foggy. But if it will get me some power, I'm all for it."

By the time the sun had fallen, I was dressed and ready for an awful night of bowling. I hated bowling. It was up high on my list of things I hate right next to Crocs and Celine Dion. To start with, it never mattered how hot you looked—once you put on those stupid shoes, your outfit was just shot to Hell. I did my best regardless, with tailored camel dress pants and a red wrap shirt that dipped into a deep V revealing impressive cleavage for my rather small frame. After spending almost an hour straightening my hair and applying makeup—I looked pretty damn good. Not to mention the glow of my body compensating for the lack of power in itself was probably enough to attract any man back to my bedroom.

As George and I made our way down the hall, we caught sight of Drew standing at his open hotel room door, leaning on the frame. Slipping a tip into the room service deliverer's hand, and holding a tray of food and a bottle of iced champagne. Champagne. I halted in my tracks, body going numb at the sight. Even if the champagne was only for Adrienne, how dare she order a whole bottle with an alcoholic sharing her room.

Drew caught my eye, too, and he shifted his weight, maintaining eye contact. I stalked over to him. "What are you doing?" I said, eyeing the bottle.

"Monica, not now. Really, it's not a good time."

I peeked over his shoulder into the room, not seeing Adrienne anywhere behind him. "Where is she? Is she the one who requested a bottle of champagne?"

"Monica." George touched my arm, in a gentle movement. Good time or not, I didn't give a shit. Drew did not need to be anywhere near alcohol.

"What are you *thinking*, Drew? This will be the second time you've been brought to alcohol because of Adrienne. Remember the first? Remember when you tore through my kitchen looking for whiskey?"

Drew flicked a grateful glance at George that suggested he appreciated the attempt. The moment between the two just made me burn that much more. "Monica, I'm fine. I'm just surprising Adrienne with a dinner."

"Dinner *and* champagne."

"Yes. Dinner and champagne. That's it."

I narrowed my eyes at him. "That's never it. Not for a recovering alcoholic."

With a sigh, he flopped against the door frame. "Monica, I haven't seen Adrienne much at all yet on this trip. I was really looking forward to tonight. Please don't ruin it for me."

"You clearly don't need *me* to ruin the night," I spat. "And if she loves you like she claims, she should be just as enraged by that bottle as I am." I turned quickly and hustled to the elevators.

19

"Oh, my Hell." I leaned back on the cheap plastic primary-colored seats and my head fell onto George's shoulder beside me. "This is even more horrible than I imagined it would be."

"Eye on the prize, baby girl. Their auras are shining brighter than Marie Antoinette's jewels."

"Can't I at least have a beer?" I whined like a child stuck in detention.

"Nope. They've got to believe we're just as holy as them. No trust, no ass." His gaze traveled back to Rob, the blond guy he'd met on the trail. "But look at him—he's never even had pussy. The boy has no clue he's gay."

"And we're gonna help him, right?"

"Oh yeah." George winked at me.

"Monica!" one of the girls on my team called. "Your turn!"

I stood up, breathless, the bowling ball feeling heavier than its eight pounds advertised. I lined up the sights and bowled a perfect split—on purpose. I loved the shouts when I was able to take down both pins. Strikes were easy in comparison. After my team hugged me and cheered, I took my place next to

George again. He stood to take his turn when Rob slid into his seat.

"Nice job. I thought for sure there was no way you'd get that spare." I looked him over and immediately understood the appeal George was talking about. Strong jaw and chin, high cheekbones. Striking blue eyes and blond hair. This kid was a walking Gap advertisement.

"Thanks." I flashed a smile and angled my breasts toward him. He glanced down—but didn't seem to notice or care. He sort of looked because he was supposed to. Like the way one looks at tofu on a menu. You know you should, but when you sink your teeth into it, it's just never quite right. Even if George and I did end up taking a chunk of this guy's life, we would be helping him overall for sure. "You got the strike last round, right? Impressive as well."

Rob rolled his eyes. "Yeah. Well, there's not a whole lot else to do around these parts other than camp and bowl."

"Somehow I think that must be a gross exaggeration."

He shrugged. "Maybe a little, though not as much as you probably imagine it to be." He made eye contact with another guy sitting across from us. "Hey, did you meet Dave?" He did a guy-like head gesture thing and Dave came over. He was good-looking as well. Not quite the picture-perfect image Rob was—Dave's nose was slightly crooked and teeth weren't the straightest I'd ever seen. But he would definitely do for the night. Like all the rest in the group, his aura was sparkling. Not quite as shiny as Rob's, again. My guess he had probably been with a woman before—once, maybe twice. Probably a long-term girlfriend he thought he was in love with or some shit like that.

"Dave, hi. Nice to meet you," I said while taking his hand. Rob stood and Dave took his place next to me, where we engaged in the normal getting-to-know-you chitchat.

A chill lightning bolted up my spine. Someone—no, some-

thing was here. It took me a moment to place the aura. Vampire. And as I looked over Dave's shoulder, Dejan stood at the bar, staring at me with cold eyes.

"So," I said, looking into Dave's dark, almost olive-colored eyes, "when do we start the Bible-study part of this evening?" My stomach clenched as I asked the question. I didn't want to be anywhere near a Bible or anything holy.

"Oh, probably after this game. On bowling nights we don't spend too much time on theology. We save the real deep discussions for Wednesday evenings. You gonna be around? It's at Rob's house this week. He's making his famous pancetta."

"Huh. You don't say?" I eyed Rob again. Pancetta. Snapping my eyes back to Dave, he had leaned in even more, his arm snaking around the back of my chair. "Yeah, maybe. We'll see." I slid out of the bucket seat, getting to my feet. "Excuse me a minute. I'm gonna get a Diet Coke."

His eyebrows twitched down ever so slightly. "Oh, cool. I'm pretty sure they have a caffeine-free one over there. We had to petition to get them to put it in."

"Oh." I feigned enthusiasm as best I could. I was certainly not going to win Best Actress anytime soon. "Great. Be right back."

Dejan had shifted so that his back was to the group after our initial eye contact.

"What are you doing here?" I spoke through a clenched jaw, whispering.

"Good evening, Monica," he said, lifting a bottle of beer to his lips. "You're looking well."

"It's been a while." I fiddled with one of my rings, spinning it around my index finger.

"Not really." The slightest smile flickered beneath his pale, bloodless lips. His skin was as pale as I remembered, but no longer starved and hollow. It glistened with a dewiness that women paid good money to achieve with expensive moisturizers. His dark eyes sparkled like two onyx stones.

"Oh. Right." I remembered six months back, lying bloody on my foyer floor. . . . Dejan fighting beside Lucien and Julian to save my soul. "What the Hell was that about, anyway?"

He shrugged in a noncommittal way, taking another sip of beer. "I like to keep tabs on you. My peculiar creation."

My face flushed and I could feel the heat burning my cheeks. "Oh? By killing innocents and branding them with my family crest?"

Dejan sneered, lip curling back before sliding a glance to me without moving his head. "You know I had nothing to do with any of these murders. But clearly someone wants to pin it on me." His shoulders hunched over more, hollowing out the space between his flat stomach and the edge of the bar.

"That's why you were at the crime scenes? The one this morning and in the town square?"

One eyebrow raised toward me. "It seems as though I am not the only one checking in," he said through a chilling smirk. "They are, however, doing a terrible job in framing me."

I paused as a server (and I use that term very loosely) came over to take my Diet Coke order. "What makes you think they're trying to pin it on you specifically?"

"Me—my kind—what's the difference?"

My beating heart pounded against my chest. Hell, this man made me nervous. And why shouldn't he? The very vampire who had changed my existence forever for the worse sat just beside me. He could rip the throat out of every human here in less time than it took most to eat a burger.

"It's nice to know I still make your pulse race." He leaned in close, inhaling deeply at my hairline.

"I assure you, Dejan—it's not for the reasons you believe. Is that the only reason you're here? Because someone is attempting—and failing—to frame a vampire for these murders?"

"And . . ." He paused, his smile barely visible and teetering on the edge of being deathly dangerous.

"And?" I repeated.

"Like I said." He finished the bottle, tipping his head back with one final glug, "I like to keep tabs on you." Reaching into a leather messenger bag, he pulled out an old book, tossing it in front of me on the bar.

"What's this?" The binding was worn almost all the way through, the pages so old I feared they might disintegrate if I touched them.

Dejan pulled out a wallet from his back pocket and threw down some money as well. "It's a Bible. Not blessed, so those of our kind can touch it. Figured you might need to borrow it for a while." He gave a nod to the group of bowlers behind us.

When I looked back to Dejan, he was already slipping out the door. "Thanks," I said quietly, as I tucked the Bible under my arm and grabbed my glass of caffeine-free Diet Coke.

20

Ireland, 1740

My bags were packed. I did not own much, but what little belongings I had fit into two small cases.

"You don't have to do this," Julian growled, pacing on the other side of the room. I folded my mother's knit scarf, placing it tenderly on top of the second trunk.

"Yes. I do. It's our only hope in stopping Carman."

He shook his head, stalking over to me and taking my hands in his. "It's not the only hope. I can keep searching. There has to be another sorcerer. . . ."

I shrugged and squeezed his hand. "Perhaps. And if you find one, come release me. But until then, we must continue with this plan."

With the tip of his finger, he traced up and down my arm. Goose bumps pimpled on my flesh beneath his touch. "I just don't understand. Why you?"

Raising a shoulder to my ear, I attempted to look casual with my answer. "He's just a little . . . curious about me it seems." Julian's eyes narrowed, his mouth creasing into a frown. "I don't think he will hurt me. He seems—well, it felt a little bit like he was trying to romance me." My mouth curved into an embarrassed smile and I tried to shrug the comment off as though it were nothing.

Julian's face dropped, eyes, cheeks, and mouth all sagging at once. "Romance? Monica—you . . ."

"Oh, Jules." I cupped his cheek in the palm of my hand, tracing my finger over his strong cheekbone. "Please don't worry. You've taught me well." In truth, I was terrified. I didn't want to leave Jules for this man—no matter how fine his linens and castle and servants may be.

Julian nuzzled my hand, then after clearing his throat, lowered my hand in his down to our sides. "You can't teleport out of his castle. If something goes wrong, you need an escape strategy."

My stomach turned at the thought. I hadn't considered that. "You're right. How will I leave?"

Julian resumed his pacing. Reaching one end of the room, he spun on his heel and headed the other way again. "You're stronger than he is. But he doesn't realize that, yet. Hide your strength as long as you can. Play up that you're a relatively new angel and don't quite know how to harness your powers yet."

"But what good will all that do if I can't leave?"

There was a pause while we both stood there staring at each other. Fear sizzled in the air and every muscle in my body felt tight, clenched. Finally, Jules broke the silence. "Negotiate with him. The only way you agree to this is if he lifts the enchantments so that angels can transport in and out at will. He probably will not acquiesce to those demands, but use your judgment. If you feel safe—accept his terms."

Lord Buckley's gold gown hung off of the bed. Julian ran a hand down the bodice, fingers barely grazing the silky material. "You must have looked exquisite in this. I wish I could have seen it on you." On a sigh, he lifted the heavy dress and draped it over his arm. His outstretched hand gestured to me, fingers twitching in a "come" gesture. "Shall we?"

I nodded slowly, placing one hand on his and the other on top of my tattered cases. I closed my eyes as we teleported. This was my job. This was my destiny. But I couldn't shake the feeling that I was Daniel heading into the lion's den.

21

"So, what do you think?" I whispered to George after the group finished its lengthy discussion about Psalms. "Can we close this deal tonight? Because I need energy. Like, now."

George's gaze skimmed the group to Rob, then back to me. He gave a short, sharp nod. "I'm pretty sure we can do this thing tonight."

"Pretty sure? George, baby, I love you, but I need a sure thing. I can't even shift away this frizz right now." I gestured to my hair, which, despite some mousse and styling, was beginning to fray at the ends.

Smoothing my locks with the palm of his hand, he pinched the ends between two fingers. "But you've got that sexy succubus-in-heat thing happening. Not many can resist." I gave him a look, rolling my eyes, calling him on his complimentary bullshit. He shrugged. "What do you want me to say? Sure things are nonexistent in our business."

I bumped him with an elbow. "Maybe for *you*," I said shooting him a grin.

George and I took our sweet time returning the shoes and

packing up our stuff until the only people left from our group were us and Dave and Rob.

"Rob says you're from Nevada?" Dave asked while helping me into my jacket.

"Las Vegas," I clarified.

The surprise registered on his face before he quickly collected himself. "Wow, how . . . exciting."

I nodded. "There are so many men and women there who need our help. George and I assist those struggling with gambling addiction and women who fall into dangerous industries."

"Like . . . *hookers*?" He said the word as though his only experience with them was a Julia Roberts movie.

"Um, yeah. Pretty much."

"So . . . you in town tomorrow night? Maybe we could grab a bite or something?"

I tilted my head to look into his eyes. "Oh, I could bite something for sure."

His eyebrows shot up, eyes sparkling with mischief that had been suppressed—dormant for far too long.

On an exhale, I released my pheromone. It was so potent, I was certain George could see a fog-like substance seeping from my lips. Dave's eyes drooped and he stared at me, mouth parted. "Dave," I whispered in my most husky voice, "would you like to drive me back to the hotel?"

He nodded, the trance-like state making the movement almost mechanical. My magic couldn't force anyone to do something they didn't already want to do. It simply made their desires stronger and more apparent. Took the subconscious and pulled it to the forefront of their minds, if you will.

My smile curved and I mimicked his nod, turning toward Rob and George. "Rob, would you mind giving George a ride back? Dave and I wanted to get to know each other a little better."

"Sure, no problem." Rob smiled at George with the sweetest, most unassuming glance I'd seen in a while.

"And you'll keep him company until I get back, right?"

His smile widened. "Of course . . . but, wait. Are you two staying in the same room?"

Shit. George's smile dropped immediately into a glare. Directed straight at me. "Um, yeah. But separate beds. Our church couldn't afford two separate rooms."

Rob nodded, his smile returning, though it didn't quite reach his eyes like it had moments before. "Yeah. Our budgets have been slashed like crazy too."

"So, I'll see you both in a bit, right?"

"Oh, you can count on it," George said, offering his friendliest grin.

I climbed into the passenger seat of Dave's giant SUV. The sort of gas-guzzling vehicle that Saetan himself wouldn't even drive. He may want to send humanity to Hell, but his goal was certainly not to destroy the environment.

"Wow . . ." I looked around the interior, noting the very polished leather and sound system. He plugged his iPod in, turning on Creed. I cringed as a grumbling singing voice blasted through the speakers. "Don't you just love these guys?" He closed his eyes swaying to the soft rock and raising a hand in the air. Barf. Don't get me wrong . . . I'm all for morality; I'm just really against terrible music.

I glanced in the passenger-side mirror, noting that my lips were a natural pink and my cheeks, perfectly flushed. My eyelashes feathered long and soft, nearly touching my eyebrows. I batted them at my reflection. My body was compensating for what my magic couldn't accomplish. Time to turn on the charm. The car purred to life and he backed out of the lot, making some inane chit chat. I didn't bother buckling up, but instead slid to the middle of the front seat, propping an elbow on his shoulder.

He shifted a glance to me before quickly diverting his gaze back to the road. "How long of a drive is it, Dave?"

"Uh, about fifteen minutes or so. Why?"

I shrugged, brushing my lips against his earlobe and running my nose down the length of his jaw. "Just determining if we need to park or not."

"Huh? What are you—"

"Shh." I placed a finger on his lips as the light turned green. He accelerated and I could hear his pulse quickening. I exhaled my pheromone again, and his body immediately relaxed. "You want me, Dave?" I flicked a tongue out and his stubble scraped the surface as I licked a portion of his jaw up to his ear.

He grunted a response and nodded. "Uh-huh. B-but . . ."

I suckled his earlobe, taking it mostly into my mouth and he groaned. "Just relax Dave. I promise, you won't go to Hell because of this one act." It was a promise I knew to be true. I cupped his erection in one hand. It twitched in my palm and I squeezed once, making sure to brush against his balls through the fabric.

"Just keep driving." My sex throbbed and ached, but that didn't matter nearly as much as getting him to come. I could live without the release of an orgasm. But I couldn't live without *his* orgasm. I positioned myself on my knees, bending at the waist so that other drivers wouldn't see what we were doing. Unzipping his pants, I smiled as his erection sprang free.

"Are you going to—Oh God!" he cried as I took him entirely in my mouth. His skin was soft and sensitive against my lips. The tiniest flicker of my tongue and his hips bucked beneath me. I deep-throated his cock and he slammed on the brakes, sending my head into the steering wheel.

"Careful up there, Dave."

"S-sorry," he panted. "I just—it's kind of hard to focus while you're . . . while you . . ." I ran my tongue around his balls, taking one in my mouth and sucking gently, then repeating the action on the other side. His grip on the wheel tightened and I moaned, allowing the noise to buzz against him. His head fell back on the headrest.

"Shit," he whispered.

"Why, Dave." I sent him a mocking smile. "Was that profanity I just heard from your lips?"

"I just . . . I'm nervous. Really nervous."

"I know, baby," I said, quieter. "But trust me. You'll be okay. You can still have a relationship with God and enjoy the sensual side of life."

"How can you say that?" His eyes twitched down to me before quickly lifting back to the road. He put a hand to my hair and gently brushed a piece from my eyes.

"You just have to have some faith. Don't do this all the time, but now . . . in this moment. It is okay. And if you love the woman . . . it's even better. God doesn't punish love."

God doesn't punish love. The truth of Julian's words rang over and over in my head, stirring the memory from long ago.

"But . . ." He swallowed, braking at another red light. "This—us . . . it isn't love. This is just lust."

I gripped the base of his dick firmly and licked him once more. "Do you want me to stop, Dave?" I held my pheromone in. I knew ten minutes ago that this was what he wanted—but he was entitled to change his mind. He didn't answer, but his cock held firm in my hand. If that was the only answer I needed, I would have continued with no guilt. But his sweet, boyish face was so worried. I sighed and pushed off his legs.

His hand in my hair stopped me from getting up. "No," he said quietly.

"No?" I was genuinely surprised. "Are you sure?"

He nodded and accelerated once more, licking his lips. "Yes. I-I really want you to finish."

"Oh, baby," I said through a grin. "You'll be the one finishing." His fingers entwined in my hair, twisting the strands in his fist; he gripped me firmly, the pain tingling against my scalp. I moaned with the little bit of pain, exaggerating for dramatic effect and looked up into his eyes. His hand held my head firmly in place. "Make me," I whispered.

"What?" He shifted in the seat, the other hand's fingers twitching against the wheel.

"Make me get you off," I said, clarifying once more. It took another moment before he fully grasped the meaning of this. And for the first time since I'd begun, a smile crept across his sweet features. He tugged my hair once more. "Oh yeah," I cried. And finally, he pushed my head into his crotch. I opened my throat as his hard cock slid all the way to the back. He determined the speed, hand still coiled in my hair lifting and pushing my head exactly as he wanted it. He chose rough and hard, lifting his hips and plunging his dick deep in my mouth while his hand on the back of my head guided me with force. With only a few more thrusts, he spurted hot and sticky onto my tongue. I swallowed him down, the rush of his soul the best high I could ask for.

22

I passed Drew and Adrienne's door on my way back to my room. A tray sat outside on the floor. An empty bottle of champagne was nestled between two plates of almost finished room-service dinner. Anger flared through my body and heated my cheeks. I had good nerve to pound on the door and scream at them both.

Instead, I took a deep, calming breath. He wasn't mine to fight for. He was barely even a friend these days. I could hold off and ask in the morning what happened. I turned to move on, when I heard a high-pitched giggle from the other side of the door. Adrienne. Her laugh was loud, uncontrolled—it almost sounded like she had during her human days. A loud thump banged against the wall and I jumped, startled.

"Oh, Drew," she moaned, loud enough that the whole floor could have damn well heard her. "Oh yes, right like that."

There was a grunt followed by a low, manly groan. *Drew*. I closed my eyes, knowing those noises all too well from our one night together. "My God, Adrienne. You are so beautiful." Oh, Hell no.

My God, Monica. You are so beautiful.

Tears strangled in my throat and I froze, my blood running cold. It was exactly what he'd said to me six months earlier while we were in the throes of passion.

Before I could stop myself, my fist was against the door pounding fast and furious. The door swung open and I found myself face-to-face with a shirtless Drew. His chest heaved up and down with each deep breath.

"What?" he snapped.

Shit. What now? "I . . . need to speak with Adrienne. About . . . the case."

"Monica!" Adrienne ran toward me in a way that I wasn't sure whether I should steady her or duck. "Look, babe! It's Marnica!" Her words slurred and she pinched a half-empty champagne flute between two fingers. She wore Drew's button-down shirt like a nightgown and no pants. I squeezed my eyes shut. Please no . . . please don't let it have already happened. . . .

I opened my eyes again. "Hey, Adrie—oh!" My words were lost as she pulled me in for a crushing hug, a bit of champagne sloshing out of the flute and landing on my pants.

She pulled back from the hug, trying to stare at me, but her eyes crossed, completely out of focus. She swayed, steadying herself on my shoulders and sniffed audibly once before scrunching her nose. "You had sex!" she attempted a whisper, but somehow managed to be even louder than her normal speaking voice.

I swallowed as Drew sharply inhaled to my left. "No—I, no I didn't."

Mascara was smeared below her big, brown eyes and her hair in rough shape. "You're telling the truth," she stated, reading my aura. Then, pointing a finger at my nose, "But you did something tonight."

"Yeah. And you're drunk," I said, stating the obvious, then looked to Drew for any signs that he was, too. His arms were crossed and he leaned on the door frame. Tight biceps clenched along with his jaw—he was pissed. Shit. Like, *really* pissed. His mouth tightened into a hard line and he chewed on the inside of his cheek. My eyes followed down his neck to the light sprinkling of chest hair across his pecs and down his washboard stomach. Black dress pants hung low on his waist revealing a thin happy trail and that V muscle just above the groin. My mouth went dry at the sight.

"Enjoying the view?" His voice was tight and I immediately forced my eyes back to his. His mouth was still set in stone, but a shimmer of humor flashed in his eyes. He liked that I was rendered speechless.

"Are you drunk, too?" I inhaled his scent, not smelling any alcohol on him. The tangy smell emanated off of Adrienne stronger than sewage.

"Maaaaahnica should join us for a drink!" Adrienne threw her hands above her head presenting the idea as if it were worthy of a Nobel Peace Prize.

"We're out. Remember? You drank the whole bottle." Drew's face softened slightly when talking to her.

"You drank the *whole* bottle? Yourself?"

"Monica," Drew said on a sigh, "do you really need to see Adrienne now? We're in the middle of . . . something."

It was my turn to glare and I shot him a look. "Yes," I snapped while grabbing Adrienne's elbow and pulling her out into the hallway. "It's important."

"Fine." His voice wasn't raised like mine was, but it was even more lethal that way. A soft, menacing threat. "Stay in the room for God's sake. She doesn't even have pants on." He stepped to the side and gestured for us to enter. I did so, Adrienne clinging to my arm in an uncharacteristic hug. I shrugged her off onto the bed.

"I'm going to get some ice. You have two minutes," he said, glaring at me.

Fuck. Never come between a man and his orgasm. My eyes trailed once more to his chest—his nipples tight in the chilly air-conditioned room.

"And you—" He pinched Adrienne's chin between two fingers, dropping a feathered kiss to her lips. "We'll pick up where we left off when I get back." My gaze dropped to his tight ass as he bent to kiss her. His back flexed with the movement and my stomach turned. I would never again have him. His body. Or his friendship.

"Can you not control yourself, Monica? Christ," he muttered catching me mid-stare. I glanced away, face burning.

"Of course she can't!" Adrienne cried out with a giggle. The sort of giggle that had more pain than humor in it. "She's a demon-whore!"

"Adrienne!" Drew's eyes grew wide and glanced from her to me and back again.

Oh, fuck. "But, she is, Drew! She like, works for Saetan and everything."

"Okay," I said, grabbing Drew's shoulders. His skin was hot beneath my hand and I flushed at the proximity. "It's okay Drew. Really, I just need a couple of minutes."

"Monica—she doesn't mean that. . . ."

"Oh, yes she does. But it's okay. Really. Go get some ice and I'll be gone soon."

He glanced again at Adrienne, who was now on her back on the bed draining the last of the champagne. Giving me one last apologetic half-smile, he closed the door behind him. "You're not a—"

"Out!" Damn, I didn't want to have this conversation. I pointed a finger at the door and after a moment's hesitation, he left.

Adrienne!" I rushed over to her. "What are you doing? You can't tell him that !"

She shrugged and licked the rim of her champagne flute. "S'not like he'd believe me anyway."

I pinched the bridge of my nose rubbing in circles just over my eyes. "Promise me . . . no more demon talk tonight, okay?"

"Fine, whatever."

"Did you two have sex?"

Adrienne giggled and lifted up onto her elbows. "Angels make *love*, Monica."

I groaned. I only had a minute with her. "Fine, whatever. Did you two make lo—" the word choked in my mouth. Gag me. "Nope, no, I can't say that. Did you two fuck or not?"

She giggled again and threw her head back. "Not yet," she crooned in a singsong way.

My chest collapsed on an exhale. "Oh, thank Hell." I closed my eyes with another deep breath. "Adrienne, you can't. Not yet. Do not do this to him."

"You're just saying that because *you* want to sleep with him." She folded her arms across her chest petulantly.

"No . . ." She dropped her chin to her chest giving me a chastising look. "Well, yes. Fine, I do want to sleep with him. But I won't. I promise. I kept my shit together for years with him until I thought I had lost my powers and . . . and . . ."

". . . and he thought I had cheated."

I nodded and the room grew silent. "I'm not the only succubus out there gunning for Drew's soul, you know? He shines with purity—he basically walks around Vegas with a giant red target on his di—er, forehead."

All the color drained from Adrienne's face. Giant tears welled up, gathering in a pool at the bottom lower lids.

"I'm sorry," I said. "I'm not saying this to hurt you or scare you. And maybe with more time he could be committed. But—he is human. And with a human, there's never a guarantee that he'll be one hundred percent true to you. By their very nature, humans make mistakes. Big ones sometimes . . . I think that's why we love them so much." I swallowed as she stared past my shoulder at the wall. Her face was no longer registering emotion except for a few single tears that streamed down her cheeks. "But maybe, Adrienne. Maybe with time when he has a chance to, I don't know, to . . ."

"To get over you." she cut me off.

Shit. "That's not what I was saying, Adrienne."

"But it's true, isn't it?" Her eyes turned to me, without her needing to move her head at all.

Holy Hell, this was not a conversation I wanted to be having. "Do you really want your first time with Drew . . . as an angel . . . to be when you're trashed? Think about it. This is such a bad idea."

"It's been months for me, Monica. When I got my halo, it's not like my libido magically disappeared."

"Oh, I know. . . ." I remembered all too well. "Just give him more time." I would repeat this a million times until it got through to her.

"Time to get over you," she repeated. Then, after another moment, Adrienne looked up at me, swiping away an errant tear from her cheek. "And what if he doesn't?"

My throat burned. I wanted to break down and cry, too. A bitter laugh escaped me lips. "He will." I swallowed. "They always do."

Her face had softened into a beautiful melancholy pout again. She was still drunk even though our conversation was a sobering one. "I'm sick of waiting." She glared at me as though it was my fault—shit, maybe it was.

She stared at her hands, not meeting my eyes. "You promise you won't sleep with him again?"

I took a breath, hesitating before answering. I couldn't lie—she would see right through that. "I promise that . . . unless there is an extenuating circumstance, I will not have sex with Drew. And certainly not while you two are an item."

"What in Heaven's name would an extenuating circumstance be to have sex with my boyfriend?" Damn. *Boyfriend.* That word was like a dagger in my gut.

"You'd be surprised at what comes up in our realms." She continued staring at me with raised eyebrows. A thought struck me—and it was almost so mean, I didn't want to say it.

"What?" she asked through narrowed eyes.

I swallowed. "I would sleep with him if I thought you were going to get him irrevocably connected to you before he was ready."

She gasped. "But, but you would steal his life!"

I nodded. "Some . . . a week, maybe. But if you fuck Drew tonight before he is ready, you'll be taking something far worse. Because in the case that he is unfaithful, you'll be marking his soul for Hell."

"That's harsh," she whispered.

"I know."

"I think I need another drink." She looked down at her champagne glass, frowning and turning it upside down, realizing it was empty.

"You are so drunk," I laughed and gently took the empty glass from her hand, placing it on the nightstand. "Like, *really,* drunk."

Adrienne fell back onto the bed, her arm flopping over her eyes. "I know! I couldn't let Drew drink any. So I thanked him for the thoughtful gesture and drank it myself so that there wouldn't be any left in the room for *him.*"

"Why didn't you yell at him? Scream, throw the bottle out the window?"

She sighed, still lying on the bed with her forearm covering half her face. "Because. We haven't seen much of each other lately. Tonight was supposed to be a romantic date night. I didn't want to fight."

"Well, I have to admit, you're kind of a fun drunk." I smirked at her and she peeked through her arm at me. "We should have done this when you were human. You could have been fun in the clubs."

"Shut up, demon-whore," she said through a smile of her own.

"Screw you, angel-bitch," I laughed and swatted playfully at her leg.

After a soft knock, the door swung open and Drew entered carrying a bucket of ice and another bottle of champagne.

"Pretend to sleep," I whispered. Adrienne nodded barely and slackened her mouth so it was hanging open.

"Who's ready for some more champa—"

I looked up at Drew and down again at Adrienne, who was doing a good job at acting passed out. Shit, maybe she really was. I shrugged at Drew. "Sorry . . . she sort of fell asleep on me. I didn't want to just leave her here like this."

"Dammit!" he whispered, dropping the items down onto the dresser.

"You should let her sleep. We have a busy day tomorrow with the case."

"Yeah, I know. Believe me. It's all she ever has time for."

"It's her job."

He raked a hand through his golden hair. "Yeah, I know."

There was a pause while we stared at each other from across the room. Adrienne grunted and rolled over onto her stomach, shooting me a surreptitious glare as she did so. Yup, just a good actress, it seemed. I suppressed a chuckle and instead walked over to Drew. "I'll take that," I said, grabbing the bottle of champagne. "Thanks. George and I will toast to you two." I scrunched my nose, peering up at him through my long lashes.

"Monica," he whispered.

I put a finger to his lips, glancing at where Adrienne lay. I had no idea what he was about to say . . . but whatever it was, I was better off not hearing it. "Go take care of your girl, Drew." I brushed past him, shutting the door behind me and ran head first into Damien.

He looked from me to the door, then back to me again. "You have got to be fucking kidding me?"

23

"Did you do what I think you did?" Damien's nostrils flared and his hands were on his hips. Clenched so hard that the skin around his fingertips was red and swollen. The hotel sconces lit the hallway with a warm, golden glow that made Damien's tan even that more luminous. Damn, he was beautiful. Even when he was irrationally pissed.

I rolled my eyes and shoved past his shoulder, walking farther down the hall until I reached the door to my hotel room. I'd already had plenty of drama for one evening and really didn't want to deal with a man who exuded jealousy despite an obvious aversion to monogamy.

"Answer me, goddammit!" he hissed, following me.

I spun around, champagne bottle nearly slamming into his impressive forearm. "*No*. Okay? No, it's not what you think. Your angel is drunk in there and I was stopping her from making a stupid mistake."

He exhaled visibly, running a hand over his five o'clock shadow. "What do you care, anyway?" I asked. "I thought you just wanted a good fuck? A chance to poke the notorious succubus—see what all the fuss is about, right?" I stepped into his chest, nudging my knee between his legs and pushing against his tightening groin.

His lips twitched into a barely there smile that dared me to continue. "A poke?" He quirked an eyebrow, amusement sparkling in his bright eyes. "I don't *poke* anything, baby." He paused for effect, snaking an arm around my waist and splaying his hand across my lower back. He tugged me in closer, his erection strong and hard against my belly. "I will impale you. Stroke you. Worship you." He traced my ear with the tip of his nose, placing his lips on my lobe, chuckling deep and throaty. "But poking? That is not in my repertoire."

I had only meant to look up at him. But as soon as my head was tilted, his lips were on mine. They were firm and demanding, and I happily submitted to them. Within seconds, he had my back against the wall, his hands on my ass, lifting me to meet him. I locked my legs around his waist and rocked my swollen sex against his. Our arousal was thick and permeated the air around us, flooding my nostrils. I was aching with need. The car, the road head . . . it had been survival, not pleasure. But as his mouth trailed kisses down my jaw and neck, it was survival of a different kind. Emotional survival. The champagne bottle was still in my hand, its weight inhibiting me as I tried to tear his leather jacket off his body.

He dropped my legs back to the floor, pulling away from me, and I whimpered. Finally allowing myself to acknowledge that I wanted him. Wanted this. Wanted more. "Don't stop . . . ," I moaned, my head falling back against the wall.

Taking the champagne bottle from my hands, he placed it on the floor next to our feet, then with his hands on my shoulders, spun me so that I was facing the wall.

"Put your palms against the wall, Ms. Lamb." I did as I was told, arching my back so that my ass curved into the air. Lost in the feel of his hand splayed on my hips, warm coils of sensation spiraled deep inside me. "Did you think you could tie up an officer of the law without any consequences?"

His arms were above my head, enclosing me against the paisley wallpaper. His groin pushed into my backside and I rolled my hips over him. "Don't move your hands," he whispered behind me as his hands slid down the wall. "I have to search you . . . make sure you're not armed." Starting with my wrists, he ran his hands along my arms, under my arms and down my rib cage to my waist. With a squeeze, he continued down my hips, then, coming back up my inner thighs, his fingers grazed my pubic area, just missing the spot where I needed him most. I groaned as they traveled up my stomach to my breasts. He stopped just below, circling his fingers at the base of my tender breasts.

"Damien," I moaned.

He paused, hands freezing. "It's Detective Kane to you, Ms. Lamb."

"Please . . ."

His hands dove under my shirt to my breasts, rolling my nipples between his thumbs and forefingers. I yelped at the sudden intensity and my hands twitched, desperate to touch anything but the wall in front of me. His lips were on my neck, tongue tracing the line down to my shoulder, and he nipped when he reached the end.

One hand stayed on my breast, caressing and massaging, while the other one trailed down my stomach. He reached the waistband of my slacks and undid the top button and zipper. Dipping his fingers inside my thong, he stroked my landing strip with tender fingers. "How long has it been, Ms. Lamb, since someone got you off expecting nothing in return?"

I panted, unable to answer. My legs quivered, threatening to give out on me any second. The question caught me off guard. I opened my mouth to answer, a whimper escaping in place of words. His stroking fingers dipped lower and feathered across my clit. I cried out, hands slipping off the wall, I reached behind me to feel his erection. He froze. All movement, all pleasure halted.

"Now, now, Ms. Lamb. I gave you clear instructions for this pat down. Palms to the wall. If you can't comply, I'm afraid I'll have to take a more forceful approach." He pinched my clit hard making me yelp in a combination of pain and pleasure. "Hands up, Ms. Lamb."

My hands trembled as I raised them to the wall again. "Da—" His other hand tweaked my nipple hard. "Ah! Detective Kane, please," I corrected.

"That's better. Please what, Ms. Lamb?"

"Please. Make me come, Detective."

His teeth grazed my ear, stubble scraping the side of my neck as he nuzzled against me.

"With pleasure, Ms. Lamb." Gathering my moisture with the tip of his finger, he used the lubrication as his finger circled my clit. With two fingers, he dipped inside me, pulsing them in and out while pressing into me with the heel of his hand. I wriggled beneath his fingers, unable to keep still with the building climax. My orgasm was screaming to get out; it needed release. I was forced to stare at an ugly hotel wallpaper when I really wanted to spin around and take Damien's lips in mine.

His pressure and speed increased and my body grew wetter with the movement. He circled the heel of his hand over my clit one final time, being sure to add pressure. It was the last straw. With a final cry, I exploded around his fingers, arching my back to feel his excitement pressed against my ass, I trembled over him and all my weight fell into his arms.

"Oh, my Hell," I sighed against him and he kissed my hairline. After taking a moment to compose myself, I turned so that my back was yet again to the wall. Arching an eyebrow, I gave him my most sultry smile. "I do believe it's your turn, Detective Kane," I said while cupping his cock, giving it a firm squeeze.

Taking my wrists in each hand, he pinned them over my head, ravishing my lips with his in another blazing kiss that left me breathless and panting beneath him. "Not this time, succubus. That one was all just for you."

A door swung open behind us and I shifted my clothing, hair, and makeup back in place quickly.

"What the fuck are you doing out here? You're supposed to be helping me, Mon!"

Shit. Damien pushed off of me and leaned on the wall next to where I'd been left panting. "Sorry, George . . . I, I got sidetracked."

"Yeah, I can see that," he snapped, glaring at Damien. "We have a job to do, you know."

"Yeah, I do know. That's how come I managed to get Dave off in his car on the way home."

George's face registered surprise then curved into a smile. "Is that so?"

I slid a look to Damien, whose mouth was dangling open. "Yeah, is that so?" he repeated, his voice holding a dangerous edge to it.

I glared back at him, lowering my eyes. "It's my job." Even though this fact was true, it didn't make me feel any less guilty.

"I was never good at sharing." His glare mirrored mine and we were suddenly in a Texas standoff.

"Then, baby, you are with the wrong woman."

"You ready, Monica?" George broke through.

"Ready?" Damien asked the question slowly, eyes not leaving mine.

"Um, yeah. I've got a guy in here that I could use some help getting into bed. . . ." He dropped his voice lower than a whisper.

Damien's eyes widened again and the staring contest was all but forgotten. "This is a joke, right? You're fucking joking?" When I didn't respond, he continued, staring at me incredulously. "You go from fucking a guy in his car to doing God knows what in Drew and Adrienne's room to getting fingered by me to a threesome?"

I shifted my weight, "I didn't have sex in the car—just a blowjo—"

Damien held a hand up, cutting me off. "Fuck no," he growled and caveman style, he threw me over his shoulder, stalking away, taking me with him.

24

"Put me *down*! What are you some sort of Neanderthal?" I hissed so not to wake the entire hotel and pounded his back with my fists. He ignored me and barged into his room, the one directly across from Drew and Adrienne's, spilling light into the blackness from the hallway. He threw me down on the bed, kicking the door shut behind him.

"What are you *doing*?" I panted. "I am not yours to order around."

He smiled a Cheshire grin. "You are tonight."

"Of all the arrogant, no-good, son-of-a-bitch things to do . . ."

"Monica!" he barked.

His sharp tone made me pause and I looked at him with eyebrows raised.

"Just shut up," he continued. "Forgive me for not wanting to share you tonight." He stepped toward me, close enough for me to run my hand down his body.

"Yeah?" I swallowed. "And what about tomorrow night? When I have to hunt another conquest? Or back in Vegas when I'm stripping again."

With the back of his knuckle, he brushed the underside of my jaw. "We'll just have to deal with those things as they come." He tucked an errant hair behind my ear.

"You realize that 'dealing' with it is not carrying me over your shoulder out of the situation, right? I'm just going to have to help George tomorrow. . . ."

Damien winced and covered my lips with a finger. "Monica, please."

I kissed his finger, running my tongue along the tip. It tasted like me—salty and metallic.

And before I knew it, we were once again kissing, scrambling to get our clothes off, a tangle of cotton, tongues, and hands, searching for each other's lips in the darkness. Neither of us bothered to find a light. I could see well despite the darkness and pulled back to take Damien in as he ripped his shirt open, tearing it away from his shoulders. He unbuttoned his pants and slipped them off his waist. All my daydreams were nothing compared to the reality of his almost-naked body. Wide shoulders, a well-muscled chest, and lean in all the right places. With taut abs and a narrow waist—he was tight, strong, and absolutely beautiful.

He leaned down again, folding an arm under my back and cupping my jaw with the other, and pulled me in for another crushing kiss. His tongue swept across mine. "Damn, you taste good."

My body flamed and I could feel the blush from my cheeks to my toes. "My lips are just the appetizer." My words were needy and panting. "The devil's nectar," I moaned as I arched into him, his tight erection pressed into my hip.

In a swift movement, he had my bra unclasped and on the floor. If he hadn't been over a century old as well, I might have found this a little unnerving. Before I could give his undergarment expertise any more thought, his mouth was over my left breast, tongue working my nipple. Nimble fingers rolled over my other nipple, creating two hard peaks. Switching sides, he moved his mouth to the other repeating the technique. The sensation shot from my nipple down south, my pussy firing to life once more.

He pulled back, blowing cool air over them to create a chill over my tender flesh. I shivered and raked my fingernails down his back. Inhaling through clenched teeth, he hissed. "Oh, succubus. I wouldn't do that if I were you," he whispered.

"Oh?" I mocked innocence and locked my ankles behind his back, pushing my dampening sex into his belly. "What about this?" Grabbing a fistful of his hair I tugged, clenching it in a firm grip.

He grunted and I rolled my hips beneath him, once more feeling the surge through my body as pressure touched just the right area. Using the bed as leverage, I flipped Damien onto his back, sitting atop his hips.

"Oh, now this just isn't fair. You already had your way with me at the strip club."

Holding his wrists, I put his hands above his head, mimicking how he'd treated me in the hallway. "Yes—and you got your kicks just now out there. I'd say we're even." I snaked my body over his, breasts pressing into a smattering of coarse chest hair. My lips hovered above his, taking in the moment. I kissed him long and deep, stroking my tongue against his.

"Succubus, we are not even close to even," he chuckled, rolling his wrists out of my grasp. He ran a tongue along my ear, closing his lips around the earlobe. "If you don't recall, you poured my fucking beer all over my naked johnson." Curling a leg around my hips, he flipped me onto my back in a movement so fast it could only be described as supernatural. I'd never really seen Damien in action and knew very little about his powers. Super speed had clearly been exhibited just now. I wondered what else was super about this guy. I imagined him in a battle, fighting with that speed and dexterity, the vision so sexy it sent a bolt of electricity right down between my thighs.

As he lay over me, perched on his elbows, some hair flopped onto his forehead. I brushed it back, running my hands down the side of his face. "Okay, elemental. Let's see what you got." I reached for his cock, dipping my hand inside the waistband of his boxer briefs. I moaned at the feel of his pulsing heat in my palm.

His face registered surprise for all of a moment, then softened into a wicked grin. "That sounds like a challenge, Ms. Lamb."

"Call it what you like, Detective Kane. But I'm all yours for the rest of the night." Squeezing his arousal once more, I raised my hands above my head, striking a pose that would leave porn directors panting. "But make it good," I whispered. "You don't get many chances to impress a succubus."

Damien peeled away my thong, then slipped his own boxer briefs down until we were both nude. He nestled his body between my legs, parting them, his dark gaze making my pulse race. I placed my palms flat on the bed. Damien bent, placing his mouth on me, running his tongue along the length of my sex in a slow, sensual lick. His tongue was hot and wet and as he moved it against me, I trembled from the sweet pleasure of it. I was losing myself in the feel of his hands, flexing and unflexing against my hips as his tongue swirled so intimately across my flesh.

He teased me with his tongue and just when I thought I couldn't take it anymore, he took my clit in his mouth and sucked. First gentle, then hard and rough. I threaded my fingers into his hair and arched against his mouth. He moved down, sliding his tongue into my pussy, thrusting in and out just as he would if we were fucking. Then, continuing the motion with a finger, he rolled his tongue over my clit, playing with the bud over and over.

"Yes, right there, Damien," I panted and banged my head against the headboard. The pressure built inside, squeezing his fingers as the pulsing orgasm began. I cried out as the first wave slammed into my body, shaking my every limb.

Once I finished, he knelt, taking my hands in a gentle caress and lowered them to my sides again. Slipping his arms under mine, he lifted me until I, too, was on my knees on top of the bed, facing him.

"Wow." His eyes traveled down my body, settling once more on my eyes. "You are a vision."

I was unsure what to make of the compliment. My legs felt like Jell-O, as though they couldn't support my own weight, and in front of me was a man who was a self-proclaimed womanizer. A man who had professed he only wanted me for a good fuck. But his actions clearly didn't match the words. Before I could answer, his large fingers raked through my hair, pulling me into another kiss. Damien didn't just kiss with his lips. His hands roamed my body, caressing in gliding motions until I was covered in goose bumps. His erection pressed into the V between my legs and I opened my thighs just enough so that he was nestled between my legs. I squeezed his length with my thigh muscles and he groaned into my mouth.

The blistering kiss left me wobbly and trembling as he brushed his hand through my hair. "I'm failing to see the payback, Detective Kane," I whispered. "Though I'll admit I'm liking this."

"I decided," he said, kissing my temple, "that tonight is no longer about revenge." He kissed the other temple. "It's about wild, insatiable pleasure." He raised a hand above us and swirled it, slowly at first. A soft breeze caught my hair and blew it off my shoulders.

As his hand spun faster, the breeze gathered more speed. With a jerk, he thrust his hand up and the window slid open—a new, cooler gust of wind rushing into the room. "Wrap your legs around me, baby. I'll buckle you in."

I did as he said, curling my arms around his shoulders and

using them to hold my weight while I climbed on top of him. His cock pushed against the entrance to my sex and I lowered myself onto him, his erection stretching me in delicious pleasure. I felt every inch of his rock hard dick entering me. His hand, still above us, circled faster, the wind picking up. It was cold and chilled the sweat that had beaded over my body. His other arm was around my waist, clutching my body to his. We were a tangled mess of skin and my hair wrapped around him as well. I found his mouth again, pulling him in for a kiss. Enraptured by his lips, I could swear it felt like we were floating. His hard length stroked me from the inside, the tip hitting that sweet knot of desire deep inside me.

His breath was deep and heavy against my ear. His skin soft and tight with hard-edged muscle straining beneath. He groaned as he pulsed in and out of me in steady, fluid movements. I inhaled deeply, his scent intoxicating—like musk and pine.

When I opened my eyes, the room was still buzzing and Damien's lips were on my throat. The wind had picked up even more and around us, the room spun in a blurring vision. I gasped at the realization that we were in the air, surrounded by a tornado's embrace. Instinctively, I clutched more tightly onto Damien, who blinked in confusion, raising his gaze from my neck to my eyes. A smile creased his face and he laughed at my terror. Hair whipped across my face and lashed my shoulders and neck.

"Oh, my Hell," I whispered. "This can't be real."

He chuckled against my throat. "Says the soul-stealing succubus." Cupping my ass, he pulled me into him deeper and I arched my back, welcoming the thrust. "It's so real, babe." He nuzzled into my shoulder, nipping. "Lean back," he said, then lowered his hand, which controlled the air. I leaned back, Damien's other arm still snaked around my waist and a cushion of wind caught me, softer than any down comforter. Sighing, I let my arms slowly arch up and down as though I were a bird flying through the wind.

"I'm close, Monica." His words were a pant; a plea. His face was strained with lines around his eyes and mouth. And with his thumb, he applied pressure to my clit while quickening his pace inside of me. We both moaned and I squeezed my muscles around him—the tightening spiraling both of us over the edge. I knew I wouldn't be able to hold on much longer as he slammed into me, one thrust after another. The climax hit me hard and I bucked against his firm body while sweet pleasure rolled through my body, quivering every limb down to my fingertips. Damien groaned and tightened against me. Hot, sticky liquid spurted inside as he came with a final burst of thrusts and shuddered into my shoulder. The air around us slowed, lowering our bodies to the bed until the room had stilled completely.

We lay there entwined in each other, his hands running gentle circles over my bare back. I closed my eyes, enjoying the silence. The room was cool due to the leftover wind. Not dissimilar to the chill of a room right after you turn a fan off. A gentle breeze still caressed us through the open window, and as one specific breeze brushed across my body, I shivered involuntarily. The smell of crisp autumn air filled the room and drowned out the scent of heady arousal. Damien flattened his palms to my arms, rubbing as though feeling my skin's chill for the first time. "I'm sorry," he whispered, then, with one flick of his hand, the wind blew the window shut.

"That was . . . incredible," I whispered, resting my chin to his chest and looking up at him.

His mouth twitched into a small smile and he pinched a section of my hair, twisting it around his fingers. "You liked that? That was just the tip of the iceberg."

"Oh, please don't tell me we have to fuck on an iceberg. If I thought the wind was chilly . . ." I let my joke drift off into silence and turned my head to rest my cheek on his body once more. "I didn't know elementals could do anything other than speak with the elements."

I felt his shrug. "If you're in good standing with the elements, they work with you. If you're not in good standing, well, then, you have to be awfully powerful to get them to do your bidding."

The room phone rang, loud and obnoxious. "Probably a noise complaint," Damien chuckled, reaching to answer.

I caught his hand in mine. "Don't," I whispered. "Let it ring. I'm sensing an encore coming soon." I rolled my hips over his, an erection stirring to life beneath me.

Damien quirked an eyebrow, amusement flashing momentarily across his face. "Is that so?"

"If you can handle it," I challenged.

That made him laugh out loud—a rare occurrence with Damien. "Oh, I think I can." I leaned to kiss him, my vibrating cell from my purse interrupting the moment.

"Shit," I whispered, pulling away from the embrace.

"Let it go to voice mail," Damien said, still kissing me.

I relaxed again into his embrace. As Damien's hands curled under my ass, I brought my knees under me, my body moistening with his touch. His erection was nestled between my legs, where a sticky wetness gathered—our juices combined. I groaned, reaching down to stroke his length, just as Damien's cell phone rang.

"Fuck," he cursed, leaning to the nightstand to answer it.

With a sigh, I fell off his body, flopping onto my back. True, I'd just had multiple orgasms in less than an hour. But a niggling feeling of unease crept through my body. This must be what Drew and Adrienne felt like all the time. Romance for them was always interrupted with work.

"Yes, ma'am. Right away," Damien said and hung up, looking over at me. "Get dressed. Another body was found." He flung his legs over the side of his bed, thrusting both hands into his hair before standing and pulling a pair of black pants on.

I did the same, finding my dress pants on the floor and my red V-neck shirt. Sure, I could have shifted my clothes back on, but I didn't want to waste any of my powers—especially not now that I knew how friggin' jealous Damien could be, I thought remembering how he'd thrown me over his shoulder just a little while ago.

Within minutes, we each were dressed and slipping our shoes on. Damien threw the door open. "Hey," he said.

"Is it George?" I called from the bed. When I stood to follow Damien, I froze, seeing Drew standing in the doorway, pajama pants loosely hanging off his hips. Behind him, in the hallway, was the Banshee, staring right at Drew with a hungry look in her milky white eyes.

25

"Oh fuck," I whispered. "What are you doing here?"

Damien shot me a weird look over his shoulder and the Banshee floated, bobbing up and down behind Drew.

"Me?" Drew responded. "I could ask you the same question."

"Huh?" My eyes were still locked on those of the Banshee, who floated over behind Drew and stared at the back of his head as though he were something to be devoured. She opened her mouth, unhinged her jaw to let out the deafening scream I'd been coming to know so well.

"No!" I shouted, holding out a hand. Drew jumped, and Damien gave me an odd look. Even the Banshee startled and she cocked her head slowly in that same curious way, staring at me as though I were a strange, unknown creature.

"What's going on? Do you see . . ." His voice trailed off as he glanced at Drew, and he cleared his throat.

I closed my eyes. *Not him. Not Drew. Please for the love of Hell.*

I thought back to when I'd first heard her in Vegas. Walking home after having seen Drew at the coffee shop carving pumpkins. Then again on the plane after boarding with Drew and the gang. In the hotel room after our interaction in the airport bathroom. Fuck. Squeezing my eyes shut tighter, I shook my head. No. Those could all just be coincidences. All those times, they were right around when we found the victims, too.

Damien cleared his throat, snapping me back to the present. "How is Adrienne feeling?"

There was pain in Drew's eyes as he looked back and forth between Damien and myself. I knew the pain. I had gone through it earlier this evening and every day for the past six months watching him and Adrienne together.

My one-night stands were one thing—those never involved emotion. But this? Damien and me equaled long-term potential in Drew's eyes. Even if Damien and I knew there wasn't much hope for monogamy here, Drew didn't know that.

Damien took Drew by the shoulders. "Let's go see her. If she's able to come to work, we could really use her." The two guys went into Drew's room, but the Banshee stayed in front of me.

"Don't touch me," I whispered. "I can't pass out again." She bobbed up and down, floating in front of me, wild red coils of hair bouncing with the gentle movement.

"Are you here to take Drew? Is that why you're coming to me?" Her eyebrows drew in together, eyes pinching as though the thought was painful. "I know what it's like to hate your job," I said to her. "And it doesn't seem like you enjoy being the fairy of death."

The Banshee's lips parted, a strangled noise escaping in a wheeze. I held a hand up to quiet her. "Shhh, don't try to speak. Nod. Like this . . . for yes." I nodded my head up and down and she just stared at me quizzically. "Come on, Banshee. Nod for yes." When she did nothing, I sighed, falling against the door frame. "Do you ever understand what I'm saying?" My head fell into my hands and I rubbed my palms over my eyes. When I looked up again, she was nodding. Her head slowly pulsing up and down, gray milky tears gliding down her cheeks. "You understand me?" She nodded again. "Had you ever seen yourself before I shifted to look like you?"

There was a pause and then she shook her head no. I wanted to laugh. And cry and hug her all at once.

"Not even in a mirror?" There was a *crack* sound and she was no longer in front of me. When I looked around, I saw her floating in Damien's room in front of the dresser mirror—no reflection stared back except for my own behind her. "Wow," I whispered more to myself than to the Banshee. "Just like a vampire."

"Well." Damien's voice boomed from the hallway despite the early morning hour. "Adrienne's pretty much useless until she sobers up." He paused, staring at me, frozen. "What the Hell, Monica? This is no time to be primping. These murders are happening faster than we can keep up with."

When I looked to my right, the Banshee was gone.

26

"We need to gather George and go," Damien said, gesturing to the hallway.

"Yeah, of course. No problem." I shifted my hair into place slowly while walking. Stopping, just as I passed Damien, I lowered my voice and glanced at Drew's door. "It was the Banshee again. I think she has something to do with Drew."

Alarm passed over Damien's face for a moment as he glanced from me to the door and back again. "We'll beef up security on him. Take turns watching out for him. He'll be safe for now with Adrienne. Even if she's trashed. That girl can kick some ass while shit-faced, let me tell you."

"So, she'll join us tomorrow?"

Damien glanced at his watch. "I'm gonna let her sleep another hour or two, then Drew will wake her up. 'Tomorrow.' " He put air quotes around the word while snorting a bitter laugh. "It already is tomorrow, baby. Besides, I don't care if she comes to the crime scene hungover, so long as she's not shit-faced. Hell, in her human days, she'd come in hungover all the time. The plight of working Vice."

"Okay, okay, I don't need to hear her life story. Let's just go get George." I walked down the hallway, digging out my key—taking a moment to listen at the door just in case I was about to barge in on something. Silence on the other side. When I opened the door, George was watching television with a scowl on his face, arms crossed, and Rob was asleep in my bed. Fully clothed. Uh-oh.

"Oh, look who decided to join us," George sneered.

I gestured for him to follow me to the hall. "Have you been waiting up for me this whole time?"

His scowl deepened and he made a dramatic moment out of joining me in the hallway.

"What do you want? I thought you'd still be having fun with your boy toy over there."

"George, I'm sorry. We'll commence Operation Manhunt tomorrow night, I promise."

"That is not the code term we use and you know it." He crossed his arms and looked to the left, obviously avoiding my gaze.

I resisted the urge to roll my eyes at him and the stupid code name we had come up with decades ago for when one of us needed help closing a deal. "Fine," I sighed. "We'll commence Operation Ex Caliber tomorrow. For now, though, we've all been called in to another scene."

His scowl dropped, color draining from his face. "Another murder?"

I nodded. "So, go get dressed and tell Rob. He can stay in the room tonight—I'm fine with that."

"Just what am I supposed to tell him? There aren't a whole lot of missionary emergencies at three in the morning."

I shrugged. "Think of something—one of our converts fell off the wagon. Or . . . uh, we got called into a brothel. Leave him a note. Anything. C'mon, George." I nudged him with a smirk. "You should be good at this lying stuff by now."

A smile finally cracked through his anger. "Fine. I'll be out in a minute." He shifted into a perfectly tailored outfit before slipping back into the room.

Thirty minutes later, Damien, George, and I arrived at a warehouse surrounded by flashing lights. "Do we know anything about the victim yet?" I whispered.

"Not a thing, succubus. Do I look like a mind reader?"

I blushed thinking back to our night and how he would anticipate my needs. I didn't answer and pressed my smirk into a straight line as best I could.

George tugged me back, whispering in my ear. "All right, just because you managed to get laid doesn't mean you have to rub it in my nose, baby girl."

"Am I being that obvious?"

"You're blushing and smiling. Not all that typical of my darling succubus."

Damien strode up to the yellow tape approaching an older man with graying hair and a widening belly. I recognized him from the news footage and press statements over the past week. "I'm Detective Kane of LVPD. I don't believe we met earlier." He held out a hand as the older gentleman took it in his.

"I'm Chief Andowe here in SLC. Nice to meet you, Kane." His voice was gruff but his eyes were kind.

"These are my consultants on the case, Monica Lamb and George er—" He shot a panicked glance to George. George had several fake last names he had chosen through the years.

"That's right," he jumped in. "George Irving." He took the chief's hand in a masculine handshake.

"Nice to meet you both. Come on in, I'll show you our victim. I tell you," he said, holding the yellow tape up so we could all duck under, "these scenes are just getting stranger and stranger. We don't even have any damned Spanish moss in this area."

The victim this time was a young man—perhaps early thirties. His hands and feet were bound with Spanish moss and vines. Dirt plugged his mouth—which was open mid-scream—eye sockets and nostrils. Stones and rocks lay at his feet and bruises marred his flesh. Celtic runes shimmered in the dawning light, still fresh from the potent magic. They twisted like ivy around each and every limb. On the victim's well-defined chest was another family crest, formed on his skin by dozens of tiny welts. There was something about the man—something very familiar. That strong, angled nose. His bronzed skin and cropped black hair. It looked somewhat like—

"The victim's name," Chief Andowe said, "is Luis Nunez-Buckley."

27

Stars. I was seeing stars everywhere. It couldn't be. It couldn't be Luis from the other night. Buckley. What the Hell was going on here? My vision was darkening on the edges and my breath—my damn breath wasn't working. A hand was on my elbow.

"C'mon, babe. Breathe." Damien's voice was in my ear. "Newbies," he said to Andowe.

"She gonna yak on my crime scene?" Andowe's voice was rough and cutting. "Get her out of here."

And with that I was moving, then sitting on something. A sidewalk? No . . . a car. I was sitting on someone's car.

"Head between your legs," Damien instructed me. "Deep breaths."

I did as I was told.

"What's the matter?" George asked.

"Luis," I whispered through my deep breaths.

"I know," Damien said, stroking the back of my head.

"Monica, are you okay? Who's Luis?" George demanded in his usual attitude.

"He was at the strip club the other night." I sat up, holding a hand to signal that I was okay when Damien began objecting. "And his name—Buckley. I-I just needed a moment." I looked back to George, who, despite his attitude-riddled voice, had concern twisting in his features. "He wanted a lap dance—from me. Just the other night. There was sort of an argument between . . ." I glanced at Damien, whose features were like stone.

"Oh, shit," George murmured.

"Yeah," I countered, then looked to Damien for guidance. "So, what the Hell do we do? Do we tell them of our connection to the victim?"

"That's a damn good question. Their own investigation might eventually lead them to your strip club, where they will easily discover the name Monica Lamb."

"But I strip under a different stage name. . . ."

"Doesn't matter," Damien mumbled. "They'll get a warrant for the girls' real names if they have to."

"Surely Lucien could fake that somehow."

Damien chewed that over for a moment. "That's true. For now, we won't say anything. We'll see what Adrienne has to say when she gets he—"

The air crackled around us. Another immortal was in the vicinity. "Something's here," Damien said through clenched teeth. "Wait here with Monica," he said and ran off, pulling a gun loaded with holy water bullets from inside his leather jacket. It's the only gun any of us use anymore.

George bristled, taking a moment to read the aura. "Vampire. It's definitely a vampire that's here."

Dejan. "Oh, shit." I hopped up from the car, feeling a momentary head rush with the sudden movement. "George c'mon! We can't let him hurt Dejan . . . or fuck . . . we can't let Dejan hurt him."

I took off running after Damien, George's footsteps pounding right behind mine. I closed my eyes, listening—a door slamming shut. The warehouse—they'd gone into the warehouse. George caught up, almost running right into me as I stood frozen.

"Damn, girl," George said, breathless. "You can run fast—"

I didn't even let him finish his sentence, but took off again for the warehouse. It was dark and looked like some sort of arts and crafts store supplier. Shelves and shelves of craft supplies lined the walls. Yarn, scrapbooks, acrylic paints, frames. George was right behind me. "Dejan?" I called out. "It's Monica. . . . We need to talk to you. Damien, if you're in here, don't shoot. Dejan is a . . ." Shit. I didn't know what to call him. He certainly wasn't a friend. ". . . an ally in this case."

"Monica." Dejan's heavily accented voice came from somewhere in the left corner. I searched the wall for a light and flipped the switch. Everyone cringed with the sudden blinking fluorescent.

Damien strolled over to me. Annoyed didn't even begin to describe his look. "You can't even follow the simplest of instructions, can you?"

"Not when you're about to make a mistake," I said, equally harsh. "Dejan, it's okay. Come on out."

His dress shoes clacked against the cement flooring before we even saw him. He stood across the warehouse on the other side with his black leather bomber jacket and tenuous glare. His black hair shined in cascading waves down to just below his chin. His eyes glistened black. He stopped about twenty feet in front of us, hands clasped casually in front of him and his head cocked to the side in a way that reminded me of the Banshee.

"Dejan—you've been working on investigating this case longer than us. What do you know?"

He clicked his tongue, tutting at me as a teacher would her student. "Now, now Monica. What's the fun in revealing *that*?"

"This is *fun* to you? You sick, demented piece of shit," Damien spat.

I put a hand to his shoulder to quiet him. This was Dejan's game.

Dejan lowered his chin, the overhead lights casting ominous shadows over his finely chiseled features. "Now, now, is that any way to treat a guest? Particularly one who is so much better at your job than you?"

"He's right, Damien," I whispered, treading very carefully. This could end in some serious bloodshed if not handled correctly. "We could really use his help."

"As much as I'd love to sit down in this"—Dejan glanced around the cold warehouse—"charming little area, this is neither the time nor the place."

"You say where," I said. "We'll be there."

"Very well. Tonight at nightfall. Richard's Pub."

"Nightfall? That's not even an actual *time*!" Damien spat.

"Dejan, please," I said, rolling my eyes. Though I wasn't even sure which one of the two I was rolling them at.

Dejan's smirk was barely noticeable. "Very well. Seven. At Richard's Pub."

"I didn't even know they *had* pubs in this awful city," George joked.

"Kane!" a voice shouted from outside. We all swiveled. The chief was peeking into the warehouse. When we glanced back, Dejan was gone. I expected nothing less.

28

We left the crime scene with notes and pictures of Luis's lifeless body haunting my thoughts. Stoned. He had been stoned to death while tied up by Spanish moss—a plant indigenous to his native New Orleans. Was it my fault he was dead? The fact that he had taken an interest in me at the club . . . could that be why he had been a target?

"This crest . . ." Damien held up his phone with a picture of the crest on it. "Do you recognize it? Either of you?"

George cradled the phone between two hands as though it were a precious gemstone, narrowing his eyes while pulling it close to his face. "I-I don't. I'm sorry."

He held it up to me and I examined it equally closely, my eyes narrowing. "I don't know—it, it sort of looks familiar." I took a deep breath. I needed to be sure before I brought Lord Buckley into this. And if I did, I needed Julian to do so. "The only reason I recognized the one on Moe Kaelica's body so quickly was because it was my own."

Damien muttered a curse under his breath. "There's got to be some section of the library where we can see various family crests. That will be yours and George's job today. Research on family crests."

George sent a glance my way, rolling his eyes. "Great. Stuffy geeks and dusty books. Right up my alley."

"And where are we going now?" I asked, giving George a look. Now was not the time to get prissy.

Damien smirked from behind the wheel. "Just as you suggested. We are off to the impound lot to get a reading on Lena's car."

"Well, why do we have to come to that? If I'm going to be in a boring library, I should take a nap first. Otherwise, I'll fall asleep on all those books."

"You're coming with me," Damien snapped, cranky as ever, "because I want to get this done ASAP. And it would take too long to drop you off first."

He turned the wheel sharply and pulled up to a chain link gate with circles of barbed wire at the top. Braking, he leaned out the window and placed his hand on the keypad. The air around us buzzed and he closed his eyes with the humming. After a moment, he pulled away and punched in a code. The steel creaked as it slid open just wide enough for a car to pull through.

Looking at me, he arched an eyebrow, gaze flitting down to my cleavage before he averted his eyes back to the road ahead. He was peacocking, fluffing his feathers before me, and I hated to admit that it was damned impressive. He took his foot off the brake, and the car accelerated through the now open driveway. Once inside, he put the car in park.

"Wait here," he grumbled before clomping out and slamming the door behind him. He chatted to a man in uniform, pulling out a piece of paper and his badge. Finally Damien signaled for us to follow.

"Yes, I recall the car. Tragic story, that one," the guard said. "She was so young. I hope you catch the bastard."

"Us, too," I responded.

"Well, here it is. You need anything else, just give me a holler." He left us standing there in front of a green Honda. Nothing spectacular about it. Anything that was considered evidence would have already been bagged up and processed. The upholstery inside the car was dank and mildewed. The smell of death and mold. Some dried papers were around the backseat—textbooks that looked as though they had been through a flood. Economics and foreign policy. Smart girl. I couldn't help but wonder what she might have done with that knowledge if she'd had the chance.

Damien opened the trunk. Again, not much there. A spare tire. An air pump. A duffel bag that was unzipped. Damien tossed it to me. "Look through it. See if anything stands out to you."

"Where does she go to school?" I asked while rifling around her gym bag. On top were some gym clothes—folded. Unused, it seemed. Tennis shoes. Socks tucked together. A lock. Just your average gym bag accessories.

"Night classes at the local community college," he muttered while flipping through one of the textbooks.

Placing a hand on the car, Damien closed his eyes. The entire car began to buzz and when he opened his eyes, he looked more confused than when we began.

"Well? Anything?"

He nodded, but still looked confused. "Apparently . . ." He swallowed and went from staring at the car to staring at me. "Apparently, it was raining inside the car. Lena died . . . no, drowned . . . in her own car." He swiveled around, sitting on the bumper to think.

I went back to searching the gym bag. At the bottom, there was a notepad. Several dates and times were scribbled in messy cursive. "Damien—check this out," I handed him the paper. "Looks like she had some meetings arranged."

He looked closer and after a moment, tossed the pad back at me. "It's written on an ordering tablet for Hooters. It's probably just her work schedule for the week."

"Do they even have a Hooters in Salt Lake City?" George asked. And I had to admit, it was a damn good question.

"We'll have to verify that, I guess, huh?"

"At Hooters? I'll verify the Hell outta that." Damien smirked.

My eyes lowered into a scowl. Then I remembered that I'd blown a guy right before screwing Damien's brains out and decided to choose my battles better. "George, is there anything in the front seat?"

"Just a bunch of CDs and some trash. Girlfriend was studying languages—a weird one, too. She's got up to level four on the 'How to Speak Serbian' discs."

"Serbian?" Damien glanced to me, looking as perplexed as I felt. "That's a weird choice . . ."

My blood ran cold. Lena *Vlasik.* "I think I know whose crest is on Lena's chest."

29

"The fucking vampire's? Are you kidding me?" Damien's voice was almost yelling. Almost, but not quite.

I nodded. "That's why he's here following the case, I bet. She's his descendent."

"That dude is Serbian?" Damien's feet pounded against the pavement as he paced back and forth.

"Damn," George muttered. "I need to find me some Serbians to date. . . ."

I nodded, shooting George another chastising glance. "Well, back then we just described that region as Balkan. But, yes, essentially Dejan is Serbian. Seems a little too coincidental, wouldn't you say?"

"I guess we'll get a chance to ask him tonight," Damien grumbled, plunging his hand into his hair. "Why the fuck is this guy killing off the descendants of immortals?"

I looked to George, whose face drained of color. "Maybe one of them is my descendant?"

"Do you know any of your descendants?" I rubbed his

shoulder and glanced at Damien, who had managed to stop pacing.

George shook his head. "Not at all."

"Well, we're in the genealogy capital of the world. And this certainly narrows down our research—we can look up specific crests of people we know at the genealogy headquarters in the middle of the city to research. Then if that doesn't work, we can expand the search."

"This is the genealogy capital of the world?"

Damien scrolled through his phone, answering halfheartedly. "Yep. It has to do with their religion—the church owns the website FamilySearch.org—you know with all those commercials."

"I had no idea that was all based here," George answered.

"I know. Strange, right?" Damien pushed a button on the rental keys and his car beeped and unlocked.

George looked to me and then Damien. "That could explain why all this is happening here in Salt Lake City, guys. Weren't you trying to find the link as to why all the deaths were here? If this is the genealogy capital of the world—and these murders depend entirely on discovering ancestry . . ." He faded off and Damien's head snapped up.

"Well, I'll be damned," he whispered and opened the driver's side door. "I'll drop you both back at the hotel first." He slid his phone into his back pocket and climbed in behind the wheel.

When we pulled up to the semi-circle in front of the hotel, Adrienne was sitting outside waiting. Dark sunglasses hid her face from the early morning sun and two fingers circled her temple as if trying to rub away a memory.

"How ya feelin', sunshine?" My smirk was itching at the corners of my mouth even though I was desperately trying to keep a straight face.

I could feel Adrienne's eyes on me from behind her shades

as we approached. "I promise you that if you rub this in, I'll douse you in holy water when you're asleep," she grumbled.

"Awww, and here I thought we had bonded."

Adrienne's head twitched to George, who, taking the hint quickly, rolled his eyes. "I'm runnin' upstairs to catch a nap before we need to hit the books, anyway." He kissed my temple before darting for the elevator.

Adrienne turned her attention back to me. "Bonded? You ruined mine and Drew's only date night. Then alerted me to the fact that you'd sleep with my boyfriend under certain circumstances. And you think we've bonded?"

I inwardly cringed. "Well—it sounds so bad when you put it like that."

"It *is* bad, Monica."

"It doesn't change the fact that I was right. Last night would have been a mistake for you."

Adrienne's chest heaved with a deep breath. "It has been months for me. Months without any sort of sexual contact. Do you know what that's like?"

My insides twisted. I definitely knew how that felt. That conflicted feeling. Adrienne was lucky—she had been taught early on that those feelings, even in an angel, were normal. I was not so lucky. And all through my angel time, I thought I was a freak. I thought for sure I could not be God's creature and still be having such impure feelings.

When I didn't answer, she snorted, then lifted her sunglasses on top of her head. "Look who I'm asking. You probably don't even wait a day when you feel turned on." She dropped her glasses back to her nose, making sure to push past my shoulder on the way to Damien's car.

30

Ireland, 1740

"You came back." Lord Buckley's face split into a grin, revealing beautiful, white teeth.

With a nod, I held out the garment for Lord Buckley's taking. "I said I would. Did you not believe me, Lord Buckley?"

His smile twitched, a hint of—what? Sadness, perhaps? "I've learned not to take the word of anyone. Not even you, my angel."

I sighed, letting the truth and bitter sadness in his voice wash over me. "Well," I whispered taking one step closer, "I hope you will allow me to prove to you that I am worthy of your trust."

He retreated, taking one step back, distancing himself once more. "I, however, am not worthy of yours." His eyes sparkled and he licked his lips while holding my eye contact.

The air between us was thick and sizzled. "I'm not so sure I believe that, my lord."

His laugh cracked in a painful, sharp way. "Then you are foolish, my angel."

He seemed a completely different man from the night before. Where he had once been warm, friendly and inviting, he was now cold. Distant. "If that is so, then why do you wish me here? Why do you agree to help us?"

His throat tightened as he swallowed rather audibly. "It is all part of the plan."

"Your vision, you mean?"

He nodded. "So, you will stay here? With me while we fight the vicious Carman?" He held out a hand, fingers gesturing once in a come-hither manner.

"On one condition of my own."

"Oh?" His eyebrow arched. It amused him that I had my own demands. The fact burned me and I felt my anger rising, ears heating at his patronizing tone. I wasn't sure what all he knew of me, but I didn't like that he considered me naïve. I was powerful. Quite possibly more powerful than he was. With a deep breath, I pushed the anger aside.

"Lord Buckley," I said, "it is not safe for me to stay in a place where I cannot come and go quickly as I please. I must be able to teleport on and off of your grounds. In and out of your castle. Julian, too."

His smile twitched and he chewed the inside of his cheek, seemingly suppressing a chuckle. "Is that all?"

My face flamed red. "I could always demand more if you choose to be so arrogant!"

"Not the other angel. But for you, my dear . . ." His smile broke free and lit his face like a flame on a torch. It brightened and he was once again carefree and beautiful. With a snap of his fingers, magic crackled around us. "There you go, my angel." He folded his hands in front of him and raised two eyebrows in my direction. "Give it a try."

I teleported inside, finding myself in the foyer. Then upstairs to the boudoir. Then once again outside in front of Lord Buckley. My own smile twitched at the corners of my mouth, but I pushed it away. Two can play at this game. "Thank you, my lord. I will admit—I did not expect you to be so amiable."

Lord Buckley's chest expanded with a deep breath and he stepped closer to me, wrapping a tendril of my golden hair around a finger and twisting it. "Oh, my angel." He inhaled just above my ear, closing his eyes while breathing my scent. "Believe me. I can be quite amiable." With the other hand, he snapped his fingers and Dejan soon stood before us.

With a finger, he pointed to my trunks and the garment that was still draped over my arm. "Take the lady to her room."

Dejan gently took my things and stepped back once more. With a bow at the waist, Lord Buckley had my hand in his once more, brushing a soft kiss to my knuckle. "I have some matters to tend to in the stables." He looked up, still bent at the waist, that playful smirk splayed across his lips. "But we will take tea together soon."

I nodded and followed Dejan into the castle.

"You are a foolish woman," Dejan's voice rasped as if from a parched throat in the middle of a desert. And he looked at me as though I were his oasis. The red sphere around his black eyes glistened and fell upon my throat. Recognizing his own stare, he quickly returned his gaze to my eyes. He held my trunks as though they were no heavier than a pebble and led me through the cold, cavernous home back to my boudoir.

There was a tug from deep in my core. He was suffering. Yes, a vampire suffering—but pain in any creature was hard to watch. It made me think of Lord Buckley and how he could possibly surround himself with these tortured creatures each day. I thought of Lord Buckley as a husband—a father. What it must have been like for him to come home to his family, slashed and bloodied. I shivered. Vampires were violent creatures. I shook away the sorrow for Dejan, remembering the countless murders he had no doubt committed through his existence.

I nodded at Dejan's remark. "I had my own conditions as well," I returned, chin raised.

"So I heard," Dejan snorted.

I ignored his pointed retort. "When you do feed, what is it you eat?"

Dejan swallowed as though the very mention of food made him thirsty. "Rats, mostly. The occasional larger vermin if we are especially well-behaved for my lord." He addressed the castle's master with a sneer.

"How frequently?"

With a bow, Dejan opened the bedroom chamber, allowing me to enter first. He followed behind, the few pieces I traveled with tucked under one arm. "Forgive me, m'lady. You'll understand if this is not a subject I wish to discuss?"

I nodded. "Yes, of course."

Large but gentle hands rested my trunk on the bed and Dejan opened it to unpack for me.

I placed a hand on top, and our skin brushed—his flesh cold and smooth, its texture reminding me of marble. "Please," I said, "you don't have to do that. I can attend to my own bags."

"Very well, m'lady," Dejan said with another bow. "Master Buckley filled your boudoir with the finest gowns." Dejan spoke as he walked to the wardrobe and hung the one I'd worn the night before at dinner. "He wishes for you to be dressed for tea."

I nodded. Of course he did. There was an uneasy feeling in the pit of my stomach.

"M'lady?" Dejan's eyes filled with concern and he took my elbow. His touch heated my flesh despite his chilled body temperature and we both looked at where our bodies touched. "Are you well? You look as though you've seen a ghost."

I shook my head, hoping to shake off my nerves as well, stepping away from his hand. "I am fine. Thank you. I will be dressed and ready for tea in just a moment."

He licked dry, cracked lips, eyes tilted down in a frown. With a final bow, he left the room.

31

"Wow," I whispered, looking around the beautiful room. It had marble floors and dark wood accents. Computers lined the walls with more archives than anything. Books and newspapers were catalogued in case you wanted to physically see the documents yourself and not just on a computer screen.

"Baby girl, this feels hopeless," George said as he pounded the delete key.

"It's not, George. There's gotta be something in here with Lucien's crest." I fell back in the leather library chair, running my hands along my face. "Let's recap—we know that Moe Kaelica bore my family crest. Sonja had Julian's. Lena wore Dejan's. And Luis . . ." I faded off, not sure of exactly what to say regarding Luis Nunez-Buckley's. I hadn't found a picture of his precise family crest yet, but I was pretty certain without it that Luis was Lord Buckley's descendent. I just didn't understand *why*.

"Hello? Earth to Monica."

I snapped back to the present, flipping the page once more. "Sorry," I mumbled.

George cleared his throat. "You know whose crest was on Luis, don't you?"

I hesitated before shaking my head no.

"Okay." George rolled his eyes. "Then you have an *idea* of whose it is, right?"

I didn't answer, simply slid a glance at him, the computer screen illuminating his face. "I have a suspicion. But nothing that I'm certain of just yet."

"All the evidence so far suggests it is someone within our circle," George continued talking more to himself than to me. "Julian said that Sonja was his descendent, right? A great, great niece of sorts. If we are looking for a pattern, then, most likely, Moe is your descendent. Lena is Dejan's. Yes?"

I nodded slowly. We'd been over all this before. We were running around in circles. The result was that it left Moe as part of some sort of long lineage of my family. "Yes. That would make the most sense." My face fell into my hands once more. "But why? Why kill our descendants? Especially since most of us don't even know who the Hell these people are? We're not emotionally invested in them. I could give two shits about Moe Kaelica—a farmer from Utah."

"Do you think it has to do with the bounty on you?" George's voice dropped even lower, wincing as he said it.

I thought of the Banshee and how no one else could see her. This was most certainly about me in some way or another. "It could." Drew. The Banshee. Fear caught in my chest, freezing my breath in my throat. There was something more to that, but damn if it made any sense. I leaned forward, typing Andrew Sullivan into the system. After some digging around, I found his current address and searched through his lineage. No names stood out to me. Nothing was connecting him to anyone else from the group. I grunted and fell back in the seat.

George leaned over to see whom I had pulled up. "Drew," he said. "What's Drew got to do with any of this?"

I shrugged. "I don't know. Just call it a gut feeling."

"Okay." George leaned over and clicked a few keys on my keyboard. "Let's print out his crest so that we have it." He winked at me in a warm way and I let my head fall onto his shoulder. "Just in case, right?"

I nodded as he sent the document to the printer. "Drew's Irish, huh?" He added as an afterthought, "You're Irish." George scrunched his nose. "Oh, fuck. Don't tell me we've got a *Chinatown* situation on our hands here!"

"Ew, no!" I pushed his shoulder and his chair rolled away from me. He threw his head back laughing and going back to his own computer.

"Well, thank God for that," he said, standing to retrieve the printed document. He came back and placed the sheet of paper between us.

I lifted it, inspecting the image. It wasn't my crest. But it was definitely Irish. I paused, pinching my nose and squeezing my eyes closed in thought. "Descendants. Damn. It sounds like some sort of . . . spell, doesn't it?"

George's eyes snapped to me. "That's it," he whispered. "It's a spell. It's gotta be." George leaned into the computer, typing something in before he jumped to his feet. Within minutes he came back with a thick, hardcover book under his arm. "Back in Arthurian times, to break an already existing spell, you would need the blood of the descendants of those who were in the room while casting it. Someone is trying to break an existing spell. It's got to be. It would explain the use of magic in all their deaths. The runes that surround each body. It would explain why they are targeting our group."

George flipped through the pages until he landed on a sketch. A woman in a dungeon chanting out the window. "The spells can be cast from anywhere with the right ingredients. We're dealing with some powerful shit here."

"So, by this theory, this all has to do with a spell that Julian, myself, and Dejan were all a part of?" *And Lord Buckley*, I added in my thoughts.

George nodded. "Yeah, pretty much. I mean, it's not an exact science or anything, but that's what it's looking like."

I leaned back in my chair. "It's got to be about me. About when Dejan turned me into a succubus."

"That's how you know that guy? He's the reason you fell?" George's face dropped, the color draining from his beautiful cheeks.

I nodded. "Yep—he's the reason. Well, one of the reasons."

"You think it was a spell he cast specifically about you?"

I shrugged. "I don't know. . . . No one was ever able to explain how or why it happened. But that would make sense, wouldn't it?" I shivered. "When I first met him, he and his master always took a . . . special interest in me." My stomach flipped and a wave of nausea lapped at the back of my throat. A shiver rolled through my body and I shoved the memory of that night away.

"Baby girl, this is bad. If this is all about you and this bounty—"

"I *know*. Okay? I know how bad this is." Silence hung in the air between us. It didn't help that the library was annoyingly quiet on top of that, too.

George cleared his throat and I looked up at him through my lashes. "Monica, if this is about Dejan's succubus-turning spell—you realize that this means Julian was somehow involved. If his descendant's blood was spilled, he was a part of this. There's no other explanation for why Sonja would have been murdered."

Fuck. I knew George was right. Somehow . . . one way or another . . . Julian was responsible for my falling from Heaven.

32

Ireland, 1740

It had been a couple of days since I had moved into Lord Buckley's castle. On the morning of the third day, I awoke just as the sun was lifting over the horizon. With a glance out the window, I could see the frost on the ground was thicker than ever. Carman's force was still in full effect. I lit the candle beside my bed, loving the smell of a fresh flame, and pulled one of the casual wool garments from the boudoir.

I slipped the dress on, Lord Buckley's magic taking over, lacing and buttoning the back for me. Then, I slipped a heavier knit over top to keep warm. The frost didn't affect me too much, but it was important to act as human as possible so as not to raise any suspicions while on assignment.

After lacing up my boots, I quietly found my way down the stairs, careful to tread quietly. With a quick glance into the dining room, I didn't see anyone stirring about the castle. I slipped into the library. Old books lined the walls with a few set out on the side tables near a large wooden chair. On top was a journal. Beneath it, the Bible. I glanced over my shoulder, making cer-

tain to listen intently for anyone's approach. I lifted the journal first. Tendrils of magic wrapped around it, and the book steamed against my skin, burning me with a sizzle. "Ow!" I dropped it back on the table, caressing my hand in the other. Dark magic. Lord Buckley had placed a dark magic enchantment around the journal—most likely to prevent myself or any angel from seeing what was within the book.

Careful not to touch the journal, I lifted the Bible from under it, flipping the cover open. An inscription on the first page caught my eye. My Dearest John, May the peace of God follow wherever your life may take you. You have my heart, Fatima.

There was a piece of twine marking a page and I flipped to where the marker held its place, scanning the page for any indication of something relevant. Job 37:10 By the breath of God frost is given: and the breadth of the waters is straightened.

I pondered the passage. He couldn't possibly believe God had brought about this frost, could he? Or maybe he was simply praying—looking to God's word for some answers.

"You're up awfully early." Lord Buckley's warm voice was quiet but sharper than any knife's edge.

I jumped, the book nearly slipping from my fingers.

A shadow of a smile played across his lips and the morning light danced in his eyes. "Only guilty people jump, Monica."

I clutched the Bible tighter to my chest. "Y-yes. I mean no! You just startled me. I was deep in thought."

His smile tilted even more to his eyes. "About what?"

"I was thinking I could perhaps help tend to the sheep today?"

His boots clacked against the stone floor, his saunter smooth and calculated. As he approached, his gaze slid down my body, landing on the Bible within my hands.

"Doing some light reading before?"

I nodded. "The Bible gives me comfort." The presence of his journal on the table beside me thickened the air. It took all my energy not to fidget and glance down at the dark-magic-possessing book.

Lord Buckley's shoulders dropped as he gently slid the book from my grasp, nodding. "Me too, my angel," he said with a sigh flipping through the pages himself.

"The passage about the frost—you don't think . . ." My words faded as I gathered the courage to ask the question that was chewing away at my insides. "You don't think this frost is God's doing, do you?"

When his gaze caught mine, his eyes were glistening and wet. Beautiful. "Isn't everything God's doing to some extent?"

I gasped at that. "But surely, you—"

He chuckled, tossing the Bible back onto the table. A sizzling sound echoed in the air as it landed on the journal, but it quickly faded after the initial contact. Hell touching Heaven. "Relax, Monica. I'm not suggesting anything. I was just looking for answers in the holy book. I did not realize you would take such issue with that."

"I don't," I whispered, not quite believing my own voice.

His smile grew. "Good."

There was a pause as we held each other's stares. The scrutiny of his gaze was enough to send my insides spiraling, but I held firm in my stance, refusing to fidget or shift my weight. After a few moments, I broke the silence. "Is your name John?"

His eyes widened, eyebrows arching, his indifferent mask slipping before he quickly shook the surprise away. "Yes. Though not many refer to me by my given name anymore."

"May I ask why?"

His lips pressed into a thin line and he reached out to take my hand in his, running his fingers along my knuckles. "When you're powerful, people simply refer to you by your title and surname. It is just how it works."

"But don't you have any companions? Friends of similar standing and titles that you socialize with?"

His eyes dropped to my hand, refusing to meet my eyes. "Not since Fatim—" His voice broke and he shook his head as though that could shake off any bad memories. When he looked back to me, any trace of sadness was gone. "Not since long ago."

"Your wife?" His nod was barely discernible.

I cleared my throat and continued when he remained silent. "My mother gave me my first Bible. Long ago. Oh, how I wish I still had it." I looked down at his leather-bound book with longing. I had a Bible of course. But there was something to having a personalized book given to you by someone you loved and who loved you in return.

He smiled, but it didn't quite reach his eyes. "What do you say we have some breakfast, then go attend to the sheep?"

We spent most of the day outside in the stables. He introduced me to his favorite sheep, whom he had named Ainsley. After milking her and the others, I lifted the bucket to carry it into the servants' quarters. Lord Buckley chuckled, taking the heavy wood bucket from my hand and setting it down at my feet. "Please," he said. "Allow me." And with a wink and raise of his hand, all the buckets lifted and floated to the servants' entrance, where several vampires waited to receive them, shielded inside from the mid-morning sun.

As we walked back to the castle, his hand found mine, fingers lacing between my own. My stomach jumped with the contact—breath hitching in my throat. His very presence made me so nervous. I shook the silly feelings away. We were both here in this moment because we had a task. "Have you given any thought to how we will defeat Carman?"

He ran a hand through his auburn hair, lips puffing out with a sigh. "I have thought of little else these past few days. And I believe we will have to physically summon her here."

The idea struck me hard. "Like a—like a demon summoning?"

He swallowed and nodded, shifting a sideways glance at me. "Yes. With a salt circle. It is a bit more intricate than that. I'm currently writing her summons spell, which is exhaustive. Furthermore, there is one final ingredient that will take me some time to gather, I believe."

"But—but she's not a demon. Will a summons circle even work?"

"She is a demon, essentially. She is a magical creature doing the Devil's work. It will take some adjustments of the normal incantations, however."

"I-I cannot be a part of such inherently dark magic!" I whispered with an urgency that made my throat burn. I thought back to the journal that was bound with thorny tendrils of magic, shivering at what may lie inside.

Lord Buckley's face flushed and I could see the color rising to his cheeks. "I did not ask you to participate, did I?"

"You didn't have to. Why else would I be here?"

His expression was hard and terrifying. His hand grasped mine firmly, even as I attempted to tug it away. He halted, pulling me two steps back to meet him. His green eyes were stormy. "Do you wish to leave?"

After a moment's thought, I shook my head. "That is not what I said. I just don't know what I am doing here if I cannot aid in the summons."

"You are here to protect me."

"I am not even sure I can offer you that."

He swallowed, his throat visibly constricting with the movement. "Your very presence is a comfort." He took a step closer, tugging my hand to pull me halfway.

"Why is that? How can that even be?"

His smirk was a teasing one that caused warmth to pool at the base of my stomach. "Because—you are a vi—"

"Your vision. Yes, I know. Will I ever learn what that vision is, Lord Buckley?" I spat his official title as if it in itself was an insult.

"You, Monica, may call me by my given name. You are a peer. Not a servant."

"John," I whispered, and it danced off my tongue. "Tell me about the vision."

His eyes danced and searched my face as though there were an answer somewhere deep in my eyes. "This was part of the vision," he responded.

I looked around us. "This? Us, out here?"

He nodded and stepped closer yet again. His chest was pressed against me, the proximity of his manhood probing into my hip made me gasp aloud. I moved to step back, but his hand tugged me against him, the other arm wrapping around my hip. "This, to be specific." And with that, he lowered his lips to mine. They were wet and lush and delicious and I wanted to taste even more of him.

I opened my mouth against his, and his tongue slipped inside, stroking along mine. I closed my eyes as his muscular thigh nudged my legs apart, applying pressure to an area that ached. The movement left me breathless.

A crack sound came from not far away—near the gate of the castle—and I could immediately feel Julian's presence near the grounds. I gasped and pushed Lord Buckley away, bringing my fingers to touch my swollen, greedy lips.

His smirk split into a deeper grin. "And that"—his eyes flicked to the area where we could both sense Julian's presence—"that was part of the vision, too." He winked and strolled ahead of me. "I will be inside. Waiting." He spun around, walking backward so he could look at me, still frozen in my spot. "Waiting for you."

33

George and I got back to the hotel, my mind still swimming with the new information. The murders had to do with me. Or with a spell cast on me? My brain felt so full that it might implode at any moment. With the hotel key in hand, I moved to insert it into the door when George grasped my wrist, eyes wide.

"Someone is in there," he whispered.

I darted a look to him. "Rob?" Then, I inhaled and felt the presence as well. Definitely not Rob. Someone—something like us. "Another succubus," I said.

He nodded. "Claudette maybe. Weren't we supposed to see her again soon?"

"Only one way to find out," I said and inserted the key, flinging the door open, ready to attack whatever lay in wait for us.

"Took you idiots long enough," Kayce said, flipping through a magazine, lying across my bed.

"Kayce!" I ran to her, flinging my arms around her neck, and she laughed, catching me in a hug as well.

"You didn't think I'd let you guys have all the fun, did you?"

"But Lucien wouldn't let . . ."

"Oh, fuck Lucien. He's not the boss of me."

"Uh . . . well, he kind of is," I reminded her.

She rolled her eyes and kicked her feet off the bed until she was sitting upright. "Figuratively speaking, of course."

"Hey, gorgeous girl," George said while taking her hand.

"Hey back at you." Kayce grinned from ear to ear. "Damn, I missed you guys. Those bitches Claudette sent were horrible."

"Do you know Claudette?" I slid a sideways glance at Kayce, who shrugged.

"Sure. I've met her once or twice. Annoyingly composed. So fucking put together. She and our Succubus Queen are best friends."

George and I snuck a glance at each other. "If she and Mia are friends, that might explain the stone." He brought a shoulder to his ear.

"What's wrong with the girls she sent Lucien?" I asked, shifting topics.

Kayce paused looking to the ceiling in thought. "These girls, they play the good-girl card on their conquests a lot. The sexy girl next door that good guys simply can't resist."

I shrugged. "In Utah, that's probably the only approach that works."

"Maybe," Kayce sneered. "But it's really annoying. In Vegas, just as many guys want the chick who oozes sex." Kayce laughed out loud, falling back on her elbows. "Oh my God, you should have seen Lucien. He was furious that they wouldn't strip. They didn't want to waste their time on souls that wouldn't give them much of a fix."

I cringed. An angry Lucien simply meant he would take it out on me once I got home. I was the one who had put him in the situation to begin with.

I looked to George. "We should probably go see Claudette, huh?"

He shrugged. "Whatever. We'll go tomorrow if we don't get to it today. You already bagged one twinkling soul. That should keep her satisfied for now."

Kayce's eyebrows shot up at the admission. "Oh yeah? I thought you looked extra spirited today."

Rolling my eyes, I pushed off the bed, heading to my luggage. I sifted through it as if I had something to do.

"And," George continued, "she and the elemental finally hooked up." He smiled triumphantly as I swiveled to glare at him.

"What? When exactly were you going to tell me this?" Kayce shrieked.

"I was going to tell you—you know—soon."

"Oh," she sneered, "soon. Of course. Maybe at your wedding you would have thought to inform your best friend of this relationship."

"Who says you're her best friend?" George tossed a pillow playfully at Kayce's head, and she deferred it with a quick slap of her hand.

"And who said it was a relationship?" I returned. Kayce and George both flopped their cheeks to their shoulders in a look that said, *C'mon.*

"Well, was he as good as he claims to be?" Kayce wiggled her eyebrows, her almond eyes sparkling.

I sighed involuntarily, immediately regretting it as Kayce and George fell onto each other laughing. I laughed, unable to help the bit of giggles rising in my chest as well. Might as well just roll with the gossip. "I think I might have to experiment a few more times before I can fully give a fair review."

Kayce winked, a big toothy grin flashing in my direction. "That's my girl."

I fished around in my bag, taking out the pilot's iPad and setting it on the ground.

"Well, well, well, you made quite a purchase this weekend." Kayce popped up, glancing down toward the iPad.

"Oh," I said, looking at the device. I had completely forgot about it. "That's the pilot's. The assassin's."

Her head snapped up and she looked sharply to George, then back to me again. "The who?"

"Didn't Lucien tell you?"

"About an assassin? Um, no. Clearly, he didn't or I would have been here within seconds."

George rolled his eyes. "Well, I guess we know why he didn't tell you, then. He didn't want you up here for some reason or another."

Kayce narrowed her gaze at him. "And that's exactly the point. I could have helped."

"Oh yeah?" I folded my arms across my chest, quirking an eyebrow. "And how is that?" Kayce had a super mysterious job. One that I knew entailed busting heads, but she could never actually reveal to me.

"Just let me see the iPad." She held out a hand, palm up.

With a sigh, I handed it to her and she flipped the cover open, turning it on. "You're going to need his passwords to get into any of the good stuff." I looked at the screen from over her shoulder.

"That's what you think," she said, hopping up and rifling through her own bag. Pulling out a mini keyboard and a few obscure-looking small devices, she plugged into the iPad and started typing madly on the keyboard. Within a few minutes, she looked up, a triumphant smile plastered on her face. "Done," she said, so simply you would think that she had finished baking a blueberry pie.

"Done?"

With a nod, she passed me the iPad. "Yep. I ran a program

that was able to pull most of his passwords. There weren't many. Dummy Aaron used the same one for several devices and emails."

"You know his name?" I looked at her through slitted eyes.

Her own face grew solemn, smile dropping at the corners. "Yes." She paused, cracking her knuckles and making a show of taking the device back. "It's all over his iPad."

I stared at her a few seconds more, not quite buying it. She'd dropped his name so casually. As though she'd already known . . .

Kayce once again interrupted my thoughts typing wildly into the keyboard again. "What do you say we figure out who was in touch with this bozo?"

Two hours and two calls to room service later, we still hadn't found much of anything. As it turns out, most assassins don't receive their assignments via traceable emails. Go figure. The good news was that his iPad was connected to his home laptop, so we could access all the files on his home computer as well. The bad news was that Aaron was a clutterbug who downloaded everything and anything, then forgot to delete the files once he was done.

"What all did you find out about this guy already?" Kayce asked, fingers flying across the keys faster than my brain could even think.

I thought back. It had only been a couple days ago, but it felt like ages. "He's a warlock. He initially attempted to put me in a salt ring, but I—um, I managed to break away. Then he said something about a spell he had started to even out the playing field with succubi. Something that was going to put him on the map." I shrugged.

George caught my eye and mouthed, *A spell?* My heart dropped into my stomach. Maybe this whole thing had nothing to do with me specifically. Perhaps it was all about succubi in general?

Kayce chewed her lip, glancing up at me from the screen. "That doesn't sound good. How'd he get away?"

"He fell on my sword."

Both Kayce and George snapped their heads up to me. George had heard the abridged version the first time—but hadn't heard Aaron's exact cause of death. Kayce's eyes immediately narrowed. "How the fuck did you get a sword onto an airplane? What are you not telling me?"

I don't know why I didn't want to tell them about the magic thing. There was no rational reason why I should keep it from them or anyone. Maybe because I wanted to perfect it before allowing anyone to see and criticize. I wasn't quite adept yet with the skill. If anything, it could leave me more vulnerable than I realized. I shrugged. "I'm not keeping anything. He procured a sword and I was able to get it from him. I didn't mean to kill him—he fell onto it."

Kayce opened her mouth to say something, but George caught her eye and gave a slight shake of his head. She closed her mouth without another word.

One particular file about halfway down the list stood out to me. It had funny blue writing and a thumbnail-sized logo I didn't recognize to be any application. I pointed to it. "Open that one," I said.

Kayce clicked on it. "Shit, it's encrypted." She typed some more and leaned back, rubbing the heel of her hand into her eye. "This one might take a while, guys."

"Can't you just run your little thingy?" George said with a flippant hand gesture.

"I'll run your little thingy," Kayce mumbled under her breath, a small smile twitching at the corners of her mouth.

"As if I was anything close to little. Child, please."

"I'm glad to see we all still have a sense of humor even while in the midst of work," I retorted. "And by 'work,' I mean my imminent *death*."

"All right, all right, keep your panties on." Kayce typed a few more things and then sat back, moving the iPad from her lap onto the bed. "There. The program will take a while to run. Probably a couple of hours."

I glanced at the clock on the nightstand. "Just in time for us to grab some dinner and meet with Dejan."

George sighed and pushed himself off the bed, shifting his appearance into something tidier. "We also have a do-over date with Rob, baby girl."

I groaned. A threesome was so not on my desirable list for this evening.

"I don't want to hear it!" George snapped. "You left me high and dry last night."

"I know, I know," I exhaled with a puff. "Operation Ex Caliber. Damien is not gonna be happy about this, though."

"Operation wha?" Kayce darted a glance back and forth between the two of us.

George filled her in while I shifted into a lavender empire-waist dress with ivory details around the bodice. Over top, I added a cardigan and a belt to make the outfit a bit more modest.

"Well, shit!" Kayce looked to me, all smiles. "If Monica doesn't want the job, I'll do it!"

"Really?" George asked, eyes wide. "You'll be my third?"

He looked to me for confirmation that it was okay—I happily nodded. It was more than okay, actually.

Thank Hell for small blessings. Today was already getting leaps and bounds better.

34

Damien and Adrienne were already waiting in the lobby for me when I got there. Adrienne sat in one of the ugly plush chairs in the lobby, tapping her foot against the coffee table leg. Damien flipped through a *Men's Health* magazine with about as much excitement as a hunter attending a PETA meeting.

He flashed a smile when he saw me, dropping the magazine back to the coffee table in front of him. "There she is," he said, standing to plant a kiss on my cheek.

"What's this?" I mocked disbelief. "No insult? No snarky comments? This can't be Detective Kane."

"Okay, succubus. Don't be a smart ass." He slapped my butt playfully.

Adrienne grunted as she stood, sunglasses still on her nose despite the fact that we were inside. And the sun had already gone down. "I don't understand how you are always late, when you don't even have to physically *get ready* to be anywhere."

"I'm not late." I glanced at my phone. It was just a little past six-thirty. "We don't have to be there until seven."

"Yeah," she snapped, slinging her purse over her shoulder.

"And we said we would meet here in the lobby at six-thirty sharp."

I snorted. "Well, no one told me that. You're lucky I'm down here at all this soon."

"Damien, let's go." She stormed past the both of us and out the front revolving doors.

"Damn, what flew up her ass?" Damien looked at me, eyebrows raised.

"What!?"

"Since she was fine with me up until you showed up, I can only assume her little outburst had to do with you."

"There's a reason they made you detective, huh?"

He paused. "Well? What'd you do to her?"

"How do you know she didn't do something to me?"

He didn't answer, but he chewed on the corner of his mouth. "Okay, fine," I continued. "Never try to come between an angel and her right to get laid."

Damien ran a hand over his face. "Shit. I didn't want to hear that. Okay, well . . . just apologize or something so we can get on with this investigation, okay?"

"Fine. Not that I really think I have anything to apologize *for*. But I'll try. Can we please go before she booby-traps my seat in the car?"

Damien smiled at that. "She *is* pretty resourceful. In the meantime, why don't you fill me in on what you and George found at the library."

By 6:53 PM, we were seated at a booth in Richard's Pub—it was technically outside of the city limits of Salt Lake City. Adrienne and I sat across from each other and Damien slid in next to me, sliding an arm over top the back of the seat.

Adrienne grunted watching us from over the top of the wine list.

"Okay." Damien jumped up once again. "I'm gonna grab a beer. Adrienne—white wine?" She nodded. "Monica, what's your poison?"

"Sex. But I'll have a scotch and water, please."

Adrienne continued to study the drink list even though Damien had gone to place our orders already. Her mouth was pinched and turned down at the corners, her pink lips a perfect bow shape.

After another minute or so, I found Damien staring at me. Once he caught my eye, his gaze flitted to Adrienne's, then back at me with an encouraging nod. I rolled my eyes and nodded back.

Ugh. Apologies. "Hey, Adrienne—about last night . . ."

"I don't want to talk about last night," she responded sharply.

"Right. Well, we don't have to, but I felt like I should say . . ."

"You're sorry? For what exactly? For stopping me from having sex with the man I love? Or for telling me that you yourself would have sex with him in the right circumstances?" She slapped the menu down on the table and folded her hands on top of it. On the outside, she looked calm and composed, but there was a swirling of emotions behind her eyes, a brewing storm. "Oh, wait . . . right . . . you already *did* have sex with him. How good was it, Monica? Because I can barely remember these days." Her voice was sour and it cracked with distaste. I wasn't sure I'd ever heard her so bitter. In her human days, we didn't really talk much—she may have been this way, but I'd just never seen it.

After a deep breath, I continued. "I am not going to apologize. But"—I hurried into my next sentence before she could cut me off again—"I do know how it feels to desire; to want sexual contact. And to be unable to get it. I was an angel once, Adrienne. I know that feeling. And back when I was an angel, no one explained to me I would be feeling those desires. I thought I was some deviant. Some terrible angel they had made a mistake in giving wings to."

Adrienne still chewed the inside of her lip, but her face softened. "It's so easy to forget that you were once an angel." She looked around and her tough facade seemed wildly more forced than earlier.

A raspy voice in my ear startled me, and I nearly jumped over the table.

"And how did you *deal* with those feelings, Monica?" Dejan's predatory smile gleamed beside me.

Luckily, Adrienne remained cool and composed, her gaze shifting over my shoulder. "Well, well. You must be the infamous Dejan I've heard so much about."

His black eyes darted to Adrienne, the smile slowly arching across his pale, chiseled face. "Good evening to you, Ms. Lauriette."

"Oh, please," Adrienne said. "Call me Detective." Her smile quickly hardened into the businesswoman I had seen the other day. I was beginning to like the no-bullshit Adrienne.

Dejan chuckled in a placating way, as though Adrienne were adorable when she wanted to play cop. "Monica, shall we tell Ms. Lauriette here why so many angels are hunted and feasted upon by vampires?" He had a lock of my hair in his palm and he inhaled it as though I were his own plate of food. "Or don't you remember?"

How could I forget? I cleared my throat. "Angel blood is a . . . a rare delicacy in the vampire world. It's sweet and delicious and acts as a wildly potent drug to vampires."

Adrienne swallowed, appearing physically nervous for the first time all trip. "We are holy," she said, raising her chin higher in the air. "The taste of our blood should bring you nothing but pain and burning."

Dejan chuckled, the sound making my skin crawl. "You would think, wouldn't you? But we are vampires—we get off on pain. That's part of what makes it so fucking good."

Damien came over, setting the drinks in the middle of the table. He cautiously took his seat next to Adrienne and slid my scotch and water to me. "Sorry I didn't get you anything. They were all out of O-neg." He held his pint to Dejan and saluted before taking a sip.

Dejan's lip curled back, a snarl rumbling in the back of his throat. "That's what you think," he answered, looking around. "This bar is full of O-negative blood."

"Okay," I interrupted. "Let's get started, huh? Dejan, what do you have for us? We already know that the crest on Lena's body is yours. And that she's some sort of relative of yours."

Dejan's face registered surprise before he quickly hid it with a terrifying grin. "You have been doing your homework over here then, haven't you?"

"Yes," Damien growled, leaning forward on two elbows. "Now what can you tell us that we don't already know?"

Dejan hissed in response, his lips curling back to reveal his sharp fangs.

Adrienne held two hands up, placing one calming touch on Damien. "How about if, instead, you tell us how you got started in the case. What made you come to Salt Lake City, Dejan?"

His snarl relaxed and he leaned back in the booth, slowly placing his folded hands on top of the table. "I keep track of all my descendants. This may be *difficult* to believe, but family was quite important to me. Human life does not mean so little to me as you may think it does. I knew almost immediately when Lena was murdered, and when I arrived at the crime scene, it was obviously something more than human. Her own car drowned her."

"Yes, we know," Damien answered.

"Of course you do," Dejan sneered. "You're an *elemental.*" He spat the word as though it were dirty in and of itself. "I was sticking around to figure out what had happened, and a couple days later, Moe was murdered." He slid a glance to me. "As soon as I saw the personal ad on the bulletin board, I knew he was yours. It was easily confirmed by looking up your family crest."

"So you stuck around to continue looking into things?" Adrienne asked, taking a dainty sip of her wine. I slugged my scotch in a not-so-ladylike manner.

"Precisely. Soon after, Sonja was murdered. Awful, brutal murder it was. Julian's lineage threw me off. I certainly wasn't suspecting your old partner in crime to be a part of this," he said, once again looking at me.

"Part of what exactly? What *is* this?"

He shrugged. "I thought I knew at first. I thought it was the lord's way of seeking revenge on all of us," Dejan answered, talking only to me this time.

"The *Lord*?" Adrienne said. "Like, God?"

I shook my head at her with a hand signal. I'd explain later. Clearly he meant my lord. Lord Buckley. "But then with Luis . . ."

Dejan nodded, eyebrows darting upward. "So you know he is Lord Buckley's, then?"

I nodded. "I assumed. You just confirmed it for me."

"Clearly he is not to blame here. That man was more family oriented than any of us."

"I thought he lost his family? Centuries ago?" *To one of your kind*, I wanted to add, but stopped myself.

"His first family," Dejan answered. "Every century or so, he would find a woman he cared about and he would have children again."

"Oh, my Hell. How many kids must he have at this point?"

Dejan shrugged. "Typically he will have one or two new

wives each century, so he's fathered many children. Most of which did not inherit his magic. And even if they did, his wives would water down the bloodlines. If you ask me, it's what he wanted. He doesn't want to see anyone's power surpass his own—not even a son or daughter he loves."

"Does he have any other kids? Does Luis have any siblings?" I asked, stopping myself from grabbing at Dejan's arm.

"One is still alive. The rest have all passed on. As I said, most had very little magic."

"Who is this Buckley?" Damien interjected. "I'd like to talk to him. Is he one of you?"

Dejan chuckled. "No. My kind cannot procreate." His gaze shifted to Adrienne. "He is like you once were. A warlock. Though much more powerful. He had the power to live indefinitely. Never aged. Never died. Not to say he couldn't die—he was just rather clever."

"And you don't know where we could find this Buckley? Does he have a first name?" Adrienne asked, taking copious notes on her iPad.

"I have not seen him in over a century," Dejan answered.

"So what can you give us now that would be helpful in this case?" Damien said, his voice getting that hard detective edge to it. He was getting annoyed and it was obvious.

"This." Dejan slid a piece of paper across the table to Damien. "This is the name and address of the only living son. He lives here on the outskirts of Salt Lake City. Quite the coincidence, isn't it? Why was it the son from Louisiana was brought up here to be killed when they could have murdered the descendant who already lived in the area?"

The shock on Damien's face would have been laughable if I wasn't also feeling the same amount of shock myself.

"That is all I have. For now," Dejan said. I felt something press into the palm of my hand below the table by chilling fingers. When I looked up, Dejan's black eyes twinkled. "I will be going now. If I have something more, I will be in touch."

Within a blink, he was already gone. I waited until Adrienne and Damien were deep in discussion about Lord Buckley's son before I looked into my palm and unfolded the piece of paper.

Meet me in the restroom as soon as you can get away.

35

Ireland, 1740

I left Julian outside the gate after walking with him for quite some time. We found a clearing void of frost where we were able to sit and talk.

"Love is not sinful. . . ." His words remained in my thoughts even after he'd gone. How could I have never known this? How could he mentor me for all this time and fail to mention this before now?

Not only can angels partake in physical relationships, but they can do so with non-angel counterparts.

The crisp smell of the frosted air blistered against my skin as I broke into a run, making my way back to the stables. The evening sun was dipping below the horizon and it was that moment just before dark.

I burst in through the double wooden doors and fell onto Ainsley, burying my face in her wool to hide my tears. She bleated from beneath my arms and I hugged her tighter, clamping my eyes shut. How does one even go about knowing if they are in love or not? Julian mentioned getting a blessing from San Michel. How utterly embarrassing that would be.

The tears quieted finally and I sat up, a few sharp pieces of hay pricking into my back. Ainsley regarded me quietly, not daring to move from her spot. She simply watched on, offering herself as a place to rest my head and dry my tears. "Thanks, ol' girl," I said, petting the top of her head. She bleated a response.

I stood, brushing the dirt and hay from my dress, and wiped my nose with the back of my hand. There was no way I was taking my private feelings to San Michel. I could figure out on my own whether Lord Buckley's intentions for me were true or not. I certainly didn't need an ArchAngel alerting me one way or another.

"M'lady?"

I gasped, spinning at the sound of Dejan's voice. Placing a palm to my chest, I exhaled in relief. "You startled me," I whispered.

He offered a small bow in return. "My apologies. Is everything well in here?"

I nodded, not meeting his eyes. "Quite well, thank you."

When I offered nothing else, he cleared his throat. "I can smell your tears, my lady."

With clenched jaw, I shot my gaze up to his and looked straight into his blood-rimmed eyes. "I'm certain I don't know what you are talking about."

"Yes, m'lady."

"Anything else, Dejan?"

"I believe Lord Buckley is waiting for you inside."

"Very well." I gathered my dress in one arm, giving Ainsley one last scratch under her chin before brushing past Dejan's shoulder. His strong grasp caught me around the elbow, halting my steps and jerking me backward.

"Tell me one thing," he rasped. "Did Lord Buckley do this to you?"

I wasn't quite sure why I gasped. Whether it was because of his sudden and firm grip, or his intense gaze that bore into my eyes, or such a daring question that almost sounded as though . . . well, as though he cared about my feelings. My cheek brushed the front of his shoulder as I looked up into his face once more. He had a little more color to his pale tone—Lord Buckley must have allowed him to feed recently. The bruises under his eyes were far less pronounced and he almost looked healthy. For a vampire, that is.

His lips were full and moist and red like berries in the spring. I raised a hand to his beautiful mouth and ran my thumb along his bottom lip. A hot breath escaped his parted lips quickly, sharply, and I closed my eyes, breathing it in. When I opened my eyes again, his beautiful mouth was still there before mine, but two sharp fangs rested along the bottom lip.

"Is this what you wanted to see? The mighty large teeth of the vampire?" His words were soft but had venom in them, and his grip on my elbow tightened.

I whimpered in pain, not wanting to cause a fight just yet. "No," I answered honestly. "Dejan, I just thought—for a moment, I thought you were beautiful."

He released my elbow, throwing me away from him. He stood on the other end of the stable, having moved so quickly, most humans would not have even seen him. "An angel can think no such things."

I shrugged, palms out. "Angels also cannot lie. I suppose we are at an impasse. Unless you do not believe me to be an angel."

We were silent staring at each other from across the stable. The wind outside howled its lullaby and a draft blew in through the opening of the door. I grabbed one of the heavier blankets and placed it around Ainsley, who seemed to look up and smile at me.

Dejan cleared his throat. "Lord Buckley awaits your return."

I nodded. "Very well." I turned to leave, opening the stable door before turning back to look at Dejan one more time. "And no—Lord Buckley was not responsible for my tears, Dejan. Thank you for . . . asking."

36

I excused myself and slipped into the bathroom. Once in the ladies' room, I washed my hands and looked under the bathroom stalls. A pair of feet were under one, so I slipped into the other stall until I heard her wash her hands and leave.

I poked my head out, still not seeing Dejan. With a sigh, I soaped up my hands once more. I'd give it two more minutes. I couldn't wait in here all night. Who knows what the vampire even wanted to discuss? Whatever it was, I'd probably have to tell Damien and Adrienne anyway.

I brushed my wet hands along my pants and headed for the door. As I reached for the handle, frigid fingers grasped my wrist and locked the door instead. A thin, hinged window along the top of the bathroom wall clattered shut behind me.

"Well, it took you long enough," I said on an exhale. "I wasn't about to wait in here all friggin' night."

Dejan moved around the bathroom like lightning, checking the various stalls to ensure no one else was around. "No one else is in here," I said, crossing my arms. Did he think I'd waltzed in and not bothered to check the stalls myself? Honestly.

Once he had fully checked and felt comfortable with the security in the bathroom, he sauntered toward me with a slow, calculated grace that made me want to shudder. I suppressed the urge and instead rolled my shoulders back, tilting my chin higher to meet his gaze. "You best make this fast. They are going to get suspicious if I don't get back soon. And even more suspicious if they come to look for me and the bathroom is locked." I gestured to the door he had bolted and wedged closed.

"We'll hear them coming before they even wiggle the doorknob," he said with a scowl. "Why are you consorting with an elemental?" He spoke fast, almost frantically, and glared at me with black eyes.

"What? He's a detective. He's one of the good guys."

"Elementals are never the good guys." Dejan's jaw was clenched so hard, the muscles in his neck were thick and corded.

"Don't get all righteous, Dejan. It clearly doesn't suit you." I folded my arms across my chest and glared back at him.

He held my gaze. "Just be careful around him. Keep an eye open for odd behavior."

"Right, right. You mean like if he pulls me into a ladies' room and locks the door?"

"I'm not joking, Monica." His eyes flashed and I rolled mine in response.

"Fine. Yes, I'll keep an eye on Damien."

"I meant it when I said I was surprised to find Julian's descendant involved." Dejan shook his head back and forth as if trying to make sense of it all. "I don't know why he would be involved. I thought for sure it was Buckley. But then Luis was found and . . . and he would never hurt his own blood."

"Do you have any idea where Lord Buckley is right now?"

He shook his head. "Like I said, I haven't seen him in over a century. All I know is he's around." Dejan lowered his voice, looking to the ceiling. I couldn't tell if he was looking around or rolling his eyes. "He's always around," he whispered.

"He doesn't still have any power . . . or hold or anything over you, does he?"

Dejan snorted. "Don't be ridiculous. Of course not. That all disappeared when—well, you know."

Oh, I knew, all right. My stomach tightened with the memory of Dejan on top of me, his fangs puncturing through my skin, venom burning in my veins. Dejan's power over me had counteracted Lord Buckley's power over him. Had Buckley known that ahead of time, I doubted he ever would have gone through with the plan. Squeezing my eyes shut, I pushed the memories away.

"Monica." His voice dropped to barely a whisper and Dejan took a step closer. I stepped back, bumping into the wall behind me. "I think you should leave. Get out of Utah . . . go back to Vegas and bide your time with Lucien. I don't know what's going on here, but I'm certain it has everything to do with you. And I'm even more sure that it's not going to end well."

I swallowed a golf-ball-sized lump in my throat. "Stop trying to scare me." My throat was parched and my voice sounded as such.

"I'm not *trying* to frighten you. But you should be scared." Dejan's tongue ran across his red lips and his gaze dipped to my throat. My heart slammed against my ribs. Dejan squeezed his eyes shut, turning his head away from me. "I haven't had angel blood since yours long ago." He shuddered—whether in pleasure or pain I had no idea. "Demon blood is a delicacy, too—and sometimes I wonder—what do you taste like now?" His eyes slowly opened, and he turned to look at me once more, his eyes now rimmed with red and rippling with blood. "I bet there's still a little angel left in that blood," he whispered, his fangs snapping out.

"Dejan," I exhaled and shoved at his chest with two palms. I was strong enough to send him across the room, but he was quick to recover and had his hand wrapped around my throat, pressing my body back against the wall.

"Did you know that Luis was following you?" His hand squeezed and he pushed me harder against the cement block wall.

I clawed at his knuckles. "Let me go!" He blinked and released me, but not before throwing me to the wall once more.

"He was following you," Dejan repeated. "He had been watching you for a couple of months after the attack happened in your apartment back in April."

I shook my head, rubbing a hand over my neck. "I didn't know he had been following me that long. But I did meet him just a couple of days before I came here. He came to the club and tried to buy a private dance. A—uh, another customer beat him to it, though."

"What did he say to you when he introduced himself?"

I thought back. It seemed like so long ago. "Just typical introductory things. His name—well, his first name. He tipped me quite generously. Made a point in showing off his wealth . . ."

"The apple doesn't fall far from the tree, then . . . ," Dejan growled.

Lord Buckley had certainly loved his money, too. "That was basically it. Then, he slipped me his business card and left. That was the last I saw him." I paused, shifting my hair to be smoother while looking on in the mirror. Dejan disappeared from view in the reflection—something I always found disconcerting—and I quickly turned back around to face him. "Do *you* know why he was following me?"

Dejan shook his head. "No. But I wish I did. I have a feeling.

A feeling it ties into that crazy bitch Lexi and the bounty that's on your head."

I narrowed my eyes at him. "What do you care? You nearly killed me yourself long ago."

Dejan's face fell, and for all of a moment, he actually looked hurt. "Is that what you think? You clearly don't remember anything correctly, do you?" he growled. "I was saving you, Monica!" His voice grumbled through clenched teeth and two large fangs appeared behind red-stained lips. He closed his eyes with a deep breath through his nose. A tiny clicking sound echoed in the bathroom as the fangs retracted.

"Saving me?" I snorted. "I would have rather died. We all know that nothing good comes when a vampire bites an angel—at least not for the angel. The vampires on the other hand are probably worshipped among their covens." I spat while storming to the door. "If you hear of anything else regarding Lord Buckley or this case, please let me know," I said over my shoulder just before storming back to the table.

I arrived back at the hotel room around eight p.m. to find Kayce lying in my bed watching television. I tossed my purse onto the floor and threw my phone next to hers at the foot of the bed. I flopped onto my back beside her. "You've been productive, I see." I quirked an eyebrow at her and she handed me a bag of Twizzlers.

I took one, biting into the sugary twisted candy. "Kourtney and Khloe are taking Florida by storm," she said, staring at the television screen with about as much enthusiasm as I felt.

"Aren't you supposed to be helping George tonight?" I asked, mouth filled with sticky candy.

"Yeah. They're doing a guy dinner thing first. I'm meeting them out in a bit."

The iPad was still sitting on George's bed and it pinged in a way that reminded me of an oven timer. Like, *Ding, your en-*

crypted file is ready! I glanced at Kayce, whose grin spread across the entire length of her face. She wiggled her eyebrows. "Ready?"

"Oh, boy. As ready as I can be, I guess."

Kayce shrugged. "It might totally be nothing. Though in my experience, people don't encrypt files that aren't important."

"And what experience would that be, exactly, Miss Kayce?"

She smirked while typing a few things into the iPad. "Oh, if only I could tell you, Miss Monica."

I chuckled and sat down on the bed next to her, crisscrossing my legs over each other.

"Here we go," she whispered and double clicked on the file. A document opened with my headshot as the main image. It held my name as well as every alias I've even used throughout my existence. There were photographs of me at the coffee shop and with every single person in my life. There was a picture of George and me at the club. Drew and me talking at the cafe. Lucien, T, Kayce, Damien, Adrienne . . . everyone who meant anything to me was a part of this file. It listed my address as well as a blueprint of my home layout; even my furniture placement was there.

"I think I might be sick," I whispered. Kayce rubbed my back with the palm of her hand, circling, in the way a mother might to a sick child.

"It's okay, Mon. This is pretty much what I was expecting. It's a hit folder. All the information one might need for an assassination."

"And you don't find that terrifying?" I whispered. My tongue felt suddenly too big for my mouth.

"It is terrifying. But it's also expected. These people know everything about everyone you've ever come in contact with."

"Who sent it?" I asked.

She shrugged and scrolled down some more. "I don't know. I doubt that will be listed on here. Anonymity is the only thing that keeps people like this in business. They wouldn't be so stupid as to list their identities on the case file." She leaned into the screen and typed a few more things. "There's something else here, though. I don't think it's to do with the job—it just looks like Aaron kept it in the same folder. I need a minute. It's encrypted differently." A cell phone rang from the other bed and I jumped up to grab it. "Whose is it?" Kayce asked, eyes still glued to the screen.

"I don't know yet. . . . We need to get different ring tones, Kayce."

She shrugged. "If it's George, tell him I'm leaving in five." On the bed—neither phone was ringing. "Uh, Kayce, do you have another phone? It's not either of ou—"

She jumped up and in a flash had another small phone in her hands and was glancing at me before swinging the door open to answer. "I'll be right back." She gave me a tilted half-smile as an apology."

I peeked out the hallway and she was already nowhere to be seen. Something uneasy burrowed in my stomach. Grabbing my room key, I did a quick lap around our floor until I heard her voice. She wasn't whispering, yet she also wasn't talking in her normal volume. The sound was faint, but I could barely make out the gruff voice she was conversing with. She was in the stairwell and I stepped back to the other end of the hallway so that she couldn't hear my breathing.

"Is it done?" the gruff voice rumbled.

"Negative. It's a delicate situation I'm in here."

"We know. It's why you were chosen."

"It's a sensitive case. One that requires more time," Kayce said.

"You have until morning." I listened for a moment more when I heard a footstep and the stairwell door swing open. I ran for our room again, leaving the door cracked open as she had and lunging for the bed. Seconds later, Kayce came back in.

"Who was that? Was it George?" I asked in my most innocent voice.

"Yep," she said and coolly tossed the phone back into her bag. Then she came over back to the bed, sliding in next to me. "Have to leave in a bit."

"New phone?"

Kayce gave me a look, the kind that said *don't ask*, before she went back to focusing on the iPad. I glared at her profile. This don't-ask, don't-tell policy she had instated in our friendship was gnawing at me. Especially now. I had a uneasy feeling that that call had to do with me.

"Aha!" she exclaimed, a giant smile on her face. "Got it." She looked up at me and her eyes flashed with concern. "Hey, you okay? You're really pale."

I cleared my throat, nodding my head. "Oh, I'm fine. Just shaken from the file."

She'd be leaving soon—out of the room to be with George. I could do a little snooping of my own.

I leaned in to look at the screen. "It's—it's a bunch of numbers. What is it . . . some sort of bank account or something?"

"No, it's a code of some sort. You know—like if someone assigns letters of the alphabet to numbers. A would be one. B would be two and so on and so forth." She wiped a hand across her forehead. "It can take a while to decode. I doubt it's as easy as the example I just gave. We'll work on it tonight after I finish George's thing. You'll be here, right?"

I nodded. "Oh, I'll be here."

Kayce shifted into a sexy, tight red dress and did a little twirl for me. "Well? What do you think?" she asked, holding out two hands.

I arched an eyebrow. "Um, I think you might want to tone it down for this crowd."

She sighed and rolled her eyes, shifting into a looser dress that covered more skin. "Fine. This town is so boring."

"You have no idea," I said with a smile. She grabbed her purse, tossing it over one shoulder. "Kayce—was there any other reason you came up here? You know . . . other than just missing George and me?"

I wasn't sure if it was my imagination or not, but I could have sworn her smile froze. After a pause, she answered. "Like what?"

I shrugged. "Oh, I dunno. A work thing, maybe? I was just asking."

She shook her head and answered calmly. A little too calmly for my taste. "Well, I'm almost always on an assignment, Monica. You should know that by now."

I smiled back, mustering up as much calm, assertive strength as I could. "Of course. Have fun tonight with George."

She nodded and left the room, giving me one last glance over her shoulder before shutting the door.

37

Ireland, 1740

The frost had taken a turn for the worse. The weather outside was frigid and biting. I lay in my bed facing the ceiling while the wind howled on the other side of the window. I thought of Ainsley and my heart squeezed imagining her outside in this weather. I knew that Lord Buckley had enchantments on the stables to help keep the wind out, but that did little to ease my anxiety. Storms used to always terrify our livestock when I was a child. I remember my father would take Mama's wool blanket she had knitted just for him out to the barn during the worst storms and sleep with the sheep to ensure they made it through the worst of it.

I blinked a few times, knowing sleep would not come to me tonight. And instead, I layered my dress and knits and wrapped a blanket around my shoulders before sneaking out the front door, running barefoot to the stables. It was not as if the weather could affect me. But I knew Lord Buckley would have objections—and teleporting would have alerted him of my leaving.

The stable doors were heavy as I swung them open. Several

sheep looked up and bleated a greeting as I slammed the door shut behind me. Ainsley stood, walking over to offer me a greeting. I scratched her head. "Aw, c'mon, ol' girl. You didn't have to get up for me." I walked over to a pile of hay, still warm from where she had been resting, and she followed me, lying down at my side.

All the sheep seemed to be quite well considering the storm that threatened outside. All the same, I felt better having seen it for myself. Tossing the blanket over my legs, I stretched out, resting my head on Ainsley's soft wool and nuzzling my cheek into it. Just as my eyes were falling, sleep not far away, the stable door slammed open, hitting the wall behind it.

I jumped up, as did several of the sheep. An outline of Lord Buckley stood shadowed in the doorway. Slanted snow and rain whipped behind him like a wintery backdrop. He stalked into the stables and slammed the door shut behind him with a quick flick of the wrist. His face was brittle, set in a scowl, and he rushed to my side.

"What are you doing here?" he boomed. Ainsley jumped up from beside me and ran to the other side of the stables.

"You're frightening the sheep!" I yelled back, moving to comfort Ainsley and the others.

"Me? You terrified me when I woke and your presence was no longer inside my home!"

I spun to face him, wrapping the blanket tighter around my shoulders. It wasn't as though I needed the warmth; I simply liked the comfort of grasping on to something. "I am permitted to come and go as I please, am I not? Am I a prisoner here?"

"Of course you're not a prisoner," he scoffed. "But it would certainly be nice if you at least told me when and where you were going. As a courtesy!"

"You, Lord Buckley, are not my father! I demand that you not treat me like a child."

"Thank heavens for that! Your father was a bitter man who could barely manage to keep his farm well organized, let alone his daughters!"

The words were like a slap across my face and I stepped back as they stung me. "How—how do you know about my father?"

Lord Buckley raked a hand through his hair and his head fell, chin to chest. "I apologize. I didn't mean that," he said, softer.

"Yes, you did."

He sighed and rubbed a fist over sleepy eyes. "I didn't mean it to be as harsh as it sounded. Your father wasn't a bad man, Monica."

"I know *that, John." I threw his name in his face as if that itself were an insult. "I also know that I was a difficult daughter to deal with. I don't need you to remind me of such things."*

"I know. I apologize."

"And you didn't answer me. How do you know of my father?"

He shrugged. "I know everything about you."

My stomach twisted in knots as I remembered my father and mother. They had warned me that teasing the boys would bring no good, but I hadn't listened. I'd loved the attention the boys afforded me when I would swing my hips around the market. When I would intentionally bend over to sort the wool we sold. I squeezed my eyes shut. Father had tried to warn me. He had tried to tell me that when a man wants something he believes you to be offering, he will simply take it without so much as a squeak of permission. Of course, the boys never got that from me. They took my life instead.

A jagged breath escaped my lips and the warmth of my breath created a fog in front of my face.

"Oh, my angel." Lord Buckley rushed over cradling me in his arms. "I didn't mean to bring such sorrow onto you. I was

afraid that you had left me. And I handled that fear just terribly. Please forgive me." I nodded into his shoulder. "Let's go inside, shall we?"

I shook my head. "I would prefer to stay out here with the sheep tonight." I looked down at Ainsley, who returned my gaze with big, brown eyes.

Lord Buckley knelt and scratched her head behind her ears. "Hello, old girl. Afraid of a little thunder, are you?"

She wasn't, but I wasn't about to tell him that. He looked up at me with the softest hint of a smile at his lips. "Then, I shall stay out here with you."

My stomach clenched. We couldn't possibly sleep next to each other, could we? "But—but we couldn't. It wouldn't be . . ."

He pressed a finger to my lips, shushing me. "My angel, you fret far too much." He pressed his lips to mine, and they were soft and warm despite the frigid temperatures outside.

He pulled away, holding me at arm's length before walking to the other side of the stables. With a few swirls of his hands and some words I did not understand murmured from those plump lips of his, a fire started in the middle of the stables. Its heat radiated, and I rushed over, Ainsley at my side, to warm my hands by it. Ainsley bleated an approval of the warmth.

I held out my blanket and sat, leaning against the hay. Lord Buckley smiled and slid under the blanket with me, wrapping an arm around my shoulders. I shivered at how close he was. His musk was masculine, and desire pooled in my stomach at the scent. "I'm certain this is inappropriate in more ways than we can count."

Lord Buckley brushed a stray hair behind my ear and smiled down at me. The fire crackled before us, and he hugged me tighter. "Love is not a sin, Monica." They were the exact same words Julian had spoken to me.

"Love," I whispered back. "Is that what this is?" I looked up into his eyes and they were wet like mine.

He cupped my jaw with his hand. "Close your eyes, Monica." I did as he asked and soon felt his lips upon my ear. "I love you, angel," he whispered.

A tear fell down my cheek and it tickled as it slid down to my chin. I opened my eyes just as he caught the tear with a finger. His grin widened and he wiped the tear on Ainsley's wool.

A man loved me. An overwhelming heat flooded my chest and flashed all the way down between my legs making me gasp. Lord Buckley's lips were on mine once again and he gently laid me down so that my back was flat on the floor. Leaning on his elbows over me, he braced his weight so that it wasn't on my person.

His firm length pressed into the burning area between my thighs; my moan echoed through the stables. The pressure against my aching body was torturously delicious and I desperately wanted more. I wanted it harder. I wanted it inside me. I stopped thinking—I was tired of thinking. Tired of analyzing every decision. My heart swelled and this felt so right. So very right. I ran a hand down his back. The muscles were roped, strained from above me. He was holding back and his eyes were burning into mine. "Angel," he whispered. "May I touch you?"

"Touch me," I repeated. Only he interpreted it as a question.

"May I touch you here?" His knuckle grazed my breast and I groaned, arching into his hand. He chuckled in response. "I take that as a yes." He palmed my breast, squeezing it. His hand traveled to my thigh, flipping my dress up past my waist. "May I touch you here?" His fingertips brushed the bare flesh on my leg.

I nodded, a throaty whisper barely escaping my lips. "Yes."

His hand enclosed the flesh, squeezing my thigh and running his palm up to my bottom. "Here?" He kissed my neck while waiting for a response and I nodded, butterflies flapping wildly in my stomach, my heart slamming into my ribs with each beat. His hand squeezed my backside, one finger slipping into my undergarments and brushing along the crease. His touch was gentle and caressed all the way down until he reached my slit and I gasped a strangled noise.

He paused, his finger just barely touching my most intimate area. "May I touch you here?"

"Please," I moaned.

"Are you sure?" he asked again, taking my chin between two fingers and forcing my eyes to his.

"Yes. Please. Touch me, John," I cried. His finger pushed inside of me, gathering my wetness on his finger before pulling it out and using the moisture on my most sensitive button at the crest between my legs. I shouted as the heat flared through my body. It was the strangest sensation—incredible, but at the same time uncomfortable. As though the touch was wonderful, but not quite satiating the itch that needed to be scratched.

He entered me again, with two fingers this time, and the pain that flared through me ached at first before delicious pleasure took over. "Relax, my darling," he whispered into my ear, his fingers moving in and out. My body bucked from beneath him.

His hard rod pressed into my hip and I felt an intense curiosity at what it felt like. I wanted to hold his manhood in my hand. "I want to touch you," I said. His smile was the only encouragement I needed.

"Oh, I would very much like that." His boyish smile gleamed in his eyes and he yanked his trousers down. I'd never seen a naked man before.

Concern washed over Lord Buckley's face. "My darling, we can stop." He grasped his trousers, moving to pull them up again.

I darted a hand out to stop him. "No. Come here." I slowly wrapped my fingers around his girth. He grunted and fell forward onto his elbows once more, thrusting into my palm.

"Oh, yes, Monica. Just like that." I stroked him to the tip, where moisture pooled at the top, and swirled a finger around

before stroking down to the base once more. Lord Buckley threw his head back and beads of sweat glistened along his hairline in the firelight. I squeezed, gathering the pool of wetness on my fingertip once more, bringing it to my lips. I put my finger inside my mouth, sucking on the salty flavor.

His eyes, half open, watched and he groaned. His fingers moved in circles over my curls before he slid my undergarments off entirely, placing them in a pile beside us. With his knees, he nudged my legs farther apart before positioning himself at my opening. I could smell my arousal and the scent was heady and thick, exciting me even more. My whole body clenched with desire. A tightness that felt as though it could never be relieved. The hay beneath us was soft, the fire warm. It was my vision of a perfect first time and I closed my eyes as he pushed into me. I cried out, his large size stretching me sending a biting pain spiraling through my body. He paused once inside me, stroking my hair with his palm.

"Are you all right, angel?"

I nodded. "Just please—go slowly."

"Of course." He stayed like that inside me until my body adjusted around him. After a few moments, it no longer felt as though I were being split apart. In fact, it actually felt a little—nice. More than nice. It felt amazing. I wiggled beneath him and he moaned, looking down at me, a strained look on his face.

"If you wriggle around like that, I'm not so sure how long I will last," he said with a chuckle.

He slowly, achingly slowly, pulled out and thrust back into me. This time, the pleasure far outweighed the pain and I panted from below him. He stroked me from the inside, my wetness growing, dripping out around his manhood and down my thighs. I raised my backside to meet his thrusts and he grunted; a guttural sound I'd never heard from a man before. It was exhilarating. That I could do that to him; that I could make him feel so much pleasure. It was . . . powerful. I felt as though I held all the power with a man for the first time and that rush swelled within my chest. I sped up my thrusts, meeting his, pulse for pulse.

A knot tightened low in my belly. Something was mounting, though I didn't know what. It felt as though someone were squeezing everything inside of me. And in a rush, it exploded. My body convulsed and I no longer had any control of my faculties. It was terrifying and amazing all at once.

"Yes!" Lord Buckley cried out, nipping at my shoulder as a rush of moisture pulsed inside of me. Was it his? Mine? He shivered above me, convulsing as we both finished, the electricity fading.

"Good Heavens," I whispered, a heavy breath catching in my chest.

"I know." Lord Buckley rolled off of me, lying on his back next to me. "Pretty spectacular, isn't it?" I nodded, staring at the beams below the roof, and closed my eyes waiting for God to smite me. I remembered what Julian had said about needing San Michel's blessing. But no smiting came. Only blissful, wonderful sleep beside a man who loved me in front of a crackling fire.

I woke with a start, unsure of how long I was asleep. I blinked as my eyes adjusted into focus. Standing, I looked down at John, who was still fast asleep, curled onto his side, the blanket wrapped around his torso. I pulled the edge up around his shoulders, taking an extra moment to run my fingers through his soft, silky hair.

I tugged the door open. The crisp smell of snow bit my nose and the back of my throat, and I quickly shut the door behind me before the cold gust woke John. The ache between my legs was a bittersweet reminder of the choice I had just made, and I looked back to the door, a gnawing nervousness eating at my stomach. It was just jitters. I had taken an enormous step tonight—what I was feeling was perfectly normal. I hugged my arms into my chest as a shiver danced down my spine.

It was still dark out with the exception of a slice of pink edging the horizon. The presence of another angel froze my body like a bucket of ice water being thrown over my body.

Julian. He was outside the gate. That's what had woken me. My body drew me up and out before my mind knew why. The thought was a little frightening—how strong our connection to each other was.

I made my way to the front gate, where he stood clutching the bars like a prisoner waiting for family. His shoulders shook when he saw me, forehead falling onto the iron bars. As I approached, he wiped at his cheeks brushing tears away.

"Oh, thank goodness. You are well, are you not? You aren't injured?" He reached through the bars, touching my cheeks, my shoulders, and down my arms as though he couldn't believe I was still alive. I nodded to the blond vampire standing guard. He wore a scowl, but obeyed my order, unlocked the gate for Jules to enter. He rushed through, wrapping his arms around my body in a locking embrace.

"Of course I am well. What has come over you, Jules?" I hugged him back before pushing him away to look at him. His face had lines I had never seen before. His eyes were red and bloodshot and his hair looked heavily oiled, brushed back from his face.

"You-you've changed," he stuttered, his eyes searching all over my body. "I can't see you anymore."

"What in Heaven's name are you talking about? I'm right here." I gestured up and down my body where I stood.

"Yes, yes, of course I can see you. But I can't see you.*" His hands twitched out in front of himself and he started pacing in the lawn, back and forth before he jolted to a stop.*

"Jules. You are making no sense. What do you mean?"

"Our connection," he snapped, grasping onto my shoulders

and shaking me as if he could force his words to make sense with physical contact. "Our angel–mentor connection—it's gone!" He ran a hand through his hair before he started pacing again.

"Why?" he continued, speaking more to himself than to me. "Why would this happen? Why would God take you from me? There must be a reason."

"God has not taken me from you, Julian. I am right here." I took his hand in mine, halting his pacing. And for the first time since his arrival, he stopped and looked at me. Looked into my eyes. His blue eyes so bright and rippling with emotion that they were two streams, rushing with fervor, concern, and affection.

"You are and you aren't. I can't see you anymore." His gaze rushed down my body, landing on my dress.

I followed his eyes, noticing a few spots of blood there between my legs.

His eyes met mine once more. "Oh, Monica." His voice cracked and I looked away, cheeks burning. I couldn't bear to see his shame. His pity. Whatever other emotions played across his face. "Oh, Monica, tell me you didn't." He grabbed the back of my neck, pulling my forehead to his. "Look at me," he whispered.

When I had gathered the courage, I opened my eyes, meeting his searing stare. His eyebrows creased and he shook his head, tears spilling down his cheeks. He pressed a kiss to my forehead.

"You said . . ." I choked back a sob, dropping my face into my hands. My head fell against his chest. "You said God does not punish love."

I felt his nod. "I hope He loves you. I hope His love is enough."

A breath staggered in his chest, the tremor causing my head to bob with it. He was fighting his own sobs, as well. He sniffled above me and as he grasped at my shoulders, his lips found my forehead once again. "I must go. Now that I know you are . . . that you are not injured, I must get back to the ill."

The vampire closed the gate and locked up behind him, his hand trembling while he stared at the blood splatters on my dress. His nostrils flared and I ignored how his eyes flashed redder.

I waved to Jules, doing my best to muster a smile. He did not wave back. He did not return my smile. He turned his back on me and disappeared with a crack.

38

As soon as Kayce had gone, I listened at the door until I heard the telltale *crack* of her teleporting elsewhere. Lunging for her bag, I tugged at the zipper. It wouldn't budge. Tiny tendrils of magic wound in and through the zipper pull. I should have known there would be an enchantment on anything of Kayce's.

"Shit," I muttered to myself. Two could play at that game. Kayce had mentioned a while ago that she only knew a few very basic enchantments—with my new abilities, maybe I was more advanced than her. I closed my eyes and allowed the foreign words to roll off my tongue. I envisioned the words—the magic curling around the zipper, spreading the teeth apart. When I looked again, the bag sat before me, open. My grin widened. I was getting pretty good at this magic thing. I couldn't tell you what the damn words meant, but somehow I'd just instinctually known some of the spells.

I sat back on my heels. Did I really want to do this? Look through my best friend's bag as though she were some sort of suspect? My chest heaved with a deep inhalation. I didn't want to—but I had no choice. If she had been up front with me about her job, then maybe I wouldn't need to do this. But it was her choice to keep her life secret. And she was the one who had received a very suspicious call. As much as I didn't want to, I had to find out the truth.

It was a small bag. The kind that rolled—damn her for thinking ahead with that. No clothes or underwear that you would find in a normal person's carry-on luggage. There were guns. A couple of small ones that would fit in a boot or the waistband of your jeans. A box of bullets. I opened the box and a bullet fell into my palm. It sizzled on my skin, steam rising where it made contact.

"Ah!" I dropped the bullet back into the bag, shaking away the stinging on my palm. Holy water bullets. There was a pair of leather gloves—no doubt so that she could load the gun without burning herself. Several opaque bottles in various colors. I'd learned my lesson—I slid on her gloves before touching anything else.

Holding one of the bottles up to the light, I squinted, trying to see if anything was in it. I shook it back and forth, holding it up to my ear. Nothing. It seemed empty. I tossed it back into the bag and picked up a glass jar with liquid filled to the brim. I unscrewed one top and smelled. Holy water—I was sure of it. In a small jewelry travel case were some rosary beads, crucifixes, and a statue of the Virgin Mary. There was also a bag of salt, lighter fluid, matches, and a small Zippo lighter.

They were the exact items needed to trap a being in a summoning circle. The exact items Aaron had been about to use to trap me on the plane.

This certainly wasn't making me feel any better about Kayce and what she was here to do. A knock at the door made me nearly jump out of my skin and I flinched as I tossed everything back into her bag, ripping the gloves off before zipping it back up and sliding it into the closet. I hopped up, shifting my hair and clothing back into place before I peeked out the peephole.

Damien. The tight feeling in my chest relaxed and I moved to open the door, just as Dejan's warning echoed in my head. *Don't trust the elemental.* I shook it away—why would I heed the advice of the creature that had banished me as a Hellspawn? I removed the chain and pulled the door open. "Hey, you," I said with a smile.

"Hey back." He looked past me into the room. "Anyone else in there with you?"

I shook my head, my grin tilting higher. His smile mimicked my own. "Good," he answered before sweeping me into his arms and kicking the door closed behind him. His lips found mine and we locked in a kiss. After a few moments, we broke apart, each breathless and staring at the other hungrily.

"As much as I'd love to continue this"—he nuzzled my ear, flicking a tongue out to touch the all the deliciously sensitive nerve endings there—"I thought we'd go check out this Buckley character's son. He lives close by."

I nodded. "Mm, okay. We can always resume this after, right?"

Damien's grin widened. "I wouldn't have it any other way."

Raul Nunez-Buckley lived in a stunning mansion on Walker Lane. It looked like something that would be featured in a Martha Stewart catalogue. And that was only judging the outside, which had Grecian-style columns and a beautifully manicured front lawn. The driveway was long and lit with sconces. Damien whistled as we drove the length of it, looking up at the mini-mansion. "Looks like someone's doing well. What do you think he does for a living?"

I shrugged. Probably nothing, knowing Lord Buckley's wealth and penchant for looking after those he cared about. "Let's go find out, shall we?"

I walked up the steps to the mahogany front door, clasped the door knocker, and almost choked when the sheep's head stared back at me. Clenching it in my fist, I slammed it into the heavy door.

A woman wearing a black skirt and white button-down shirt with a lacy apron tied around her waist answered the door. Damien and I looked at each other. How long had it been since I'd seen a maid actually wearing a maid's uniform. Sure, it wasn't the exact sexy Halloween costume most of us pictured, but it was quite formal.

"May I help you?" she asked, turning her head to the side to look from Damien to me and back again.

Damien flashed his badge. "We need to speak with Mr. Nunez-Buckley," he said, his voice full of authority and testosterone.

"Yes, of course. He's been expecting you," she said quietly, stepping to the side. "Please come in and I will get him."

I slid an uneasy look to Damien while walking through the foyer.

She gestured to a sitting area just inside the front door. "May I get you some tea or coffee while you wait?"

My eyes widened. Coffee. Real coffee. Before Damien could answer—I could see the *no* about to come out of his mouth—I nodded. "Yes. Coffee would be wonderful, thank you." She curtseyed and left the room, her feet barely making any noise walking along the solid marble floors.

Damien tucked his hands in his pockets and moseyed around the room before taking a seat in a large, plush chair. "Wow. Look at this place." He ran a hand along the leather club chair's arm. "And this seat. Holy shit, it's so soft. Seriously, like butter."

"Yeah. Calfskin doused in butter," I muttered.

"Aw, succubus. Do I have an animal rights activist on my hands?" His smirk was condescending and it made me want to slap him across his easily impressed face.

"No, I wear leather. I just ensure that when I do buy leather, it's from a responsible seller. One that does not torture its animals."

Damien rolled his eyes. "Sure. And just how do you ensure that they're telling the truth?"

"I visit the farms."

He narrowed his eyes at me and after a moment snorted. "No, you don't."

"Fine." I rolled my eyes. "But I always meant to."

"Ms. Lamb." A deep voice from the bottom of the stairwell startled me and I jumped to my feet at the sound of his voice. Damien, however, remained seated, one foot casually resting on his knee as though he were at home about to watch the big game.

I arched one eyebrow. "I'm sorry, have we met?"

"Not exactly." Raul offered a warm smile and approached with one hand out. He looked almost identical to Luis and the resemblance nearly took my breath away. He was tall with skin the color of creamed coffee. His jet-black hair was clean cut and he wore an expensive suit, tailored to perfection on his beautifully chiseled body, despite the fact that it was evening and well past working hours. I took his hand, but pulled my body farther from his with the handshake. "Ms. Lamb," he said again, cradling my hand in his. "But it's so lovely to finally meet you. My father spoke of you often."

Damien's eyes shot to me and I could feel them burning into the side of my face. I cleared my throat. "Did he? I would have thought he'd forgotten completely about me once I left. He didn't seem all that . . . invested in us in the first place."

Raul's mouth tipped into the smallest frown. "He would be so terribly sad to hear you say that. He only spoke of you fondly. Monica Lamb. His unrequited love."

I snorted at that and yanked my hand from Raul's grasp. "Uh-huh. Funny as I've been around for centuries now and haven't heard a single word from him. It seems as though a man of his standing could have come to me at any time."

"He feared you. I never heard the whole story, but he knew you would never take him back. Whatever it was, it seemed as though he regretted his actions terribly."

"Is that so?" I forced my hands to my sides—no fidgeting. And relaxed my shoulders so that they weren't clenched by my ears. "And he told you this? What with being in love with your mother and all?"

Raul shrugged and his smile was soft and warm. It almost made me want to trust him. Almost. "He and my mother were quite happy for a long while. But with a man such as John Buckley—he's lived such a long life. After centuries of living, one is bound to have more than a single love in an existence."

"Yes," I sneered. "I suppose you are right. A man like him is apt to have multiple conquests—oops, I mean loves." I thought for a moment, sliding a glance to Damien, who watched the two of us like a Ping-Pong match. "Just how did you know who I was? You knew immediately . . . as though you were expecting me."

"I was expecting you. For quite some time." He gestured to one of the seats. "Please, sit down."

We all did so just as the maid came in with a silver coffee set, and placed it on the table in front of us. She poured me a cup and I fixed it light and sweet just as I liked it. The smell of smooth, oaky roast flooded my nose and I had to suppress a satisfied moan with that first sip. Oh Hell, that was a good cup of coffee. It could almost put Drew's to shame.

While I sipped my coffee, Raul continued talking. "Luis mentioned he went to see you. I still don't know why he did it. He seemed to have taken quite the interest in you. Then, just a couple of days ago, he came here to see me. He said he was onto something, though he never went into detail." Raul's voice cracked and he paused, bringing a fist to his mouth.

"We're very sorry for the loss of your brother," Damien offered. "Were you two close?"

Raul cleared his throat and looked to Damien. "I'm sorry, we haven't been formally introduced yet. I'm Raul." He stood, holding out a hand, which Damien took with one firm pump.

When he sat back down, his smile was a sad one. "We were twins. We were very close, though recently we had been growing apart. He was more of the risk taker of the two of us. Unfortunately, a fact that I'm afraid may have been his demise."

Raul's eyes filled with tears that danced around the bottoms of his eyelids but never quite spilled out over his cheeks. I almost felt sorry for the man. But then again, he was a Buckley. I cleared my throat. "So, he was 'onto something.' What does that even mean?"

Raul leaned in, pouring his own cup of coffee which he sipped black. "I honestly don't know. But it involved you. Luis was worried for you. I'm not positive, but I think Father may have asked him to keep an eye on you. Luis ran a very lucrative and well-respected private security firm. He has locations all around the country."

Raul's eyes met mine; they were large and dark brown. His lips were the color of caramel and, when he was in a relaxed state, always seemed to be tilted into the tiniest smile. He seemed warm, genuine. I shook the feelings of trust away and stood to look around the room. There was a glass case across the room with antique articles. I made my way over to it.

"Raul—were you born with any of your father's . . . abilities?" I glanced over my shoulder, the cup of steaming coffee warming my palms.

He chuckled. "Far from it. That was Luis. He got most of the magic of the two of us."

I stared into the glass case—and sitting there on the shelf was Lord Buckley's journal. It still glistened with dark magic, the same enchantments twined around it like a thorny vine. "Then why do you have your father's spell book?" I nodded to the case, spinning around to face Raul once more.

He shrugged, not seeming guilty in any way. "He gave it to me. Asked me to look after it. He didn't want it in Luis's hands since in theory Luis could have potentially used some of the spells. He knew I wasn't even powerful enough to open the thing."

"Your father," Damien cut in, "do you know where he is? I would very much like to talk to him about his son's death."

Raul shook his head. "I wish I knew. Even throughout my childhood, he wasn't around much. He would pop in for birthdays and holidays. It wasn't until my mother passed away when Luis and I were twelve that he became a consistent part of our lives. And even then,"—Raul's gaze darkened only slightly, but enough that I noticed—"he was more interested in Luis's powers, and in nurturing them, than he was in me."

"You seem to be well cared for here," Damien said looking around.

"Of course. Father would never outwardly treat us differently—he would never give Luis more money. It was just—how he looked at us. The sorts of attention he gave each of us were different. He gave me the academic attention. Always making sure I had the highest education a boy could need. Luis received the affection. It's hard to explain. But he had so much more time and interest to teach Luis than he had for me. I spent my time building my life as a businessman. Everything I learned was from life experience and books. Everything Luis learned was taught to him by Father."

"One last question," Damien said. "What brought you to Salt Lake City?"

Raul took another long sip of coffee before placing it down on the tray in front of him. "There's so much religion here. So much community—I fell in love with the place. Luis and I grew up in New Orleans, but when I first visited Utah, it just seemed so pure. The complete opposite of the drunken party town I grew up in."

I was still staring into the glass case, when I saw her reflection—the Banshee's. I gasped and swiveled around to find her almost directly behind me. Murky tears cascaded from her eyes. I glanced past her at Damien and Raul, who were still engaged in some sort of conversation. "What is it?" I whispered. "C'mon, speak!" Neither man seemed to hear or notice me talking to nothingness.

She glanced to the door, then back to me again, her eyes widening. My gut wrenched. "Is it Drew?" She didn't respond, but more tears spilled down her cheeks.

"Oh, my Hell," I said, louder than I meant. Both men turned to look at me. I rushed to Damien, grabbing his arm and pulling him to his feet. "I-I just remembered, I have a thing. A meeting. Back at the hotel. We have to go—"

"But—"

"We need to go *now*."

Damien looked at me curiously, but knew better than to argue. "Okay." He nodded and took Raul's hand once again. "Thank you for your time, Mr. Nunez-Buckley. If we have any other questions we'll be in touch. Or if you think of anything that might be relevant, don't hesitate to call." Damien passed him a business card.

"Absolutely," Raul said, taking the card between two fingers. "Ms. Lamb . . . do you have a card as well?"

"Don't push your luck." Damien put his arm around my shoulders and ushered us out into the night.

39

Ireland, 1740

Days had passed since John and I had committed ourselves to a relationship. For the first time in my existence . . . and despite centuries of being alive . . . I felt like a woman. Although we had vampires who did our cooking, I would make the occasional meal for us in the same way a wife would for her husband.

His castle transformed almost immediately into my own home and I moved into his bedroom. As much as I enjoyed the proximity each night, I was restless. Centuries of never sharing a bed made the extra weight on the opposite side jarring. Every stir, every noise he made would wake me.

I walked around the library, running my fingers along the various bindings. Some looked ancient, as though they might disintegrate if I lifted them from the shelves. His journal sat on the same side table, the Bible still beside it.

Afraid to touch it again, I pulled my sleeve over my hand before lifting it. The dark magic still clung to the book, a sparkling web of sorcery. I was able to flip open the cover, but each page was blank. I could tell from the arcane enchantments that they were not really blank—simply locked for no eyes but his own. I went to place the book back down on the table and it slipped from my sleeve. Without thinking, I reached out with my other hand to catch it, my sleeve slipping up past my wrist. The book was hot to the touch, but didn't sizzle against my holy skin as it had several days ago. I gasped and clutched the book in my left hand. I threw it down onto the side table and it sizzled as it came in contact with the Bible. It no longer burned me. . . . Why would a book with dark magic not burn an angel?

I backed away from the room—not even wanting to be in the journal's presence any longer. My back came in contact with someone and I screamed, turning around coming face-to-face with John. I exhaled and placed a hand to my chest. "You startled me."

He smiled warmly down at me and kissed me lightly on the lips. "I'm sorry, angel. I assure you, it was not my intent." He walked into the room past me and picked up the journal, tucking it under his arm. "You were going into the market today, were you not?"

I nodded, rubbing my palms over my arms. "Yes. I would like to get out a bit, I think. We've been cooped up in this house for days."

John wiggled his eyebrows at me, his grin widening. "There's a reason why, you know?" He wrapped an arm around my waist and tugged me in for a kiss, his tongue nudging my lips open. I happily obliged and stroked his tongue with mine.

He released me and brushed his forefinger along my jaw. "I'll miss you. I have to prepare the final spell for tomorrow. The words must be exactly correct or it could be a detriment to the entire operation." He cupped my face with his free hand and tilted my chin up to his. "You ready for this? It will be rather intense."

"I'm ready to defeat Carman. It's well past time."

"It bloody is." He grinned and I flinched at the language. He

gave me an apologetic half-smile. "Sorry. It's a terrible habit. One that's difficult to break." He took my hand in his and placed a soft kiss upon my knuckle. "Enjoy the market. How long do you believe you will be gone?"

I shrugged. "I plan to enjoy the day out. I will be back by dinner time."

He smiled. "Fantastic. I will have Dejan cook up something delicious."

I wasn't at the market for long before I started to miss John. It was amazing how quickly someone could get into your heart. I couldn't go for minutes without seeing something that reminded me of him. I walked along the market, finding a leather-bound journal. I turned it over in my hands and paid the merchant for it. A new journal—for a new life.

I purchased some bread, which was admittedly not the most appetizing looking due to Carman's frost and the lack of grain. The old woman's eyes lit up at the sale and I gave her a little extra for her effort.

I didn't want to purchase anything else, so since there was plenty of time until dinner, I decided to walk home as opposed to teleporting. The cool air felt good as it whipped my hair from the knot at the nape of my neck. And instead of tucking it back away again, I pulled my hair free, letting Carman blow it every which way she pleased.

I approached the castle and the gate creaked open as Ulrich let me in with an acknowledging bow. I smiled as warmly as I could at the beast. The only vampire I trusted in this house was Dejan—and even him I only trusted while John had him under his power. Even if the idea of a coven of hungry vampires terrified me, I trusted that John knew how to control them. Despite their thirst.

I could feel the vampire's eyes following me as I made my way to the house. I opened the door to home. My home. My cas-

tle. The thought was a strange one. "John?" I called out. "I'm back early." No one answered, so I skipped into the kitchen to put the bread away. Dejan was there, stirring a pot over the fire.

He bowed when he saw me, his eyes dropping to the scant loaf of bread in my basket. "You do know, m'lady, that we make our own bread here."

I shrugged and handed him the basket. "I know. But the folks at market so desperately need our support."

Dejan's mouth twitched into a barely there smile, and his throat rasped as though he were parched. "That's very kind of you."

I narrowed my eyes, my gaze drifting to his mouth and throat. "You are thirsty," I stated. It wasn't a question.

"I am always thirsty, m'lady." He turned away from me, away from my stare.

"Yes, but you are particularly thirsty today. I can hear it in your voice. How long has it been since Lord Buckley allowed you to feed?"

Dejan checked on the pot of boiling water over the fire—even though we both knew it needed no such attention. "Who can keep track anymore?" he whispered and I wasn't sure the response was even meant for me.

I turned out of the kitchen. John had to let them feed. I could convince him, I thought with a smile, running my hand over the curve of my waist. I was certain of that. Besides, they needed to be strong for our battle with Carman tomorrow. Tomorrow. It was hard to believe it was already time to take her on.

I climbed the stairs and peeked my head into John's study. Empty. I moved along the hallway, hearing some noise from the boudoir. Not our boudoir—but my old boudoir, the one I had stayed in prior to John and myself consummating our relationship. The door was only slightly ajar and I pressed my palm to it. It silently opened a few inches, opening just enough that I could see a sliver of the bed. A woman I had never seen before lay in my bed, her perky breasts and tight nipples heaving with her moans.

John's face was between her legs, his bare backside in the air. He moaned against her dark curls and her face twisted, legs wrapping around the back of his neck.

I fell back against the wall, unable to look anymore. Their pleasurable moans still flooded my ears and I placed two hands over them to drown out the noise. I should have felt something, right? Anything? A gut-wrenching pain? But I felt nothing. Absolutely numb. I walked slowly back down the stairs, leaving the journal on his desk in the study before walking out the front door. I made my way to the gate, where Ulrich bowed once more and let me out.

Numb. My arms and legs felt disconnected from the rest of my body. I knew I was walking but with no intentional direction to go in. The sun was starting to dip below the horizon and I found myself outside of mine and Julian's headquarters. The little cottage outside of town where up until recently we had been tending to the ill.

The door swung open; he had sensed my presence almost immediately. And he knew. With one look at my face, he cradled me in his arms and all sensation came back with his hug. My feet, my hands, my fingers and toes. They were all there again and my heart—my throbbing heart stabbed with pain.

We stood there in silence until I finally pulled away from his hold, looking up into those soft, blue eyes. "Why would he betray me?" My voice cracked as I asked.

Jules regarded me a moment before answering, eyes flitting over my face. "He had nothing to lose. His soul already had a black mark on it."

"What?" My throat was dry and the word could barely escape through my parched lips. "You knew he had a black mark and didn't tell me?"

Julian's eyebrows dipped into a scowl and he stepped back. "I tried to warn you. I told you to get the blessing from San Michel."

"You did everything except come out and tell me the truth! You knew I wouldn't give my—my heart to someone who was destined for Hell!" With my palms to Julian's chest, I pushed with all my might. He stumbled back, but in a controlled way. As if he had known that was exactly what I would do.

"I could not physically tell you anything about Lord Buckley!" he yelled, spinning back into my personal space. "I tried, but I couldn't. But I did my best to warn you. This was your choice, not mine. Don't blame your indiscretions on me."

"You could have tried harder." A single tear rolled down my cheek. "You began with all this talk of love and angels having the ability to-to—"

"Because I thought you were finally acknowledging us." He was back to his calm self. No longer yelling, he was cool as he turned to straighten the room, tidying what sparse items we had in there. "Go home, Monica."

"W-what? This is my home!"

"Not at the moment, it isn't." He turned to face me from the other side of the room. "We have a job to finish. No matter what happened between you and Buckley, you need to stay on his good side until Carman is defeated." Before I knew it, Julian was in front of me once more, nose to nose. "Go. Home. Act as though nothing happened."

My tears were cold as they rolled down my cheeks. I backed away from Julian—my angel. My friend. The person I most trusted in this world. And even he was using me. Angels were supposed to put humanity before themselves. It was a fact I knew, and yet, I had never before seen it in action when it affected me so greatly. Julian didn't love me enough to defy his angelic position.

"You didn't love me enough," I whispered and with a crack and a heavy heart, I teleported back to the manor. The table *was already set for supper and Lord Buckley trotted down the stairs to greet me with a kiss on the cheek. "You're tardy, I see. No bother. Run up and change. Dejan will keep supper on the fire a little longer."*

He grinned at me in that boyish, lopsided way again. It took all my effort not to grimace. Instead, I walked steadily up to our boudoir to dress for dinner. My limbs, once again numb.

40

Damien raced us back to the hotel in record time, swinging wildly into a parking spot near the front. Before his car was even in park, I was hopping out and running through the front doors.

I rushed for the elevators, pressing the button again and again as though that would help the car come faster. After a few seconds, I abandoned the elevator, making a run for the stairs.

"Monica!" Adrienne's voice echoed in the lobby and I halted mid-sprint, turning to look for her.

She was standing in the middle of the lobby, hands out at her sides as if saying, *What the fuck?*

I ran toward her. "Where's Drew?" I called out.

"He's right over there." She gestured flippantly to the restaurant right off the lobby. "We saw you charge through here like a bat out of . . . well, you know."

"Oh, my Hell." I collapsed against the wall. "He's okay? Nothing's wrong?"

"He's fine. . . . We're just having a late dinner. What happened?"

"I-I saw the Banshee," I gasped, catching my breath as I bent over with my hands on my knees. "And I c-could have sworn Drew was in danger."

Damien came running up behind Adrienne. "Goddamn, Mon. Everything okay in here?" He looked to Adrienne, who nodded.

"Of course he's fine. What do you think, I can't do a simple protective detail?"

Damien chewed the inside of his cheek and put a hand on my shoulder. "See? He's fine."

"I want to see him for myself," I said, glaring at Adrienne.

She rolled her eyes. "Fine. Let's go."

We headed to the restaurant, where I saw Drew staring at us through the window in front of their table.

As we walked, Adrienne talked behind me, more to Damien, I believe. "You're telling me that she's the only one who can see this fairy of death? All we're going on with this is Monica's interpretation of some red-headed hag?"

"I know what I saw, Adrienne. Drew is a target. And being that he's *your* boyfriend, I'm surprised that you're not more concerned by this."

Her sigh was exaggerated and audible from behind me. "It just seems a little—excessive, that's all I'm saying."

"I'm glad to hear you say that," Damien said, looking through his phone and checking an email. "I got a call from Andowe just now. He wants us to pay a visit to Sonja's ex-boyfriend. Tonight would be preferable."

"What?" I hissed, spinning to face them. "You can't leave Drew here alone. It's not safe."

"We won't leave him alone." Damien slid a hand around my waist and pushed me along. "You'll keep an eye on him, right, Monica?"

Adrienne clicked her tongue and Damien flicked a glance back to her. "That would be okay, right, Adrienne?"

"Oh, sure. Just peachy."

"That is, if you think you can handle it, babe?"

"Don't be stupid. Of course I can handle it." But as I looked through the window at Drew, that little gnawing in my gut was unsettling.

After Drew finished his meal, we were back in his room watching television. "You know"—he cleared his throat—"you really don't have to stick around with me. I'll probably just pass out."

I shrugged knowing this would be the hardest part—convincing him to let me stick around while Adrienne and Damien were out. He was spread out on one bed and I was on the other with my back propped against the headboard. "I know—but what else would I be doing back in my room? I'd just be watching the exact same TV as you are. . . ."

"Really?" he said, glancing at me with a smile. "You'd be watching *American Choppers*?"

"Um, yeah. I love a good hog." My face split into a smile and Drew's grin widened.

"You always were a terrible liar." He laughed and threw a pillow, which I caught between two hands. I tossed the pillow behind my back for extra support.

"Okay, fine. I wouldn't be watching this exactly. But I'd just be in my room watching *something*." He shook his head, directing his focus back to whatever American flag motorcycle they were building this time. "You ever ridden on a bike?" Drew asked.

I nodded. "A few times. It was fun. Cold . . . but fun."

"Yeah, that's part of the reason why that crowd wears so much leather."

I snuck another glance at Drew's face. He was unshaven, reddish stubble peppering his jaw and chin. He looked relaxed around me for the first time in months. Granted, a large part of that reason was probably that we were on separate beds. But still. It was a nice change.

"So." He cleared his throat. "You and Damien, huh?"

I could hear the pain in his question and it made my stomach twist. But then again, he was the one who had made his choice. He'd chosen the angel. I nodded. "Yeah. Me and Damien," I answered even though I wasn't even sure if I was speaking the truth. We'd hooked up once. In our worlds, that does not make a relationship. Not even close.

Drew played with the drawstring on his hoodie and put on a brave smile. "That's good. I like Damien—he's a good guy."

The lump caught in my throat. Drew's acceptance was like the final dagger in our chance for love. The fact that he wasn't even going to fight for me.

"Yeah," I whispered. "He is a good guy."

"I mean, he's still not good enough for *you,*" Drew added quietly, looking up from his hands to meet my eyes. "But he's better than most of the assholes I see you with."

Warmth swelled in my chest and I tried to surreptitiously wipe away an errant tear that sprung from my leaky eyes. "Monica." Drew swung his legs over the side of the bed so that he was sitting up. "If he makes you happy, why are you crying?"

His green eyes burned into mine and I bit my lip to stop the cascade of tears from spilling over my cheeks more than they already had. "Because I miss you," I whispered. "I miss my best friend."

I closed my eyes and heard rather than saw him come over to the bed I was on. I felt the weight as he sat next to me. Felt his arm slide around my shoulders and pull me into his strong chest. His stubble pricked into my face as he held me close and I didn't mind the scratchiness of it one bit. "I miss you, too," he whispered. "You're going to come back and work at the coffee shop after all this, right? I mean, you didn't really quit, did you?"

I swallowed and nuzzled into his chest more, shrugging beneath his warm hands. "I don't know. I have to think about it. We may be better off not working together every day. It doesn't mean I wouldn't still be your number-one customer. . . ."

"For my sake, I hope you stay."

I shrugged again. "I might. But I should start thinking more long-term."

He sighed. "You know—I've been debating selling the cafe."

That caught my attention. I jolted up, staring at him, my mouth gaping open. "What? That's . . . that's crazy. You love that place!"

With his thumbs, he brushed away my stray tears and angled my chin to look at him. "I love the community. I don't know that I love the business. Hell." He chuckled. "I don't even really like coffee all that much. Besides"—his voice was barely a whisper—"if you're no longer there, it won't feel the same, anyway." He looked down and smiled. "You know," he said with a sigh, "I've always wanted to see Alaska. It's been a dream of mine to live way out there. I love the snow—damn, but I hate Vegas heat. I hate crowded cities."

"So, why not? Why don't you go?"

Drew shrugged, a wistful look creeping along his features. "Adrienne hates the cold."

I decided to let that one go and instead nuzzled closer, enjoying the closeness after feeling stripped of our friendship for so long. "What have you been doing here during the days while we were all working this case?"

I felt his eyes roll. "God. I feel like I've done everything this city has to offer. I've been hiking, rafting. Saw the sites, saw the town. There's a great bookstore you'd love. I'll take you there tomorrow—if you have time, of course."

I nodded. "I bet I can make time."

There was another pause before he interrupted the silence again. "Monica, what's going on lately? I know I'm not a 'consultant' like you or a detective like Adrienne and Damien, but . . ." He trailed off and sighed. His chest rose and fell from beneath my cheek. "Something's up. I know it. And I can't help but feel like everyone's keeping some huge secret from me."

I pulled back and looked up into his green eyes. They regarded me with warmth, but also skepticism. As though he might not believe whatever was next to come from my mouth. Could I tell him? I know it's against every rule Saetan and Mia, Queen of the Succubi, have set up for us . . . but he was surrounded by all of us so much more than most humans were. I opened my mouth, not knowing what exactly I was about to say.

The door pounded on the other side, making us jump apart. Drew swiped a hand down his face, guilt weighing heavy in his features. He stood, walking over to the door.

"Wait." I held out a hand to stop him, grasping for his wrist. "Don't answer that!"

"Why not?"

Why not? A damn good question . . . one I didn't have an answer for.

"Monica!" Kayce's voice on the other side of the door made my heart jump into my throat.

Drew gestured to the door. "See? It's just Kayce."

"No!" I whispered, squinting my eyes closed. She could of course hear everything on our side of the door. "Drew, don't let her in here," I whispered as quietly as I could, crossing my fingers that maybe she didn't hear that. I could easily be overreacting about the phone call I'd heard, but my trust with her was waning. She was the last person I wanted to see at the moment.

He rolled his eyes, ignoring me. "Monica, don't be ridiculous." He took the chain off the door and it swung open. Kayce's eyes flashed with anger as she looked around the room, gaze landing on me. She looked as though she could have spit bullets right into my skull.

"Oh, hey, Kayce." I did my best to put on a casual smile.

" 'Oh, hey?' " she mimicked. "Are you fucking serious? Why didn't you want him to open the door."

I glanced from her to Drew and back again. "We were . . . having a moment."

Drew looked at me with wide eyes, mouth gaping open at me. "We were . . . uh . . ." He coughed into his fist, not daring to meet either of our eyes. "Uh . . . well, that is we were . . ."

"Oh, my god," Kayce said, rolling her eyes and slamming the door behind her. "I don't give a shit that you two were about to make out or *whatever*." Her head snapped to look at me. "I need to talk to you. Now."

"Yeah, Kayce . . . this really isn't a good time."

"Why not?" Drew butted in. "We're just watching TV."

My teeth ground together. Why did he always have to stick his nose where it didn't belong?

"Besides"—Kayce held up Aaron's iPad in her hand—"this is kind of important."

"Fine," I said, falling onto the bed. "But we'll talk in here."

"Okay." Kayce hesitantly took a seat on the bed across from me, glancing at Drew.

He cleared his throat, obviously feeling the tension between us. "Okay. Well, I'm just going to hop in and take a quick shower while you two . . ." His words faded; then he rolled his eyes and headed for the bathroom. ". . . do whatever it is you're going to do."

Kayce tossed the iPad on the bed between us. "I decoded the message. Not that you even *deserve* my help."

"Excuse me? What are you talking about?"

"You went through my things, Monica." Kayce's eyes narrowed and her voice held venom that sent a shiver down my spine. She sounded more than angry. She sounded . . . deadly. "And I couldn't help but thinking . . . why would my best friend be snooping in my bags?"

"Can we just talk about the message first?" I swallowed and swiped my finger across the iPad screen.

"Oh, sure. Whatever Queen Monica wants." Kayce yanked the iPad from my grip.

"Hey—!"

"It was easy to decode. This guy's a moron. Probably the worst assassin they could have chosen, lucky for you." She shoved the iPad back into my hands with one eyebrow raised. "Once I figured out his code, I plugged the sequence into my program and it decoded the message for me."

"Thanks," I mumbled, looking down at the screen. "So, what is it?"

Kayce shrugged. "Not sure . . ."

"It looks like a poem . . . a weird poem. 'Shriek and toil and burn and snare; eye of toad and newt's mad glare. When you look around and find, your actions will forever bind. Take care and when foils foe; you will burn, your innards glow.' " I felt the magic winding around my tongue, taking hold of my breath and seeping out of my body. "Oh, shit."

"Right?" Kayce exclaimed. "That was like the worst fucking poem ever. God, this guy is stupid in so many ways."

"It wasn't a poem," I whispered, bringing my fingers to my lips, which still tingled. "It was a spell." A spell I had just completed in some way or another.

I braced myself for what was to come. Something magical—a pop or a crack signaling that whatever I had read aloud had changed anything in my existence. But nothing happened. The room was filled with silence; dead air hung around us.

"So what?" Kayce said, her voice filled with annoyance. She

was getting to her breaking point—I knew the sound. And the feeling. "It's not like either of us can activate it."

"Yeah," I answered, my body feeling numb. I didn't seem to have spurred anything from the spell and after another moment of sitting in silence waiting for something—anything—to happen, I breathed easier. "Yeah, you're right." I looked back down at the iPad. "Pretty lame spell. They're so much better when they're in the ancient language."

Kayce rolled her eyes. "Tell me about it. Aaron is such a loser anyway. I can't believe you were about to sleep with him."

I shrugged. "It never happened or anything."

"Still." Kayce's lip curled.

"How do you know so much about him?" I asked cautiously.

She was silent for a second before answering. "We run in similar businesses."

"You mean, you run in the same business."

Kayce dropped her hands in her lap and they hit her jeans with a slapping sound. Outside, thunder rolled in the distance and wind whipped against the window. "What are you talking about? You know my job is secretive." She lowered her voice, placing a hand on my knee. It took all of my power not to recoil from her touch. Everything about my best friend seemed so disingenuous now. "It's for your own safety. The less you know the better. Seriously, Mon."

I didn't mean to do it, but her words made me flinch and she pulled her hand back, anger hardening her face. "What? What is it, Monica? Grow a pair and tell me what's bothering you."

My throat felt tight, constricted. Talking without crying was going to be a feat. With a deep breath, I steadied myself for a fight. "The phone call earlier," I said quietly, but with no less venom in my words. "I listened in." I narrowed my eyes at her, to which she twitched her head to the side.

"Okay . . ."

"And it sounded an awful lot like you were here for your own hit."

"You know I have a wild job. This is not new information."

"Yes, but . . ." After another deep breath, I forced the tension to release from my shoulders. "Everything in your bag is exactly what Aaron also had. And it makes me wonder if you were sent to complete the job he couldn't finish."

Kayce's eyes widened and her mouth rounded into an O. I had rendered her speechless. For the first time since I'd known the girl, Kayce had nothing to say to me. "Monica, no—" She reached out a hand to grab mine and I wrenched it back.

"Don't!" I held up a hand, palm out as another thunder clap echoed outside. "Don't *touch* me."

Kayce held both hands out in front of her as though I were holding her at gunpoint. "Okay. Okay, I won't touch you. I promise. But Monica, this is not what you think . . . just ask Lucie—"

Drew came out of the bathroom wearing a T-shirt and workout pants. He rubbed a towel through his hair and flung it over his shoulders. "Sounds like we're in for one Hell of a storm, huh?" he said, looking up and finding Kayce and me in a standoff.

He paused, staring at each of us. "Did I—did I interrupt something?" he asked, clearly already knowing the answer. "No," I said, not daring to remove my eyes from hers. "Kayce was just leaving."

"I'm *not* leaving. . . ."

"Yes, you *are*!" I shouted in response.

Another louder thunder clap sounded outside and the wind blew the window open, whipping the curtain around in a frenzy. Rain splattered inside, and both Drew and I rushed to the window to close it.

The magic slapped into me before I knew it was coming. I

could see the tendrils of the arcane spinning through the room and Kayce was pinned to the wall by the force of the wind.

The curtain ripped from its fixture and wrapped around Drew, tying him in place. I raced to push the window closed and it wouldn't budge from beneath my hands. Outside, standing in the grass below, I saw the Banshee looking up at me and crying. Her jaw unhinged and she let out a scream. I covered my ears and bent at the waist until the shrill sound ended. When I opened my eyes, a man stood before me.

I froze, the wind whipping my hair every which way, and he smiled in a way that was anything but friendly. "I know you," I whispered, eyes widening. He touched my forehead and everything went black.

41

Ireland, 1740

I set my fork down beside my plate of meat and potatoes and folded my hands in my lap.

"You hardly touched your supper, angel. Are you ill?"

I shook my head, not raising my eyes just yet. I didn't trust my body's response to making eye contact with the man.

"Just . . . nervous about this evening. When did you say we are to begin?"

"Soon, I believe. We are waiting on . . . well, on a signal from a silent partner."

This made my head snap up to lock eyes with him. "Shouldn't Julian and I be privy to all the information regarding this battle? Or is there a motive behind keeping us in the dark?"

He looked visibly hurt and shocked by my reaction. Standing, he wiped his mouth with his napkin before walking to my side of the table. "Monica, my angel, what in Heaven is the matter? You know that there are aspects to my work you as an angel should not know of. It would be detrimental to your status."

I sneered at that. As if he gave any consideration to my sta-

tus. He brushed a finger across the top of my cheekbone. I swallowed, forcing myself not to flinch at his touch. "Monica—what is it?"

Pebbles from outside slapped against the window and I startled at the sound. Jumping up to see what was out there, I saw nothing but darkness and the vampires standing guard.

Lord Buckley's eyes flashed. "It is time."

Within minutes, we had all congregated in an enclosed room within the manor. Julian refused to meet my eyes and instead stared at the floor. I looked around the room that I had never before been witness to.

Lord Buckley, Dejan, Julian, and myself all stood in a circle. "We are to do this together. Each plays an integral role in this evening's summonings. Angels—you are to keep watch, and while I know you mustn't interfere, before we begin, I need your word that I am protected."

Julian nodded. "You have my word. The council has approved and we may fight if Carman is not yet imprisoned and it appears as though she may escape. That is the best we can offer."

"Dejan," Lord Buckley said, "bring the sacrifice. Be quick with it." The room was empty except for one wooden chest, which John opened, pulling out stones and salt. With a stone the size of his palm in one hand, he drew three circles along the smooth stone floor, and covered the lines with salt.

Lord Buckley met Julian's gaze and gave a nod, which Julian returned with a scowl. The tension among all of us was a palpable fourth party in the room. A knock at the door sounded, and Dejan entered with Ainsley tethered behind him.

"Wh-what is Ainsley doing here?" I asked, my eyes wet and wide. They shot from Dejan to John. No one answered me, but Julian's large hands on my shoulders were meant to be reassuring. I shrugged them off. "Answer me!" I stepped into Lord Buckley's chest and stared up at him, my face flaming.

"Angel, we must spill the blood of an innocent creature. Un-

less you wish that creature to be human—an animal must be sacrificed."

"Not this one. It doesn't have to be Ainsley."

"Enough!" His lips pressed together and his face hardened in a way that I hadn't seen before. "Step back, angel.*" It was the first time he had called me "angel" in a way that was meant to be anything other than loving.*

"No!" I cried, the tears streaming down my face one after another and falling onto Ainsley's wool. She bleated and pulled back. Dejan held her reins firmly in place, but I could feel her fear. I placed my hand on her nose and kissed her head—my touch having an immediate calming effect on her.

Julian pulled me off of her, and I forced myself to stand tall beside my angel counterpart.

"Let Buckley do this," Jules said. "Your sheep will save thousands."

Lord Buckley grabbed Ainsley's reins and tugged her toward the first circle with little regard for her fear. He had claimed this was his favorite sheep. There were several down in the stables. Why not one of them? Why Ainsley?

She bleated, her eyes wide and terror gleaming in the reflection of the knife John held. He slit into her front leg, letting the blood spill inside the circle. He moved the next with the same action. Her pain echoed in the empty, cavernous room and I covered my ears with my hands. On the third circle, he slit her neck, dropping her convulsing body into the circle with little regard for her life. Dejan handed him a rag, licking his lips and eyeing the spilled blood as a man eyes his bride on their wedding night. Lord Buckley wiped the blood from his hands as though nothing had happened. It was the same way he had wiped his hands after finishing supper.

"Oh, Ainsley," I whispered as her twitching body drained of the last bit of life.

With palms in the air, Lord Buckley whispered incantations.

A strange language I'd never before heard and the circles lit with fire. The room hummed with his magic and Dejan held the journal from the library at John's eye level. For the most part, Lord Buckley needn't even look at his notes. But now and then his eyes would flutter open and scan the page before him.

The wind swirled around us, smelling of frost and death. Ainsley's blood filled the air with its copper scent and I laced my fingers together, squeezing tightly as a reminder to breathe.

The air fizzled and popped around us, and I blinked as two men materialized before us and flickered in the center of their separate circles. The first was thin and wiry with long black hair that flowed beyond his shoulders and came to a widow's peak at the center top of his forehead. A scowl marred the space between his dark eyes and his cheekbones were high and defined.

The second man had dark hair and eyes as well, only was of stronger build. Olive, tanned skin and hair that fell in waves to just below his chin. While the first man flung himself at an invisible wall enclosing the circle, the second stood, simply staring out at each of us, like a caged animal preparing for its attack.

"What comes next?" I asked Jules.

"I'm not positive; however, I believe once Carman arrives, he will have to hold the bindings tight. If any of them get out, he will have to kill them. And we will have to help."

"Who are they?"

"Carman's sons, Dub and Dother. She has one other, who supposedly has nothing to do with this frost."

"Aren't we interfering if we fight?"

"Not if their attack physically comes first. Which it will."

"But what—"

"Monica," Jules whispered, closing his eyes. "Shhh."

Resenting being shushed, I reluctantly turned my attention back to the summoning. Lord Buckley had both hands in the air, palms facing out to the circles. Sweat was dripping down his temples and his features twisted as though he were in pain. The words grew louder off his lips and in the center circle, a woman began to appear. I could see through her at first. Her body was tall and thin, a similar body type to the first man who had appeared. But her face—it was the face of the second man. Its heart shape accentuated her high cheekbones. Her eyebrows were perfect arches over two sparkling, silver eyes. Dark hair fell to her waist in large, full curls, and though her skin was pale, it had that same olive tone to it that her sons bore.

A flash of red caught my eye in the corner of the room. Standing and watching the display was the Banshee, and a breath caught in my throat.

Julian gave my arm a squeeze. "I see her, too, this time. I think we all can."

"You can see the Banshee?" I repeated and felt his nod in response.

"No!" Carman shrieked and pointed to the Banshee. "You, out! Out of this place!" She fell to her knees and raised two hands to the ceiling. Veins corded her neck, the muscles so tense they appeared as though they might burst through her skin at any moment.

The larger son's eyes fell on me, and a smirk tugged at one side of his mouth.

The ground below us started quaking as Carman threw a blast of her magic with the elements in our direction. A rumbling sound groaning from deep in the Earth. Lord Buckley stumbled, losing his footing and his focus for all of a second—but a second too long.

The bindings around the circles faltered and Carman, along with Dub and Dother, charged us. Carman ran to Lord Buckley first and raised her hands to his stomach region, a bolt of lightning sizzling from her fingertips.

Julian pushed me aside, running to step in front of Carman's attack. With Julian as his shield, Lord Buckley rushed to help

Dejan, who fought Dub, the lankiest son. His teeth were bared, and in a crouched position, they circled each other.

Wind swirled around me and I ran to escape it, only to find the tunnel of gusts followed me. Dother, the muscular son, grabbed me by the throat, lifting me off my feet and slamming me into the wall. I looked around the room, and the Banshee walked between us all, staring mostly at me. Jules fought Carman and rain poured from the ceiling. Dejan and John almost had Dub in a hold.

Angels couldn't die. I knew that rationally and yet in the moment, panic and fear convulsed through my body. With a rabid scream, I pushed him off of me, clawing at the hands that surrounded my throat.

He fell back, startled, and I pounced on top him, my power far outweighing his— something he couldn't have expected of an angel. For they knew we were to not interfere in their affairs, yet here we were defending the lives of a sorcerer and a vampire.

I flipped him onto his stomach and shoved my knee into his lower back. Fisting a handful of hair, I slammed his head into the floor. Blood splattered against the stone tile and trickled out from beneath him. He grunted, still alive. We were supposed to take them alive, not dead. Angels did not murder.

I looked to my left, where Lord Buckley had a knife to Dub's throat. "Enough!" His voice boomed over the battle. Dub gurgled something and Dejan tightened his hold on the man. "Carman," Lord Buckley said, and his voice had a calmness to it that was chilling. "If you wish your son to continue living, get back to the circle."

Carman advanced toward Lord Buckley, who dug the knife into Dub's arm. He screamed in pain, writhing against Dejan's hold. Dother struggled beneath me and I grunted while tightening my hold.

"No!" Carman shrieked. The rain above us came to an immediate halt.

"Next will be his throat," Lord Buckley growled. "Back in the circle now. I will not ask again."

Carman's eyes spilled over with tears as she darted a look back and forth between her sons. The wind died down in the room and her arms lowered to her sides. "You will keep your word." It was a statement more than a question.

Lord Buckley nodded one time only in a staccato movement. "You have my word."

With her chin high in the air, she strolled back into the center circle, slowly spinning back to face us. "Very well." She looked at each of her boys. "S'agapo," she said and placed a palm to her heart.

Lord Buckley nodded. He looked at both Dejan and me. "Hold them steady until it is time to throw them into the circle."

"Yes, sir," Dejan rasped and I simply nodded. Dother looked up at me through the corner of his eyes. I quickly looked away, unable to hold his gaze much longer.

With hands in the air, outstretched toward Carman, Lord Buckley began his incantations once more. The air hummed, and as he finished, the room stilled once more.

"The circle is closed," Lord Buckley whispered. "All that is left is to banish her."

Julian's gaze lowered, and he glanced at John through the corner of his eyes. "Well, then, what are you waiting for?"

Carman glared at Lord Buckley, eyes blazing. "Let my boys go. I did as you asked."

The Banshee's scream echoed through the room; her jaw unhinged, she looked to the ceiling like a wolf howling at the moon.

"No," Carman whispered, her face dropping as though she could see into the future.

Lord Buckley darted to Dub, sinking his knife into his chest and tearing it down to his belly button. Dub's screams combined with the Banshee's as his innards oozed from his body. Dejan's mouth trembled and he dropped the body, stepping back from the blood pooling at his feet.

"M-my lord," he rasped, smelling the blood that stained his fingers.

"Out!" Lord Buckley commanded. Dejan's eyes rippled with red, but he obeyed the orders, rushing out of the room.

Carman shrieked from her circle, falling to her knees crying. "You will pay! You will all pay!"

"Monica," Lord Buckley yelled. "Bring me Dother!"

"Monica, no!" Julian shouted at the same time.

Lord Buckley charged us both, knife in hand still dripping blood. He was fast—but I was much faster. I stood, taking Dother with me, and tossed him into his circle, standing as a shield in front of it in case Lord Buckley got any ideas about opening the circle again.

Julian exhaled in relief behind him, but John's face was stern. Beyond angry. Not that I cared in the least. Nothing about this man was loveable anymore.

"Why did you disobey me?" he snarled, raising a hand to slap me. Again, I was faster and caught his palm in mine, bending his arm backwards. I could have kept going. I could have bent it until I heard a pop. But I didn't. Instead, I let him go, throwing him across the room.

"Perhaps you could have spared Ainsley. Another sheep—one that was not a pet to me. Or," I added more quietly, "perhaps if you had had the ability to be faithful, just for the small amount of time it took for you to use me—perhaps then I would have 'obeyed' you." I spat the word obey as an insult to his face. His eyes widened as I strolled over to him coming in closely. "Was she delicious?"

"Angel—" he started and I cut him off.

"Don't call me that."

"Monica," he tried again. "Part of the ingredients for this spell—for an angel unknowingly to spill holy tears onto the sacrificial lamb. I needed Ainsley specifically for this."

Again, he had used me. He had orchestrated a relationship between Ainsley and me for the sole purpose of slaughtering her. The news ripped my soul apart.

I spun and walked to the other side of the room again, glad not to hear his footsteps behind me.

His throat cleared and he moved to the center of the room. "I'll deal with you later, Monica. For now, I have to finish what we started. And fix your stupid mistake." With a rag, he wiped off the knife. "The circles are closed and shall not be opened again unless by the council."

"Finish the banishment, John." I would not refer to his title in this moment. He was no lord to me.

"With my blood. It is the only way to banish—by using the blood of the sorcerer who created the circle." He dug the knife into his palm and scarlet tears oozed from the fresh wound.

Carman and Dother stood staring at each other, hands against the invisible wall as though they were palm to palm. "Do not worry, Mother," Dother whispered. "Dub shall be avenged."

John flicked his blood onto each circle, and the ground below them opened into a dark hole. They, along with the circle of salt and fire and blood, disappeared into the floor.

42

My eyes blinked open, a hanging orb of light swinging above me. It flickered as though the lightbulb might go out at any moment. My tongue felt fuzzy and my head pounded.

Drew was lying to my left, his feet and hands bound together and his eyes closed. I wanted to reach out and touch his face, feel that stubble beneath my hands once more. When I shifted to move, my hands were bound, too. I looked down; only the ropes tying me were entwined with magic. I struggled against them anyway in a futile effort to twist my hands out of their hold. On a frustrated exhale, I let my head fall back to the stone floor.

The room was dark and a bit musty. Brick covered the lower half of the walls, and then white paint took the other half up to the ceiling. One sliver of a window was at the top, revealing the night sky. We were in a basement. Chalk circles that looked erased and drawn again several times over covered the cement floors.

That face—the man who had appeared—he had been so familiar, but I couldn't place him exactly. Dark hair and dark eyes. Strong build. Olive skin. I squeezed my eyes tight. *Think, Monica, think!*

I pulled at the bindings, whispering an incantation. I felt the magic leave my tongue, but the spell binding my hands was too strong. Drew stirred beside me, turning onto his back. A goose egg swelled near his temple and a trickle of blood oozed out a small cut at the crest.

My spell might not break my bindings, but it could sure as Hell untie Drew! It wouldn't mean jack shit if he wasn't awake, though.

"Drew," I whispered, sliding my body over to his. "Drew!" I said more urgently, though still quietly this time. I nudged him with my knees.

He moaned and his head turned toward me, eyes fluttering open. "Monica?" he responded in a most groggy state.

"Yes, Drew! Open your eyes. Look at me." His eyelids were heavy, but he was focusing on my face.

"Wh-what happened?" He rolled his shoulders to move his hands, only to be met with the rope. "What?" His voice was panicked and he started pulling at his hands and thrashing around on the floor.

"Drew! Stop, quiet!" The last thing we needed was for the man to come back down here. "Drew!" I threw my body on top of his and our torsos connected, my nose touching his. "Stop. We can get out of this, but you need to be calm. Okay?"

He panted from below me, but nodded. "Why are we here? What's happening?"

"I don't know yet. But we've been kidnapped . . . for something."

"*Something*? That's all I get? I'm hit over the head and tied up in some cult's basement and I still can't get any answers out of you." He shook his head and looked up to the ceiling. "Ridiculous."

"Look, Drew, I don't *have* answers right now, okay?"

He turned his head toward me again. "And if you did, you would tell me everything, right?" I stayed silent and he rolled his eyes, turning away from me again. "That's what I thought."

"I think I can get you untied. But, if I hear him coming again, I'll have to at least make it look like you're tied up again. Okay? When I get you out of the ropes, check the window." I nodded my head to the window above, and he followed my gaze.

"You think I can fit through that tiny thing?"

I shrugged. "It's worth a try, unless you have any better ideas?"

"Yeah. When I'm untied, I'll undo yours and we can fight this guy off together when he comes down again."

"He's . . . I think he's stronger than you think. I'm not sure we could take him."

"It's worth a shot."

"Only if the window doesn't work. Besides, I don't think you'll be able to untie my ropes. They're, uh, a little more intricate than yours."

"Well, I can't wait to see how you untie me with your own hands bound," he sneered.

"Just—" I took a deep, cleansing breath. "Just try not to freak out, okay?"

He didn't answer, but continued to stare at me with the most annoying look of doubt on his face.

I closed my eyes, focusing all my effort on the ropes around his wrists and ankles. The words flowed from my lips and I imagined them swirling to Drew in a dance. Those words locked around his ropes and loosened them.

"What the Hell?" Drew whispered, and when I opened my eyes, his face was blanched of color and staring at me in horror. "How did you do that?" The ropes hung loosely around his feet and he pulled his hands from the open loops, glancing down at them as though they held the answers.

A lump constricted my throat. "There's a lot to tell you, but now isn't the time. And you will probably see a lot more that seems crazy tonight. Just—try to breathe through it and know that we all love you."

"Huh? We, who?"

"Go check the window. Be careful getting up. It looks like he hit you over the head pretty hard."

"But—"

"Drew! Go!" I nodded to the window, but instead he came to me and knelt by my side.

"Let's untie you first." He reached for the knots around my wrists and I heard a crackle.

He stumbled back on his hands and ass, looking even more horrified than before. "What the—it's like . . . it's like there's some weird sort of . . ."

"Magic," I finished for him and he held my stare.

Jumping to his feet, he rushed the window, checking the edges. "Let's get the Hell outta here, what do you say?"

"Oh, I wouldn't do that if I were you." A deep voice came from the dark stairs. I saw his feet first, bare, with faded jeans rolled a few times above his ankles. I scanned up to his chest—shirtless. He was tanned with just the slightest bit of chest hair sprinkled over his Adonis-like muscles. Dark wavy hair that hung to the middle of his neck in glossy strands.

Drew hesitated for all of a moment before he charged at the man to attack. With a flick of his wrist, a gust of air flung Drew across the room and pinned him to the wall. Drew shouted and writhed against the hold. With a roll of his eyes, the man turned his attention to me, a wry smile curving his lips.

"Recognize me, do you, Monica?"

I stared at him—I did recognize him. But recognition and remembrance were two very different things.

He clomped toward me and even though he was barefoot, his step was so powerful that the ground shook with each movement. "Think back. You of all people should remember me, specifically. We had a very special moment shared between us."

"Monica!" Drew yelled. "Who is this?"

"Dother," I whispered. Carman's son. My body started trembling involuntarily. I thought back to that night—the night we'd captured Carman. Lord Buckley had killed his brother. I shook my head. "But I—but I saved your life."

He snorted at that. "Saved? You fucking imprisoned me. Banished me to the depths of Hell!"

"What the fuck is he?" Drew shouted again, fighting the pressure of the wind holding him against the wall.

Dother rolled his eyes and with another flick of his wrist, the wind swirled around Drew's head until his eyes rolled back and he fell to the ground in an unnatural heap.

"No!" I screamed, fighting my own restraints. "Is he—did you . . ."

"No, no. Calm yourself. He's just passed out." His jaw muscles clenched and released as though he were grinding his teeth.

"But you were banished from this realm! How are you even here?" I struggled against my ropes.

He chuckled, the noise sounding maniacal and distant in my head. "That's the beauty of our world, Monica. I was able to offer my services in ridding this world of you. And poof"—he held up two hands with arched eyebrows and a small smile—"banishment lifted."

"Who? Who lifted it?"

He tutted and stepped even closer. I could have reached out an arm and touched him. He tucked his hands into his pockets and bent at the waist to lean in toward me. "You don't expect me to answer that, do you?"

"No," I said through gritted teeth, "I suspect not."

"So!" He straightened and clapped his hands together, the sudden change in tone and volume causing me to flinch. "Let's get this show started, shall we?"

He turned and, from underneath the stairwell, pulled out a box of items. Beginning with chalk, he drew two circles. Even though he'd just eyeballed them, they were perfect spheres. From the box, he grabbed salt and lined each circle with a thin, perfect pour of salt.

"Why our descendants?" I asked. The more information I had, the easier it would be to stop him. Or at least delay him.

He paused a moment to look at me before he went back to work on the circles. "I could have used all of you. But humans are so much easier to capture and kill. Why make it harder on myself? Besides, you were the only immortal I *had* to capture for this bounty. And I knew that wouldn't be hard. After all—" He stopped and stood straight, his eyes flicking to Drew. "I know your biggest weakness. Hot blondes, right?"

Hope sprang to life in my gut. If Drew was only the lure to capture me, maybe he would be spared. There was certainly no reason to kill him. "So, then, let the human go. There's no point in keeping him if your intent was solely to capture me."

"Don't be ridiculous. He's part of the plan, too." He had a can of lighter fluid in his hands and on top of the salt, he poured a steady stream of liquid around the circle. None of it leaked out and it was far from any walls or wood.

Drew was part of the plan? I squeezed my eyes shut in thought. He had all the descendants, didn't he? There was me, Lord Buckley, Dejan, Julian . . . no one else had been there the night of her capture.

One by one, Dother pulled jars containing blood from the box. Opening each, he poured its contents into the center of only one circle. When all the jars had been emptied, he tossed them back into the box and kicked it back under the stairs.

He whistled. "Here, boy! Baxter, come here!" A wave of nausea hit me as I saw the yellow lab descend the stairs, tail wagging and happy. He sat for Dother, ears perked, tail sweeping across the floor. "Good boy. Stay."

"Oh, Hell," I whispered. I knew that dog. "We're at the—the Morgansons', aren't we?" I thought back to the couple who had found Sonja on the trail and how Mrs. Morganson had clung to the dog's neck in tears.

"Well, done. I followed them home after you and that angel interviewed them."

"Where are they?" Panic rose in my throat like bile. "What did you do with them?"

That same evil smile crept along his face as if he enjoyed every second of this torment. "Let's just say that Baxter here is now an orphan. But not for long—he'll join them soon."

"Why? What did they do?"

Dother shrugged, his eyes dead. "Do? They're only humans. Fuck. Even some angels know how meaningless human existence is."

"But . . . but why Baxter? He doesn't need to be a part of this!"

"I need a sacrifice to complete the circle. Why are you acting as if you know none of this?"

I ignored his question. "You've sacrificed *four* people already! You don't need the dog to complete the circle."

"Not Mother's circle. *Your* circle."

I paused at that, holding his stare, mine equally vicious. "Can you at least untie me?"

His eyebrows arched and a smile twitched at his mouth. "I highly doubt that you would simply sit there and watch as I kill your lover here. The bindings stay."

"Just what do you expect me to do? It's not as if I'm a powerful angel anymore. I suspect these enchantments are all over the house as well?"

He shrugged. "A few."

"So what could I possibly do? You afraid of a little ol' succubus?"

He snorted. "Nice try. You're staying bound."

With an outstretched hand, he snapped his fingers. "Human."

Drew's body, still lying in a heap on the floor, lifted with a gust of wind and was carried to Dother. "Awake," he whispered and the air swirled around his head and into his nostrils.

Drew gasped awake, eyes fluttering, and he looked around, getting his bearings once more. His gaze landed on Dother, eyes pinching together in a scowl. With no warning whatsoever, Drew threw a punch that connected with Dother's jaw. He smiled with the hit as his head snapped to the side. Drew went in for another punch to his stomach, which he quickly dodged, locking Drew's arm behind his back. "You done, human? As if you could fight me," he sniggered.

"Don't hurt Monica," Drew rasped, still fighting Dother's iron-grip hold. "Take me instead and let her go."

"Oh, so chivalrous," Dother said with a dopey smile and an eye roll. "Monica, dearest. I find it hard to believe a demon like you could stomach being around a toothache like this and not get a taste of that sugar."

"How do you know I haven't?"

Dother snorted a laugh. "Your lifestyle choices spread far and wide, my dear."

He tossed Drew into the circle and he landed on his back, head slamming into the cement. I snaked my body over to where Dother stood. He pulled a knife from the back of his pants and, leaning into the circle, swiped at Drew. Drew dodged the hit, backing away just in time. I got to Dother just as he lunged again and sank my teeth into his ankle. His blood pooled in my mouth and he screamed, kicking at my face. I felt my own blood gush from my nose and I sat up, shifting the wounds closed.

When I opened my eyes, Drew was staring at me, jaw dropped. That one second of delay was all Dother needed, and his knife slid across Drew's neck, spurting his blood all over the circle. His body crumpled and Dother laughed as he caught him, pulling him away from the salt ring.

"No! Oh, fuck, Drew," I cried. He coughed and blood ran down his shirt; his head turned to the side, he stared at me, reaching a hand out to mine. I shimmied over to him and the smell of a fire crackled in the air around us. The circle was almost complete. I closed my eyes and incanted a spell. Carman's laugh sounded around me—a noise that made a shiver run down my spine.

I looked into Drew's eyes, repeating the foreign words over and over again. A new ripple of power coursed through me and I licked my lips, still tasting some of Dother's blood. Had I ingested some of his power, too? Drew's wound began to close, starting on either end and slowly stopping the gushing blood. I smiled through a sob and kept repeating the incantation. The cut was almost healed when I looked over to the circle. Dother stood around it with his hands in the air, wind swirling around him, grabbing his hair and blowing it around his face. In the center of the circle, I could see a transparent Carman materializing.

Drew snatched my hand in his, squeezing it, and I met his eyes again. Both filling with tears. "Whatever you are . . . ," he whispered and I put a finger to his lips.

"Sh, don't try to talk."

He shook his head. "Whatever you are . . . it's—it's incredible."

I squeezed my eyes shut and a tear rolled down my cheek landing on Drew's face. "Oh, Drew. You don't know the half of it."

A laugh from the circle brought my attention back. Carman stood in the center, not entirely materialized yet. Wind outside the house howled, and Dother looked around at the ceiling and the one small window.

"He's here, Mother. The prodigal son returns," Dother said with a psychotic laugh.

A clomping sound came from the top of the stairs, where, in a blink, Damien stood at the bottom. He chewed the inside of his cheek, his eyes narrowed, as he scanned the room.

"Ah, Dian!" Dother gestured in an exaggerated welcoming way. "Come, brother. You're just in time."

43

My heart wrenched into my throat. It couldn't be. Not again. I squeezed my eyes shut. The man I'm fucking cannot be here to kill me.

"Let them go, Dother." Damien fisted his hands at his sides, and his cracking knuckles sounded through the room.

Dother cackled. "Dian, you're telling me that you'd choose a human and Hell's whore over family." He put a palm to his chest, his melancholy tone a gross exaggeration. "Over your brother and mother? The woman who is responsible for the magic you use daily?"

"It's Damien. Not Dian. Not anymore."

Dother's eye roll was so big his neck mimicked the movement. "Come now, don't be ridiculous. This ruse you keep up of being human must be growing tedious by now. Masking your powers. Hiding your true nature. Your name . . . your very essence means violence."

Damien snorted. "So, we'll just be one big happy family again, will we? And just how do you plan on completing this circle, Dother? I believe you're missing an important facet."

Dother's smile was tight and thin-lipped. "How could it be missing when it's standing just before me. Besides"—he darted a glance over his shoulder at Drew and me—"I don't know how she saved him, but the human must die."

"As must I, isn't that so?"

"Well"—Dother's voice was a hoarse whisper—"you were the one who arranged for our family's defenses to be down the night of the summoning." They both growled, chests puffed out, ready to strike.

Damien—Dian—whatever—had been part of that night in Ireland centuries ago? I thought back to the start of the evening. The pebbles that had splattered against the window with no one around to have thrown them. Carman wasn't only a sorceress . . . she was an elemental. It made perfect sense, though. She and her sons controlled the elements—the weather.

Dother leapt at Dian, a crack of thunder sounding outside the house, shaking it all around us. Carman stood in the center of her circle, watching. Observing quietly with the smallest pleased smile curving her lips. She was as beautiful as I remembered her to be. A hardened, vicious beauty.

Damien and Dother charged each other, their movements so fast and violent, it was a blur. Wind swirled around the basement, a bolt of lightning striking the stairs, splitting the wood. Baxter yelped and cowered in the corner, shaking.

With the brothers busy fighting and Dother's blood still fresh in my mouth, I attempted another spell to free my hands. The incantation whistled from my lips and lashed at the dark magic binding my limbs. They snapped open and my stomach flipped inside my core. I hated the fact that I had some of Dother's dark magic in me, but fuck if I was going to turn away the help when I needed it most.

I tugged Drew to his feet, his weight not an issue. With his arm around my shoulder, I looked up into his eyes. "C'mon." I ran for the stairs, slowed down by the extra weight on my back. I was still faster than any human but not fast enough.

Without so much as a word, Carman's arms stretched out, aimed directly at us. The wind knocked us backwards, pinning us once again to the wall on the other end of the room.

Kayce ran down the stairs, directly to us, and she was lifted off her feet, back slamming into the ceiling before she was dropped onto the cement floor. Blood splattered from her face, which she quickly shifted away. Carman laughed, her voice cracking with the foreign sound. She lifted and dropped Kayce like she was her own puppet. With a final slap to the floor, Kayce whimpered, still managing to shift her wounds closed. Her limbs trembled as she pulled up to her hands and knees, glancing at me from the floor. "It wasn't what you think," she whispered and even I could barely hear her over the roaring wind around us. "When they contacted me for the hit, Lucien told me to accept. Because we wanted to learn who was behind it."

I nodded at her, unable to say more as the wind swirled around my nose and mouth, sucking all the air from my lungs. I looked to Drew, eyes blinking, fighting to stay conscious.

Adrienne, George, and Raul rushed in, Raul sweating and pale. George shifted into an animal—a tiger—and lunged at Dother, ripping his flesh open. A finger flew across the room and Dother's screams outdid the howling wind. Even Carman, from inside her circle, seemed to be tiring. How long had it been since she had practiced magic? In her imprisonment, magic certainly wasn't allowed.

Dother put George, who was still in tiger mode, in a head lock, cutting off his oxygen, and Carman shot another bolt of lightning to Adrienne, who fell through the cracked stairs.

I had Dother's blood—if I tried, just maybe I could counter her spells. I looked to the fight where Kayce was pinned to the floor. George was flickering back to his human self, exhausted. There just simply wasn't enough energy to feed the power. Dother's eyes flared, angrier than ever, skin hanging open in raw, angry gashes. Blood covering his entire body.

Raul opened a book—John's journal—reciting the spell. I recognized it from long ago. The spell that had initially bound Carman and Dother to their circles. His magic crackled around the existing elements in the middle of a war. He had clearly undersold his abilities. His powers were practiced. Eloquent. The flick of his fingers perfectly sending the magic to the circle. But he was expelling a lot of the force in the spell. He was sweating, his legs trembling, and something flickered around his person. As if he wasn't able to maintain two spells at once, a mask lifted, and quivering behind the beautifully sculpted Cuban face, I could see John. Lord Buckley performing a spell.

I clamped my eyes shut, cursing both Dejan and myself for being so stupid. Of course after a few centuries of practicing magic, he was able to use glamour. There was no twin brother to Luis; it was simply an alias formed to mask Lord Buckley.

Carman's laugh pulled me back to my present situation. Pinned against the back wall with crushing winds sucking the air from my lungs. It would be so easy to give in. I glanced again at Lord Buckley—Raul—and his gaze met mine. He flickered again and his eyes turned from dark brown to green. His mouth twitched into that infamous half-smile that made the stomach acid burn in my guts.

The ancient Indo-European language came easier this time, and against Carman's winds, I raised a hand pointing the elements back to her. The wind caught in my hand and I felt the gust enter my body, rushing through my blood and brain. It was like a hit of ecstasy and I felt invincible. I fell to the floor, landing in a crouch, and Drew crumpled to the ground coughing. Out of the corner of my eye, I saw Adrienne run to Drew, who braced his body around her as she cried into his shoulder, holding him.

Carman's face registered what was happening, and those beautiful Greek features twitched with uncertainty. She darted a glance to Dother, who was still in the throes of battle with Damien. She threw a lightning bolt, which I caught, and it oscillated through me. I chanted the ancient language and threw the elements I had absorbed back to her. Wind and a lightning bolt entered her circle, and she doubled over as the tunnel of air swirled around her, lightning flashing a sliver of light above her head. Using the last of her energy, she calmed the elements, falling forward, hands on knees. She wheezed between her legs, and I, too, was unable to stand any longer. I fell to my knees in an effort to catch my breath. She couldn't keep up. . . . I knew it—she wasn't so practiced anymore.

Drew, Adrienne, and Baxter were in the corner, and Adrienne was applying pressure to Drew's bleeding cuts.

George limped over to me, helping me to my feet as well. The wind still swirled around us from Dother and Damien's fight. Thunder clapped inside the basement.

"I'm okay," I said to George. "Go help Kayce."

"Kayce will be okay. I still have some energy—let's fight," he whispered.

"Don't deplete yourself entirely—"

"I'm not."

He helped me to my feet. When Carman blew another tunnel of wind at us, I managed to hold it at bay.

Damien was bleeding now. His eyes were puffy and red. Lip was split open. And even though Dother was just as bloody, he seemed to have more energy. Their magic still swirled through the basement, but they had resorted to a brotherly fistfight on top of that. Dother circled Damien, arms outstretched. He smiled. "What now, brother? I was attacked by a tiger and still am stronger. Evil wins every time."

Adrienne rushed Dother's back with a flashing speed, launching herself at him. He caught her in a wind tunnel, slamming her body to the ground. I whispered an incantation, lifting her body and bringing her over to George and me. "You okay?" I asked.

She nodded. The wind had been knocked out of her, but she didn't seem to be bleeding.

Drew was on his feet, bracing his body against the wall, he walked over to where we gathered, me still holding Carman's blasts at arm's length. It was getting more and more difficult to hold her powers back. "We need to get Dother into the circle," I whispered quietly, hoping that elementals' hearing was not as good as ours. She nodded and a flash of red caught my eye.

The Banshee! She had been there that night, too. Her murky tears stained her cheeks, and she stood before Drew, hand hovering over his face. "Drew's your descendant," I said, more to myself than anyone. Her head snapped to me, eyes shimmering as much as they possibly could in their milky state. Her face was twisted, and Drew's breathing seemed more labored. The Banshee's chest sobbed, but her tears were a silent wheeze. Slowly this time, slower than I'd ever seen her before, she unhinged her jaw.

"No!" I screamed and she looked to me first.

The distraction was all anyone needed, and a flash of blond hair and muscle ran past all of us. Drew slammed into Dother's body, throwing him into the center of the circle with his mother. The Banshee followed him, her scream shaking the walls of the house.

The ground beneath us trembled, the circle turning into a swirling black hole. I screamed, leaping to jump in after Drew, but Damien caught me around the waist. "Don't be stupid," he shouted.

The ground swallowed Carman, Dother, the Banshee . . .

and Drew. The house was still; all that was left was a singed floor, smoking in a perfect ring.

Adrienne fell to the floor, face dropping into her hands. Her shoulders shook.

"How did that fucking happen?" Lord Buckley—still glamoured as Raul shouted, running over to the circle. "The tears of an angel were needed to banish them to Hell!"

"Oh, no." Adrienne's voice was a whisper. Her cheeks still stained with dried tears. "It was me. I-I cried."

"You cried in the circle?" Lord Buckley rushed to Adrienne, his eyes swirling with anger and authority.

"No!" she countered. "I cried on Drew—but he . . ."

"He ran into the circle," John finished for her. "Angel tears were shed on the sacrificial lamb." His voice was void of emotion.

We all stood around the smoking circle, bleeding, panting, mouths agape. "We've got to get him back," I whispered. "There's got to be a way to get him back!"

"He's in Hell," Damien said, eyes unblinking, staring at the ground.

I advanced on John, grabbing him by the collar of his perfectly starched dress shirt. "Cut the shit, John. Get him back!"

"You can fight me all you want, angel. It won't bring him back." His facade flickered until finally fading, leaving me nose to nose with the man I'd wanted to hunt down and hurt all these years.

"Don't you ever call me angel. I'm not a fucking angel anymore," I spat.

His mouth tilted into a half-smile and I slapped him. My sudden outburst only made his grin widen.

"Monica—" Damien touched my arm, but I just slammed John harder against the back wall.

John took my hands in his, removing them from his lapel and brushing it off as if I had dusty hands that needed to be cleaned.

"Why is it you think I came when I felt the magic in my sector, Monica?" His eyes flashed and he glanced around the room at the other faces surrounding him. "Do you think I cared at all about the lives of any humans? That I cared whether or not Dian was sacrificed by his own brother? I came for *you*."

"You have a funny way of showing love."

He shrugged. "Don't you see? When you were an angel, we could have never been together. But as anything else—" He stepped in closer, my reflection glimmering in his green eyes. They were a similar shade to Drew's, but maybe a touch darker. "I knew Dejan's obsession with you. I knew he would save you back then. As he would save you now. Of course, even I couldn't have anticipated that you would transform into a succubus." John took one more step, his hand outstretched, aimed for my face. "Think of the power couple we could be, Monica."

I flinched away from his touch, stepping back toward my friends. "You can bring Drew back. I know you can. And if you don't know how yet, I will make your existence a fucking misery until you come up with the spell that will save him."

Sorrow twisted John's face for only a moment before he clicked his tongue and rocked back on his heels. "I see," he said. "The funny thing about that . . . is you'll have to find me first. You will come around to me again, Monica." He snapped his fingers—and then he was gone.

44

Ireland, 1740

"Julian." I grasped at his sleeve, tugging him closer to me. "I cannot stay here a moment longer. Please. May we go home?"

His eyes were clamped shut, and on a deep breath, they opened to meet my eye contact. "You cannot. Your home is no longer with me." He swallowed and shifted his gaze to the floor.

It was like a punch in the stomach. All wind was knocked from my lungs with that statement. "Why?"

He glanced quickly to John and back to the floor again. "I was told only that you mustn't return with me after tonight. I know nothing else."

"Horse shit!" I shouted the expletive, immediately covering my mouth with a hand and releasing his sleeve. "Oh, dear," I whispered. "I-I didn't mean to say that. How did—why did that . . ."

"You should have known better than to react as you did with Lord Buckley," Julian said, his teeth gnashing together even as he said it.

"Who says I cannot come home? The council? San Michel?"

"You made a grave mistake, Monica." Julian's cheeks flushed

red. "I-I don't think you'll be cast out of Heaven. But I cannot see you being an angel after they deliberate."

I was lost in thought, staring at a speckle of blood staining the wall. "Then, go," I whispered, not bothering to look at him. "Go home without me." He moved to step away, when I grabbed his arm again. I could feel the sobs rising and pushed them down instead. "But know . . . this is partially your doing, as well. You pushed me into taking this mission. You failed to inform me of—of all the rules of being an angel. But most of all—you could have professed your love for me at any time over these last few centuries. But you didn't. And you waited until I thought I had found love elsewhere." I gave his bicep one last squeeze and pushed him away. "Now. With that, you can go."

I turned to go find John. I didn't know where I could stay tonight, but I certainly would not stay anywhere near the man. Ainsley's face flashed in my head. The brutal and careless way he had murdered the animal he'd claimed was his pet.

"Monica," Julian's voice called out. I didn't bother stopping. I didn't bother looking back. "Monica!" he shouted again, more urgently this time.

When I turned the corner of the hallway into what was once my boudoir, I came face-to-face with John. From down the hall, I heard the crack of Jules leaving.

"Angel," John sneered. A glass of something amber colored and pungent was in his hands, and I could smell the alcohol on his breath.

"Not for much longer," I muttered, pushing past him. I tore the clothing from my body—one of the fine gowns he forced me to wear. The character he made me play. The life he'd convinced me I'd fit into. I found my wool dress—the dress I had worn before John had swooped in and tangled into my world a web of things my life had no room for. I swallowed a lump in my throat.

Surely, John and Jules were partially to blame, but this was still my fault. I made the poor decisions that led to this point in my life.

"I'm leaving," I said while turning to face him.

He laughed, his voice cracking with the bitter sound. "You are? And just where will you go?"

I shrugged, not caring. "The climate does not hurt me. I can procure any garment I need. I do not require food or drink to survive." I took a step closer, pressing my body against his in a way that was anything but sexual. "And I am far, far stronger than you ever believed me to be." I nudged past his shoulder. "As long as I am an angel, I have no need for you or any man like you."

I turned and closed my eyes, waiting for the cracking sound to teleport me outside the manor's gates. Nothing happened. I opened my eyes and John stood there, one hand in his pocket, the other holding the almost empty glass of whiskey. His smirk lifted on one side, and he raised his glass to me before throwing his head back and finishing the rest in one last gulp. He threw it to the floor, the shattering glass bouncing and biting at my ankles. His stride as he advanced on me was smooth and angry. "I can change that. Make it so you need a man."

I turned and headed down the hall to the top of the stairs. Just because I couldn't teleport didn't mean I couldn't walk out of there on my own two feet. From the boudoir came John's voice just barely above a whisper. "Feed," is all he said and there was a crackle of magic in the air.

I took the stairs quicker, throwing the front door open and running for the gate. It was already significantly warmer than it had been in months. The frost beneath my feet was melting into puddles that splashed my calves and shins as I ran.

The pounding of footsteps behind me was just as fast as my sprint, if not faster. And before me, two vampires at the gate crouched, their pale skin reflecting the moonlight. John's final word echoed in my mind. Feed.

"Oh, Heavenly Father . . ." I slowed my pace until I stopped. There were five vampires total surrounding me. Their eyes were red. Their stomachs growled. I could sense their thirst. I was not only the first meal they would have had in ages . . . but I was probably the first meal that didn't walk on four feet and eat garbage. Dejan was nowhere to be seen. Was he refusing? Did John specifically want to keep him from me?

I was strong . . . but I knew I was no match for five hungry vampires. I knelt down, cast my eyes to the sky, and did the same thing I had done when my human life had expired. "Our Father, who art in Heaven. Hallowed be thy name . . ."

The first vampire lunged, his fangs piercing the first open flesh he could find on my arm. The poison spread through my body and my arm felt as though it had been tossed onto a flame. Soon more vampires were on me, feasting on my essence. My blood was draining. Could this kill me? Could an angel die this way? I didn't know. . . . There was still so much for me to learn.

Ulrich, the gate's guard, knelt between my legs. Pushing my knees apart, he licked his lips, staring at the space where John himself had feasted many a time. I closed my eyes ignoring that little spark of heat that rushed to the region down there.

A snarl above me made my eyes snap open. Breathing was hard and I felt too weak to even turn my head toward the noise. "Away! Enough!" he growled and I recognized the accent immediately. Dejan.

The other vampires growled and snapped their teeth at him as well, but they listened, backing away from my drained body. All except the one kneeling between my legs. He licked his lips, a chunk of blond hair falling in his face.

"Ulrich, no," he purred.

Ulrich smiled before baring his teeth and sinking them into the soft flesh between my legs. I cried out—it felt both terrible and painful, yet satisfying. My hands fisted into the wet grass.

My body convulsed with the movement and the world around me seemed to be fading. Dejan tackled the vampire and they wrestled in movements so fast, I couldn't keep up. Not with the loss of blood. My breathing was heavy and the scuffle quieted. Two arms nudged under my back and legs.

When I opened my eyes, I looked up at Dejan, the world around us a blur with how fast he was running. I turned my head and saw trees whipping by us, wind slapping my face. His running slowed, and he lowered me onto some moss.

"Wh-what will come of m-me now." My teeth were chattering on top of my breath being staggered.

Dejan growled low in his throat, the hunger rippling through his eyes. He eyed my bloody, open wounds and swallowed. "You will die if we do not turn you."

"Angels can die?" I asked, never once believing this to be true.

After a pause, he answered. "I didn't believe so until this moment."

"Turn me?" I repeated and attempted to turn my body over for him.

"No." He placed a hand on my shoulder, pushing me back to the moss. "Stay. Rest. Do not move." He swallowed again, raising his hand, now covered in my blood, to his nose. He inhaled and closed his eyes, a smile tugging at his mouth. "Do you realize how long it has been since I have had the blood of anything other than sheep and rats? Let alone the delicacy of angel blood." He licked the length of one finger and moaned, eyes snapping back to me. "We must turn you now. Before I drain you completely."

Turn me. Turn me. *The thought rolled over in my brain still not making sense.*

"What happens when an angel is bit by a vampire?"

He inhaled the night breeze, raven hair blowing back from his face. "You will be one of us. A vampire."

"Just leave me to die, Dejan. Feast on me. Use me. Do as you wish."

"Don't talk like that!" he growled. "You won't be an angel—but you will not die here like this. You'll be . . ." His tone changed as suddenly as he had appeared, and he sucked the blood off another finger. "You'll be mine, though. All mine."

He sunk his teeth into his own wrist. Blood gushed down his arm, and he shoved it against my lips. I turned my head, the warm, thick liquid, splattering against my face, gagging me, I coughed and sputtered it out. "Drink!" he demanded, tilting my head back and pinching my nose so that I had little choice in the matter.

It slid down my throat and I swallowed, unable to fight any longer. I coughed as he released his hold on my head. He, too, knelt in the same position as Ulrich. He was gentler. Tender even, as he placed a hand under each of my knees. He looked into my eyes once more. "This is going to hurt," he whispered.

There was no pain worse than what I was feeling in that moment. Or so I'd thought.

When I didn't answer, he closed his eyes, inhaling through his nose. I wasn't sure if he was smelling my blood, or my sex. From his position, it could have been either. Or both. "From my blood, breeds your blood. From my mouth, to your mouth. You will feed on man. You will hunt at night. My blood, to your blood. My mouth to your mouth."

His teeth sank into the inner part of my right thigh and I screamed out. If the other bites felt like fire, this felt as though lava now flowed in my veins. He drank from my lower half until I felt his presence above my face. His lips on mine were chilled and the blood he pushed into my mouth tingled against my tongue. It wasn't nearly so vile as the first sip of his own he had given me. He tongue brushed against mine and I could feel his erection pushing against my moist sex. I resisted, pushing him away, but as the blood entered my body—sliding down my throat, warming my stomach—something inside me changed. Heat flared everywhere. An awareness of my curves, my breasts, my nipples— my swollen sex was hungry and aching. I threw an arm around his neck and pulled him into me for a deeper kiss. He grunted and thrust his hips against mine once again, his erection hard.

"Fuck me," I grunted. "Fuck me now."

His eyes flashed with humor and he kissed me again. "Yes, m'lady."

45

Damien and I sat outside of the cafe, sipping our iced lattes. Baxter sat at Damien's side, at the end of a leash, and Damien scratched one of his ears, making eye contact with the dog, but refusing to look at me.

"I still don't quite get why you couldn't just tell me about who you were—are. . . ."

Damien sighed, taking another sip. "I couldn't. There was too much risk. The threat of anyone knowing my lineage could have meant imprisonment for me with absolutely no trial. I couldn't risk it."

"But that's how you knew I was an angel? And how you just knew so much about me in general before we even met?"

He shrugged, but didn't answer. It had been three months since we had all been in Salt Lake City. Damien and Adrienne had stayed a few days to clear up their part of the investigation and clean the Morganson's house. It was apparently pretty easy to make it look like Mr. Morganson had been the guilty party.

For three months Drew had been gone. The time had done

nothing to ease the aching hole in my chest. I'd searched for John, but knowing he could glamour himself to look like anyone—and on top of that, his ability to mask his powers—it felt rather hopeless. Yet, there were times I could feel his presence. As though he didn't dare to stray too far from me. I knew he was watching me.

Outside of Buckley, we'd all tried everything to requisition to get Drew back. And apparently, short of going rogue and venturing into the depths of Hell to save him ourselves—something I just might do if there are no other alternatives—Julian claimed the council could do nothing to save him. He had to make it out on his own.

"I'm sorry," Damien said finally, interrupting my thoughts.

"I know you are." I dipped my finger into the foam that sat on top of my latte and swirled it around the tip. I dipped the creamy froth into my mouth and swallowed. "I should really get back in there. With Drew gone . . ."

"And you as the new acting owner. Yeah, yeah, I know."

I nodded. It was an excuse I had given him many times over the last few months when our conversations would wane.

"Hey, succubus." He cupped my jaw with his palm, turning my face to his. "I'm not giving up on us yet, you know?"

"I know." Nor did I want him to give up just yet.

I entered the cafe and went back to work, slipping an apron around my waist and a hat on my head.

With every jingle of the bells—the signal that someone was entering—my attention would jolt to the door. For a moment each time, there was hope that it could be Drew coming home. And yet, it never was.

A beautiful woman entered. She was petite with porcelain skin and sharp, blue eyes. I watched as she walked over to our coffee bar area—a new service implemented by me so that during the busy times, customers could pour and fix their own drip coffees—and filled a small to-go cup with coffee and placed a lid on it, black. She walked over to me and tucked a strand of red, curly hair behind her ear.

She placed two dollars on the counter and smiled at me. I took the money and put it in the register. "Do I know you?" I asked.

Her head tilted to the side ever so subtly and she turned, walking quickly out of the cafe.

"Genevieve, watch the register!"

"Hey!" I called as she walked away. The sun in front of her seemed to shine down directly on her body, casting a halo around her. The Banshee. She'd been released from her imprisonment . . . with a kind act. "You saved him, didn't you?"

She stopped, freezing mid-step. Only instead of turning, she took a sip of her coffee, glancing toward the parking lot, then continued walking.

Something was tucked on the windshield of my Toyota. I walked over, lifting it out from under my wiper. It was a blank postcard from Alaska. I turned it over in my hands. No stamp. No writing. Just a GREETINGS FROM ALASKA! phrase on the front with an image of the state's snowy landscape.

I pulled my cell from my back pocket and called Kayce. "Hey." I smiled down at the postcard, running my thumb over the edge. "We can cancel the rescue mission. Drew's okay. He's no longer trapped."

"What? Then where is he?"

I tucked the postcard into my apron pocket. "I don't know, but he'll be back eventually. I'm sure of it."

It's called Sin City for a reason. Nowhere else are the temptations so great, the sex so good, and the demons so bad! Turn the page for a special excerpt of Katana Collins's

SOUL STRIPPER

PROLOGUE

She lay on top of his body, her bare breasts pressed against his tight muscles. His breathing was steady against her chest. She lifted herself up quietly so as not to wake him. She hadn't known her date for long, but he seemed nice enough.

She walked to her bathroom, not bothering to turn on the light. A candle glowed on the sink, and she ran the faucet to splash some water on her face. A tendril of red, curly hair fell over one shoulder, and she could taste something bad in her mouth—what was that? Morning breath? She grabbed her toothbrush, which hadn't been used in ages. Every now and then to spruce up before a date, but really—she had no need for one other than keeping up appearances. She scrubbed the bristles against her teeth, the action feeling foreign, and stared at her reflection.

It was dark, but her succubus vision was sharp.

There was something next to her mouth—a crease? It couldn't be. Succubi don't *get* wrinkles. She closed her eyes and shifted, thinking about what areas she wanted to change. Where there would normally be a tingle—some shiver of magic running through her body—she felt hardly anything. A few goose bumps rose on her arms. When she opened her eyes, the crease was still there, though slightly less visible. She spit the minty foam into the sink and tossed her toothbrush down, bringing her face in closer to the mirror to investigate.

She was naked with the exception of the beautiful anklet dangling just above her foot—a gift from the man lying in her bed, fast asleep. Her breasts brushed the cold porcelain of her sink, making her jump back slightly. She closed her eyes and shifted into clothes. The power was still there, though barely. She looked down, now wearing a sheer camisole and panties. It wasn't what she had in mind, but at least it was something. Her head was spinning and she was dizzy, faint from the energy spent.

The light behind her clicked on and she jumped, turning to find her date standing behind her. His eyes, which had been so kind only hours before, now seemed like empty, bottomless holes. "Trouble sleeping?"

She shook her head, fiery hair tickling her collarbone. A pull came from deep in her gut, feeling his aura's shift from earlier in the night. It was red—a purplish red. She sent him the sweetest smile she could muster and casually tossed her hair behind her shoulder. "Not at all. Just wanted to freshen up before round two." She reached for the sink, grabbing her porcelain hand mirror from the vanity and slowly brought it to her face. She kept one eye on him and managed to act as though she were looking at her reflection.

His chiseled jaw clenched, and his face twisted into a sadistic smile. "Come now, Savannah. We both know there's not going to be a round two. I can smell your fear." From behind his back, he pulled out a knife with a serrated blade. He moved quickly, lunging at the succubus, but even in her exhausted state she moved faster.

She smashed the porcelain mirror against the counter, the

glass shattering, leaving her with the pointed shard of the handle. She swung the shiv toward him, just barely missing his arm. They each stood in a crouched position, ready to strike.

He laughed at her. His head tipped back, the low chuckle escaping his throat like the soft rattle of a dangerous snake. With no warning, he threw his knife, the blade slicing through her bare foot, staking it to the hardwood floor.

She screamed, her body crumpling into a heap, and yanked the knife away. She sat there, blade in one hand, shiv in the other, waiting for her foot to heal itself. Waiting for regeneration that didn't come. He cackled above her. She looked up to find him standing over her, another knife in his hand.

He knelt, eyes cold like stone. "You're waiting for something that's not going to happen, hun. You are practically human. Nothing's going to heal itself this time."

Her breath became shorter—panic. She had not felt true fear in such a long time. Not since she was human. She forced her breathing to slow down. Forced herself to stop the tunnel vision from closing around her. She still held two weapons, his knife in one hand and her shiv in the other. She would not go down without a fight. The small tingle of power coursed through her veins, reminding her she still had a touch of magic left—she would find the right time to use it.

She swiped the knife across his bare chest, and the blade slid into his tender flesh. He fell back, a scream echoing in the bathroom. In the moment it took him to gather his composure, she leaped over his body, running to the bedroom. Her leap was not high enough and he raised his knife, cutting her deeply behind the knee.

Both legs were damaged. She could hardly stand; most of her weight rested on her hands, leaning on the dresser. She had lost the knife somewhere along the jump, but the shiv was still clenched so tightly in her fist that her palm was bleeding. The blood from her knee traveled down her leg, over her calf, and as it dripped across her beautiful anklet, steam rose with a sizzle, as though the anklet were absorbing the blood. The blood that hit the anklet dropped to the floor, still steaming and sizzling, creating burn marks like a chemical spill.

He walked slowly toward her, knives dripping with blood. His, hers—did it matter? "It's over, Savannah."

She shook her head, eyes wide and wet. "Why?"

His eyes creased, and he smiled in that evil way again. He shuddered with pleasure as her body trembled in fear before him. "You kill for a living. And now, so do I."

Adjusting her body, she forced herself to stand so that she was leaning only against one arm—the shiv stretched out in front of her. "Then come and get me, fucker." Despite her tough exterior, her heart hammered against her ribs.

He ran toward her. As he did, she shifted into a serpent with her last remaining power. Her fangs sunk into his abdomen just before his knives slit her throat. A handful of scales fluttered to the floor and a fang ripped out of her mouth as she choked on her own blood. She fell to the ground, transforming back into her human form. A bloody goddess with lifeless eyes.

He chuckled softly and licked the blood from his knife, his body radiating with the power of fresh blood and a new kill. Her magic entered his body with her blood, slithering down his throat like a fine cognac. He bent down and ran his hand down the length of her lifeless body. Using the edge of the knife, he gathered a pool of blood on the blade and scraped it across two small test tubes. "I'd fuck you one last time, but I fear it would somehow wake you," he whispered to himself. "Such a waste." His fingers trailed down her hips, across her ass, and down her thighs until he reached the anklet. He ripped it swiftly from her body, pocketing it before taking off.

1

The smell of coffee always turns me on.

Well, it might not be the coffee as much as it is my manager *at* the coffee shop. Drew. I liked to repeat his name in my head. Drew. *Drew. An*drew Sullivan—one of the best men I've ever met. Which might not be saying much for him considering the degenerates I hang out with. I wiped down a table with a few stains, thinking about those dimples of his. He always had the faint aroma of coffee on his clothes. And under his cotton T-shirts, I could see the slightest ripple of muscles. Long and lean. The muscles of a soccer player.

I stood there wiping the same spot over and over, my nails scraping against the tabletop. I imagined Drew's lips gently brushing against the dip in my neck. His growing erection pressing into me as he tenderly nibbled the soft skin above my collarbone. *Monica, Monica,* he'd moan. . . .

"Monica?" His smooth voice snapped me out of my dream. "I think that table's clean." His lips curled into a playful smile, eyes sparkling with mischief. He turned his attention back to the faucet, wrench in hand, fixing the constant drip that had been annoying all the baristas over the past week.

"Oh. Right, of course. Sorry, Drew. I'm sort of lost in my own thoughts today." My eyes traveled to his tight ass; his signature dirty towel was hanging from the back pocket of his jeans. Disoriented, I turned to move on to my next task and slammed into a customer closing in on the table I just cleaned. His iced coffee spilled onto my chest. Ice dribbled down my white T-shirt, and cold coffee covered my now-tight nipples.

"Oh shit." I looked up at the regular customer whose caffeinated beverage I was now wearing. He looked angry—which for anyone else might have been a problem. But for me? This was an easy fix for any succubus over a century old. That's what I am—a succubus. And whatever notions you have in your head about succubi are probably wrong. Just because I am a minion of Hell doesn't necessarily make me an "evil" being.

I used to be an angel and am apparently the *only* angel-turned-succubus known within the demon realm. I guess this sort of makes me a celebrity. They call me the golden succubus—the nickname makes me cringe. It's a bit too reminiscent of a particular "golden" sex act.

I looked up at the angry man standing over me and felt the tingles as my succubus magic handled the situation. My bottom lip pouted naturally when I spoke. "I am just *so* sorry." As I took a deep breath, his eyes fixed on my nipples pushing out my wet T-shirt. "I'm such a klutz!" Running my fingernail along his forearm, his face softened.

"It's really no problem." He flashed a smile after licking his lips. "We should really get you out of that shirt." He lifted a hand to his mouth, and I noticed a wedding band on that ring finger of his.

Fucking men.

I opened my mouth to answer, but before I could, Drew

stepped between us, his eyebrows low over his eyes. "You can go have a seat—we'll bring you another coffee."

"*Iced* coffee." The married man smirked and looked past Drew, meeting my eyes.

"Iced coffee? What's the matter—can't take the heat?"

"It's Vegas, man. Who drinks hot coffee in the middle of the desert?"

Drew's mouth tipped into a barely visible smile. "*I* do."

The customer ran a hand through his dark brown hair. "Fine, whatever man."

Drew was still standing protectively in front of me, and I touched his arm lightly, an attempt to break him from his aggressive stance. As he rocked back on his heels, Drew's face cracked into a friendlier smile—one that was much more appropriate as the owner of the coffee shop. He clapped the man on the bicep in that weird way men do to each other. "Just messin' with you, man. Have a seat. I'll get your iced coffee."

Once the customer was out of earshot, Drew swiveled around, his smile entirely gone, replaced again with the anger I had seen a moment ago. He leaned down, his face suddenly close to mine. "Do you have to come on to every friggin' customer?" He grunted and pushed past my shoulder, heading back behind the counter.

"*Me?* I don't know if you saw the whole thing, Drew—but that guy came on to *me*. Not the other way around." I was whispering so not to create a scene in the crowded café.

"You don't even realize how much you flirt."

I paused, taking in his vibe. "We're not talking about *him* anymore, are we?"

He snorted and slammed some of his tools around, not answering right away. After a few seconds of silence, he stood with his hands on his hips, not meeting my eyes. "That was a long time ago, Mon. Trust me, I'm not exactly sitting at home pining away over you."

"Six months is not that long ago." Ever since I started working for him here at the coffee shop, I knew he was bound to ask me out at some point. He managed to hold out longer than most men—almost two years after we first met, he invited me to dinner. And I for some stupid reason still have a conscience—that little bit of angel left in me—and had to say no. I couldn't take that risk with Drew's soul.

He sighed. "It is in the dating world. You should know that."

I resisted the urge to roll my eyes. "Whatever. I'm happy you've moved on." I swallowed. His lips pressed together and one eyebrow twitched into an arch. Maybe he knew I was bluffing, maybe he didn't. It didn't exactly matter anymore. We held each other's gaze for seconds too long. I broke the eye contact first and joined him behind the counter, pulling out a new cup of ice for the customer's replacement coffee.

Drew cut me off, taking the cup from me. "Why don't I refill this for you? You're still a little bit—eh—indecent." His eyes flicked toward my breasts.

"Oh. Right." I glanced down at my shirt. Brown stains covered my hard nipples. "And—I really am sorry. About spilling the coffee," I clarified quickly. "I feel off my game today. Spilling stuff, drifting off, daydreaming . . ."

Drew smiled at me, turning back into his normal self. "It's fine, Monica. Really." He tossed me the hand towel that was hanging in his back pocket.

I smiled back. "Well, feel free to take the refill out of my hips—oops, I mean, *tips.*" I smirked, exaggerating the flirting.

He rolled his eyes. "There you go again." He smiled, lines creasing around his mouth. "I have an extra shirt in my office, if you need it."

I headed to the bathroom. "No, it's fine. I think I have one in my bag."

I shut the bathroom door and slid the lock to the left. Can't have anyone walking in while I'm shapeshifting. In actuality, my shapeshifting is just a mind-trick on mortals and immortals. A mirage of sorts. I took a look at the reflection in the mirror. My dark blond hair still looked in place, parted on the side with a slight curl at the ends. But my shirt was a mess. I focused—closed my eyes. A familiar prickle surrounding my body as I shifted into another clean, white shirt.

The idea of stealing souls for Hell makes my stomach twist. Even though I am technically a demon, you could say I sort of play for both teams whenever possible. Ethical souls are the nutrition. They're like eating fresh vegetables and free-range chicken. The bad souls, well, they're the fast-food equivalent. I'm essentially sustaining my existence on this mortal plane on a diet of chocolate and potato chips. My body certainly craves something better, but I allow the indulgence only when absolutely necessary.

I looked away from the mirror. I wasn't always such an immortal vigilante. There was a time I accepted my fate as a succubus. A time in my existence I wasn't exactly proud of.

Maybe I should try a new hair color—go blonder—surfer bleach blond . . . like Drew's new girlfriend, Adrienne. Ugh. I couldn't even bear the thought of it—Drew with a girlfriend. A *blond* girlfriend. It was just so . . . so . . . obvious. I mean, okay, my hair was blond, too, but mine was natural. I hadn't changed my looks much since my angel days, partially because I liked my cherub features but also because the art of shifting takes a lot of power. It simply takes less energy to adjust the looks I already have in people's minds rather than create a new vision entirely.

I thought again of Adrienne and her platinum blond hair. The sort of white blond that looked as though it had been singed at the bottom—brittle and crisp. It just screamed Pamela Anderson. Sighing, I walked out of the bathroom to finish up my closing shift duties.

I finished cleaning the tables and restocked the sugar, and as

I carried another bag of arabica coffee beans to the front, I inhaled their scent and thought of Drew. That sweet smell that hits you at the back of the throat. That scent will get me through the end of my night job. The strip club doesn't always have the nicest men . . . or the nicest smells, for that matter.

"Aren't you going to be late for the club?" Once again, Drew snapped me out of my thoughts.

Nine p.m. Which meant yes . . . I was going to be late. I flashed him a smile. "Yes, probably. With any luck, I'll be fired." I laughed to myself at the thought. Lucien would never dream of firing me. I'm his best dancer and the closest thing to a sister that he's got. As my ArchDemon, Lucien is in charge of Nevada and the entire Southwest region. He may seem threatening to most, but when he pitches his fits, I only ever see a petulant teenager stomping his feet and raising his voice.

Drew took a few steps closer to me and placed his rough hand on my elbow. They were the hands of a carpenter. A hard worker—rough and masculine. "Maybe you should quit. I could give you a raise here." His green eyes grew wider with hope—and perhaps a slight hint of desire.

My mouth tipped into a sad smile. "You can offer me a thousand dollars per night?" *Not to mention the easy access to men's souls.* The strip club is the best way to meet bad boys and avoid the good ones. The degenerates that come into that club give me just enough energy to keep running. I glanced back up at his green eyes, his warm breath tickling my lips. Drew's soul was clean. Pure and totally Heaven-bound. Sure, he was quite the flirt—even with a girlfriend. But that alone doesn't warrant a one-way ticket to Hell. He deserved better than me. Even still, when he was this close to my body, my ethical stance became fogged.

Drew chuckled, and his laugh reminded me of water bubbling over a fountain. "No, I definitely can't offer you that."

His hand was still on my elbow, and his fingers moved in gentle circles over my skin. "But I can give you unlimited coffee and an extra two dollars an hour."

"That's a *tempting* offer," I teased, "but somehow I'm not so sure I can sustain my life on coffee."

"I could find other ways to keep you happy here." His breathing became more shallow and his face lowered closer to mine. I knew he was just reacting to my succubus pheromones. It wasn't Drew talking—it was simply his carnal desire coming through. No man can resist a succubus in heat. And though I rationally knew this, I still couldn't pull my gaze away from his. I could feel the need from deep within my body, an itch to have sex with someone so deliciously pure and good. I looked down at my nails and they were glossier, with a sheen most women paid good money to get. My powers were running low, which meant only one thing—I needed to sleep with someone tonight. Everything about me was designed to draw in humans. I'm like a shiny, intricate spiderweb, waiting to catch my prey. As my body requires a recharge, my hair gets shinier, my eyes become more vibrant, and I emit a pheromone unlike any a human has ever produced.

We stayed there, eyes locked, as the bell above the door chimed. I sensed Adrienne's aura before even hearing her acrylic heels clacking against the floor—another succubus perk. Being able to sense most auras—human and demon. I quickly broke away from Drew's grasp and grabbed my bag.

"Well, hey there, handsome!" Adrienne came up behind Drew and wrapped her orange, faux-tanned arms around his shoulders. Her platinum hair fell into her eyes, making her black roots even more painfully obvious. *Ugh, a typical Vegas girl,* I thought. Which was admittedly ironic, since *I* was the stripper out of the two of us. Her aura shone as a bright red. That usually meant one thing—adultery. I'd seen her aura just the other day and it had been green. She must have recently finished the deed. I inhaled, and though I couldn't smell the stench of sex on her, there was something different about her scent.

Drew's face faltered and he withdrew his hand from me as if my touch burned. His eyelids drooped in that way that a man's does after watching golf for a few hours.

"Hey, back at you, gorgeous." His voice sounded genuine, for the most part. It strained a little bit on the word *gorgeous,* but that also might have just been my imagination.

Without thinking, I groaned. Adrienne darted an agitated look in my direction and Drew's head dropped to the side, his eyes rolling at me in a chastising way that made me feel like a teenager.

"Oh, um, sorry. I can't find my costume for tonight. I thought I had it in my bag." Adrienne narrowed her eyes at me, obviously not buying my story. Maybe I'm not as smooth as I thought.

Drew sighed. "Don't mind Monica, babe. She's our resident cynic here at the café."

I shrugged at Adrienne. "Well, I'd better get going. See you tomorrow, Drew." I rushed past them, bumping her shoulder in the process.

But before exiting through the door, I saw the married man from earlier. The one whose coffee I spilled. His eyes went directly toward my tits, acting as though if he just stared hard enough he'd develop X-ray vision. I ran up to him, grabbing my card from the bottom of my bag. "Here," I said, handing him the card. "If you're interested, I'll be dancing there tonight." It simply had my stage name, *Mirage,* listed with the strip club's name and information.

His eyes sparkled and he licked his lips as he glanced down at my card. "Oh, I know this place," he said.

I looked back again at Drew to find him staring at me. His

lips were pressed into a thin line, eyebrows knitted in the center. *Good,* I thought, *be jealous.* I turned and headed for the exit, glancing over my shoulder one last time to look at Drew. Instead, I found the married man staring at my ass. Sometimes it was just too easy being a succubus.

The itch between my legs simply would not go away. As I drove down Las Vegas's dusty roads, I knew I had to take care of my desire, and soon. I hoped the married coffee shop guy would show up, or I'd be forced to sleep with one of the other regular assholes who frequented Hell's Lair. That's the name of the strip club—real original, huh? I shifted myself into my stripper look while driving, which was becoming increasingly hard to do as my powers lessened. I made my hair a dark brown—almost black—as I tried to decide which costume to wear tonight. Schoolgirl seemed too obvious. Cowgirl was *so* overdone here in Nevada. And dressing like an angel hit a little too close to home for me. Maybe a 1950s housewife character tonight? Or even better—I'll go vintage chic. Classy but naughty. I shifted into a tight black dress that was backless but left something for the imagination. Underneath, I put on lacy black underwear that was styled in a retro fashion, with thigh-high stockings that had a seam running up the back of my leg and a garter belt. As the finishing touches, I added a pillbox hat, black elbow-length gloves, and a long cigarette holder. Like the one Audrey Hepburn had in *Breakfast at Tiffany's.* I had to make my shift gradually so that the other drivers on the road didn't notice anything funny. Luckily, Lucien's club isn't in the heart of Vegas. Being off the beaten path makes it a little easier to not only attract the scum of the earth but it is also perfect for bringing in the immortal crowd.

I parked and ran inside, feeling completely out of place. The costume didn't even look like a stripper's costume. Grabbing one last look at myself in the full-sized mirror at the entrance, I had to admit it was unusual for a dirty strip club but still incredibly sexy.

I walked into the dark, smoky club and saw a few of the girls dancing on the stage. Hell's Lair was frequented by both mortals and demon-folk, and the seats around the stage reflected the lowest of low from both worlds. The floor was slick with oil, grease, and probably bodily fluids that I didn't let myself think too hard about. To the right and left of the stage were two bars. I crossed next to the crowd of men who were circling around the stage, each turning to look at me as I made my way past them, the smell of my sex hitting their noses—among their other regions. I nodded at T, our bartender and bouncer, and he winked in my direction. T got his name because he wears jewelry like Mr. T, and although he has a similar coloring and height, that's where the resemblance ends. Where Mr. T had muscles, T simply has fat.

Standing in front of the stage entrance blocking my way was Lenny, the annoying new manager Lucien had hired to run the place. He stood there, arms crossed over his man boobs, tapping his foot with his eyebrows knitted together. I inwardly rolled my eyes. He's shorter than me, probably somewhere around five foot four, and his greasy black hair combed over his balding scalp resulted in a zebra striping pattern along the top of his head. His belt was cinched tightly around his hips, and his belly spilled out over top. I could guarantee that at some point during the night, his shirt would come untucked, revealing his dimpled belly fat.

"You are late! Again!" He pulled out his clipboard and scribbled something down.

This time I rolled my eyes so that he saw me and brushed past him to go backstage.

He followed at my heels like some sort of balding, ugly

puppy. "Monica! *Monica!* Are you even listening to me? I'll fire you if you continue this pattern."

At that threat, I twirled around to face him. A slow smile spread across my face. I spoke quietly and calmly—and continued to give him a biting smile through my gritted teeth. "No. You won't fire me, Lenny. You can't and you *know* it. Now get the fuck out of my dressing room." I sat down at my mirror and dabbed on some lip gloss.

His chin dropped to his chest, creating even more jowls. "You're on in fifteen minutes," he muttered, dragging his feet behind him.

For tonight's music, I chose an old jazz tune with a lot of bass. The curtain opened and the spotlight warmed me. I started center stage, and as the first beat began, I smoked my cigarette from the long holder, taking the time to inhale deeply and slowly. The smoke streamed from my lips and swirled around the top of my head. After slipping the gloves off one at a time, I tossed them into the audience. As I slowly pulsated my hips to the rhythm, the dollar bills shot high into the air like statues in my honor. Starting with an older gentleman to my left, I allowed him to unzip my dress and peel it down over my body. His knuckles shook nervously as they brushed the smooth flesh on my back. When it reached my ankles, I opened my legs to him and stuck my hip in his face. Giving me a shy smile, he tucked a twenty into the garter belt. I danced away, moving on to the next man in the crowd, but not before I let my fingernail travel down the older man's cheek.

I stood at the edge of the stage, moving my hips in rhythm to the music. At the back of the crowd, I met eyes with a sexy man. Despite the dark bar and bright spotlight, I could see him clearly. Thank you, succubus vision. He had dark brown hair that tickled the tops of his ears and thick eyebrows that sat low over his eyes. I held his gaze for a few moments. He broke eye contact first and turned to leave the club. Some men just can't handle a forward woman.

Pivoting, I found my next tip, and that's when I noticed him against the edge of the stage. There, in the front row, was my married man from the coffee shop. His knuckle was raised to his lips, and low and behold—he had no wedding ring on his finger. Tsk, tsk. My lacy panties grew even wetter. He was no Drew, but he was definitely hotter than most of the men in this joint. Not to mention the most nervous. The beat wore on, the neon lights hit his eyes, and I sauntered over to him, crouching down so that my breasts were in his face. I was sure he could smell my sex from where he stood below me. I took another drag from the cigarette and blew it into his face. He drank in the smoke—and his eyes flashed with lust. I was his cocaine—his drug of choice, sweeter than any alcohol, more addictive than nicotine, and far more dangerous than any hallucinogen. I passed him the cigarette and he took a drag as I unhooked my corset, letting the straps drag over my arms and fall to the floor. My nipples puckered as the men around me gasped.

Through my peripherals, I saw more dollars fly into the air. I winked at my married man and continued on to collect the rest of the money. I moved fluently around the stage and finished my dance in nothing except heels, thigh-highs, and the pillbox hat.

After my set, I quickly shifted into my original dress, sans the panties and corset, and headed back out to the club. Every man I passed called out to get my attention. Propositioning voices circled around me as I walked straight for my married man. I was done waiting. I needed my fix now. The needy feeling was not one I ever got used to—an itch that is so uncomfortable, if we wait too long, it actually becomes painful. With the types of men I sleep with, I'm lucky to make it forty-eight hours before I need to find my next fix.

Ignoring everyone else, I plopped myself down on his lap.

His eyes darted around the club. "My name is Erik." I smiled to myself watching him glance nervously about.

"Really?" It was less of a question and more of a bored statement. No need to feign any interest. "Well, Erik, I don't give a fuck what your name is." I took another drag of my cigarette and looked into his mundane brown eyes. "Buy a private dance."

"Oh, um, well . . . I-I don't know about that. You see, I'm a newlywed and I was just curious about this place . . ."

"Erik, please." I rolled my eyes. "You knew what you were getting into by coming here. Especially after a personal invitation from me." I lowered my face so that my lips brushed his as I spoke. "So . . . buy a fucking private dance. Now." I paused once more, giving a second thought to how forceful my voice was. "Unless, that is, your wife satisfies you fully."

If the stress lines around his face were any indication, I'd bet that he was sexually frustrated. But for a moment, his face softened at the mention of his wife. I thought he was going to push me off his lap. Go running back to his wife for some plain old meat-and-potatoes missionary sex.

Instead, he simply nodded, drool practically dripping from his lips. "She's a prude. Only ever cares about her work."

I sighed. Men are such shits. In the couple of centuries that I've been around, that's never changed. I guess I couldn't be too annoyed by him though—it was that lack of morality that would give me enough energy to survive the next couple of days up here on Earth. I grabbed his hand, leading him to the back room. I yelled to Lenny as I passed the pot-bellied manager. "Gotta private one here, Lenny." He marked something on his clipboard.

I shut the door behind me. "Money first, *Erik*."

"Right. Uh, how much again?"

"Four hundred dollars. Plus tip."

"Four hundred? Dollars?"

"Plus tip."

He gulped. "Wow, I don't know that I have that much . . ."

I slipped my tongue in his ear. "Trust me. I'm worth it. What I'm about to do to you would typically cost much, *much* more." I pressed my breasts into his back.

"You're killing me. . . ." He groaned and exhaled between barely open lips. It was unclear whether he was referencing his wallet or his libido.

Ha. "Oh, sweetie. If you only knew." I nibbled his earlobe.

He reached into his back pocket, opening up an expensive-looking leather wallet. A few wallet pictures of a baby fell to the floor. I bent to pick them up and studied the beautiful child smiling back at me. She couldn't have been more than six months old. A knot formed in my throat, and I instinctively placed a hand on my stomach. "Is this your daughter?"

Erik grabbed the photograph and tucked it into the folds of his wallet. "Nah. It's my brother's kid."

My eyes narrowed as I studied his aura. No shift in color—he was telling the truth. I sighed, my tense shoulders relaxing.

He handed me the cash without any more debate, plus an extra twenty. Cheap-ass. You don't come to a strip club with several hundred dollars in your wallet and plan on leaving here innocently. It definitely made me feel better about what was to happen. Nevertheless, I always marvel at how easy it is to get men to cheat on their wives.

He sat in a chair in the middle of the room. I slowly undid the buttons of his shirt and slid it down over his shoulders. Surprisingly, he had an amazing body. Much more fit than I thought he would be. Grabbing his bottom lip between my teeth, I sucked on it while undoing his belt and lowered his pants. They dropped to the floor with a clunk.

"What do you have in those pockets? Rocks?" I smirked, tilting my head to the side. He was already hard, standing at full attention.

I left him in the chair, his pants pooled around his ankles, and danced around him, lifting my leg over his shoulder. It offered him close-up view of my sex peeking out from under the black fabric of my dress. "You want to taste me, don't you, *Erik?*"

He cleared his throat, allowing his eyes to travel up my thigh and land on the glistening flesh between my legs. "Uh-huh." His eyes were wide and dazed.

"So? Go ahead. Give me your best tongue."

He flicked his tongue out, lightly brushing over my skin. The contact made me moan softly, yearning for more. He slowly ran his tongue along my lips and into my folds until finally covering my clit with his mouth, sucking. I grabbed his hair and pulled him into me harder. Two fingers entered me. I was so wet, I begged for a third. He quickly obliged, pulsating them in and out with a "come hither" sort of movement. My muscles tightened around him. It wouldn't take long for me to come.

"Just your tongue. . . ." My voice was hoarse and breathy. He followed my orders, removing his fingers and delving his tongue deep within me. In seconds, I was coming on his face.

As my tremors finished, I grabbed his hair and pulled his face back so that he could see mine. "How'd I taste?"

"Amazing." His voice was gruff. The shy stutter was completely gone, replaced with lust.

"Tell me I taste better than your wife," I demanded.

"You taste so much better than my wife. She's nothing compared to you."

I turned around and had him unzip my dress, slipping the soft fabric off my body. The movement made my already-hard nipples even tighter. Naked, with the exception of my thigh-high stockings and heels, I straddled him.

"Wait." Concern suddenly filled his eyes. For a moment, there was hope for his soul. "Don't we need . . . protection?"

I laughed a sultry, throaty chuckle. "Not with me, baby.

That's not an issue. Relax. . . ." I dropped to my knees and lowered my mouth to his cock, running my lips along his shaft and twisting my tongue around his tip. I loved the feel of a cock slamming into the back of my throat. I increased my pressure and speed until he was ready for me.

I sat up, facing away from him in the reverse cowgirl position, and lowered myself down. It felt incredible having him fill me entirely. He sat there, not moving at all. And it figured. For four hundred dollars, of course he expected me to do the work. I lifted myself up, enjoying the sensation of his dick pulling away from me, and just before I lifted up entirely, I came back down hard. He groaned and grabbed my breasts, tweaking my nipples. I continued bouncing on him, feeling his size grow larger as he got more and more excited.

"You like that?" I asked, much louder than before. "You like being fucked by someone other than your wife?"

"God, yes," he cried out.

"Tell me!" I turned so that I could face him and grabbed his face roughly with one hand. "Say it again." I continued fucking him hard, squeezing my muscles as I reached his tip. My wetness grew with each thrust—so much so that I could feel it dripping out over my lips.

I slapped him across the cheek, perhaps harder than I intended to. "I *said,* tell me!"

"I love being fucked by you. You're so much better than my wife."

My itch raged on, worse than before, almost unbearably so. It wouldn't be relieved until he came—my release would come when he did. I could tell by his suddenly larger girth stretching my insides that he wasn't going to last much longer. I rolled my hips in circles over him, and his velvety tip rubbed just the right areas. The swelling felt amazing. He grabbed my ass and pulled me down onto him hard. His body trembled and his juices filled me. I groaned in delight at both his release and the life I was sucking from him. The orgasm was good, but the high from his soul was even better.

In a flash, I saw a movie reel of his life. Like a flipbook, I caught a quick glimpse of what was to come in Erik's life and what the world would lack by my stealing a portion of it. I saw him playing catch with a little boy, signing divorce papers, and finally . . . I saw him sitting quietly in a rocking chair, eyes closed. I exhaled, and it wasn't until that second that I realized I had been holding my breath. You just never know until that moment what exactly you're taking from your conquest. Knowing he was going to die peacefully in his rocking chair allowed my stress to melt away.

Seconds later, my human form radiated with life—*his* life. Muscles deep inside me tensed, and the sweet release of my own orgasm squeezed every last drop from him. With a forefinger, he flicked my clit and I screamed as the tremors rolled through my body again.

Pulling away from his body, I could feel his cum dripping down my thighs. I put my other leg back up on his shoulder. "Lick me," I demanded.

"But, I-I—" he stammered, staring nervously at his juices combined with my own.

"Shut the fuck up and *lick* me." I spoke through clenched teeth.

More hesitantly than before, he brought his tongue to the dripping area between my legs, tentatively licking.

"Harder!"

His tongue stiffened, and the tension built inside me once again. My muscles pulsed, squeezing the cum out of me and onto his tongue.

"How do I taste *now?*"

"Still amazing," he said. He slapped my ass, squeezing my cheek with one hand.

His sudden force caught me off guard, and I moaned as my

body convulsed in yet another orgasm. After, I leaned down and licked the juices from his lips.

We finished dressing and he came up behind me, kissing my neck. "That was amazing." He reached in front and caressed my breast through the material of my dress. "*You* are amazing. I had no idea it could be that great." He tucked another hundred dollar bill between my cleavage. "Can I see you again?" He was speaking fast, and I could see the effects of succubus sex affecting him already. It acts as a sort of high, making my victims more manic and stronger than they normally are. One of the many ways we succubi keep them addicted, coming back for more.

I rolled my eyes, and even though he couldn't see me, he probably sensed my annoyance. "Well, of course we'll *see* each other again. You're in the coffee shop every fucking day."

He turned me around so I was face-to-face with him. I didn't realize before how tall he was. My eyes were about level with his pecs. "That's not what I meant." He brushed a piece of hair from my face.

"I-I know." I stammered slightly, feeling uncharacteristically bad for the man. "But I try to keep my two lives separate. My dancing life and the café life. Inviting you here was a . . . a momentary lapse in judgment."

He tilted my chin toward his and gave a small tug on my almost black locks. "I like this look. Is it a wig?" Then with the same hand, he cupped my jaw. For a second there, I really thought he was going to kiss me.

"Something like that," I replied.

"So, I can visit you here at the club?"

I nodded, sadness washing over me. Leaning in, he brushed his lips against mine. It was so intimate. So atypical for me. Intimacy was not something I experienced on a sexual level. It had been decades since I had felt that sort of sexual affection and actually acted on it. My stomach clenched; a rush of sorrow flooded me for . . . everything. For his wife. His deceit. Because of me, he would die a week sooner than he should have; I stole part of this man's soul and suckered him into cheating on his wife. Okay, well, maybe I didn't sucker him, but I certainly offered temptation. He may have gone his entire marriage without any infidelity if it hadn't been for me. Maybe I was the reason he'd be signing those divorce papers in the future. I needed to get away from him—away from this club.

I broke free from his kiss and headed toward the door. "I'll see you around, Erik." It was the first time I said his name without dripping sarcasm.

As the door clicked shut behind me, I instantaneously felt Lucien's presence. Seconds later, he stood before me. And he did not look happy.

"My office, Monica. Now."